Elizabeth Worth was born and raised in Leeds. After graduation from Bath Spa University College with an Hons. Degree in Literature and Creative Studies, she spent several years living and working in Cheltenham. She now lives with her husband in Powys, Wales.

In her spare time she is a keen amateur dramatist.

THE VIRGIN
&
THE WHORE

Elizabeth Worth

The Virgin
&
The Whore

Vanguard Press

A CIP catalogue record for this title is
available from the British Library
ISBN 1 843860 63 5

*Vanguard Press is an imprint of
Pegasus Elliot MacKenzie Publishers Ltd.*
www.pegasuspublishers.com

First Published in 2003

**Vanguard Press
Sheraton House Castle Park
Cambridge England**

Printed & Bound in Great Britain

Dedication

For William, and in memory of my father,

With love.

Prologue

"Well, that wasn't so bad, was it?"

"Tough enough," he shrugged. I was about to hug him in congratulations, but his silence of indifference halted me. I thought he would have been happily relieved. The dreaded informal talk and the following question and answer session was over. And we'd come out of it pretty well, I thought. His new book had received the kind of response that we both hoped it would.

And it was a heavy topic which hit on a lot of sensitive issues that everyone has a strong opinion about. Everyone including victims, police, the judiciary, perpetrators, psychologists, MPs, the public at large...

Something was bugging Dominic. I had noticed his off-handedness with me, which was unusual. He was usually friendly and easy-going. I had dismissed it as nerves. But I think I was wrong. It felt like *I'd* done something wrong. I glanced at my watch. Lunch time, so this room wasn't scheduled to be used for the next writer for another hour.

"What's the matter Dominic?"

"What makes you think anything is the matter?"

"Well, you've just had a lot of positive responses on your new book, and you look like you've just been to a funeral. I thought you'd be pleased."

"I am pleased."

"You don't look like you're pleased."

"Daphne..." He looked at me a long moment. As if he was about to tell me something terrible.

"It's something else isn't it? Do you want to talk about it?" Dominic gave a strange look. His eyes rose to heaven and there was a bitter twist to his mouth that I'd never seen before.

"Is it Roberta? Is she OK?"

"I haven't even told her yet."

"Told her what?"

"About you."

What was he talking about? Not told his wife what about me? Dominic made it sound like we had some sort of secret from her. What on earth was he going on about?

"I want to show you something," he said mysteriously. I waited as he turned to get his jacket and searched through the pockets. "Here, read this." He handed me an old newspaper cutting.

He watched me as I unfolded the well worn piece of paper. I looked in his eyes. There was a strange emotion there that I couldn't read. My eyes scanned the words of a well known story.

My story.

My body went cold, and my heart skipped a beat. The article told of a twenty-nine year old woman having been knocked over by a lorry. A single mother. Knocked over dead. She'd left a three and a half year old little girl behind. By the name of Daphne Pemberton.

I felt a wave of emotion wash through me, something like loss. It was many years ago. A lifetime ago. But many days passed now when I didn't think of her. Then something would remind me of her blood in my veins.

"Why have you got this?" Was he investigating me or something? Checking up on me? Or was this his idea of some sort of sick joke? I shielded my emotions from him. I had thought Dominic was above such suspicions. I'd trusted him as a friend. What on earth was going on here?

"Do you know who that is in the picture? Do you know who they're talking about there?"

I looked down at the black and white photograph next to the article. I had looked at a lot of photos of her. For a long time. Wishing her back to life. Feeling her love beyond the grave entwine me in its arms at nights. I saw again her long, deep black hair, the light catching her dark dancing eyes. Her head thrown back laughing.

The picture faded into the pictures in my head. The last time I'd seen her alive, she was wearing a long white t-shirt, with slits up the side, and black leggings half way down her calves.

She was holding a shopping bag with groceries in. I was standing on the pavement. Standing nowhere. I'd been looking in a toy shop window. Mummy was wanting to cross the road. She called my name. I turned. There was a blur. A rush of people. A push. A cyclist. A lorry. A loud screech. No Mummy's hand holding out to me anymore. But a body that belonged to Mummy flying through the air. I remember a scream. I don't remember if it was me. I remember her face. I touched her warm arm. Blood trickled down from her nose and I wiped it away.

"Mummy, your nose is bleeding." Her body was twisted unnaturally. "Mummy?" She never answered. She didn't move. But she was still warm. I remember an ambulance. Lots of uniformed people. I don't remember anything else. I'd suddenly been removed from real life and transported into a horror film. There were gaps in time, and places missing from my memory. The following months squashed into a few minutes. I remember Uncle Ben and Aunty Gail hugging me tightly, and lots of tears. I remember a dark funeral with a coffin but no Mummy. And starting to live with two loving strangers who I had not met before. And lots of nightmares. And missing her, missing her, missing her, missing her…

"Of course I know who it is. Why are you showing me this?" I didn't look at him.

"Well, who is she?"

I looked at him angrily. "You know perfectly well who she is, or you wouldn't be showing me this. But what I want to know is *why?*"

"She's your mother isn't she?"

"Why do you want to know?"

"Isn't she?" He was relentless.

"Yes, damn it, she is. Was." I caught myself before saying anything more. I felt a silent war thicken the air between us. I was angry with him, and he was angry with me. And I had no idea why.

I thought we'd stand there forever, staring at each other in a deadlock, surrounded by unknown questions. Finally he broke the silence.

"You don't know do you?"

"Know what?"

"Do you have any brothers and sisters Daphne?"

"What is this, twenty questions?"

"Do you?"

"No. But I don't see what that has to do with anything."

"You're wrong. You do."

"Look, I think I would know if I had any brothers or sisters or not. And I've been an only child my whole life, Dominic."

"You have a brother. A twin brother."

"What are you talking about?"

"She's my mother too." I stared at him uncomprehendingly. "I was adopted," he continued, "given away pretty much the day I was born. You're my sister." He was totally dead pan. He wasn't joking. He was *serious.*

"But *how?*" I asked incredulously.

"I've known for some time that I had a twin sister, who wasn't adopted. But I've only just found out who that twin is. And it's you. You're the one mother didn't give away. Didn't abandon and totally reject since the day you were born."

I fumbled for the nearest chair and sat down. "But I don't know anything about this. I'm sure Dad would've told me about something like this… I mean, God, I didn't know…" I said rather lamely. A twin brother. I had this very fuzzy feeling in my stomach. But in my head I heard this click of the last piece of jigsaw falling into place. All my life… I had a brother. A twin brother…

I looked at him. He looked confused and vulnerable. I suddenly felt a very strong truth without any history flood my being. I felt as if an arm that had been amputated had now returned itself to me, and I could feel the fingers physically move for the first time, instead of just imagining it.

"Why did she do that?" he asked, in a hollow sounding voice. "Why? What was so right about you, and so wrong with me?"

My mind raced. I thought back through all that I'd come to know about Mum. The past that she'd shared with Dad and Isabel. I thought about the book that Dominic had just written. And why he had written it.

"There's nothing wrong with you Dominic. Nothing at all. You were just born the wrong gender." I felt the truth of this

14

statement as it announced itself in the air without having thought about it at all. Call it instinct.

"What does that mean?"

"Dominic, there's a lot to tell you…"

Chapter One

Leeds, West Yorkshire

Isabel Farmington Age 9

The house was dark. Mum'd gone out – to the shops or something, Sissi was with her. I quite liked the dark, no-one could see you or guess what you were thinking, or judge what you were doing, or complain about what you were wearing. The stars twinkled at me from above and the house was quiet and small, letting in the night light and the night shadows. I crouched underneath the kitchen table and closed my eyes. I felt the breeze breathing on my face and on my arms, and ruffling my t-shirt, as it gently fluffed up and squeezed down again. The street outside didn't shout any of its alarms and screams and engines through the window at me for a change. A cat somewhere crept too far and upset a dustbin lid with a clatter. It disturbed the night air for a moment, like a thrown stone's ripples on a lake, and then disappeared.

I liked playing games when I was in the house on my own in the dark. Games in my head – like I was a princess, trapped in a big, old creaky house, deep in the woods, and everybody would be looking for me, wanting to bring me back. They were unhappy without me, and needed me to come back and restore peace, love and happiness to the kingdom, and everyone was worried about me. And no-one could find me, or find out who had captured me and taken me away, cause there wasn't anyone holding me prisoner. I'd just gone off by myself and got lost and taken refuge in this big, dusty, cobwebby old house, and sat in the dark under the kitchen table to gaze at the stars and listen to the wind and the birds. And I was going to stay there until Teddy and Fippy came, and said they had come to save me. I'd look at

Teddy with his blond locks and blue eyes and his cheeky grin. He was cute and he could always make me laugh, and I'd look at Fippy with her very black plaits down either side of her face and wonder again at how dark and smooth and creamy her eyes were, as they smiled mischievously at me. Come on Izzy, they would say to me. And I'd shake my head and say I'm not going back to that horrid white palace, and plastic servants who don't know how I feel and parents who don't care. Smelly boring classes on how to sit and how to talk and how one day all these lands will be mine... blah blah... I don't want to go back to that. Fippy would start plaiting my loose, shaggy auburn hair, and Teddy would nod and say, "Let's run away together then," and I'd go, "Where?" Teddy would shrug and Fippy, still trying to tame my wild hair would say "Let's stay here and play – they'll never find us here." I'd go "Good idea."

Squeak, spring, snap – that's the gate.

Mum and Sissi are coming back.

I snap back from my fave daydream and sigh inwardly thinking of the boring kitchen strip light that will come on and chase all my secrets and specialness away, and mum'll say, "Clean off that dirty face of yours," and Sissi will say, "Your hair's a mess again Izzy," and want to brush it harshly. And they'll be rough meat and hard potatoes for tea. I was just about to get out from under the table, and dust my faded jeans off, when I heard a soft "Ssssshhhh – don't move" behind me. I felt a tingle of excitement and smiled in the moonshine now falling on my face, making puddles of white amongst the long shadows.

"Fippy!" I say.

"Sssshhhh, someone might hear," she says, as she crawls under the table next to me. Fippy wasn't allowed in the house. Mother didn't approve. She said Fippy would lead me astray and that Fippy came from a 'bad home'. But I liked Fippy, and she slithered in and out of the house as it pleased her, when no-one noticed, when Mum was out. She didn't live far away, but I'd never been to Fippy's. She always came to mine, or we'd bump into each other in the street.

"Did ya Mum shout at you about the teapot?" whispered Fippy. Phillippa was Fippy's 'grown-up' name, with two l's and two p's, but Fippy had introduced herself as Fippy when I first met her and it'd stuck.

"She didn't say owt really – just gave me one of her stares, ya know – like she does, and put it in the bin." Mum's special cold, blank stare, reserved just for me, with her lips shut very tight in a thin line. Fippy had accidentally (on purpose) smashed Mum's old teapot last time she was here, but I'd told Mum it was me. "Then she went into her room and I could hear her crying." It had felt worse than her just shouting at me, but I didn't tell Fippy that.

"She's got a new one then?" I followed Fippy's gaze to the dusty surfaces of the washing machine (that broke again last week and Roger, the bloke next door was on hols. and Mum can't afford someone else to fix it) to a shape that could just about be made out – in the gloom – as a teapot.

"No, Mrs Jones from Corner Shop was gonna chuck it out, cause she'd just got a new one, and she gave Mum it instead."

"That's nice," Fippy said, though she wasn't interested anymore. Fippy's 'accident' had been a dare actually. Fippy had dared herself to do it – and I said she wouldn't, but she did. I wish I could do outrageous things like her, just for the hell of it sometimes. But I daren't. I was too scared.

"Sissi and Mum'll be back soon," I say. Fippy understood the warning, but didn't care.

"It's OK, I saw 'em take the long way round." This meant they'd gone to the supermarket over the hill and passed the haunted church that no-one had been to for fifty years or something.

"I thought they were off to Corner Shop," I said. Fippy shrugged.

"Wanna play a game?" she asks, and I feel pleased that she wants to stay and play with me and a bit scared, 'cause I know I might well end up in trouble again.

Chapter Two

Ted Hawkins – Aged 15

"Mum, I'm home."

"I'm in the kitchen, Ted love."

"Come in," I motioned for Elaine to go through the lounge doorway before me. "Ya can dump your bag down there if ya like. Yo' OK?" She nodded. She was so pretty. The first girl I'd ever been serious about. Izzy and Fippy both get on well with her too. That was such a relief. Otherwise I always have a hard time convincing prospective girlfriends that I'm not romantically involved with either of them, just 'cause I spend a lot of time with them.

Mum came bustling in, apron on. Smudges of flour on her face and hands, and down her front.

"Mum, this is Elaine. Elaine – my Mum."

"Hello love. Make yourself at home. We don't stand on ceremony here. Would you like something to drink?"

"Squash please."

"I'll just go see what I've got. Do take a seat. Switch telly on if you like."

"Mum, we're jus' gonna go up to my room, do a bit of homework before tea."

"Is baked potato and salad all right, Elaine? And there's cake for afters."

"Er, yes, that's great. Thanks Mrs Hawkins."

"Oh, call me Trish. Do sit down. Ted, put Yorkshire on fer me will ya? I want to hear the local news."

"It won't be on yet."

"Yes, I know that, but put it on for me anyway, will ya?"

I did as asked, then turned to the attractive girl stood behind me. "C'mon Elaine, let's go up."

"Er, Ted, can you gimme a hand in here a minute love?" Mum had hearing like I don't know what! Annoyingly!

"You go on up, I'll be there in a tick. It's the second door on the right."

"Ask Elaine in ere an all will ya? I want to make sure I'm giving her something she likes." I rolled my eyes heavenward, and sighed. Elaine giggled. Good job she understood about having fussy mothers.

"I'm sure it'll all be fine Mum. Elaine's not fussy."

"Well, I want to ask her. Is there any crime in that? Now go set the table for me, dear. Elaine, do you like tomatoes?"

Mum proceeded to go through a whole list of foods, while I set the knives and forks on our set of three small tables in the lounge.

"Right, we're gonna do some study now, Mum."

"OK love. What are you studying?"

"Oh, science."

"Is that tonight's homework?"

"Yeah."

"For Mr Delfinchy? Are you both in the same class?"

"Uh-huh."

"Well, I'd rather you didn't go upstairs now. Tea'll be ready in a few minutes. Why doncha settle yourselves down on the sofa in front the telly, and I'll bring it through shortly?" It was an order made to sound like a question. Mum was good at that.

"Mum, we've got a lot to do." Well it was a white lie.

"Well, it can wait till after, I'm sure. It's not going to be that long, you'll have no sooner started than it'll be time to stop again, and you'll lose your thread. Now go sit yourselves down, go on." I hated this game Mum played. Yet again I was rail-roaded into doing what she wanted me to do.

I tried to contain my exasperation. "Mum, I'd really like to get started on it now…"

"Oh tush! On with ya. If ya start in an hour's time, after tea, it won't make a blind bit of difference I'm sure." Really she wanted to vet Elaine. And make sure we didn't spend all that much time together, alone, in my room. Didn't Mother trust me or something? I gritted my teeth against making an angry retort. If I did, I knew I'd regret it. Mum would play the injured party, and wonder why I was getting so uppity. She'd lay on the guilt trip, and make me feel bad, just for wanting to do what *I* wanted to do, which wasn't getting in the way of anything after all. It wasn't like I wanted to do anything terrible or owt. In fact, Mum was preventing us from studying, which is the opposite of what parents are supposed to do. Still, I didn't want to provoke a row, especially not in front of Elaine. So I let it go. And me and Elaine went and sat in the lounge.

It would have been different if I'd had brothers or sisters to share the limelight with. Or if Dad hadn't have died. I wouldn't be the sole focus of Mum's relentless attention then!

But Dad was dead. And I was an only child. And I couldn't go up to my room to get to know Elaine better. And that was that. For now.

"I think we'll go to your house next time," I whispered to Elaine. She smiled at me and winked. We held hands until Mum brought in our meals.

Chapter Three

"Isabel?" Mum shouted from downstairs.

"What?" I yelled back as I uncrossed my numbing legs, and leaned back against my head board again.

"Have yer seen Sissi?"

"No." Siss could be anywhere. And I didn't much care where.

I felt mildly annoyed at Mum's interruption. I bit my pen, and reflected on what I'd just written in my diary.

Dear Diary,

My whole world now seems to be consumed by one question, one word. Why? Is this what adolescence is all about? An endless stream of questions with no answers?

Instead, I hide in my room and read and listen to records, on the nights when I can't see either Ted or Fippy, 'cause they're out on dates. Ted's still dating Elaine. They've been together about four months now. And Fippy's going through a string of guys, who always seem to be at her beck and call.

But me? Well, I'm just a lonely spinster on a shelf. No, that's not true. I do like being single. But it <u>would</u> be nice if guys did take an interest in me, but they never do. And even if there is a particular guy that I fancy, they always fancy Fippy, not me. And she inevitably ends up going out with them at some point.

Perhaps I'll put some Bon Jovi on next, vent some of my frustrations, and just dance round my bedroom. Stop feeling so restless and caged, and just relax.

Not really much room to dance in here, but I love prancing up and down in front of the mirror, holding my hairbrush as a microphone. I make believe I'm a famous singer onstage, in front of thousands of fans, thinking how good I am at singing and dancing. Wish I really was. Hate not being able to sing for shit.

I remember when all my fantasies used to consist of being a princess, hiding in a dusty house, and playing simple games with Teddy and Fippy. Now I fantasise about having my Dad back, or having an older brother who sticks up for me against Sissi.

Fippy asks me if I mind her going out with such and such, and I always say no. Even if I do fancy them. My friendship with Fippy is much more important to me than any guy we might both like. Well, if they like her, and she likes him, I'm not going to stand in the way and make a fuss, and just end up with Fippy resenting me for curtailing her freedom in her choice of boyfriend.

I didn't *really* want to get involved with any of them anyway. Not seriously. The whole idea of having a relationship scares me too much, it's all just a bit too physical for my liking. I just like fancying them, and fantasising about how it might be between us, how romantic and spiritual it would be. How tender, loving and caring he'd be. But in reality, I know they're all just really immature boys, who can't offer me the love that I need. So I don't envy Fippy's relationships.

I do feel really naive though, not having had any experience with boys. Especially at this age. Everyone expects ya to have had at least one boyfriend. Only Ted and Fippy know I've never been out with anyone. I wouldn't know *how* to act in a relationship, not know what I'm supposed to do, or how to behave, or what to say to him. So, in a way, I'm quite relieved that I don't have to worry about being in a relationship with someone. I don't think I'd be very good at it anyway.

And I like my own space too much. Don't get enough of it as it is. What with Sissi barging in and out when she feels like it, always wanting to be centre of attention, always causing a commotion.

I suppose when it really comes down to it, I don't want a boyfriend at all. All those complications and sex and thinking of each others' feelings. I just want to be loved and protected.

I miss Dad. Still. Even though I never knew him. Don't even barely remember him. I've seen some photos in Sissi's room though, hidden from Mum in her dressing table. I wonder how life would be now if he'd stayed. Sissi told me a little bit about him, but not much. She's still really angry with him I think, for deserting us. She hardly ever mentions him in fact, these days. Except to taunt Mum with something like, "Dad would've let me!"

I feel so sad sometimes. Despairing. Like Mum does I think, sometimes. That he left and didn't care enough to ever come back, or even stay in touch.

It's left this huge ache in my heart, my gut, my stomach. And I don't know how to get rid of it.

I miss a father figure, my Daddy to run to. I wonder if Ted feels like that sometimes. At least his father didn't *choose* to reject him. He just died of natural causes, heart attack I think. He doesn't talk about him much either.

But it's different for a girl, not having her father around, than it is for a boy I think. Not sure I could explain how, but I feel that it is.

I wish he'd come back. Say he loved us all. Say he didn't know how he could possibly have left us and not called since. That he'd missed us all terribly, and all he'd really wanted to do was to come back to us, and make everything all right again.

And we'd forgive him, take him back with open arms, and perhaps Mum would find a way to be happy again. And Sissi would stop being so horrible to me. And I'd be a normal girl again, with two parents, like Fippy, and I could date boys, and have more confidence, and flirt with them like she does. I'd be attractive and like being wanted by guys. It would be fun. And me and Ted and Fippy could all go out on dates in six-somes, to cinema and stuff. It'd be great.

Why did he go away and leave us? Why?

Why didn't he ever write or call? Not even birthdays or Christmas. Mum said it was better to behave just like he never existed. But he did, otherwise I wouldn't be here. And so there's this void that I can't fill. And I'm unattractive, and Sissi hates me, Mum doesn't care about me, Fippy gets all the attention, and Ted has someone to kiss and cuddle and no-one cares about me at all.

No, I know that's not true. I know Fippy and Ted do care about me a great deal, but I just get so low sometimes, when I haven't seen either of them for a bit. I just feel a bit neglected. I like to be centre of attention too sometimes. All the time. So I know that they still like me and still care. How can I be so sure of it, when they're not here, but doing other stuff with other people?

Just then Mum called up to say tea was in the oven, but she was off out, so I was to help myself. I locked my diary away under my bed. My music taste picking fingers changed their mind, and dwindled from Bon Jovi to Meatloaf's 'Bat out of Hell II'. I put side two on first. I was really in the mood for *Objects in the Rearview Mirror*. I switched the light off, then went and sat on the narrow window sill to stare out at the stars, thinking how they looked like sparks from a firework frozen there forever.

My daydreaming/nightgazing was cut short by Sissi's loud insistent return. She always tried to act so grown up, but I always thought she was dim and a bit up herself really.

"Oh Izzy, look ya haven't even cleaned the kitchen or nothing!" She loved ordering me around, copying what she knew Mum'd say to me, but she hadn't done owt either to help Mum. She'd probably just been down to the shops buying a new lipstick or nail varnish, or both, in a colour she didn't have yet, but couldn't live without. She'd a huge collection of both.

Mum never said owt to her about it. Dunno why.

The sun glared in through the hot windows and I longed to open 'em and let in the car fumes and next door's stinky cat and the quiet birdsong in the background. I needed to let some life in. The air was stale, I was feeling stifled. But Felicity (Sissi for short) didn't like her hair put out of place when she was indoors – and would complain of 'that draught' again, even though the temperature was in the mid-eighties.

Once Sissi had had her share of the food, I told her, "It's your turn to wash up, Sissi." She frowned at me. She hated it when I called her by her baby name.

"Well I can't do it. I've got a date."

She always had a date. I grimaced slightly. I knew what that meant. I'd be left to do the cleaning up again or Mum would have my guts for garters, and Miss Felicity would get off scot free! – as usual!

"Who is it this time, Sissi, that spotty Mike fellow from down the road?" I couldn't help but tease. But Felicity was in an even less good-natured mood than she usually was. Jeez, she could be a pain sometimes!

"Isabel! You're such a cow! Just 'cause you can't get dates. No-one'd touch <u>you</u> with a barge pole, and just for your info. yes it *is* Mike, and he's NOT spotty. *And* he's gonna take me out in his new car tonight, so there!" She paused. "And before you think about squealing on me to Mum, don't bother, she already knows." And she got up, and left.

I boiled with anger. I wanted to shout, to claw her pretty face till it bled, to smash all the dirty crockery in the whole stinking house. But Mum came in, tired and weary and on the warpath.

I swallowed my pain and frustration and said, "I'll take those Mum, you go through. I'll fix you a cuppa and then I'll do the kitchen." I took the bags of food from her arthritic hands. She didn't even look at me. She went through to the lounge to collapse in her favourite chair in front of the telly. It was obvious her morning had been really bad. She hadn't levelled one hundred and one complaints at me, before even getting to the lounge door.

Chapter Four

"Sissi – hey, how ya doin'?"

"Oh, it's you." I was used to Izzy's sister treating me like this. She really had no tact or any awareness of anyone other than herself.

"Yes, hi Fippy, it's nice to see you too. How've you been?" I tease her. I was about to indulge in some more sarcasm when I notice her tear stained face. I jump up on to the crumbling wall next to her and start swinging my legs, enjoying the sun's warmth on my skin and the breeze through my hair. Shame about the view. Crowded terraced houses, grafittied walls on the corner shop, empty cigarette packets and crisp packets fluttering in the gutter.

"Push off squirt. I don't need your smell hangin' round."

"Cheers Sissi, love you too. Come on, spit it out, it's boy trouble ain't it?"

"How would you know? You don't know shit!" I could tell she was warming to me.

"You'd be surprised Felicity, how much I know." Maybe it was because I used her full name, or because I said it with absolute confidence, or because I refused to be baited by her insults, or 'cause of her own desire to tell someone about it. Though I still half expected her to tell me to piss off again. Instead she blurted out "He's dumped me."

Oh, I really had to bite my tongue on that one. With great difficulty I restrained myself from going "Oh – tough shit" and decided to hand out a little tea and sympathy instead. Goodness knows why I felt so good natured towards Izzy's selfish, self-absorbed sister, perhaps I felt pity for her, pity for her in her patheticness.

"When did this happen?"

"Just now," she sniffed, and rubbed her eyes as she turned

slightly away from me, as if I couldn't tell she was upset! "Mike were just here, and he says, he says to me... he says," she gulps some air and I remain quiet till she calms down. "He's wiv someone else. He's got another girl." That sounds like a line from a song I know.

"Any chance you'll get back together yer think?" I ask. Sissi shakes her head dolefully. "What will ya miss bout Mike then?"

"How d'ya mean?"

"Well, if he ain't around, what will ya miss?" Straight forward enough question methinks.

"I dunno. Er..." she takes a moment or two to think about this. "Er, the sex," she says flushing a little.

"Nar," I say, "ya can get that anywhere; owt else?"

"Well I shan't miss his smoking. Or his rude jokes that only he thinks is funny. Or his smelly feet. And I certainly won't miss him slapping my arse in public or the way he drinks his drinks – or slurps 'em rather. And I shan't miss him droning on and on and on about what a rotten world it is and how no-one does owt bout it, least of all him!" I've set her off now!

"So you're not missing much then, you'd have dumped him in a few days time. He saved yer the hassle *and* the guilty conscience." I say.

"Yeah," she sniffs, "yeah, yer right. Why didn't I think a that before?" I feel pleased with a job well done. "She's a cow though. Just you wait – I'll get me own back!" And Sissi storms off, with her seeds of revenge and I sigh. Sissi has a very limited range of feelings, and for once I don't give myself a hard time for feeling superior to her. Life's too short.

Chapter Five

I couldn't believe Sissi! – and how she'd treated me. I was shaking with anger and fear. I needed to talk to someone. Fippy. She'd understand.

Sissi had walked in on, and interrupted me doing my homework yet again. She'd a habit of disturbing me from that. I could never get anything done. It was mid-afternoon, and I hadn't heard her come back. She'd said some horrid things to me, how Mum never really wanted me around and only loved her, Sissi, and why was I being so difficult all the time and getting in her way, on her toes, under her feet, in the way, on her toes, under her feet... and so on. She made me cry and made me cry some more when she saw I was upset. She was three years my elder. Mum had only wanted one child – her – I was an accident, unwanted, unloved, selfish; I was the reason Mum and Dad had split up. Everything had been fine before, okay before, all right before, before I came. I took Mum's love away from her, I took Dad's love away from her and Mum too, it was my fault, all down to me, to me, I'd caused it all. If it wasn't for me she'd be happy, she'd be accepted, she'd have a career and money and parents to take her on holiday to places she only saw on telly. I knew some of it wasn't true, but I couldn't help but feel awful and guilty, and guiltier and even guiltier. Maybe it was all my fault. Maybe Dad would've stayed and they'd've all been playing happy families together; Mum and Dad and Sissi; Dad and Mum and Sissi; Sissi and Dad and Mum... no Isabel, no me, no I, not anything of myself – how would the picture have looked then? – or would it have been Sissi and Mum, Mum and Sissi, pining after Dad, instead of three of us pining after Dad? Would that have been more bearable? The tears flowed, wave after wave after wave, hot and salty, like I'd been saving up tears for years and I couldn't think of a single word in my defence. I felt too weak to retaliate and say anything back. I just wanted to curl into a ball in a dark corner and have the world forget about me! I was about to leave, I couldn't take Felicity's tirade any longer, and she said, "Where do you think you're going, you little minx?" and before I could answer she'd pinioned me to the never-to-be-white-again door of the pantry, always three quarters empty, no matter how much food Mum brought.

"I haven't finished yet."

"Please let me go, Sissi."

"Don't whine, you pathetic little cow."

"Please Sissi," I couldn't struggle against her, either physically or emotionally, at that moment she had all the power. I'd none.

"You make me sick you little shit," her words were a curious mixture of one of Mum's many rebukes and some selected vocab from the 'really-rough-gang' that always hung about on the corner of our block, opposite the corner shop that Mum always warned us to steer clear of. I was shocked. Sissi had never sworn at me, never directed it towards *me* before.

All of a sudden she let me go, but then struck me across the face with her right hand. I dunno where she went next, if it was outside or upstairs, I was blind for a moment and my cheek stung. I slid to the floor, my legs shaking like jelly. I sobbed tearlessly for a few moments; the emotion welling up in my stomach and pushing past my throat; but the tears were all gone, all used up, till next time. I don't know how long I sat there, just feeling the sobs rack my body and spill out into the quiet air – just listening, half embarrassed to my sounds, that I don't often hear. Feeling the cold tiles of the floor against my sweaty, clammy palms. My throat was parched.

I pressed the flat of my hands to the paint chipped door, and hoped their strength would support me, as I slid up the door. I checked my legs mentally, and decided they would withstand my weight. I spied the last clean glass on the counter beside me and took the two steps to the sink. The tap flowed for me a glass of cold refreshing water. I let its iciness touch my empty insides. I could feel it slosh in my tummy as I listened to it. Grasping the side of the sink for the moment, I let the water magically soothe me from my shock, and I felt the desperate urge to talktalktalk to someone. Fippy. I wasn't sure where I'd find her, but she was usually hanging around somewhere nearby.

I went out onto the street and let the sun heat my back. I felt unnaturally hot and cold at the same time. Hot skin, sweat gathering under my arms, but cold inside, like I wanted to wrap a blanket round me. I headed off down the street.

I think it's no. 47 – Fippy's, that's down and round the corner a little way. I hope I don't meet any of the 'rough-gang' as my Mum terms it – as I wasn't going to be able to face them in my currently fragile condition.

As I rounded the corner, and neared Fippy's house I was suddenly taken with a bout of hesitation as to what Fippy would think if I suddenly came to her unannounced. She'd always said it wasn't a problem but British politeness was! A sudden flash memory of Mum's emotional distance, and Felicity's cruelty and my own stark messy room at home to return to; I knew I couldn't go back there – not at the moment anyway. I needed Fipp. Her understanding and reassurance.

I came to her front door, beyond the small patch of overgrown front garden. The door too was almost covered over in out-of-control shrubs and bushes that hid the downstairs windows. The door was a midnight blue colour, dirtied, but still had a soothing effect on me, ever such a little, and my jarring feelings subsided a trifle at its welcoming. I knocked lightly – no answer. It creaked open, and I stepped into the musty hallway.

It smelt damp and fusty, even in the heat of the summer's peak. There wasn't much light. Curiosity and the welcoming door emboldened me to tread further. I popped my head round the door that led into the lounge. It was gloomy and cluttered, too small, much like our own front room but this one was littered with baby toys. Fippy had a younger brother, only two. Something inhibited me from calling out for Fippy and I carefully stone-stepped across the living room floor to the back where the kitchen would be. I quickly poked my head round the doorway.

There was a strange sickly smell, like that of out-of-date baby food, or puked up baby food not cleaned up and gone rotten in the heat. I creased my nose up and quickly withdrew. There was only the upstairs; three small bedrooms, one for

Fippy's parents, one for Fippy, and one for baby bro.

Fippy's Dad often came home drunk and beat Fippy's Mum. Those were the nights Fippy would hide in her bedroom world and shiver and cower at the noise and untold emotions, or she'd slip round to our house sometimes and sleep in my room.

After briefly viewing the other bedrooms and ascertained that they were totally absent of any two legged living creature, I ventured toward the last door. I was just about to open it when I heard a funny sound, a sort of scuffle, and a few heavy breaths, a moan, then silence. How strange. My hand slowly turned the door handle. It slid open silently, slowly. I couldn't see very much at first. Just strewn clothes on the floor, a few teddies and a heap of bed clothes on the bed, which twitched. I was just about to come closer to the bed, when my eyes saw two heads poking out of the sheets as my eyes accustomed to the dimness. There was some huffing and puffing and ungainly grunting and somewhere amongst the pile of arms and legs and bed sheets was Fippy. Our eyes connected. I was confused. I received Fippy's silent communications, backed out of the room, quietly closing the door and exited the house.

Out in the street again, my lungs gratefully inhaled fresh air. My mind spinning.

But Fippy doesn't have a boyfriend – or she would've told me. But she's only 15 – same as me. She's never mentioned anything to me about... such a thing as this. So who was he? I couldn't get my head round it, yet the facts were indisputable.

She didn't seem such a girl anymore. But why hadn't she told me? I wouldn't have balked, been shocked or cut her off in disgust. I'd have just listened, surprised, amazed a little and curious. I didn't get it. Questions swam round and round behind my eyes. There would be a lot to chat about next time I saw Fippy – Phillippa rather. 'Fippy' didn't have sex. But 'Phillippa' did. I had to make that distinction all of a sudden, my brain trying to come to terms with this new knowledge.

I didn't want to go home after that. I wanted some space to think my own thoughts – undisturbed and undistracted. I decided to head toward the park. It was only a few streets away. 'Ave to watch out for the 'rough-gang' though. They liked to hang in the park.

I walked through the alternate shade/sun/shade/sun under the trees as the sun leaked through.

"Tell your mother I saved your life," a voice suddenly rattled off at me in a whirlwind of speed as someone jumped out from behind me. I turned round, half expecting one of the 'rough-gang' ready to punch my face, but instead I saw Ted's laughing eyes.

"Don't do that!" I said, not impressed at all.

"Sorry, Izzy – didn't mean to scare ya," he said grinning, his arm dangling from my shoulder. We fell into step with each other as we continued through the shadow dappled pathways.

He was still grinning. I was still scowling. "Come on Izz, it was just a joke." I knew he was just joking around, but I couldn't laugh very easily at the moment. I felt his arm fall away.

"What's up, Izzy?"

"Nothing."

"C'mon. I know you better than that. What's biting ya?" he says as he links his arm through mine. It felt nice and comforting, we weren't an item or anything, though people often teased us about it, Ted was my male best friend, like Fippy was my female best friend. The three of us were best friends together. There wasn't any romance. We did that with other people. Well, them two did anyway, I just wasn't into it at all. Too much else on my mind.

"I had a big row with Felicity," I said, wanting to avoid the other issue and simultaneously remembering my initial upset.

"What's new there then?" he smiles.

I suddenly felt exasperated and misunderstood. "Is everything a game to you Ted? Sissi blamed me for how Mum is, for why Dad went away, for us all being so poor, and then she slapped my face and you just go 'What's new then?'" I finished, and the pain inside resurfaced and expressed itself in big sobs as Ted held me and stroked my back, apologised, told me it was all okay, I couldn't get Fippy's face out of my head, telling me to go – this wasn't the time – someone else was there – someone more important than her best friend upset – someone male and grunt like. I cried into Ted's chest. I felt his warmth, felt his breathing stomach out of sync with mine. Smelt his smell exuding from his neck and shoulders and I, breathing him in, breathed in his comfort and solidarity, breathed in his strength, hoping it would steady me, calm me, reach into my inner depths and ease the pain away.

He held me for a long time and didn't say anything. It was nice. I listened to the birdsong of birds I'd never know the name of and the distant sound of kids playing.

"I'm OK," I finally say and Ted draws back a little and looks in my eyes.

"Sure?" I nod. We walk on, hand in hand in an easy silence for a while. I can't tell him about Fippy.

Chapter Six

Fippy sat on my bed next to me. Statue like. Not looking at me. I began to feel awkward. I'd asked her about the man in her room. And Fippy started talking as if she wasn't really there…

It sorta happened all of a sudden but gradually if ya know what I mean. Mum and Dad'd slept in. Benji was gurgling happily away in his cot, staring at his mobile. A mate of Dad's had slept over on couch downstairs. He'd come back with Dad, from one of their late night binges. He was one of Dad's old-time drinking mates. And also Dad's boss. A little overweight and a bit hairy, but good-for-a-laugh my Dad always said. Mum weren't too keen on him though. I'd come downstairs in my jimjams to get a glass a water. I didn't know he was there. He was sat up on the sofa holding his head. I tried to be as quiet as poss. 'cause I knew what Dad was like in the mornings and was well trained not to make any loud noises. I was tiptoeing along and he looks up and says, "You're Ed's young un aren't ya?" I says yeah. He then motions for me to sit next to him, looks like he wants to tell me something.

So I goes over and sits down. He dun't say nowt for a second or so, then he says, "You're mighty pretty you are." I says thanks and asks if he wants a drink, as I can get him one. He says no, but he'd like a kiss though. I'm a bit surprised and before I know where I am, his mouth is slightly against mine, and his tongue flicks over my closed lips, and then it's over. Then he's sat with his head in his hands again and I wonder if it really happened or if I imagined it.

Then he looks up again as if he's aware of my staring at him and he smiles, gives me a longer kiss this time. I can taste beer, and feel his gentle warmth. It feels exciting and naughty. It weren't like kissing any of the other boys, 'cause he were older and more experienced. Then he stops kissing me, as we hear some creaking upstairs. I feel a bit strange, like I dunno what I'm supposed to do.

Dad was gonna be in his usual foul mood when he got downstairs, 'cause he'd have a stonking hangover and Mum'd be in a foul mood 'cause he'd stayed out late again.

Then he, Brian's his name, well then he gives me this tenner, ya see, and tells me to get mesen somert nice, like a pretty dress or somert; says he'll see me Dad on Monday as usual. Then he goes. I didn't spend much time thinking of it – any of it really – just that he were a bit odd.

She stops and her eyes wander to a very distant spot where only she can see the past. My eyes follow hers, but all I see is the greying colour of my bedroom walls in the growing darkness.

Next time I saw 'im was about two weeks later. Had forgotten about his mouth on mine and only vaguely remembered it when I saw him again. He'd come round to pick me Dad up before goin' to one of their usual haunts together. He'd had a couple of drinks already, and were a bit merry, but he were clean shaven this time, and spruced up a little and smelt of ol' spice, dressed in clean t-shirt and jeans and denim jacket. He weren't bad looking I guess. Mum were out on one of her girly night outs at a mate's talking about diets and hair-gone-wrong and how there were nowt on tv these days, but they all watched it anyway! She'd taken Benji with her, to play wi' other toddlers. Dad weren't back yet, from wherever he gets to.

I asked him if he wanted owt whilst he was waitin'. He smiled his smile again. He looked sorta friendly but secretive at same time. He said he were fine, but would like to talk to me. I sits down in a chair, and he says, "Do I smell?" And I looks at him puzzled. He says "Yer can sit on sofa next to me, I won't bite yer know." I moves across to him saying wi'out thinking that he smelt nice actually. He said, "Thanks very much". We sat like that for a couple of dead silent seconds. I was just about to ask if he minded if I put some music on or telly or somert, and he asked if it would be all right if he could kiss me again, as he'd liked it the last time. I didn't know what to say. The kissing'd felt sort of nice, but wet, and I wondered what it'd be like to smell his smell nearer to me. So he leans over and kisses me lightly and then his tongue slides into me mouth and it's wet and spongy and fiddling with my teeth, just like Ian did when I went out with him, and Stuart did that too. He pulls back a little and says "Do I still smell nice?" and I says "Yes" I couldn't think of what else to say. He smiles, and kisses me more. He starts moaning a little and getting hot, and worked up, and I likes his heat, and the touch and this new warmth so close to me. I felt this tingling in me tummy that I'd never felt before. I could smell his smell which was quite heady when surrounded by it as I was. Then he puts his warm hand on my thigh and strokes it a little, and my tummy were still murmuring pleasantly. He brings his hand up and up and he's stroking my inner thighs and I'm not thinking of owt except this fluttery feeling and his heat and taste. Then he puts his hand actually right up me dress to feel my heat down there and I dunno why but I froze. I stopped kissing. I was panicked I guess. He withdrew almost immediately and said, "Hey sorry babes I get carried away sometimes". We sat there for a couple of seconds, and 'cause I couldn't think of owt else to do, I asked if he were sure I couldn't get him a drink. He smiled at me again, patted me knee, said he were sure, and that he'd best get off, things to do.

I felt a bit at a loss – a bit cold and upset. He was there and warm, and alive and real and making me feel real and then he was gone. I felt a bit guilty about having frozen like that.

I wanted him to come back, to feel his skin next to mine. I thought about how disapproving Mum and Dad'd be about me dating an older man!

I wondered when I'd see him again. It were pretty soon. He came round next day to go drinking with my Dad again, but he totally ignored me. I felt really bad. Why did he do that? What was wrong with me all of a sudden?

Then later, much later, I was downstairs, watching a video, I couldn't sleep for being upset about earlier, couldn't get Brian out of my head, and then he came in with Dad. Quite merry they were, but not nearly as out of their heads as they usually gets. Mum was in bed, after taking a sleeping pill, after she'd sulked for hours about Dad's behaviour.

They'd come in. Dad went into kitchen to get 'em a couple of beers from fridge, and then went to the loo for a piss.

She wouldn't look at me. I felt her becoming more distant.

Brian went right over to her and started massaging her shoulders. It felt real nice. She relaxed. I wish she hadn't done that. He kissed her neck. I remember she thought that was sexy. Something that none of the boys she'd gone out with before had ever taken time to do. They faced each other. He put her numb fingers on his flies. Down, down, down. The zip went so slowly. It caught on his brown shirt. I remember thinking it might tear a hole in it, and everybody would notice it. He smirked. He didn't care about that. She couldn't understand why he didn't care about his brown shirt. He took her hand and rubbed it up and down him. She felt him getting harder. Wetter. He asked her if it felt good. It felt really strange. Surreal. She didn't know what to say. He kept doing it, said that it felt very good to him too, as if she had agreed with him.

Fippy hung her head. I thought she wasn't going to continue, but after a while she resumed.

Then his hand went between her legs, and she let him this time. It felt dangerous but he was really getting into it. She wanted to make up to him for the last time when she'd froze. She didn't want to be rejected. Again.

Then he whispered to her, "We're going to do something really special now," and he pulled her body to his and fumbled around a bit. She didn't want to. But she couldn't get away from his arms. She remembered the hole that had not been ripped in his brown shirt as he forced himself inside her.

She hadn't expected it to hurt like it did. She tried to push him away from her.

"C'mon, I know you want it, don't pretend you don't."

"No, Brian, I don't want this, I don't. It hurts, please stop."

"I can't stop now, and neither can you."

"I'll scream." He stuffed a hanky in her mouth.

"Shush baby, it's ok, it's always like this at first, but you'll like it, you'll see. You'll get used to it, you'll like it." She was terrified and hurting. He used her until he'd finished with her. She could smell his ugly sweat.

She stopped again. I was holding my breath.

I bled afterwards. Kept bleeding. I remember thinking I would never stop bleeding. That I'd never be able to sit down or walk again. I imagined having to live my life in a huge nappy to keep all the blood in, stop it leaking out everywhere I went.

Then Dad walked in. It was obvious what had happened and Brian goes, "Yer don't mind me and your lass here just having a bit of fun do ya?"

Dad, save me, beat him, throw him out, smack him, kill him, he's broken me, I screamed at him inside my head.

Dad looked at me. He didn't see me though. He saw nothing. I was nothing. He just said to me, "Don't just stand there girl, go get dressed will ya!" He switched on the telly. There were cartoons. Brian and Dad sat down. Together. And had a drink. Together. I watched Tom and Jerry running round after each other. I wondered what it all meant.

I don't remember moving. Or walking out of the room. But I guess I must have done, as the next thing I remember was standing in the shower. I stood there for a long time. The water was cold.

I couldn't think of anything to say. A whole new white terrifying world yawned before me, and Phillippa had kept it all hidden from me, until now.

A week went by. Dunno where Mum was, she was never there when I needed her. Dad and Brian came round again. I was in my room listening to my fave records.

Dad came in.

He told me loverboy was waiting for me downstairs. I didn't know who he meant. He said yer know, your boyfriend. Paul? – I thought.

"Brian's here," he says and I shake my head and say I don't want to see him. "But he wants to see you."

"Why?"

"Wants a word with ya that's all."

"I don't wanna see him Dad, really I don't, tell him I'm ill or somert."

"Hey, I'm not gonna stand in the way of you two getting it on, he told me all about you two lovebirds, don't worry, your secret's safe with me."

So he had Dad's blessing. I felt trapped, didn't know what to do. Then Brian came in.

He was all nice to me, and said for me not to be scared. He said he were real sorry if he'd hurt me last time, he hadn't meant to. He smiled at me, and put his arm round me. I didn't like it too much, but he seemed really sorry bout before. We just sat and talked for a bit. And I felt a bit more at ease. Then he started kissing me again. I kissed him back, half scared but half wanting to.

"I wanna be inside yer again," he says. "It felt so good last time." I told him I didn't want to, didn't like it. He said "I promise it'll be better this time." I said no still. Then he started getting nasty. He said I'd do as he said or he'd sack my Dad, and then there'd be no money, and we'd all be homeless, out on the streets. I said he couldn't do that. He said sure he could, and he started to walk out the room. I stopped him and said okay. He was real nice to me again then. But I hated him. And it hurt just as much as it did before. I don't feel anything when I'm with him. I don't feel anything anymore.

Silence.

I felt a pain inside me that wasn't there before. I could only think that Phillippa's pain must be a million times worse, and I just couldn't imagine it.

"But Fippy..." I wanted to be friend, comforter, outraged defender, put her rights forward, say she's not to live like this, it's not right, she can tell someone, her Mum, be protected, be okay...

"Don't!" she snaps. "I'm not Fippy anymore." And she's right. She's not.

"Phillippa, yer Mam would understand, she wouldn't let Brian..."

"Isabel, you so much as breathe a word of this to anyone and I'll never speak to you again. Whatsmore I'll deny every single word you say." I feel shocked, and hurt at her rebuke.

"I just wanna help..."

"Well I don't need your help. Can't you see? I don't want everyone to know that I'm... not me anymore, that I'm, well, about what's happened to me. It's nobody else's business but mine. Nobody would believe me, or if they did, they'd blame me, and we wouldn't have anywhere to live and... you're not to tell anyone, promise me!" Phillippa was stubbornly resolute.

"Phillippa," she looks at me, "OK, I promise," I say, and she turns and hugs me for a long time, and I hold her tight in the quiet dark, but strangely, I feel as if I'm the one being comforted.

41

Chapter Seven

There goes the bell. Break's over. English next. My best subject.
I also liked Miss Thames, who took the top set that year. Me and
Phillippa came in from the playground, amidst numerous other
pupils. I desperately needed a wee. Phillippa followed me to the
bogs.

So hot today. I could feel a slight sunburn on my exposed
shoulders. I didn't know how Phillippa managed to get through
the day wearing her brown polo neck, and trousers. Most of the
other lasses were in short sleeved blouses, and skirts.

As we flowed down the crowded corridors, I could hear
Phillippa groan, as she pulled alongside me. "I hate English. I
might not bother coming." Phillippa was doing this more and
more at the moment. She'd never knocked lessons before... But
now she just said she couldn't be arsed with it all.

"Oh, don't desert me, Phillippa. Remember, we're doing
discursive essays today. Ya can pick any topic and tear it apart.
C'mon it might be fun."

Phillippa gave me a cynical look. "Come on Iz, since when
have I ever enjoyed English?" You used to quite like English
actually. Especially doing things like polemics. But I didn't say
anything.

We arrived at the loos. We managed to get through the
throng to enter the smelly, grafittied room. Six cubicles, three on
each side, sinks in the middle. No soap as usual. And a drier that
was *still* out of order.

Phillippa didn't like a lot of things now, that she once used
to. And her behaviour had changed in other ways too. She wasn't
as loud in lessons as she used to be, and when she did speak out
it was usually to level criticism at something. She was no longer
witty and funny. She was just angry and withdrawn.

One day she told our maths teacher Mr Ticktale to go and

screw himself as he didn't have a clue what went on in the real world, and what real life was all about. I remembered what she'd said to me after that lesson, walking down the school playing fields.

She'd said, "It doesn't prepare you for life at all. They never talk about real things and real people. Just stuff out of books. Well I can read them mesen without having to come to school everyday." 'Real' was her buzz word at this time. "They never talk about real *life* and feelings and families and relationships and bills to pay and how people get stressed and drink themselves stupid to forget about it. They don't talk about sex or love or hate. Or self esteem and self hate. Or cruelty and beauty and contradictions and things not making sense. They just go on and on about the syllabus, the meaningless tests and exams. that don't mean shit in the real world. All they want is for everyone to get A-C grades in their GCSEs so that they can look good when the inspectors come round, so no-one cares about whether the kids are taught anything real, 'cause no-one fucking talks about real stuff in the big wide world either."

Phillippa had been breathless and sobbing by the end of this torrent, one of the few times Phillippa had ever cried in front of me. I tried to comfort her, but she'd just said, "You don't understand," and turned to walk away.

I'd felt rejected and hurt. But I hadn't wanted to let her go by herself in the state she was in. And then I'd had one of those moments, one of those flashes of wisdom you occasionally have, and you somehow know the right thing to say.

"Phillippa, I know I don't understand. But I am here to listen. And I do care about what you're feeling and what you're saying."

She'd turned and faced me. We'd looked at each other for a very long second. Worlds apart, yet threaded together so closely.

"Thanks Iz. You're the best." She'd given me a short hug, then drew back. I still looked concerned, so she reassured me the way a parent might. "Don't worry. I'll be fine. I just want some time alone."

I'd let her go then, feeling slightly shaken, and not having said all the things I'd wanted to say. My belief in education and its purpose to help you 'get a better job' seemed to pale in the face of Phillippa's passion.

I decided to try a different tack to persuade her to join me in English. "OK, so it'll probably be boring as hell, but I'd rather *not* be sat in English on my own." She caught my meaning.

We had the misfortune that year, to have been put in the same set as Sally and Petula Cleary. The terrible twins. Apparently they were only seven minutes apart, but they were as horrid as each other. They usually stuck together. They both had long mousy hair, with hazel eyes. But that's where the similarities stopped. Thank God they weren't identical. I dread to think of the mischief they would've got up to.

Usually, we managed to avoid the Cleary twins quite successfully. But not this time. And to make matters worse, quite a few of their friends were in our class too. They were much worse in a group, than by themselves. They seemed to enjoy being even nastier when they had an audience.

"OK, I'll come." I smiled gratefully. I slipped into one of the cubicles whilst Phillippa held the door closed by holding her foot under the door.

When I was done, I came out, and washed my hands. "We're going to be late," I said.

"Never mind. Miss Thames is always late too. She might not even be there yet."

We hurried along the bare corridors to room 37.

We were the last ones in, but Miss wasn't at her desk. There was a message on the blackboard to take one of the photocopied sheets from the top of her desk, pick three of the titles from the list and make notes on our ideas for an essay.

We both took a sheet then sat at our usual table, door side of the room, in the middle of the row.

The twins were in the next row over, further to the back. Their main supporters, Paula and Naomi were sat at tables adjacent to them, on the window side. They were getting blinded by the sunshine, and there were no blinds to pull to alleviate their distress.

We took our pencil cases out of our bags and started to look at the sheet.

There was the usual rowdiness and nobody was doing any work. Just chatting to their mates, scribbling on bits of paper, sat

44

on the tables at the back laughing loudly.

Then Miss Thames popped her head round the door. She came further in when she saw the disarray. The people at the back, Tommy and Clarissa, Lee and Shelly clambered off the tables, and back into their chairs. The noise subsided to a gentle hubbub.

"Good to see you're all working hard in my absence, class," her sarcastic tones scathed our ears. "I want ideas on at least three of those titles from each and every one of you when I get back in ten minutes. Upon my return, we will discuss your ideas. So you better make sure you actually have something that's worth talking about. Tommy! Naomi! Ten minutes. Get writing. In silence." And she left us to it once again. Despite her curt words, we just didn't have the self discipline to stay silent for more than a couple of minutes. The chattering started up again, but at least most of it was now focused on the text before us, instead of what we'd done last night. And things might have gone as smoothly and as uneventful as any lesson, but for Sally and Petula having decided they were feeling more bitchy and spiteful than usual.

"I hear you've got a boyfriend." I didn't register that the voice and the subsequent cat calls were directed in our direction at first. Then I saw Phillippa stop writing, her posture frozen in position.

"You got a boy-friend Philly-poos?" She hated being called Philly. So they used it as often as possible.

"Ignore them," I said quietly to her.

"Have yer sucked him off yet Philly?"

"Had him in yer mouth yet, have yer?"

"Has he licked you out? Did you like it?"

"She hasn't got a boyfriend, so shut up!" I called back.

"Bet she'd like one though."

"Yeah, someone to poke her up the arse."

"Yeah, and eat her tits. I can hear her now. Yes, yes, oh yes, just there."

They all laughed.

Phillippa was struck rigid. Just staring unblinkingly at the wall at the front of the class. If they'd taunted her about anything else, I know she would've been in the middle of a huge slagging match with them by now. But this was different. This was more cruel than they could know.

"You'd like that wun't ya Philly?"

"Yeah, does he ever get ya in a threesome, licking each other off, while he sticks it up yer..."

I stood up and faced them. "Just shut up and leave her alone, you arseholes." OK, so it wasn't a very good insult, but it was the best I could think of at the time. My legs were shaking, and my palms were sweating. I hated this sort of thing.

"Well, no-one'd be seen dead with you, Isabel. You skinny cow. Look, she ain't even got no tits. Who on earth would want to touch her?" Sally said. More laughter. While I was trying to think of something just as nasty to say in return, Phillippa had leapt out of her seat, stormed over to Sally, grabbed her by the collar, pushed her backwards till she was up against the back wall, and struck her a stinging slap across the face. Petula then joined in, and tried to push Phillippa away from her sister, but Phillippa gave Petula a hard push that sent her backwards over a chair, hitting her hip on a table in the wake of her fall. Petula slid on to the carpeted floor groaning, holding her side.

My brain was just getting in gear to get me walking over towards Phillippa, when she grabbed Sally's long mousy hair, and dragged her forward, down the classroom, to a table near the front. She slammed Sally's head on to the table, amidst the struggles. Despite Sally's wriggling, Phillippa kept her head against the hard table surface, and screamed at her, "You piece of shit." Sally's eyes were running, her hands were at Phillippa's trying to scratch them off.

"Lemme go you bitch." Everyone else was just stood/sat watching, enthralled. I could see Petula getting her second wind, and was about to attack Phillippa from behind. I knocked a chair into her path, and pushed her away. She glared at me, scared to retaliate. She gave me more power than I had.

"Admit it Sally. Say it! Say you're a filthy piece of shit!" and she banged Sally's head on the table again. "Say it," she demanded.

"I'm a piece of shit." Her eyes were absolutely streaming now, with the pain.

"A *filthy* piece of shit," Phillippa corrected her.

"Phillippa! Let Sally go. Now." Miss Thames's low and dangerous tones cut the air like a knife. We hadn't noticed her return. We were for the high jump now. Phillippa released her grip on Sally, and blinked as if surprised to find herself there.

"Everyone back to your seats." The silence in the room was palpable. We all moved back to where we should have been. The only sound amidst the shuffling of chairs, was Sally's whimpers.

Miss Thames remained rooted to the spot. Her face set. Her eyes raked over our faces, one by one. I avoided meeting her eyes, when they fell upon me. The seconds ticked by, not a word was said. We awaited the storm of fury that was surely going to come pouring out, but Miss Thames held herself in check, as if the silence would yield forth the guilty parties.

My heart thumped in my ears, as I sat demurely next to Phillippa. I tried to catch her eye, but she intently stared at her lap.

"Phillippa," Miss Thames waited for Phillippa to look at her before continuing. "Sally." And Sally stopped wiping her snuffly tears for a moment. "Petula," and Petula turned a sullen, angry face in Miss's direction.

"Isabel." I jumped slightly, my heart racing even more. "All four of you stay behind after class." Then she turned her back to us, as she wiped the blackboard clean. Then she faced us again, "Right, I now want to hear all the wonderful ideas that you'll no doubt have made copious notes on whilst I was away."

A discussion slowly got going, from people's half thoughts and semi-ideas. We painstakingly went through the whole sheet until Miss Thames felt somewhat satisfied that most of us had at least one theme we could go away and write about in some detail.

The dreaded end of lesson was soon upon us. Once the rest of the class had packed up their things and left, Miss indicated for the four of us to line up in front of the blackboard.

Miss Thames stood in front of us, leaning on the back of her chair which was tucked in under her desk. I looked nervously at her, and wondered what Phillippa was thinking.

She looked at each of us in turn, painfully slowly. I felt my cheeks grow hot and red. I just wanted this to be over!

"What happened, Isabel?" Why me? Oh no. Don't pick on

me to explain it all!

Just as I was trying to gather my thoughts together, the terrible twins erupted into their versions of what had occurred.

"Miss, Philly pulled all my hair out. You saw her!"

"And she pushed me over, and then Isabel kicked me." I started to protest my innocence to that one, as more of their accusations flooded out. Then Miss Thames silenced us.

"Enough! I asked Isabel for her point of view. Last time I checked your names were Sally and Petula. Wait your turn girls." She turned her burning eyes back to my glowing face.

"Well, Miss, er…" But then Phillippa came to my rescue.

"Miss, the twins were teasing me about this boyfriend they think I have. Isabel stuck up for me, Miss. But they insulted her too. So I pushed Sally up against the wall and slapped her. I slammed her head on to the table. Petula tried to stop me, and I pushed her out of the way. And then you walked in Miss." Just like that. Straight to the point. No stumbling or bumbling along. No excuses. Said right into Miss's eyes. Just so matter of factly. Phillippa even made herself sound like the villain in the whole scene.

"But Miss, Sally and Petula said some really horrid stuff to Phillippa," I said. Someone had to point out the real villains here.

"And what was your part in this exactly Isabel?"

"Well, I just told 'em to shut up, when they were saying all those horrible things to Phillippa. And I put a chair in Petula's way, and pushed her over, to stop her from attacking Phillippa," I said shamefaced.

"Do you disagree with any details of their account?" Her attention zoomed in on the twins. Her tone invited only the truth. Heads down, they both shook their heads.

"Detention. All of you. Phillippa, double detention for you. You can do yours tomorrow after school. Sally, yours is on Wednesday. Isabel, Thursday. And that leaves you Petula, with Friday. This room 3.30 sharp. Your parents will all be receiving letters. I don't ever want to see such disgraceful behaviour from any of you, again. You may now go to lunch." She watched us get our things, then followed us out of the room, and locked the door behind us.

The Cleary twins went one way, and we went the other. I linked my arm through Phillippa's as we walked down the corridor. We'd dump our bags in our own form room, then head down to the shops to get somert from the bakery, just down the road.

"That's so unfair you get twice as long in detention as the rest of us." Phillippa didn't say anything. "Phillippa, are you OK?"

"Well, I was the one who committed most of the violence."

"They deserved it! They said some horrible, horrible things. Are you sure you're OK?"

"Bit shook up, I think. How about you?"

I nodded. "Me too." Phillippa slipped her arm away from me as we went through the doorway into our room. We dropped our bags at the back.

Then Phillippa gave me a hug. "Thanks Isabel."

"What for?" I said, hugging her back. "I should be the one thanking you."

"Don't mention it." We drew apart, smiled, and walked back out to the corridor. "I'm starving. Let's make a run for the shops."

"OK," I agreed, feeling like that was the last thing I wanted to do.

***

Ted nudged me. He tapped his watch meaningfully. I looked closer. 3.25. Science was nearly over. Nearly there. Only five more minutes to go. I loathed science. But at least it was biology today. The lesser of three evils.

Mr Pines finally drew the lesson to a close. At last! We could pack up, and then GO HOME! Ted put our petrii dishes and microscope away. I tucked my science book and pencil case into my bag, right next to the letter for Mum, informing her of my 'misbehaviour', and saying I had a detention on Thursday for 45 minutes. I wasn't looking forward to giving it to her. If I was lucky, Mum would be in one of her 'I don't really care about anything' moods, rather than going totally overboard with her torrent of verbal abuse. Depended on what sort of day she'd had.

But just before Mr Pines said we could go, Miss Thames entered the room. She whispered something to him. He nodded.

"Right everyone. Don't forget, homework to be in on Friday. Isabel, Miss Thames would like a word with you before you go. Right, the rest of you, go on, get out of here," he chuckled.

Ted and I exchanged looks. I'd told him about what had happened in English earlier. Ted still didn't know about Brian though, so he didn't understand quite as much as he thought he did as to why Phillippa had lost it so badly.

People swept past, as we hung back. I wondered what she was going to say to me now.

"Do you want me to wait for you?"

"No, you go on ahead. I'll meet you and Phillippa at the gates, if you like."

"OK, I'll see you in a bit. Don't let the Thames water drown you."

"Very funny," I said, but smiled.

When there was just the two of us alone, Miss Thames indicated for me to take a seat. I hoped this wouldn't take long.

Miss Thames took a stool at the bench beside me. "Everything we say here and now, will be held in the strictest confidence. What happened today is most unusual, and to be honest Isabel, I'm very worried about Phillippa."

This was the last thing I had expected to hear. I didn't know what to say. I hoped she wasn't going to ask me any difficult questions.

"You don't have to say anything that you don't feel comfortable with, Isabel. And I'll be talking to Phillippa myself later. I don't expect you to break any confidences between you. But if you could help me out at all, it would be very helpful, and whatever you say, I promise won't go any further than between the two of us." I gulped a dry throat.

"Does Phillippa have a boyfriend, Isabel?"

"No Miss." Well that was the truth.

"I've noticed Phillippa's work isn't up to its usual standard. Is she having any problems at home? Anything troubling her?"

"Sort of." I instantly felt guilty, as if I'd be damned forever now, for betraying Phillippa, even in this small way. But I felt I could trust Miss Thames, and if she could help Phillippa, that would be great – wouldn't it?

"Hmmm. I know her parents aren't particularly supportive of her. So she's not in any sort of serious relationship with anyone? Or has been?"

"No, not really." Please don't ask me anymore.

"Sorry, Isabel, I know this isn't easy for you. But could you just tell me definitively if Phillippa is very upset about something at the moment?" I remained mute, not really knowing what to do. "I'm not going to ask you what. I just want to know if there *is* some particular reason, whatever it is, behind her recent odd behaviour. Just nod if you like, if there is definitely something." I nodded.

"Are you meeting Phillippa to go home?" I nodded again, glad I didn't have to say anything. "Then I won't keep you, Isabel. But I'd like you to do something for me. Tonight, if you could write down a factual account of everything said and done, and by whom, and when, as clearly as you can remember. Everything that occurred in today's lesson. Hand it in to me first thing tomorrow. And I promise I won't be offended by any rude words, or swear words," she smiled.

"OK," I said.

"See you tomorrow, Isabel." I fled, glad to get out of there. I'd just tell Phillippa that Thames had given me extra homework. It was a half truth.

Chapter Eight

"Delilah?"

"Yes, I'm home. I'm in here."

Melissa came into the living room, where I was sitting, English books open on the table in front of me, but I couldn't really concentrate on marking. She kissed my brow, my frown ceased aching for a moment. She planted a welcoming kiss on my lips, and asked me how my day was.

"Not too bad, how was yours?" I asked, watching her undo her anorak.

"Just got caught in the summer rain. Other than that, pretty bobbity-boo really," she said smiling. Her shorthand for things chugging along nicely. "Jerry was off sick today, so I had to cover for his work load mostly. But thankfully, it wasn't so busy today! Think he's got flu. Hope he's better for next week."

"Sorry?"

"You haven't been listening have you?" I shook my head and smiled an apology. "I'll just get myself a drink, then you can tell me all about your 'not-too-bad' day." She understood my shorthand too, for 'it was a lousy day really, but hey…'"Do you want one?"

"No, it's OK, I haven't finished this one yet."

She plonked herself down beside me, armed with her pure orange juice, and an unlit cig. She said just holding it made it easier for her to give up. It seemed to be working thus far.

"So did the little rat bags at school give you hell today then?"

"No, nothing like that. Just a little worried about one of my pupils. Her behaviour's changed suddenly. Quite violently. Negatively. She's… I dunno. She's not interested anymore. It's very strange, because normally she's quite bobbity-boo about things."

Melissa held her cigarette between her lips a moment, as if she was about to light it, then held it between her slender fingers again.

"What can you do about it?"

"Well, there's nothing much I can do really, if she doesn't tell me anything. I've got her in detention on Friday. I'm going to take her for a five mile jog, help her to exercise her demons, or at least some of her rage anyway."

"You and your individual detentions. Shame other staff don't use your techniques."

"Hey, you never know one day it might catch on!"

"You never know!" She drank down her juice, and I felt suddenly thirsty for another drink myself. She studied my worried face. "Even if it is what you think it is, you've no way of knowing. I'm afraid you're powerless to do anything, darling." She put a comforting hand on my knee.

"In any formal sense, you're totally correct."

"And informally?"

"I can help build her self-esteem. Give her something to strive for, something to push against. She has a lot of anger, and that's good. She'll need it to get her through, if she's gone through what I think she has. She can harness that anger, that energy, and take control of something in her life."

"Something?"

"I know she's good at games. I'm going to have a discreet word with Lucy. She could perhaps make her captain of the hockey team or something, give her some sort of responsibility, something to chew on. It'll also serve as a good external focus, other than home, and other than study."

"You've thought about her a lot, haven't you?"

"Yes." Melissa wiped a tear from my cheek.

"You could be wrong you know, darling. She might not be going through anything like you did."

"I know. I hope I am wrong. Well, if I am, giving her some responsibility will do her good anyway. So she won't lose out in that respect, either way. All else I can do, well, bugger all really! Unless she comes to me."

"Is that likely?" I shook my head.

"But maybe I am just reading too much into it anyway.

Perhaps it's just her natural rebellious stage against authority that she's acting out." But I couldn't help but think of the conversation I'd had with Isabel earlier today. And my gut instinct about such things told me something was up. But I don't have anything to back that up with, no evidence, no proof.

"Perhaps that is all it is." She stroked my thigh gently. I was so glad she was here to talk to and share everything with. "Well, you've got a course of action darling, and it sounds like good sense to me. There's nothing else you can do, so I *suggest* we either go out and have a damn good game of badminton to relieve all your frustrations, or we can go out and socialise and take your mind off everything. Alternatively, I can rustle us up something delicious to eat, and we can have a cosy night in with a video. Whatever you like best."

"But Melissa, I've got marking to do and all this…"

"Delilah! I'm not going to let you sit here and strain to give attention to all those adolescent scribblings, when really you're worrying like sick over this pupil of yours. C'mon, you know a total change of activity is just what the doctor ordered. If we're quick, we can still fit in about half an hour on the badminton court, and we can grab an Indian and a video on the way back, my shout. What do ya reckon?"

"I reckon the doctor's right as usual! I'll just grab our stuff. Shall we take your car or mine?"

Chapter Nine

I'd been trying to get hold of Ted all day. This wasn't something I felt I could ask Isabel. But I hadn't shared any lessons with him today, and when I did spy him on the football pitch earlier, he was busy canoodling with Elaine (as usual). I hated to interrupt!

End of the bleeding last lesson at long fucking last! Time to go home, but that didn't make me feel any better. Might as well hang round in the park or something for an hour or so.

I got to the school gates and Ted was there. With her. Doing the usual. Well I was bloody well going to butt in this time. If I wasn't going to get to ask Ted about it today, I don't think I'll ever get the words out. I'll just have to go it alone otherwise. I put my hands in my jacket pockets, so he wouldn't see them shaking. It's now or never.

"Ted, have you got a sec?" I said, patting his arm, to make sure he was aware I was there.

He pulled himself away from her embrace slightly. "Yeah sure, hold on a tick Phillippa." His gaze remained on her. "I'll see you tonight then." An extended kiss ensued. I looked away discretely. Them two were so soppy it made me wanna puke!

"Bye Ted." And that voice of hers! Like fucking syrup! It made my stomach churn. I used to like Elaine. I did. But these days she just got on my nerves. Big time! They kissed. *Again!* Probably for my benefit. She's started getting really precious over Ted lately. Christ! – could they not leave each other alone for more than two fucking seconds! Finally! – one last lover's glance. She'll fall over in a minute if she doesn't look where she's going. Ted stares after her. Elaine actually does bump into some other pupils and finally decides to walk *forwards* like everybody else.

"Hello! Loverboy? Earth calling Ted Hawkins!"

"Sorry Phillippa. You now have my undivided attention."

He said with a mock bow.

"Have I? It's not skittering off somewhere, thinking of what you two gooey love birds will be doing tonight?"

"Well, now that you mention it..." he laughed. I didn't. He sobered up. He could tell I wasn't in the mood. "What's up?"

"Let's go for a walk. Your Mum won't mind yer bein' a bit late home tonight will she?"

"No, course not." She'd grill him about where, when and wherefore no doubt though, when he got back, as to why he was late. She was a sweety his Mum, but she went a bit far sometimes. Still, at least she cared. Not like my Mum.

We went down to the stream at the start of the woods, at the bottom of the playing fields. I watched my shoes getting wetter from the grass. It took us about ten minutes to get there. We walked in silence. I ran over in my mind what I was about to ask him. My stomach churned again. I thought about the *thing* growing inside me. Stop it Phillippa! Stop it now! I forcibly blanked my mind – otherwise I'd just change my mind and wouldn't say owt at all to Ted. And I really needed to about this. It was too big to cope alone.

We stood on the bridge, watching the excuse for a stream trickle a few feet below us.

"What's on your mind?"

"I've got to go to the clinic." Ted looked at me. Seriously. Concerned. I couldn't look at him.

When I didn't say anything he asked me if I was ill.

"No. I'm pregnant." He was shocked.

"So that's why you've been acting strange lately." I let it pass.

"I'm going to have an abortion." I schooled my face and turned to him. "Will you come with me?"

"Yes, of course," he immediately responded. I gave a very brief smile and turned my head. The tears were there, but I pushed them back. He put his arm round me and I welcomed his support. My legs were none too steady at the moment.

"Is the father anyone I know?" I shook my head, unable to speak. I could taste today's dinner threatening to join the leaves beneath my feet.

We stood like that for a while. Bird song occasionally

erupted and died away. The occasional car could be heard in the distance. There was no-one else around.

"Does Isabel know?" Again I shook my head. "I won't tell her," he said kindly. He knew I would tell her if and when I wanted to. I couldn't speak my thanks.

"The appointment's for next Tuesday. 3 pm. I just need someone to hold my hand." To protect me.

"I'll be there." He didn't say anymore. He didn't need to. Why did I instinctively choose Ted to turn to, and not Isabel? Probably because Isabel knew about Brian. And probably 'cause she would empathise too much, the grief would feel doubled. I just needed Ted's quiet strength. No questions asked. And I knew I could rely on Ted for that.

I wish I could stand here forever and not face life again. Should I say this aloud? No, I don't think Ted would know what to do with such a heavy statement.

"C'mon, let's go home," I finally say. We walked back up the playing fields. Good job Elaine can't see us now. She'd have a fit! But then she was having a normal life, and having a normal relationship. She didn't know how lucky she was.

"Do you want to come back to mine for a bit? Mum won't mind."

"Elaine's coming though isn't she?"

"Not till seven. So we've a couple of hours clear before the green-eyed monster rears her beautiful head."

I laughed. "OK, sounds good."

Chapter Ten

"Isabel!" My Mum called me from downstairs.

"What?" I shouted back.

"What are you doing?"

"Nowt." I always said that. I never told her what I was up to. I just wanted to stay here in my room and do my own thing. Undisturbed.

"That'd be right," she retorted scornfully. I ignored my anger, and continued looking back through my dream diary. I filed all the dreams into different sections, as I often had serial dreams about the same thing, but different things happened in each.

There was the 'Wasp Dreams' section. Dreams of human sized wasps, and of swarms of wasps chasing me, threatening to sting me. I had lots of them.

'Time Anxiety Dreams' were another section. These were the dreams where I had got to go somewhere important, like for an exam. and I had to be there for a certain time, or else I'd fail, and they won't let me re-sit it at any other time. But I dream I'm late for it, or I dream that it's the day after the event, and only then do I realise that I've forgotten to go to it.

I had a section on 'Man Dreams', where I dream I'm a man. Often married, and I have an affair behind my wife's back. But not always. One dream I had was like an epic film, it went on for ages. And I was this bloke trying to rescue his girlfriend. And we were both running away from all these people who kept trying to kill us.

I was just flicking through the 'Being Chased Dreams', wondering what they all meant.

Dream Four: I was walking down a street at night, on my way into town, towards the shops. It was black as pitch. I was walking down this alley way, there were two men behind me. I was terrified. They might do something to me. Anything. And no-one would know. They were catching up to me. They had their arms round each other. One of them was holding out a baton, like you would conduct an orchestra with. I couldn't wait for the horridness to come to me, so I turned round to face them. I reached out for the baton, to touch it. And they walked right by me, and entered one of the late night restaurants open at this time. I breathed a sigh of relief. They'd had no dark intentions toward me. They were gay. Then there was another guy behind me, catching up to me. I started to run. He caught up easily, and rushed past me. He was only interested in going into the light of one of the cafes/food shops.

Dream One: It was blackness. No walls. Trapped in some sort of basement perhaps. One bright spotlight of white light shining on to a ladder, and on to the floor. The ladder wasn't resting against anything, and it didn't lead to anywhere. This man was holding a gun, he kept chasing me round the ladder. He wanted to kill me. I kept dodging him. He could've just shot me at any time, but I continued to dodge him, as I went round the opposite side of the ladder to him. It went on and on for ages. I felt terror, waiting for the strike to come, but it didn't.

Dream Three: He chased me up the stairs of my house, even though it was a house I've never been in before in real life. I locked my bedroom door behind me. He pushed against it. He banged on it, but I wouldn't let him in. I was leaning against the door. He screamed and shouted at me through the door, but there was no way I was going to open it to him. I was so scared. But he wouldn't go away. Wouldn't leave me alone.

I'd read somewhere, in one of my dream interpretation books that when a woman dreamt she was being chased by a man, it meant she wanted to be loved. Funny way of showing it, if you ask me. But I suppose it made some kinda sense if I thought of it in terms of my being scared of being loved. But the violence, the threats… what's that got to do with love?

I looked at the clock. Seven pm. I'd better get a move on if I was going to meet Ted at the cinema tonight. I'd twisted his arm to come and see a comedy *The Paper*. As I was interested in becoming a journalist, I thought it would be right up my street. And I'd decided this was the ideal way of getting Ted to forget for a couple of hours about Elaine having dumped him for someone else.

***

"What did you think of the film?"

"Was OK."

"Oh, come on, I saw you laugh."

"Yeah, it wasn't bad."

I didn't push him on it. I watched our feet fall in time on the night time pavement. The regular fall and miss of yellow streetlights lighting and darkening us.

"I wonder what Elaine's doing now. I wonder if she's with *him*."

"You deserve someone better than her Ted."

"But I love her."

What could I say to that? Only time mends a broken heart – too corny. There's more fish in the sea – too cliché.

"I know," was all I said. Ted linked his arm through mine in solace.

"Phillippa's not seeing anyone anymore is she?"

"No." Not in the technical sense.

"What happened to Christopher Jenkins, do you know? She's not mentioned anything to me."

"She called it quits."

"I thought she had. Did she say why?"

"No." She didn't have to.

"She's been a bit strange lately, hasn't she? I mean, stranger than normal. Do you think she's OK?"

"She's got a lot on at the moment." So she hasn't told Ted about Brian then.

"It must be hard putting up with her Dad when he beats up on her Mum like that."

"Yes."

"Do you ever think of your Dad, Iz?"

60

"Yeah, sometimes. I wonder where he is, and what he's doing. But I don't think he'll ever get in touch again."

"Do you want him to?"

"Yes and no. If you'd have asked me a while ago, I would've said definitely yes, but I dunno if things would be any better if he did. Maybe Sissi and me might stop fighting like cat and dog."

"No, that would never happen. You're so unalike. You'll always have stuff to argue about."

"Cheers Ted."

"I'm worried about her."

"Who?"

"Phillippa." Or does he know, and he thinks maybe I don't know?

"Me too." I said honestly.

He paused and then said meaningfully, "Did she tell you?"

"Yes." So he does know.

"That's a hell of a trauma to go through."

"Yes. It is. But she won't tell anyone."

"Hardly surprising. Don't think I would want to either."

"But wouldn't you want to tell the police?"

"And have my name dragged through the mud and have everyone talking about me? No I certainly wouldn't."

"But it's a crime."

"There are worse."

"I can't think of any."

"It was only underage sex Isabel, not murder."

"Underage sex! Is that what you call it! Call it what it is for god's sake Ted."

"Well, she wasn't raped, was she? I mean..." We stop and look at each other, caught in the yellow limelight. "You mean she *was* raped. Oh my god! I didn't know." He looked shocked.

"But I thought that was what we were talking about," I said puzzled.

"No, I didn't know. I assumed it must've been Christopher's."

"That *what* was Christopher's?"

"The baby."

"What baby?"

"The aborted one. You didn't know." I shook my head in silence. I was at a loss for words. The bastard! Poor Phillippa.

We continued walking a while, absorbing this new distressing information about our best friend. Every now and then a car slid by, the white and red lights glancing off us.

"We've got to tell the police," he said after some time. "He can't be allowed to get away with this."

"But we can't. Phillippa said if I breathed a word to anyone she'd deny it all."

"Then we'll have to persuade her to go then."

"She won't do it Ted. She doesn't want people to know."

"Who is the guy anyway?"

"Brian Thurston. It's her Dad's boss. He's done it a few times." I felt sick and shaky.

"It's happened more than once?"

"Still is I think," I said tremulously.

"We've got to stop him! No wonder Phillippa's been so weird lately."

"*How* can we stop him?"

"We can tell her parents, they'll want to put a stop to it, and they'll want her to report it, and put this guy behind bars where he belongs."

"Her Dad already knows."

"*What!*" I explained what Phillippa had told me. "What a bastard! What a total shit!" I'd never heard Ted swear before.

"She'll never talk Ted. She doesn't want to!" How could I make him see?

"But she's *got* to. We'll talk to her, tell her we'll stand by her and see it through with her." I shook my head. This wasn't good. I felt the same way as Ted, but I didn't want to go against Phillippa's wishes, what was I supposed to do? How else could we stop Brian?

"She won't do it Ted. She really won't."

"Well, we can at least talk to her about it, and see what she says."

"I don't want to do that."

"How else is she going to be protected? She hasn't got anyone else Isabel, only us." I knew he was right. I felt I should've done something or said something earlier.

"What are we going to say?"

"We'll talk to her about it tomorrow. Perhaps, once she knows she's got our support, she'll want to talk to the police anyway. Don't worry Isabel, it'll be fine." But I did worry. It didn't sound fine to me.

We didn't talk much more on the rest of the way back. We got to my gate eventually.

"Bye Isabel, and thanks for trying to take my mind off Elaine."

"That's OK." Just had Phillippa to worry about as well.

"I'll see you tomorrow."

"Yeah, OK." We hugged and said goodbye.

I worried all night about Phillippa and what would happen tomorrow. I didn't get to sleep till about five, only to wake again about six.

***

I couldn't eat any breakfast the next morning, and I didn't hear anything that was said in registration, assembly or maths lesson. I just couldn't focus. I couldn't think about anything else except Phillippa, and telling her, and for her to tell or not to tell, and all the possible ramifications that I just couldn't work out.

The three of us met up at break time. We went down on to the football pitches, out of earshot of everybody.

"What's wrong with you two? You're acting like someone's just died!"

"Sorry Phillippa. Last night, when we were walking home from the cinema together, we sorta got talking and…" This was difficult.

Ted jumped in, "and we were saying how worried we were about you and…" Phillippa raised her eyebrows and looked at us amused.

"And we misunderstood what each other was talking about…" I continued and trailed off.

"I know about Brian. And Isabel knows about the abortion." Nothing like blurting it out Ted. I saw Phillippa's face go blank, and she looked at us coldly. Not cold, as in hateful. But cold as in removed, distant. I felt my heart thud loudly in my head.

"Sorry, Phillippa. I really am. I thought he knew you see, and he thought I already knew and..." I rambled.

"It's OK Isabel. It's fine. I would've told both of you at some point anyway." Her reassurance was genuine, but she was still a million miles away, unreachable.

"I think you should tell the police," Ted said, and I cringed inside.

"You do, do you?" Phillippa said oddly.

"We can't stand by and let you keep getting hurt like this Phillippa. We care too much. It's not right. You don't deserve this."

"Don't I?" I didn't like her simple reflective questions. I would've preferred her to blow up at us and lose her temper and tell us to get stuffed, rather than this detachment of emotion.

"He needs to be punished for this. And you need to be protected."

Phillippa was silent a moment, and so was Ted. I looked at them both, Ted's concern and demand for justice, and Phillippa crushed like a wounded animal. I'd never seen her like this before. I waited for Phillippa's 'Do I?' It didn't come but it was in her eyes.

"I don't think you understand Ted," she finally said, her eyes glistening, as she turned away from us slightly.

"You can do this Phillippa, we'll help you. We'll come with you if you like. We'll see it through together, the three of us, each step of the way. But we've got to stop him doing this to you."

"OK." Did I hear right? Did that small voice belong to Phillippa? Did I hear her correctly? She'd agreed? "OK, I'll do it," she said more forcefully this time, "but let's do it now, before I change my mind."

The bell went for the end of break just then. It was now or never.

"OK then." Ted agreed and the three of us went down to the bottom of the field and out through an alleyway into the next door neighbouring estate.

Their concern made me giddy. Their sympathy made me feel sick.

We walked the crazy streets in a fog of nothingness. Somehow we were on a bus to the police station and a crazy world passed by. And I felt heavy dread in all my limbs, like I was weighed down with lead. My torso didn't exist, air passed through it. I felt sick if I looked at the ordinary world crazying by. I stared at my hands that didn't belong to me. I couldn't look at either of them.

We crazed floatily off the bus into the station. I wouldn't let them come with me to the interview room. I didn't want them to know...

Phillippa didn't tell us what was asked of her or what was said. She still looked terrible. She looked vacant, like she was there, but not really there. I wished we hadn't gone and that Ted had never insisted on it. It was too much to comprehend, too much to take.

I didn't know if I'd made the right decision or not in the end, suggesting we went to the police. I look at Phillippa's ashen face and wonder if even we can provide the support she needs. I hate feeling so powerless to do anything to help. The afternoon felt so futile somehow, yet surely now, the police will bring this piece of dirt in, and Phillippa will be safe?

Chapter Eleven

After the police station, Ted and Isabel went back to school. I went back home. I didn't tell them that I hadn't told the police after all. I spent the time reporting some vandalism that had happened in the local area, but that hadn't taken very long, as there wasn't much I could tell them and not much they could do. So I spent the rest of the time in the ladies toilet, till I thought enough time had gone by... I just couldn't do it. I just couldn't tell a stranger all the horrible intimate things... I couldn't do it. They wouldn't believe me anyway. And what about Dad's job? And the house, and money and food... And everyone *knowing*... I couldn't bear it.

But then I thought, if I tell Mum and Dad about it, make Dad see what was really going on, and if *Mum* knew, and then if they were behind me, then I'd tell the cops, because everything would be OK then. They'd take care of everything. If they backed me up, I'd do it. I would.

It didn't work out that way at all though. I should have known better. I should have known. How could I have been so blind, hoping so blindly?

Dad happened to be at home already. He'd had a doctor's appointment.

He hit the roof. Went ballistic. Lost it. Big style.

"You did *what?*"

"I told them Brain raped me." Well, I hadn't yet, but I will.

"You wanted it you lying slut!"

"That's not true!"

"You're a disgrace to this family. You know that? Running round telling such outrageous lies. Bring the whole family down you will. And Brian's gonna be none too pleased to hear about this."

"I don't *care* about what he thinks."

"Well I damn well do. The money he gives me pays for the food you and me and your mother and your baby brother eat. Do you want us all to starve? Is that it? Is that what you want? See us all on the streets, and our little Benji going hungry, crying out on the streets?" But part of me realised that a lot of that money went on booze. "Is it? Is that what you want? 'cause you're going the right way about it my girl. But don't think we'll be out begging food for you. Oh no! You can forage for your own damn food."

Mum just sat there. Mute. Stone like. Statue. Horror on her face. She only got chance to utter three lines in the whole sorry episode. "Is it true?" "What sort of mother am I?" and the last line only contained two little words. Very little words. Very meaningful words. Very overlooked words. Very ignored words. Words I'd screamed a million times in my head, in bed, every night, every shower, every second of being in this shit hole of a house. Her last line echoed in the dead wake of my father's storm. The last words I heard her say before I walked out the house.

"This is all your fault, you lazy good for nothing. You shouldn't have come down in your pyjamas that time. Then it would never have started and you wouldn't have put us in this terrible mess now. You can damn well tell the police you didn't mean a word of it, and admit to them what a liar you are. You can do that right now, this very minute my girl, and no bones about it." I was not his girl. I was never his girl.

I didn't cry though. I felt surprised at my lack of emotion in front of him. I did cry later. I cried my soul out, till I felt my body held no more water, but before the man who liked to call himself a father, I donned a coat of ice, and he chipped bits off my corners every now and again with the words he was throwing at me.

He saw his words trying to break the ice coffin I was surrounded by, and he failed time after time. There was the odd crack, but my ice was thick. So he did the only thing he knows how to do. What he's been practising on Mum for years in his drunken rages.

He hit me.

It was the first time ever. And the last.

Normally there was a code of 'non-touching' that was heavily enforced, between him and the rest of the world; the rest of his family.

He struck me hard. Slap. Right across the left side of my face.

I fell backwards. I could feel the sting, and my eyes watered, and something trickled down from my nose on to my top lip.

I stared at him in shock.

I could feel hate, fear and anger mixing up the air and I couldn't tell which feeling belonged to whom.

"Get out of this house. And don't you ever, ever come back. I can't stand the sight of you." He looked away then.

And from somewhere I heard a voice that I suppose must have been mine, but I couldn't feel the vibration of my voice, or feel my lips moving, and my ears didn't register the sound as coming from the space my body occupied, but there was no-one else there to say these words but me: "I'm going, and I never *want* to come back. You're worse than Brian and *I* never want to see *you* again." He didn't respond.

"Oh no," she said. That's all she said. "Oh no. Oh no, no, no, no, oh no!" I know better than anyone the complete uselessness of those two words. "Oh no." It doesn't stop it happening. It doesn't make it better. But worst of all, it doesn't get *heard!* No-one hears it. No-one listens to it. "Oh no." No, don't hurt me. No, don't call me a liar. No, don't betray me further. No, don't let our only daughter walk out like this. No, I don't believe it. No, don't do this. *Don't do this.*

It's so important and so ignored. "Oh no."

I didn't even go to my room to collect anything. It wasn't my room. It hadn't been for a long time. This wasn't my home. And they certainly weren't my parents. And Benji… well good luck to him – he's going to need it. But at least he isn't a girl. I think if he had been a she, I would've taken her with me, and rescued her from ever feeling the way I did right then. I couldn't look at Mum as I walked out the door, but even so I knew what her face looked like.

I didn't know where I was going. Or what I was doing. I just walked out and kept on walking. Kept on walking like it was the only bodily function I knew how to do.

It was a still day. Still Friday. Still sunny. Still a pavement. Still a road. The world hadn't changed so much.

It was still a school day. And people were still in school. School was still. That didn't move. Didn't change. It would still be there. Everything else was, so school would be too.

It was the only thought I could hold in my head as my feet stepped one in front of the other of their own accord.

Still school. School still be open.

Left foot and right foot knew where to go. To the stillness.

I didn't know what lesson I was suppposed to have this afternoon, but my feet knew and walked me straight into English, and there was Isabel with an empty chair next to her, where someone I used to know used to sit. All the other faces were familiar, but their names floated free of their bodies meaninglessly. I saw the whole classroom with me stood in it, just inside the door, and simultaneously saw Miss Thames looking at me instead of the book she was holding in her hands.

I saw myself take one critical step forward into the classroom. Then my feet decided they would stop walking now.

I saw the distances between myself and the door, between me and Miss Thames, between me and every single other breathing body in the room.

Yet the whole time I was staring into Miss Thames' face. Our eyes connected for only moments, yet forever spun out of it. I saw the look on her face, a knowledge passed between us. I hadn't said anything and neither had she. I didn't even blink. I couldn't move. I didn't know how to move anymore. Everything was frozen in time and place. Only this existed: seeing Phillippa Pemberton stood in a classroom in the middle of an English lesson, with all the pupils and the teacher staring at her; and Miss Thames' face. Just that. The two weren't superimposed. They were separate, yet whole within themselves. They both existed in the same time and place, and all was ever so, ever so, still.

Chapter Twelve

I was in the middle of reading the list of essay questions out to the class.

I had vaguely noted in the back of my mind that Phillippa Pemberton was playing truant again.

I was reading and I suddenly stopped. There was a quiet in the room and in my head. I looked up before she came in, before she even opened the door, as if part of me knew, had expected her to enter just at that point.

She opened the door, left it ajar and stood, one step, two steps inside the classroom and stopped. Dead. She didn't speak. She didn't go to her desk. She didn't apologise. She didn't come up to my desk. Her stillness shocked me. Our eyes connected. And I knew. In that terrible moment I knew. I just knew. I rose, told the class to read to the end of the chapter. I went to Phillippa, placed a hand on her shoulder and steered her out of the room. I closed the door after us, firmly, deliberately.

I took her hand and led her to the sick bay. She followed like a lost child and still said nothing.

I sat her down on the long narrow blue bed in the private cubicle. I sat opposite her in the orange plastic chair.

"Phillippa? What's wrong?"

She looked at me strangely, as if focusing her attention on who I was and where we were for the first time.

And she said, "my Father hates me." And burst into tears. I sat on the bed beside her and she cried in my arms and couldn't stop. She cried and cried and cried some more. Her tears flooded.

Time announced that English lesson had ended, and she still cried.

Mr Jackson, Head of English looked in on me, to see who was in the sick bay. I motioned for him to go. And he did silently. Phillippa hadn't seen him.

I knew I could rely on John to take care of my next lesson for me.

She cried through the second lesson of the afternoon.

Home time came, I could hear the footsteps, calls, chatting, shouting, tripping, open and closing doors, bags dropping, as pupils piled out of the school.

Phillippa still grieved in my arms.

I reassured and comforted her in her grief, allowing it all to come out in this safe space.

Four o'clock came. I gently told her it was time to go home.

"I've got no home," she said. It was the second thing she'd said all afternoon.

"I'm going into the office for two minutes Phillippa. You stay here. I'll be back here in just a couple of minutes. Stay here till I get back." I didn't move until she looked up at me and nodded.

I spoke to the secretary and got Phillippa's home telephone number and returned to Phillippa.

"Phillippa, I'm going to take you with me, back to my house. We'll go in my car. I just need to collect my things from the staff room. Do you want to wait here?" She shook her head. "Do you want to come with me whilst I collect my things?" She nodded.

I took her by the hand and I guided her down the corridor to the staff room. I nodded at John and told him I was taking Phillippa back to mine, and that I would phone her parents from there and let them know where she was and that she was safe, and I'd speak to him tomorrow. John offered to ring them for me. It would be great if he could, and I'd ring them as well later.

I took Phillippa out to the car. Her sobs had stopped. Her tears had stopped.

She fell into a deep sleep on the way back.

Melissa was home thankfully, when I got there. She made up the spare bed for me, whilst I carried Phillippa in.

I took off her shoes and threw a cover over her and drew the curtains.

I wrote a note and put it on the bedside table. Just saying where she was, and to shout or come find me when she woke.

Then I went downstairs to phone Mr and Mrs Pemberton.

"6 3 9 double 2 1."

"Is that Mrs Pemberton?"

"Speaking."

"Hello. It's Delilah Thames here. I'm Phillippa's English teacher. I believe John Jackson called you earlier to tell you that your daughter is with me?"

"Yes, yes he did. Oh my god. Is she OK?"

"Well, she's sleeping soundly at the moment in my spare bedroom. I didn't want to disturb her. She's deeply distressed, Mrs Pemberton. Could you shed any light on the matter?"

"I don't know what's going on. She came home today from the police station saying that my husband's boss had raped her, but he says it's all lies and there was a terrible to-do and Dave hit her, he's never hit her, and it was awful, and he raged, and I'd no idea what was going on, or that the poor thing could have been in any, oh but Dave went on in a rage, and…"

"Is that Phillippa's teacher?" A male gruff voice suddenly said into the phone.

"Yes it is. Is that Mr Pemberton?"

"Yes. Now don't you go believing all that my wife says Mrs er, er…"

"Miss Thames."

"Miss Thames, 'cause she doesn't know her own mind. And neither does my little girl, you got there with you."

"Has your daughter been raped, Mr Pemberton?"

"Of course she bloody hasn't. She's making it all up. Just to get attention. She just dun't want her boyfriend no more, see, and this is her way of going about it."

"Your boss sounds like someone too old to be just a boyfriend, Mr Pemberton, and he's certainly breaking the law if he's had any sexual relations with the girl, as I'm sure you're aware." My voice was cold and steely. Did this man have no idea?

"Oh yes, of course, and I've tried to discourage it of course, but you know what youngsters are like these days, eh?"

"I know that youngsters who cry for a solid two hours or more are not upset for no good reason, Mr Pemberton. Might I suggest she stays here for the night, so she can get her bearings, then we can all discuss this tomorrow when tempers have calmed down and emotions aren't running so high."

"But she's such a liar you see, always making things up…"

"I'll tell you what, Mr Pemberton, I'll give you my number, should you wish to contact me before we meet, to alleviate any worries you might have."

"Er, that's very kind. Er, thank you."

"I'll speak to you tomorrow." And I hung up. Then I dashed to the kitchen and retched, but nothing came up.

"Is this the girl you were talking about?" Melissa asked. I nodded. "Go sit down. I'll sort out something to eat. And then we can talk." I nodded and smiled gratefully.

I went through to the living room, then came back through to the kitchen again. "Actually, I'll make the tea and stuff. It'll give me something constructive to do." Melissa nodded, understanding. She went and sat in front of the telly, and I envied her the ability to switch off.

I opened and slammed cupboards, clattered cutlery, and banged pans around with not enough satisfactory noise, as I proceeded to prepare the food.

Chapter Thirteen

When I awoke I felt warmth and peace. I snuggled and snuggled under the cover on this comfy soft bed, which felt so different from mine. It smelled different too. And I was still in my clothes – how odd. I squinted my eyes open and felt for my bedside lamp. It was further away than I remembered it, and the switch wasn't in the right place. I found it eventually, to see a very unfamiliar room.

Softer shades. Cleaner. Tidier. Colour coded in soft blues and a vague sense of lavender wafted across the room from the twin identical pots of pourri on either side of the bed. Either this was a dream or my bedroom had undergone some miraculous makeover in the night. Yet when I looked at my watch I was amazed to discover that it was only nine o'clock.

Then I spotted the handwritten note propped under the lamp. The idea of Alice in Wonderland popped into my head for a vague second.

'You're at Miss Thames' home. Come find me or shout when you awake.' said the handwriting that has marked so many of my English essays. What was I doing here? How did I get here?

I remember Dad hitting me. I felt the side of my face and winced. I don't remember much after that.

Why had Dad hit me? Oh. Yes. That's right. And it all came back in a most unwelcome flood of memories.

My horror and insecurity swamped my being, and I suddenly felt I wouldn't ever be able to move from this bed.

I'd told Dad I never wanted to see him again, and that I would never set foot inside that house again. But where would I go?

And how did I get *here*?

I didn't quite feel ready to face Miss Thames and other parts of the outside world yet. So I laid still in the warmth of a safe bed, and remembered Miss Thames' arms around me, holding me as I cried like I never had before. I wish everything would just disappear and I could just stay here undisturbed in the peace and quiet. Make myself a new person again. One that was as clean and tidy as this room.

I felt myself start to feel sleepy again, and I think I must have drifted off again for a good half hour.

But when I reawoke, I felt restless and pained. And the bed no longer held such bissful ignorance as I sought. The cleanliness seemed to emphasise my inner dirtiness. But through my aching pain, I realised a fact plain and simple that had not occurred to me before. I was now free of Brian.

And with that thought, I swung my feet out of bed. I had things to sort out. I was going to sort out somewhere to stay, even if it was a park bench, there was no way I was going under that roof ever again. Not tonight, not ever.

To my relief Miss Thames and her partner Melissa didn't ask me any questions. They were very gentle with me but didn't treat me like I had a contagious disease. I also found to my joy that I didn't need to sleep on a park bench for tonight, or go 'home' either. I was to stay the night here. I felt I had air to breathe, that I hadn't felt this way since forever.

Unfortunately, I also learned that I was to step into that house just one more time. But I swore to Miss Thames that it would be the *very* last time. She didn't argue with me, or try to convince me otherwise, like I thought she would. She just said she understood. I'd never been shown so much... thoughtfulness, before. She made me feel like a valid human being with valid desires and reasons – valid reasons. She accepted what I said. It was so new to me. I felt like an adult for the first time.

She made it clear that she was there for me to talk to, should I feel like it. I had a choice. And it was OK to talk to her if I wanted, I knew she would listen. And it was OK not to talk to her, I knew she would not hold anything against me if I didn't take her up on the offer. Either choice was right. Whatever I decided. I felt a certain space created around me that I never had when I was at home. A sort of mental space. A thinking space. A feeling space. And all that happened in it was safe and fine. Nothing to hide. Nothing to be punished for.

Miss Thames was my velvet cloak that I could wrap up in or discard as I needed. I wish she had been my Mum. Being at home was to continuously face a wall of large sharp nails, that snared me and pricked me, each with a different pain.

Miss Thames didn't even mind that I wanted to shower so often, and used up so many of her towels.

It was Saturday today, I had to remind myself. And it was pouring it down. I felt glad it was raining. I felt the sky was crying for me, so I didn't have to. Miss lent me some of her old clothes that she'd grown out of, but never got rid of, as I didn't have anything to change into.

Melissa stayed at home, and Miss Thames took me in the car – back 'home'. My stomach churned. I was not looking forward to seeing my ex-father again. And I couldn't bear to see my ex-mother. I just wanted to burn the whole house down, and everything that had ever happened in it would vanish.

Miss Thames turned to me in the car, after she'd pulled up outside of the house, before we were about to go in.

"I realise this will be hard for you. I'm giving you my car keys," (and she did), "so if you feel like you have to get out of there, you have the option to come out to the car and wait for me here if you want to." I had an escape route. Thank you Miss. Thank you so much, I said in my mind.

It was an awful day, and I don't think Miss managed to get through to ex-dad. I don't think anyone could. I don't want to dwell on it. I couldn't look at ex-dad at all without feeling like a no-thing, or a bad-thing. I had to block out his voice in my ears, his lies. His lies.

Mum and me were alone in the kitchen at one point. She tried to talk to me. Tried to comfort me. Tried to connect with me – hold my hand. I told her she was too late.

"I don't want you sleeping rough Phillippa darling. I worry about you."

"Worse things have happened whilst I was in my own bed."

She was quiet then. I could tell I'd hurt her. And part of me wanted to. She hadn't been there to help me, protect me. She never stood up to Dad.

"I love you Phillippa. I'd do anything to take your hurt away. I'm so sorry I didn't know." I could see tears in her eyes and I felt myself on the verge of them too, but I held it in.

"Leave him Mum," I said. "Leave Dad and we can just live together, just you, me and Benji."

There was a moment, a brief moment where I had hope. Hoped we could just junk this old life and start afresh together, the three of us, and maybe for once, feel the love that Mum wanted to give me.

But she shook her head, and tears fell down her cheeks. "I can't." I despised her in that moment. I just couldn't understand how she could stay with him after all this. I couldn't think of a single reason.

"Please Mum." I hadn't noticed I'd started to cry too, a tear slid off my nose. "We can do it." She smiled, that sort of smile that says 'you're too young to understand' or 'it's too complicated to explain'.

"I love you darling, but I can't…"

"Don't talk to me." And I fled then. The room. The house. Her. Him. I opened the car door, and sat there waiting for Miss to come out.

Chapter Fourteen

"Delilah?"

"Yes?" I turned to Melissa, her gaze upon me.

"Is there anything I can do to cheer you up today?"

"I dunno."

"Other than make it possible for Phillippa to live here with us, which I really can't do."

"No-one can."

"That's a big sigh." She plonked down beside me on the bench in our conservatory. She gazed out at the lawn, the flowers we'd planted last spring, the garden shed, the big pine tree at the bottom of the garden, the hole in next door neighbour's fence. "She'll be fine in the home, darling. A lot better off there than with her parents. She's only got so many months there anyway, before she turns sixteen."

"She needs a loving home and loving guidance and she hasn't got access to either."

"You can't change the world Delilah. You already do all that you can. *You* offer her loving guidance, and she knows that you're here whenever she needs someone."

"But she probably won't. She likes to handle things herself. But she doesn't realise that what she needs is…"

"That she needs help, assistance, love?"

"Yes."

"She has to find her own way. Give her time."

"What else is there?"

"You got her out of a very negative family situation. Don't keep on at yourself."

"And now she has *no* family."

"Now she has a *choice*. And freedom. And opportunity. As you say, she likes to do things her own way. And she will. Have faith in her, that's the greatest tool you can give her right now."

"OK, Miss-I'm-so-Wise, how about us getting the hell out of here for a bit?"

"Where would you like to go?"

"Anywhere."

Melissa laughed, jangled her car keys and said, "Your wish is my command dear lady."

Chapter Fifteen

I'd been in the home a while now. It wasn't too bad. Very strange being with so many people. Different set of rules and regulations, but I still felt freer here than I had been at ex-home. I still see Delilah on a regular basis, though I've dropped school completely.

But today, on my wonderings, I came to see Ted.

"How's the revision going?"

"Not bad."

"You look like you've got something on your mind other than exams."

"Are you going to be all right Phillippa?" I looked at his scattered notes all over his floor and bed. He was more laid back about the upcoming GCSEs than Isabel was. Personally, I didn't see the point of it all.

"I'll be fine Ted. Don't worry so much."

"I do though." We didn't talk about 'it' much, not since the police station. I just wanted to do normal stuff. Wanted to see what else in life there was other than pain. I didn't want the experience to be my whole life. But it kept jumping out at me and wouldn't be ignored sometimes. But with Ted and Isabel, I just want to be the same old Phillippa with them. Even though I wasn't. But it always made me feel uncomfortable when they started getting concerned about me. It bothered me, I don't know why. I just couldn't talk about any of it to them. Things were different, though I tried hard to deny it.

It's different with Delilah. She provides this comfort zone for me, where it's OK for me to be 'Phillippa who was raped'. I wasn't 'Phillippa pretending not to have been raped', or the 'Phillippa whom they don't know was raped, but has this dirty secret'. Nor was I 'The Raped' with no Phillippa attached to it at all. I could be 'Phillippa beyond the rape' with Delilah. She offers me possibilities. She never judges me, and she's a source of information. She hasn't told me very much about what happened to her, but I know she knows my pain, and that helps.

Sometimes we go out for walks, and I can just blurt out any old stupid stuff that comes into my head. Sometimes I won't say anything at all. Her and Melissa have taken me out to ruined castles, and picnics in the country. She says 'Nature is so much bigger than yourself' and so is always a place of comfort. But I've known uncomfortable trees, just like there are friendly buildings.

"You just make sure you get an A in maths, so you get into college to do your A-levels."

"You could too, if you wanted to." I just looked at him. Him in his unchallenged marigold room. His books. His maps. "You could. You're intelligent enough Phillippa. You could easy do this stuff."

"But I don't want to. So gimme a break Ted." We'd had this conversation before. I was tired of both him and Isabel trying to 'convert' me to their way of thinking. They couldn't seem to understand that I thought a different way.

"OK. Sorry."

"Apology accepted. I'm gonna go, I think I'd best let you swot up for next week."

"Are you coming to the cinema on Saturday night with me and Isabel?"

"Yeah, I'll be there. 8 pm at the doors, don't worry. I'll see meself out Einie," (short for Einstein), "don't get up out of your mess," I grinned at him.

"OK, see you then then."

I bade goodbye to Ted's Mum, who was in the kitchen baking cakes again! She was a born baker that woman, she really was.

I didn't feel like going back to the home quite yet, and decided to take the bus into town for a wander.

I reflected on how difficult it felt to have a flowing conversation anymore with either Isabel or Ted. The river of words somehow didn't flow as easily as they used to. We kept hitting rocks, we'd flow round them and over them, but we remembered the feel of the bump of the rocks as we went on our way.

Chapter Sixteen

Two Years Later

On one of my weekends home from college, I went round to visit Phillippa. I'd do some study in the mornings and evenings, avoiding Mum and Felicity as much as possible and go see Phillippa and/or Ted in the afternoons, if I could.

Ted would take time out from his A-level studies and we'd go out for a drink and a chat. He'd ask me about how the world of journalism spun. Phillippa never did. She never asked. It seemed she didn't care. She'd drifted apart from both of us.

This coming September Ted was off to university, and hopefully I'd be in my first job on a magazine.

And Phillippa... Well... She didn't seem to care about hardly anything at all these days.

Phillippa and I sat on my bed, like we used to do. But we weren't as we used to be.

Phillippa had just finished reading part of my diary I'd given her to read, I thought it would be something we could share, something that would bring us closer again.

I looked down my list of fears. My list of rules I'd made in my life, that I always adhered to, that were always on my mind. Phillippa said I was crazy, but I couldn't help it. She said most rapes were carried out by someone you knew. She said rape had nothing to do with sex. But I didn't understand. I just lived in fear of it ever happening to me. I was always on the alert.

Take the name and number of the taxi driver.

Make sure he knows I'm meeting someone at the other end, that I'm expected for a certain time.

Paranoia, Phillippa called it. I couldn't understand why she didn't behave the same way. She said she was alert too, but she didn't fear *all* men the way I did.

Never go in a lift with only a man/men in there.

Always cross the street if there's a man walking in the same direction as me, on the same side of the path.

Walk slowly, so that he has to overtake, so he's no longer behind me, but in front where I can see him.

She said not all men were capable of rape. I didn't believe her. In my eyes every man was capable of it, and I half wondered why they didn't all do it. She tried to explain it to me. She said if every person had a gun, that didn't make everybody a potential murderer. Only some people have the capability of taking another's life for no apparent reason. And just because every man had a penis didn't make them all potential rapists. I didn't believe her. I didn't understand. Every man was capable of it until proven otherwise. I held every man in distrust.

Never get drunk in pubs/clubs.

Never lose control.

I'd rather die than be raped, I told her. She said nothing. She turned away and said nothing. I'd rather be murdered than have to suffer being raped, I said. She said she'd already been murdered *by* the rape, and now she was trying to live. She gave me the look, the one that says I could never understand. Silence ensued.

Never return to a bedroom alone with a man I don't know.

Phillippa took strange men to bed often. They paid for the privilege. I didn't understand. I didn't understand. I didn't understand.

"How can you be sexual?"

"It's nothing to do with sex. Don't you understand? They're just bodies. They have no power, they give that power to me. I'm the one in control."

"But how?" I was referring to my first question, and she knew this.

"How can my soul be stolen?" she countered, anger and pain shook in her voice, in her hands and in her eyes. "And *how* could I have participated in it?" I shook my head. I had no answers. I wasn't even sure I understood the question. I couldn't think of anything to soothe her despair, I felt powerless.

She made to leave. She didn't want to speak of any of it again. Not to me. I tried to convince her to stay, but she shrugged me off.

I heard the door close after her, and I felt the tears slide down my face. I felt like I'd lost her... lost her friendship... lost who we'd been.

I couldn't repair the unbroken silences between us, didn't know how.

Chapter Seventeen

My world was consumed in work. I lived and breathed it. The deadlines, the travelling, the writing, the appointments, the interviews... I heard from Phillippa and Ted only occasionally. Birthdays and Christmas and a little bit in between. Phillippa travelled all over the place too, seeing 'clients'. And Ted had met someone at Uni. who he seemed to spend most of his leisure time with. We were all 'too busy' for each other.

And then I met Reg. A photographer. Very nice chap. And for the first time in my life, I let a man in, let him get to know me. A man other than Ted that is. But we seemed to be knowing each other less and less these days. And when it came to sex, I froze. He was happy to wait. But I was frustrated. He left me feeling cold and dry. Nothing 'happened' like it was supposed to in the films, in the books. Was that incredibly naive of me? I don't know.

***

Just got news this morning. Ted's getting married. To the lass he met at Uni. I don't know why, but I felt my stomach plummet as I read the invitation, all very nicely embossed in gold on a black background. And I didn't want to invite Reg along as my companion, or partner or whatever. So I haven't told him about it.

I'll go alone. Must get in touch with Phillippa and ask if she's going... what she's going to wear... what she thinks of Lily – his fiancée...

***

"What's wrong?"

"Nothing. Why?"

"Come on Isabel. You can't fool me. You've got that look again."

It was the day of Ted's wedding. We'd arrived early and were freshening up in the ladies'. I assessed the stark contrast of my sky blue, cotton, knee length dress next to Phillippa's silk red jump suit, in the mirror above the sinks.

"What look?"

"That look Isabel. The one you're wearing now." Our eyes met in the mirror.

"Oh, that look."

"Yes, that one." We both smiled.

"It's Reg."

"Go on." Phillippa prompted. We'd had one of our major disagreements. It wasn't really an argument, just a refusal to see things from the same side of the net. I wasn't really sure what it was all about. The usual I guess. He wanted some sort of commitment from me, but I needed my space.

"We're just going through a rocky patch at the moment."

"What sort of rocky?"

"I don't know."

"C'mon Isabel. What's eating you up from the inside out?"

"We haven't slept together yet," I blurted out.

"Is that an issue between you?" I looked away from Phillippa's reflected eyes, down into the sink.

"Yes."

"How long have you been together now?"

"Five months." I raised my eyes to meet her mirrored ones again.

"Don't you find him attractive?"

"Yes, I do. I don't get it."

"What's holding you back Isabel?"

"I'm not sure."

"Do you love him?"

"I'm not sure."

"Maybe he's not your Mr Perfect." We both smiled again. It was never 'Mr Right', he *had* to be 'Mr Perfect'.

"Maybe that's it. But he's awfully sweet and pleasant to be with, but I just... I dunno. When we kiss, I either feel empty or

86

kinda strange."

"Strange, how?"

"Strange as in... I just wanna push him away, even though I *do* find him attractive, and I would like to, but something inside me keeps him at arms length, keeps pushing him away. And he gets annoyed, but somehow it just doesn't feel right."

"Is there someone else you like?"

"No, of course not."

"You sound very convinced," she said sarcastically. My reflection frowned at hers.

"What do you mean?"

"I mean, I don't think you're being honest with yourself, Isabel."

"I don't understand."

"I think Reg is jealous." What on earth was she talking about? Phillippa turned to the real me. I faced her.

"Jealous of what?"

"Ted."

"Ted! Why on earth should he be jealous of him? He knows we've been friends for aeons. That there's nothing there and never has been... Why, they've met and drank and chatted. They get on fine."

"But Ted's marrying Lily, Isabel." That didn't follow on at all, made no sense whatsoever. What had Ted and Lily got to do with me and Reg? But then I suddenly found myself in floods of tears. Why was I so upset?

Phillippa hugged me to her. I tried not to let my tears soak into her silkiness.

A good couple of minutes passed before I managed to compose myself.

"Why am I crying, Phillippa?"

"Just admit to what you're feeling, Isabel. It's OK."

What I'm feeling. What was I feeling? I wasn't sure. "What am I supposed to be admitting? That I don't really want to be with Reg? That I need to tell him that? That I hate Lily? That I think she's no good for Ted? He picked the wrong one to marry. She's not the right one for him, she's not..."

"Miss Perfect?"

"Right."

"And who is, Isabel? Who would you like Ted to be with?"

"Me." Where had that come from? The word shocked me, but it rang true deep within my body.

"You love Ted, don't you?" I nodded, as tears fell silently down my cheeks.

"How did you know?" I asked.

"Call it a hunch."

I suddenly felt a dreadful panic. "Does Ted know?"

"No, he's as blind as you are, darling Isabel. He doesn't have a clue." Phillippa took my hand in hers, and rubbed her thumb across the back of it.

"What am I going to do?" I whispered.

"You have a choice Isabel. You can tell him. Or lose him to Lily."

"But I *can't* tell him. It would ruin everything. He *loves* Lily. And I'd just end up wrecking our friendship."

"You do have a choice, Isabel. It's up to you. Only you can decide which way to jump."

"But *you* think I should tell him."

"*I* would tell him if I was in your shoes, but I'm not. I'm not you. You're you, so you have to make a decision on what you think is best. You can tell him, and take the chance. Or not tell him, and so doing, lose him till death do them part."

"Why have I only just realised now, when I can't do anything about it?"

"I think you could surprise yourself. I think Ted might surprise you too."

"Ted would never leave Lily for me."

"You don't know that for sure. Not unless you give him a chance."

"No, I can't. I absolutely can't, Phillippa. It would be a big mistake. I'll just have to live with it. That's all."

Then we hugged for a long while. Somehow I had to get through this damn ceremony and do my best not scream out when the moment of silence came, where the vicar would ask if anyone knew of any reason why the two of them should not be married.

Chapter Eighteen

I made my way back from the doctors still in shock. The whole journey home I operated on automatic pilot. Not very reassuring considering I was driving.

I was relieved when I eventually reached my garage, attached to my castle of protection, my detached home in the Yorkshire hills. Years of working in London and Manchester on various magazines, but with the advent of e-mail and the world wide spider web, as a freelance worker it's good to be able to work from home sometimes. Cuts down on the amount of travelling!

My feet carried me through the interconnecting door into the house, and into the kitchen where I poured myself a brandy.

Then I went through to the dining room at the back and stood looking out through the patio doors, to the fields ahead and beyond. Where the sun had no right to shine on the luscious green grass. And the first daffodil heads had no right reflecting the sun's yellowness back. It had no right to stare out of its blue haze, with not a single damn cloud in the sky.

No, all the grey and black clouds, all the rainy days and frost-bitten flowers were in me. Inside me. In my womb. The day had the nerve, the cheek, to be so fine, as if life was dandy, whilst other people continued their 'normal' lives. But I, I shuddered and shivered and hid in the corner, afraid of my own dark void swallowing me up from the inside out.

I couldn't have children.

That's what the doctor had said. There I was trying for a child, by myself. No man to share with, to make it with. No man I wanted. Not any I'd met. Well only one, but Ted was married. So I pretended I was a lesbian, and how about getting a sperm donation for one of my eggs. What could be simpler? But nothing's ever simple, is it?

Infertile. The word echoed round the dank chambers of my

head till it detached itself of meaning.

I was defunct. Out of action. My choices were stolen from me.

The unfairness of it swelled inside my stomach, the fingers of pain threatening to scratch and crawl their way up my throat and push itself out of my mouth like a fist.

I'd been cursed with a second rate body, one they didn't have all the spare parts for. None in stock at the moment. So, I got the rejects that healthy people had sent back.

Self pity swamped me. My tears fell freely down my cheeks, dripped from my chin on to my top. I'd run out of words to voice my thoughts with. Yet there were too many words, and not enough of them. No words at all.

Chapter Nineteen

The issue of Phillippa's prostitution had arisen once again. It was usually something I didn't mention, but my concern and disapproval was a continuous backdrop to our friendship.

Phillippa didn't rise to the incredulity in my voice. "Take a look around Izzy. Tell me what you see." I frowned in puzzlement at her and she made a gesture for me to do so.

I gazed round the en suite room. Five stars this hotel had been given. It was more than nice. It was positively luxurious, airy, spacious, air conditioned. Pastel shades on the walls, wooden floor. Wide screen tv, wine bar, Jacuzzi.

"Nice linen, good decor, lovely carpet, nicely kitted out," I say shrugging.

"So everything's good, nice and lovely," she laughs, and I loved her freeing laughter. "Think what we had in childhood." I think. I don't want to, but I comply with Phillippa's request. She sees me frown, as sadness, dissatisfaction and frustration glide across my displayful face. I don't have to say anything. "Do you know how much something like this costs?"

"Yes, but money aside Phillippa, the erm, well you know, the other side of things..."

"Control. That's the name of the game Izzy. Control." I involuntarily felt a shiver down my spine. I felt just a tad uncomfy with this unfamiliar side of Phillippa's character. But then she laughed, and she was back to being my loveable, bubbly, up-beat Phillippa again. "Look at this way Izzy, I get to say what I will and will not do with my body. I decide my hours, and with whom I work and when. I make a lot of people happy, I get lots of money to spend my free time just as I feel fit to do." I was just about to protest at the word 'people' and insert 'dirty bastards' instead, but Phillippa continued. "Whereas you are tied into a nine till nine job, pretty much everyday, at the beck and call of Mr X and Miss Y and that schedule and those deadlines, for a non-negotiable amount of money, you get what you're given, and only get a certain amount of time off and only then if it fits in with others. You spend evenings being exhausted and just catching up with yourself ready for another adrenaline-junkie day, and by the weekend you're stuffed. By the end of Sunday, you're a recharged human being again, but all your energy is devoted to work once again, so you never get chance to spend time and effort on other things you'd really like to do. You're stuck in a rut Isabel darling, and you can't even see it. You're yet another slave of patriarchal capitalism. Don't you ever feel the need to lash back and rebel against that?" I watched Phillippa and thought about my response for a moment.

"But you're as much a part of the system as I am, but in a different way."

"You're wrong Isabel," she shakes her head, "I'm outside the system, because I get exactly what I want, whenever I want it."

"And the clients get what they want," I say, gently, not sure how Phillippa will take this.

"Of course. There's a price to pay for everything, and it's a price I'm willing to pay." I shook my head showing my incomprehension.

"But Phillippa…"

"Damn it Isabel. Why do you have to make such a big deal about it all?"

"I just want you to take care that's all. I don't understand why…"

"Damn right you don't understand. So I'd appreciate it if you just kept your nose out of my business."

"But you're worth so much more, Phillippa. I'm only saying all this because I care, you know…"

"Oh, don't give me all that caring bullshit Isabel. I don't need 'caring'. I need space. Don't you think I know how much I'm worth!" No, she didn't. Not one bit. "I live my life just the way I choose. Just like you live your life the way you want. I don't expect you to take the moral high ground and quit your job, just because I think all journalists are scum of the earth. But you are one. You *want* to be one. No doubt you *like* being one. But that's not me. Just like this isn't you. I understand your view point perfectly. It's crystal fucking clear. But you don't have a fucking clue when it comes to my job, and the world I live in. I give them an orgasm. They give me money. Fair exchange. It's the oldest fucking career in the history of humankind! It's always going to fucking be here. I can take care of meself Isabel. You *know* that. So I wish you'd just get off my fucking case about it."

We stood still. In the centre of the room. Staring at each other. Phillippa was breathing hard, her rage subsiding, I hoped. I didn't quite know what to say.

"Isabel?" she ventured, as mute silence continued. I looked away.

"I'm sorry Phillippa. I didn't mean..." What did I mean? A tear slid down my cheek. I loved Phillippa. I didn't want to upset her. I just... wanted more for her than this ritual self abuse she was putting herself through. But I couldn't make her see that. I sighed. What was the use?

"C'mon you ninny. I'll shout you lunch." And she hugged me to her, as we walked out of the room, and down the stairs. Just like Phillippa – let's move on to the next thing, no point in dwelling on something we can't change.

We lunched at this restaurant just a few streets from her hotel. It was sunny, but breezy. T-shirt and jeans weather, and we were suitably attired.

We ate and chatted. But I could feel the gulf between us. It wasn't just Phillippa's job. She'd changed so much over the last few years. We didn't seem to agree about much these days. She said I was naive. I thought her harsh. It was painful, because we still loved each other, but we led such different lives now.

"You're an idealist, Iz. Always thinking you can change the world. Journalists don't change it, they just report the bad bits. And even then they don't always get their facts straight." She said as she drunk her beer. I refused to be baited. We'd been here lots of times before too. There was no way I could convince Phillippa of the benefits that media's mass communications brought us. She was such a cynic when it came to the media, too contrived, she would say.

"What about a husband? Children?" I had asked her on many occasions.

"Ah, that old stone age tradition. Who wants them milestones hanging round your neck? I certainly don't." Or something as equally mocking would be her reply.

We didn't get to see each other very much these days. About once a year, if that. We always knew we were there for each other, if we ever needed someone to turn to. But Phillippa didn't readily confide in me anymore. Not like when we were younger. I knew I could tell her anything. But something always held me back. I didn't want our friendship to be one-sided, me confiding in her, and it not being reciprocated. But she never seemed to need any comfort or advice, and that made me feel redundant.

We parted with a hug and a kiss on each cheek. We said we'd be in touch with each other soon. But really, underneath, we knew it would probably be months before we spoke to each other again. Perhaps months and months.

Chapter Twenty

I put the phone down, numbed. Lily means it, she really does. I'm to pack my things and go. She's going to stay at Mum's till then.

I look round the place we built together. The colours that we painted, the lilacs, the creams and the blues. We'd picked them together. Got so messy together and laughed so much during the paint fight we had. We eventually stopped painting each other long enough to actually get some colour on the walls. The whole place spoke of the two of us entwined, and the volume was too loud.

I walked through the kitchen, to the connecting door for the garage. Got out my keys and sat in my mint green fiesta.

But I couldn't turn the key. My hands wouldn't reach for my seatbelt even. I just sat there, limp like a peeled banana skin. I just keep wondering, where did it all go wrong.

Lily had finally said it, the words I so dreaded. But now that they were out, it was almost a relief. I could stop living in fear of their utterance. Now all I had to do was live through the trauma of their consequences.

Divorce.

What a cold divided word. For a divided world.

I don't measure up. I'm not quite right. I don't somehow fit as neatly as I should into Lily's life. Whatever I do is *never* enough. I've tried everything. Perhaps I tried too hard, I don't know. I look back on the downward spiral of Lily's happiness and can't remember where it started. I really can't recall when they started to take up more time than the smiles, the fun, the lovemaking and laughter.

Maybe if I'd paid more attention... I must've missed the point, the exact point, where I could have made things right. Brought us back to how we were when we first got wed.

It's only been two and half years. Over so quick and yet so long.

If things were so wrong for Lily and me, how come we hadn't known sooner. How come it had taken this long to find out?

It had felt so right. I can't believe this is happening. I never thought I would ever end up in a failed marriage. But I guess everyone thinks that. Because if we had the least suspicion, then we wouldn't even get through the vows, would we? Failed marriage. Failed husband.

I just want her back. Start anew. I can't let her go. How am I ever going to walk away from this in one piece?

I dig out my wallet, from my back pocket. There's a bride and groom smiling up at me, two faces I once knew. It seems a lifetime ago.

Single again. A divorcée. Life without Lily. How can that be?

I look at my numb lifeless hands, hanging in my lap. I remember them holding Lily, her body alive next to mine, whispering her love to me. The whole world's gone blurry. The finality of her words sinking through my disbelief, cutting through my memories like scissors to ribbons.

I wonder where those sounds are coming from, and why there are damp droplets falling on my trousers. I lean my head to the steering wheel, and let the storm break over me.

Chapter Twenty-One A

Is that Ted? No, it couldn't possibly be. Looks like him though. Gosh, I haven't seen him for such a long time. How long? Months and months. I don't know how long. I wonder if Isabel is with him. But then why should she be? I haven't seen her for way too long either.

A familiar blond, slightly chiselled face bobbed between many nameless faces in the crowd. Saturday. Busiest day. Sunny. So many sweaty people, all wanting different things, at that very second. How tiring! I almost wished it was raining, but then you would have to avoid all them big umbrellas knocking your eyes out as you dodged between the shops.

I'd only come out to get some new leggings and a top for my keep-fit classes. I didn't really need them, but had decided some nice retail therapy was just what I needed on the worst day to be in town. What was I thinking of?

Yes it *is* Ted. I can see him properly now. Just going into… oh, lost him again. No, there he is, stood outside a jeweller's window. He hasn't changed much since I last saw him, when was it – a couple of years ago maybe, I forget time. It just passes me by. Wonder if he's thinking of buying a pretty ring for his pretty wife, or crying over a pretty ring he feels he needs to pawn.

One way to find out.

"Tell yer muther I've saved yer life," I pounced on him playfully. He jumped, and looked at me startled.

"Phillippa! My goodness! I didn't expect to see you here. You look well. How the hell are you?" He grasped me in a bear hug. I laughed, trying to get my breath.

"Great to see you too Ted. Listen, why don't you come up to the flat and have a drink? We can catch up, and not have to deal with overcrowded tables, and irritating waitresses?"

"Sounds good to me. You've a flat here? London's a long way from home."

"Ah, was it ever home Ted? We lived there, but was it home?"

"Don't get philosophical on me!"

"And don't you use big words on *me!* C'mon it's this way. I tend not to stay in the City for too long if I can help it. Too many people I might know!" I take his hand, and lead him through all the milling tourists, lost kids, screaming parents, tight arse business chappies (even on a Sat'day) and bored inhabitants.

We made our way over to a five storey block of flats. I typed in the code, and slid through the opening door.

"Very nice," he commented.

"I'm on the top floor. Hope you don't get out of puff so easy!"

"Me, nah. Fit as a fiddle." I laughed. I didn't believe him, as he huffed his way all the way to the top.

"Make yerself at home," I called, as I slipped into the bathroom, to amend my hair and refresh my make-up.

"Wow, not bad at all. Quite luscious in fact," he said whilst squidging his feet into the inch thick carpet, rubbing his hands over the leather suite, and taking in the pretending-to-be-personal paintings dotted around the walls. They didn't belong to anyone. Just came with the flat, so it looked like someone had been there for ages, but really, people just came and went staying only till the little hand had passed through the numbers once, or maybe twice.

The next couple of hours, me and Ted spent just catching up. He was a successful systems analyst. He talked about enjoying working with linux instead of windows. I followed it a little. Some of my clients worked in computers. Ted seemed to be doing very well for himself. He hadn't mentioned Lily though. An ominous omission.

I made him dinner – well shoved a lasagne in the oven anyway. Which is kind of embarrassing, as I'm actually a very good cook, but I only do it for special guests, not just for one. And Ted had been a bit of a surprise.

It felt like old times again. The years just rolled away as we talked. I'd forgotten how easy-going Ted was to be around. I'd forgotten what it was like to be with a male friend. Someone I could trust and just be myself with. Hadn't done that for so long.

We chatted away through the meal and a couple of bottles of mineral water, and a glass of wine.

I started to feel buzzy and glowing. Relaxed for the first time in ages.

Ted still hadn't mentioned Lily, so I asked.

Divorcing. That was a bit of a shock. And yet not a surprise at the same time. Instinct had told me that Lily hadn't been quite Miss Perfect for him. But all the same... I reached for his hand and gave it a squeeze. Words deserted him for a moment, and then it all came flooding out.

I listened as he poured forth about Lily and all his mixed feelings. I ached for his loss of happiness. He had so believed in his happy-ever-after with Lily. I wondered what it was like to have that hope in the first place with someone. I guess I thought I'd just die a lonely old spinster. The old cliché of having loved and lost flittered through my mind as I listened to him. I didn't say it. I just wondered at the wisdom of it. After all, if you've never felt the joy of requited love, you've never felt the despair of abandonment/loss after.

I listened as he related his confusion to me, the arguments he couldn't understand, the gradual increasing of misunderstandings and hurtfulness breeding like maggots on mouldy bread, when once they'd been 'so in tune with each other', knew 'exactly what the other was thinking'. I wondered at Ted's innocence, and Lily's spoiling of him, taking him for granted. Ted was blind to her failings. He couldn't see it. Convinced that he was entirely to blame for messing up their lives, and being a miserable old bastard now.

"No, Ted, you're absolutely wrong." He looks at me. I know he's not going to be persuaded out of his self-blame reverie right now. "You've always been a miserable old bastard." He looks at me in disbelief at first, and then bursts out laughing. I join in, and it's like a wind of laughter has entered his body and taken him over, and he can't stop. It gets beyond being funny, and we're both in hysterics.

"Thanks Phillippa, I knew I could count on you!" he wheezes out.

"Takes one to know one," I say, raising my glass to his, hoping my lightness of voice doesn't belie the empty swell I feel inside. I couldn't have hid it as well as I thought I did. It's a sobering moment as Ted's hand relaxes on mine, on the table and strokes gently. His concern and tenderness make my eyes sparkle a little too bright. I am not going to cry in front of him. I am not.

"Would you like some more wine?" I offer him. Lame excuse for a change of subject, but nothing else sprung to mind.

"I'm sorry, I'm hogging the conversation."

"I'm not sorry you are. I can't tell you how good it is to listen to it, I mean, not that it's good about you and Lily, I mean, just to talk and to…"

"I know what you mean." His tone was a little too low. A little too intimate. A delicious shiver chased down my spine. "I've missed you Phillippa. I really have."

"And I've missed you Ted."

"It's such a terrible waste of time. How did we get so out of touch?" I'm not hearing his words correctly. I'm suddenly imagining his hand stroking gently elsewhere. What is wrong with me? "Phillippa?"

"Yes?"

"Does the loneliness get any easier?"

"What loneliness Ted? I don't feel lonely." But my voice caught. And I cursed myself for being so transparent.

"But you were always so alone." Alone? Me, alone? Well, isn't everyone? I think he's talking about his lonesomeness, now Lily's gone.

"You're not alone Ted." And my lips brush his. It's as much a surprise to me as it is to him.

"What am I going to do Phillippa? I'm a failed man."

"A failed marriage doesn't make a failed person. It just means you weren't as right for each other as you first imagined. You'll walk through the other side of this dark tunnel Ted, I promise. And at the other end there will be someone who you can be really happy with."

"And what about *your* dark tunnel?" He was so serious, and so gentle, and so hurt. I knew he was reaching out for me, with the pain that he was feeling, to try to comfort whatever hurt I

100

was harbouring.

There was some crazy chemistry in the air making all these little connections between us. As if we were a string of fairy lights, and the missing bulb had been fixed, so they lit up, one by one in a row. But it was crazy. This was Ted, who I'd known since forever.

"I have a torch," I whispered. I was half aware of his hand stroking my cheek, and my face inching closer to his. "And lots of batteries."

"And where do you recharge them, or get new ones from?" His breath was in my hair, and my head was feeling dizzy. Was this just the drink? It felt like drunk haze, but we hadn't even polished off our first glasses of wine yet.

"I don't know." And in those three words I felt a release from pretending to Miss Invulnerable all the time. My mind went sailing through sweet oceans blue as our bodies both entered into free flow. They seemed to know what they were doing. I got drunk in his eyes, and fed on the raw emotions that played in his twin blue depths.

Our nakedness presented itself as new. And natural. I felt virgin like and experienced at the same time. My body wasn't new, but these feelings were. Which made me new. My body behaved as I had never known it to before. But there was no shame. Ted welcomed me. Needed me. Teased and reassured me. And I played the tune of his desire, sweeping it back and forth, drawing him in, lapping him up. Washing myself in this friendliness, this trust, this new bond we were making. This old bond we were re-forging.

Then he stopped. He stroked me away from him. "We don't need to do this. I love you as you are Phillippa, we don't need to..." He was going to throw it all away. Chuck it away on a far away island, and call us 'friends'. No, he doesn't want to take advantage, and spoil our friendship. But I want to take advantage and know him as a lover. I want this. I felt so sure of the moment.

"I know we don't need to. But I want to Ted. I want to. Take me into you. I want to know what it's like there." He still needed to be convinced. I place my pulsing hand against his heart. "Let's not lose this moment, please Ted. Let's just follow what we feel right here and now."

So we did.

We met like foreigners in a strange land.

Lily may have taken Ted's virginity, but this night, I gave it back to him. He found someone else he never knew he could be. He trusting me with his vulnerabilities. He felt release too. Release from restraining his emotions for so long, scarred by Lily's rejections. Her many little rejections, before they even split up.

In the aftermath of our heat, I listened to the rhythm of our heart beats slowing, as we continued breathing each other in.

"Phillippa?" It was strange now hearing my name on his lips.

"What is it, Ted?" And his name felt strange on mine. The old words held new intimacies in their notes.

"I don't know. I feel…"

"Then just be happy to feel," I interrupted. I didn't want words spoiling what we'd just shared. He looked up into my face, into my smiling gaze.

"As long as you are."

"I'm very happy to feel." An emotional lightning streaked its way through me, and fizzled out into the warm glow that we'd created. I felt clean.

Chapter Twenty-One B

"Tell yer muther I've saved ya life." I nearly jumped out of my skin. It was Phillippa. Here in London. She'd caught me looking at a similar ring I'd bought Lily for our wedding. What was Phillippa doing here? Could we catch up? No, we hadn't seen each other for a good few years. We hugged, and she laughed as she led me through the teeming people to her flat. She looked well, with her laughing eyes, in her floaty, blue, summer dress.

She cooked a lasagne and apologised for not having anything better. I assured her it was fine. She'd heard from Isabel more recently than I had, and we caught up on the latest news about people we still knew. I tried not to bore her too much with talk of work. I knew Phillippa wouldn't be interested in all the ins and outs of computers and networking.

We ate and talked and drank. It got late. I told her all about Lily. I hadn't meant to. It just came pouring out. I didn't realise just how much I had left unexpressed until then. We'd been so in love, but by the end, well, I seemed to repulse her. I never knew what it was I'd done wrong. I never seemed able to rectify the situation. When I tried, I seemed to make them worse rather than better.

I told Phillippa about me wanting children, but that Lily had adamantly *not* wanted them. Lily had said it was selfish of me to want to physically imprison her with a child. I couldn't believe it. I'd just wanted a family to love, to be close to, but she made it sound like a crime. I didn't want to imprison her. I'd be there to look after our son/daughter too. We would be a team together, I'd said. But Lily didn't want to take time off from being a surgeon, to play Mummy to a screaming baby.

I guess that was something else we'd fought about. Or she thought we fought about it. Yes, OK, so I occasionally felt a bit miffed when she was off working funny hours, or was called in on an emergency, because there was no-one else to do it. But for the most part I understood. But I think Lily felt guilty or something. She didn't believe me when I said I was fine with it all.

I rambled on for quite some time I think, and finally there came a pause. That sort of pause where neither of you is quite sure what to say next.

I knew a little of Phillippa's life, from brief talks with Isabel, though Phillippa and I had not talked about her life, her 'job' or anything like that the whole evening really. I wondered at her pain, her past, all the things she kept private and wouldn't talk about even to me.

What happened felt so easy, so right. But I doubted it for one moment. Was this wrecking everything? Was I in some kind of emotional turmoil it would be unfair to wrap Phillippa up in? What were we doing? And why were we doing it? But she wanted me still. And I needed that, and gave into it. And she made it feel so inevitable.

Phillippa made the moment important, of what we needed there and then. Consequences and meanings and time were to be relinquished. It was just the here and now.

Afterwards she fell asleep while we were still one. I smelled her freshness and lightness and wondered at the wisdom of our bodies. But she didn't want questions or regrets, and I didn't either. I didn't know what it meant. But everything was OK in this minute, so let's leave it as it is. So we did.

In the morning, she made me breakfast. She didn't have to, but she bustled round, said she had a lot to do that day. She was wearing a different dress. A red one. A fiery one.

I felt at ease with her, and although we'd never been in this situation before, it somehow felt familiar. And before she left for her 'busy day' she kissed me a cheery goodbye on the cheek. Then she was gone.

I'd forgotten to ask her what time she would be back. I assumed she'd be back at the flat that night. But she wasn't. I hadn't even got her number.

Days passed, and although I watched out for her, and tried to get hold of her, there was no reply. No answer. Nothing.

I felt strange and new, almost reborn, and then suddenly bereft. Where was she? Why didn't she get in touch? What did all this mean between us now?

***

Eight days and not a word from Phillippa. I'd rung, I'd gone round, I'd written to the last address of hers that I had. Still nothing.

It was a normal Tuesday morning, and I was doing my usual slow-wake-up routine before going to work. I was contracted out for six weeks to set up and ensure the smooth running of Cooper's new server and network, which ranged across three different sites. My second day today. I stifled a yawn, as I went to pick up the letter that had kindly been pushed under my door by Deborah. She had the flat above me, and she often picked my post up at the same time as hers, and brought it up for me. She went to work early that girl!

Strange. Air mail envelope. French stamps. I returned to the kitchen counter, to finish stirring my tea, then I went and plonked myself on the sofa wondering who I knew in France. No-one I could think of.

I sipped my tea, too hot. I set it on the coffee table to cool. I ravaged open the envelope, curious. I pulled out a single sheaf of blue air mail paper. I unfolded it, my eyes immediately flicking to the name at the end of it. Phillippa. I brought my foot up, to cross it over the other one, and promptly kicked my tea all over the floor. Shit. I dashed to the sink, and got a wet cloth and a tea towel from the railing. I gave it a harsh rub all over with the cloth, then laid the towel on top of the damp patch. I'd have to make another one now. Damn. I'll read the letter first.

Hungrily, I read and re-read her short letter. At least she was still talking to me, we were still friends. Good, we hadn't thrown that away. I still felt confused though. No reason given as to why. I re-read it again.

Dearest Ted

I want you to know that you are and always will be a very special person to me. But we both know we were not meant to be together as a couple. Our night together is something I will

105

always treasure in my heart and in my memories.

Take care of yourself Ted.

I know you will find Miss Right to make you happy in the future.

Keep smiling. Stay in touch.

All my love, Phillippa xx

Chapter Twenty-Two

Here I am, sat in this satin black negligée, on a bed that would take me half a life time to save for, if not more. And outside in his fucking pristine gardens, trim hedges, perfect lines and colour fucking coded flowers, he owns it all. This mansion, these grounds, the staff. And he thinks he fucking owns me too. Just because he's paid me for the fucking week. Nobody owns me. Nobody. I own me.

Ah, look, a robin. Free. Flying. Perching. Flittering from tree to tree. Sat watching an organised fucking mess.

Wondering where to catch your next worm birdy? He doesn't own you, does he? He can't touch you. He can't pay you. He can't fence you in. You come and you go, or maybe not even come at all. Where do you fly to robin?

I'll be flying soon too. He won't like it, but he's going to have to face the hard fact that I'm as free as you are robin. I also can come and go as I please. And as of this Sunday, I please to go. And not come back. Maybe back to England. OK, so they don't have as much sunshine there, but there's a strange familiarity in its drabness sometimes. A nice familiarity. It's nice to leave, and nice to go back to.

And monsieur and his fucking mademoiselles (literally) can go fuck themselves to their hearts' content, and Sir can damn well pay a different pair of eyes and a different body to partake of his little games.

Jesus! What was I thinking? This is the last time I settle for an 'easy-life'. And where was the fucking Prince Weirdo now? In the spa? One of the many bedrooms with one of his floozies? Fucking one of his tarts? Three more days to go. I can last that out. Good money though. Christ – too good. But I don't do fucking live-in pretend wife, not for free and not even for this much! I can't stand this fucking guy!

The voyeurism I can handle, but it sure as hell gets boring after a while. How can someone with an ego as big as his require more massage? His insecurity must be as big time as his fucking wealth. Mr Fucking Pristine Pervert. What a serious head fuck.

What on earth was I thinking? It wasn't his sexual tastes that bothered me so much, if he only liked his own tastes and was into them himself. But he never let go, in any scene. He never came. He was always the cold and calculating one. I did think he got off on seeing the others get off with each other, and the things they did together. But I don't think so now. I think it's the control he gets off on. Knowing what turns them on, how far he can push them.

But the deception he uses to do it! As if he was *in* the scene instead of just fucking orchestrating it. But I think he's a passionless man. And if he hasn't got passion in that department, I can't control him. That spells danger. I don't like that. A man's passion is predictable, can be sated, can be controlled. But if he holds out all the time, and knows what other people's buttons are… no I don't like that one bit.

He thinks he knows my buttons too. I'm not that stupid. He's not the only one who can pretend.

"Lenola! Dar-ling!" Oh shit, here he comes. Deep breath Phillippa, just a few more days, then I'm gone, on the wind, like the robin.

Chapter Twenty-Three

P: Isabel?

I: Speaking.

P: It's me, Phillippa. Can you…?

I: Yeah, OK Andrea, be on it in a minute. Sorry Phillippa, what were you saying?

P: You're really busy, never mind.

I: *Since when did Phillippa care for pleasantries?* Phillippa? Are you crying?

P: No, no, no. It's fine.

I: Tell me. What's wrong?

P: Oh God, Isabel, I feel like I'm dying.

I: Hang on a sec while I take this in my office. Andrea, can you put this through to me? Cheers. *I sped through to my office in a flurry.* Got it. *I heard Andrea click down. Must be something very bad for Phillippa to call me at work. And in tears. So unlike her.* What's up? What's happened?

P: I've given up. I've given it all up.

I: What are you talking about? *I heard her laugh bitterly.*

P: I don't take clients anymore. You'll be dead proud Isabel, I'm going clean. *Her sobs caught in her throat and at my heart.*

I: Where are you? *This was so difficult on the phone!*

P: In a room in… oh, you mean… I'm in Edinburgh.

I: Listen, tell me where you are, and I'll get the next flight up to you.

P: Don't be silly. You're busy and you've got…

I: Nothing more important on than coming to see you, when you're so upset. I won't hear any arguments. I'll just tell work it's a family emergency.

P: I can't talk you out of this?

I: Absolutely not. Now where are you exactly?

***

Phillippa was renting out a grotty room in a cheap hotel. I wasn't sure why. Maybe it was the first thing she came to in her present state of mind. I knew she wasn't strapped for cash.

She was huddled in a ball, knees tucked up to her chin, when I came in her unlatched door. Horrible thoughts ran through my head of what could possibly have happened to her. I tried not to think about it too much, but braced myself for the worst.

I sat down beside her. I said her name, but she didn't respond. After a brief silence, she turned to look at me, and then I was cradling her in my arms, as she sobbed her heart out for all the world as if I was the mother comforting a small child, as if I could mend her broken heart.

I didn't ask her any questions, just reassured her, held her, stroked her back, let her cry it all out, whatever it was. The dam had burst and her avalanche of emotions rocked through for a good while. I let it ride its own storm out.

I'd never known Phillippa to be like this. She was always so in control, so focused, determined, almost invulnerable.

Her grief, whatever it was, was amazingly strong. I continued to rock her and hold her, her tears still coursing, making puddles on my blouse. I think it was at least a good forty minutes before she calmed, but the tears still flowed. She cried a lifetime of tears, it felt. I held her head, and stroked her hair, my other arm round her shoulders, her face still buried against me. My heart ached for her, and I tried to keep my unruly thoughts under control. I was longing to hear everything, but I respected the time she needed to tell me.

Another half hour of silence passed. I gave her some tissues. I usually carried some with me. She mopped up her remaining tears and blew her nose. She started to shiver, her emotion spent. I bundled her into the bed, under the bed clothes to warm her. I gave her a drink of tea from my flask, which she gulped down.

"I can't do it anymore, Izz. I just can't do it," was the first thing she said. Her shivers were starting to abate.

"What can't you do?"

"Go on the way I have been. I'm jacking it in Isabel. I'm not going to sell my body to another, ever again."

This was good news, but I sensed something darker in the background.

"Can I ask why?" I held my breath as I awaited the horror story that must surely follow.

"I got attached to somebody." This certainly wasn't the answer I'd been expecting.

"How do you mean?"

"I let someone in. Someone got close."

"Did they betray you? Hurt you in any way?"

"No, just the opposite. He honoured me." I was confused. Surely this was a good thing?

"Is this a client of yours?"

"Goodness, no! Not a chance!"

"Are you seeing this someone? Are you together?"

"No. Not at all. We'll never see each other again, well not in that way anyway." She saw me frowning, trying to understand. "He's a married man. Well as good as." OK, that explained everything then. Didn't it? No, it still didn't sound quite right.

"You're upset because you've fallen for a married man, and can't be with him?"

"Yes. No. Not really. No, that's not the point. What I mean is, he made me feel, Isabel. Damn it! He made me *feel*. I can't forget it. I can't go back, as if it never happened. I can't shut it out anymore. I can't switch off with a client anymore. I can't tune them out. I can't numb myself anymore. It doesn't work. It's all changed. He made me feel again. Somehow my barriers didn't work with him. I had a choice, and I took it, and it was a good choice. But now I feel everything. All the things I never wanted to feel. And I can't..." she began to break down again.

I sat beside her on the bed. She laid her head in my lap. I squeezed her shoulders tightly. Her sobs threatened to engulf her once again, but she reigned them in.

"I'm falling apart Isabel, and I don't know what to do."

"It's OK Phillippa. Let it all come out. God knows it needs to. Everyone falls apart from time to time. It's OK."

Through her re-emerging sobs she repeated, "What am I going to do?" I handed her another tissue. It was a rare occasion

111

when I was the one handing out advice to Phillippa.

"I think you need a different focus. Something new to pour your energies into."

"Like what?"

Good question. Erm… "Anything. Something you like doing. Something new and different. Be adventurous, you're good at that."

"Yeah, you're right." I could tell an idea was forming in her head, there was a new calmness to her. She seemed to have spied a buoy in the rough of the storm.

The room started to get dimmer, as the sun set in. Even though there was a lamp on in the corner, it seemed to add to the darkness rather than alleviate it.

"I never thought this would happen," she said after some time. "I didn't think it was possible."

"Who is he?"

"Oh, it's not important. Nothing's going to happen, or rather, nothing *more* is going to happen."

"He won't leave his wife?"

"His what? Oh yeah. I mean no. That's right." She looked to the distance, I wondered what she saw there. I was puzzled, something still didn't quite fit somewhere, but I'd no idea what. "Isabel, I love you," she suddenly said, and sat up to embrace me properly.

"I love you too." She kissed my cheek, then suddenly sprang out of bed with a new energy. "I know, let me get changed. And we'll go out for a meal. Dunno about you, but I'm ravenous." And there was my old energetic, smiling, whirlwind Phillippa, back in full force.

The rest of the evening she spent being her usual charming, entertaining self. She wouldn't hear of me staying overnight with her, insisted I should get back, and that work was probably piling up, waiting for me to get back to it. I said sod work, I came to see you. I felt confused and a little rejected, as she said she was fine and dandy, thanks ever so for coming down, I was there when she needed me, but now she could pick up her pieces and get on with her life, she didn't want to hold me up more than was necessary.

"You sure you'll be OK?" I asked again, before getting in

the taxi.

"Stop fussing nanny. I'm fine now, honest."

"Call me straight away, if and when you need to." I still wasn't convinced.

"Yeah, OK."

"Promise me, Phillippa."

"OK, I promise. Now go, or you'll be late."

"Promise me you'll ring me tonight anyway, and tomorrow."

"Isabel!"

"For my peace of mind Phillippa, please?"

"All right then, mother hen. I'll ring tonight and tomorrow and let you know that I'm *still* fine! And Isabel?"

"Yes?"

"Thanks again. I mean it. You saved my life today." Tears sprang in my eyes.

"That's what I'm here for," I said, as we hugged one last time.

Chapter Twenty-Four

I couldn't sleep. Every time I dozed off, I started dreaming about Lily and Phillippa and then ending up alone. It was tonight's repetitive nightmare. It was the only film my brain would show, just in case I didn't get all the detail of the horrible feelings the first time round, or even the fifth time round.

I'd woken up. Again. The terrible pressure of loneliness and betrayal in my chest. Again. I couldn't take anymore of this.

I clicked on the bedside lamp and looked at my desolate room. Half lived in. Clothes on the floor. No pictures on the walls. I felt like I'd been living in this empty space forever. The place had that 'temporary' look about it no matter what I did to it. Like I still hadn't managed to put my stamp on it. Or hadn't bothered to. I wasn't sure which.

My alarm clock told me it was 3 am. I groaned to myself. I'd have to be up again in four hours to go to work. But it was no use, sleep, or at least peaceful sleep was just so damned illusive tonight.

I picked up my latest unread book, from the floor (like everything else!). It was the latest Stephen King. I did enjoy it – my monthly read, of about five pages! My eyes followed the words on pages 126 and 127, and I realised I didn't have a clue what I'd just read. I put it down again.

I didn't want Lily back. So why did I keep dreaming of our lovemaking? And then she'd turn into Phillippa. But it all felt hurried and frenzied in the dream. There was an underlying fear about something, but I didn't know what. Then I'd be alone, making love to thin air, but the desperation still clung to me. And I'd wake sweating. I didn't understand the emotions behind it at all. Nothing horrible happened, but the mood was feverish. And I felt hemmed in by it. Surrounded.

But in real life it had never felt like that, with either of them.

I felt a yearning for Phillippa still. To be with her again. I didn't understand. Why hadn't she wanted to continue our affair? See where it would have taken us. Deeper into the knowledge of each other. It's obviously not meant to be. At least I haven't lost her friendship. But she acts now like it had never happened.

Perhaps I'm just lonely. Need someone to hold. I (surprisingly) don't feel... *attached* though – is that the right word? I do feel happier, or relieved maybe, that things between me and Phillippa are just the same as always. I feel contrary. There's a word!

There's a calm part of me that's at ease with the fact that nothing did develop between the two of us, which would have left Isabel hanging on the outside. The three of us have always been equal in our triangular friendship, I feel. It would be top-heavy somehow, out of kilter, if the balance changed like that. I'm not sure that makes any sense, even to me.

Yet a part of me, I don't know... To be with Phillippa that one night, and it didn't finish or start anything. It's like it's suspended in animation, an event all of itself that doesn't connect to anything else. Yet it's not something I could classify as a one night stand. That's too crass a terminology for it.

I did feel accepted though. Just for myself. And strange though it is, throughout the few years that I was with Lily, I don't ever remember feeling as comfortable as I did that one night. It's crazy looking back on it, but *only now* do I realise I felt I had to live up to a certain standard, a specific expectation of Lily's, but was never really sure what it was, so I never knew if I fulfilled it or not. Forever in suspense.

There wasn't any sort of tension with Phillippa, as there was so often with Lily. I think we fed off that tension. It was the source of our love and hate for each other. No, I didn't hate her, that's too strong. Too unkind. She drove me to distraction sometimes, admittedly. The only thing I really hated was when my continual efforts to please were continually shunned. Meet me half way, can't you, damn it Lily!

Perhaps we never should have got married. But there were good times too. Everything had been so *magic* between us to start with. Maybe that was the problem. Things had been *too* good. Too perfect to be true. And when we really got to know each other deep down, or deeper anyway, we just weren't compatible.

There wasn't any peace, just more arguing and less making up.

But I wouldn't take Lily back. Not now. I can see that there's just no continuance, no possibility of it, with me and Lily. I could never go back to the pretence of us two, after feeling something so different and new with Phillippa.

I wonder where Phillippa is now, what she's doing. If Phillippa called now and said she'd met someone, a real someone, a true someone that she could be with and share things with, I'd be very happy for her. Which makes no sense at all, when I think of us together and I want to feel her touch again, yet I'm happy to let her go. Maybe it's just biology. I don't know. Or just missing someone being here to be warm with in bed at nights.

Or maybe I'm just having a mid-life crisis at 25!

3.15 am. Oh, long night. I'm gonna feel like a damn zombie in the morning. Maybe I should pull a sicky. Haven't had any time off sick this year. Maybe tomorrow I'd could just take a walk in the park, go for a swim at the leisure centre and come back and finish my Stephen King.

Very tempting idea.

I switched on the radio, see if they could may be play me something soothing to send me to sleep.

I don't believe it! They're having a flipping 'Lurve Night' All those soppy couples dedicating unrealistic love songs to each other! I switched it off again. I'm not a cynic or anything, but all those hours of gooey love songs just do my head in and do nothing to soothe my head, heart, groin, or anything else.

Love songs were always way OTT in their expression of 'romance or bust'. So way off the mark, most of them. They never sang about the subtleties and complexities that real relationships have. The little things you know about each other, the little irritations, and vulnerabilities. The times spent together forgetting about the rest of the world, the times alone together wishing you had some space of your own to retreat to, the love story off the screen, not in the book, not in the song. The unspoken being togetherness whilst doing something boring like washing up. The planning a weekend together camping, and still having fun even though it pisses down and the tent collapses on you! The muscles in the body that react to a certain touch that only you know. The messages in the eyes and the unspoken thoughts, read, communicated and shared.

Am I imagining things or did me and Lily once share that deep understanding I now long for? I think I thought we did. We must have done on some level, or we never would've got together in the first place.

But somewhere along the line, messages got misread, or not sent, or received too late, and the other wondered why their messages were not responded to as was needed. Our synchronicity of language was lost. And we never seemed to recover it, no matter how hard we tried. But by the time I realised we might have been talking, or rather arguing over different things, the storm had already blown over and the ice had already set in.

Our antennae for each other got faulty and we couldn't get the right engineer out to fix it. Or even if we could, we'd first have to find their number. But then we would only end up arguing over which number to use. And then I'd give in on the one Lily had decided, and then it would promptly be lost, and we'd blame each other for the nuisance of it all.

So the engineer never even got their call out, never mind a foot in the door! There were too many other words in the way to misinterpret and pick over.

But when we did make up… there was fire, but it was never sated. We couldn't find a way to answer each other's needs, well not in the right way anyway.

Oh, it was way too late, or way too early depending on how you looked at it, to be mulling all this over.

I could maybe call Ian and we could have a good thrash on the squash court or something. We could be naughty school boys together and both call in sick. Yeah, that's a better plan. I might just do that. I'll give him a ring first thing. 3.33 am. Time to attempt some more sleep methinks.

Chapter Twenty-Five

I stared up at Patrick's backside.

"Take it in," he yelled down to me.

I tightened up the rope on my belay device, and Patrick hung from it twenty-five feet above, his feet braced against the rock. He'd gotten to the difficult bit of the climb and needed a rest while he mentally figured out how to get over the overhang facing him.

The sun beat down on us, and the birds called to each other in the trees. I wondered at how long it had taken me to discover rock climbing. Isabel was right, all I needed was a different focus. And ever since I'd bumped into Patrick, or rather, ever since he'd taken me to the hospital in a mad dash, I'd done hardly anything else but climbing.

"You OK?" I called up.

"Yeah, just resting. How the hell did you do this bit Phil?"

I smiled. I seemed to have a natural talent and daredevilness when it came to climbing. I loved it. There was no room in my head or my body to think or feel anything but the present stance and the next move up to the top. It was all consuming, and it felt so healthy! Which is a 100% improvement on how I felt a couple of months ago.

Seeing Isabel did help. Being with her was comforting. I wish she could've stayed and stayed and stayed. But I could never tell her who it was. It would alienate her from me totally. Break her heart. I feel I betrayed her in some way. I've never been so consumed by guilt before.

But when she'd gone, I felt lost. Wandering round and round, in my head, on the streets wondering what to do with myself.

I called her as promised. Lied, and said I was OK. What else could I do?

But a few days wore on, and the despair became everything. I thought I was going mad. The anguish and pain that I'd blocked out for years... It had all been waiting for me, and it all collapsed down on my head, all at the same time. Eating became impossible. Getting out of bed was the worst! I just wanted to die beneath the covers, too much emotion to face. The weight of it was totally crushing. I was nothing but a body of despair. A void. A black hole. I couldn't talk to anyone, or interact at all. I just wanted to sleep and sleep and sleep forever.

All those men I slept with and not one of them could remove Brian's marks on me, they just smudged them, like a dirty rubber on pencil markings. Then Ted. And the burnt imprints of Brian erased for a little while. I felt new again. I felt worthwhile. I was worth something again. I was worth loving. But too much loss, too much grief... That I hadn't let myself feel before. There's pain in feeling happiness again. All or nothing. I can block out the pain, but that numbs me to everything. All of life.

But I sure as hell felt the razor blades cutting ribbons of red from me in the hot bath. I wanted to feel pain again. So I could find me again. But I couldn't stand all of that pain. Suicide. The only way out, I thought. I can't keep living like this. I couldn't even talk to Isabel about it. I didn't know how to.

But it obviously wasn't the plan for me to leave this existence like that. Along came Patrick. The door wasn't locked. I'd overran my time in the motel room. Was supposed to have been out of there by noon. Patrick came in and saw it all.

Hell of a way to find new friends!

He's also a fucking good climbing instructor and I booked him everyday.

"OK, gimme some slack," he called. I let the rope out, so he could continue climbing. At least he hadn't had to put the gear in, he was just collecting it! I sure had fun doing that! Still, it wasn't a particularly hard climb. Only HVS 5c, but it had some interesting bits to work out along the way.

But the thing that had turned my whole life around in a wonderfully different perspective, and turned my world on its head, was when I found out I was pregnant.

My periods are as regular as clockwork these days, and I

was late. PG test time. Positive.

It was like someone flicked a switch. It was the most incredible feeling, and certainly one I thought I'd never be prone to. A complete revelation. Where it came from, or how it came about, I've no idea! But it's here, and it won't go away. I feel so different, I never would have thought it. Not of me. Not in a million! I couldn't stop crying for a couple of days, from happiness and sadness.

My daughter was growing inside me, becoming a loving living being. Ted's daughter. Of course I haven't told him. That would just end it all, wouldn't it?

So I now have two major focuses in my life now. Daphne. And climbing. I haven't felt so full of life for such a long, long time. Everything was fun at one time, about a hundred years ago. And now things are starting to be fun again. I feel like I'm breathing fresh air again, after being suffocated for years.

I cry everyday for about an hour or more, just to give relief to my intense pain inside. But I also feel joy and happiness. I look forward to climbing, the feel of earth and rock beneath my hands and feet, so primal. And planning for Daphne's arrival, which I look forward to with excitement and dread. It's going to be hard, but it's going to be love.

I feel challenged, and interested and interesting. My future suddenly looks so vastly different from what it did so not very long ago.

Patrick thinks if I keep up the way I am now, I could take the exams and be an instructor myself and freelance. Sounds like fun to me. I'm now reunited with my estranged friend – Fun.

I raided the local book shops for baby books and climbing books, and am reading both avidly.

"Your safety's sure as hell in well and good." Patrick shouted down, as he continued to use the nut key to batter away at the nut I'd lodged in a crack.

"Thank you kind sir," I shouted back with a laugh.

Chapter Twenty-Six

It was dead of night. I couldn't sleep. My body still hadn't got used to being in a different bed, a hard hospital bed.

The main window showed the full moon winking at me through the passing clouds. I could hear the breathing of the other new mums in the ward. Happily breathing in the new memories of their new beloved children. Dreaming of their futures.

My mind reeled back and replayed in slow motion Daphne's birth. And his.

I knew I'd been acting hysterical. I just couldn't help it.

My beloved Daphne was born. I had known instinctively that I was carrying a girl. She was all well and good, all the bits in all the right places, kicking and screaming, full of life.

And then out came him. Her twin brother.

I had looked at his small new face. And I'd seen Brian's face there instead. I screamed and wailed, and it had taken me some time to calm down again, even after they'd taken 'im away.

Brian's dead son. That's what I thought I'd seen. He'd come back to haunt me in this new baby. To seek vengeance. I couldn't bear to have him anywhere near me.

I tried telling myself that he was OK. He was Ted's son. He was as pure and clean as Daphne. But every time I think of that small male body being lifted from my insides, I just want to throw up.

No matter how much I try and rationalise it to myself, I have to blank him out. It was better to believe he had nothing to do with me, he was some sorta mistake, a freak of nature. But he wasn't really the same spirit as Brian's aborted scum. How could he be? But he might be.

Besides, I'd never wanted a son. Never. How could I possibly know how to bring him up when our bodies were so different; held different kinds of knowledge within them. He would grow up to desire bodies like the one I have.

I hastily sat up in bed and leaned over the side and retched. But nothing came out. I retched nothingness again. I sat very still, but nothing more happened. I plumped up my pillows, and laid back, releasing my breath noisily.

But Daphne was a part of me. She was of she. Of me. I'd encapsulated her small, warm vulnerability within me for nine months. I'd read baby books. Cultivated a whole style of up-bringing in my head for her, so she'd grow up to be wise and strong, loving and fearless. Her body would know the secrets of the female body, how it felt, how it ticked, how it ached, how it gave and how it asked. I understood that. I felt the affinity between us. And I'd felt the shock of one becoming two, as her own individual shape took form in front of me. She will have her own likes and dislikes. Her own passions and cravings. Her own fears and challenges to meet in life. She'll probably desire different food and drink to the ones absorbed from me through pregnancy.

I had a good view of the main entrance from here, the drive and the car park. I could see the occasional headlights of cars glinting through the tree lined road that ran past the hospital.

I stared at the halo round the moon, clouds now framing it, letting the big night torch shine down on us.

He was different though. He of she. Why didn't men give birth to boys, like women gave birth to girls? It used to make perfect sense to me as a child. A very small child I was, when I believed that all dogs were boys, and all cats were girls. So one of each species had to come together to have puppies and kittens. I'd been most surprised to learn that there were she dogs and he cats. That little piece of knowledge had altered my view of the world. It was only a small change, but a fundamental one.

This little he body that I had no knowledge of what to do with. I'd never experienced boyhood. I didn't know what it was like, how they should act, how they felt. He was an alien to me. A totally alien thing. Distant. Remote. The opposite of everything I was.

And I just couldn't get it outa my head that he knew about the previous baby. The one that was nearly a boy. They'd both come from the same womb after all. What if it shared secrets like that? Told him this was the grave of another 'him' long ago. Wouldn't he hate me for that?

How the fuck did Brian still have power over how I felt and how I acted all these years later? Would he never die? Could I never kill him off? Would he never leave me alone? The bastard!

My eyes fell on my empty water glass, at my bedside. I would dearly love to throw it at the window, welcome the crack, the smash, the splinters, the cold night air stealing in, the cries of alarm it would raise, the rushing nurses in a panic, all the lights being turned on, the other mothers disturbed from their fucking blissful dreams. And they'd worry and flurry, going here, there, everywhere, cleaning it up, reassuring everyone. Giving me strange looks.

And I'd shout, "There. Look at it, you ignorant cows. Look at all that smashed glass. That's how I feel. That's me. Angry enough to burst, and feel the pain of all my shards on the floor. Do you get it now? Do you fucking understand?" I would have felt pleased to have caused such a commotion, to finally spell it out to everyone. And I could pretend to myself that they would've understood. Would've cared. Would've seen it immediately.

They would say, "Of course you don't want to look after him. That's perfectly natural. We can understand that. What a terrible ordeal you've been through. We had no idea. We're so sorry. It's important that you do what's best for you, and we'll respect that."

And all the strange looks, the accusing looks would stop.

The splintered glass of myself would be a big 'fuck you' to them all. But they'd see that I was perfectly justified, had every right. They hadn't been through what I'd been through. They'd be so apologetic, and they'd take him away from me forever, and never ask me about him again.

But I didn't throw the glass. And I didn't smash the window. Because although it would clearly express myself, how I felt and everything else, in my eyes; in their eyes they'd just think I'd fucking lost the plot and wasn't stable enough to even look after Daphne. And I was damned if they thought they could take her away from me. Absolutely no fucking way.

I watched the clouds wash over the moon, they almost completely swallowed her up.

Well, what did I care about any of them, anyway? They'd no idea, and I wasn't about to tell them.

I'd leave the hospital, take Daphne home with me, and make a life for the two of us. Together.

Chapter Twenty-Seven

I decided I was going to go out and get drunk tonight. Well and truly slaughtered.

Wearing my red silk shirt and blackest jeans, I was gonna hit the clubs. Any of them. All of them, I didn't care.

Where the hell was my wallet?

I hunted round my flat, tipping up piles of papers hidden under heavy computer books. Being tidy always feels like too much of a luxury, and a waste of time. I looked under and round the bits and pieces of odd furniture I'd acquired since...

Damn it. Where was it?

Then I remembered. It was still in my jacket pocket from this morning.

I tramped my way through the mess to the door where it was hung up, and promptly nearly fell over the damn cat! "Misty!" Neighbour's cat. Very fond of exploring.

Just as I was about to take my jacket down, my eye fell on it again. The letter. On my small post table. The top one of the pile. I should've destroyed it already. Ripped it into a thousand pieces. Burned it. Or never even read it in the flipping first place.

What did Lily think she was playing at? Sending me an news update on her fucking happy life? With Steve. Their unborn baby kicking away inside her. I gripped my jacket with one hand, and put my hand over my mouth with the other trying not to throw up. I gulped. Breathed. Recovered. Staring at the piece of paper, Lily's scrawl easily visible from here, I almost picked it up, to murder it into shreds there and then. But it wouldn't let me.

I reached for the door handle. Checked my keys were in my pocket. Slammed the door shut after me. Threw my arms into my jacket sleeves. And ran helter-skelter down eight flights of stairs.

It was more than a year now. Since the divorce. Why was I getting so worked up? I reached the ground floor. I yanked open the door and strode forth into the ignorant cold night.

Perhaps she just felt sorry for Steve. She couldn't really love him. She must be only marrying him out of pity. It can't be the money, Steve doesn't have any. Or perhaps the pregnancy had really been an accident, and she only wanted him around for the child. But Lily had always been so *careful* not to let any accidents happen. But she can't really *want* to have children with Steve! She'd not wanted children. Period! Well, not with me anyway! No, it must've been a lapse on her part. Perhaps she'd been drunk one night. Yes that was it.

I suddenly realised I didn't have a clue where I was going. I stopped and took in the houses, the traffic lights, the occasional car passing by, their lights momentarily highlighting me. Well I would get to a pub sooner or later. I carried on walking.

What about her *precious* career? What about taking time off from healing all her patients to clean her baby's dirty bum? Probably Steve would be house-husband and father, whilst she worked. But she wouldn't make that compromise with me. I would've done that. I told her that. I didn't mind staying at home with our child. But she wouldn't have it. Didn't she trust me? Had she so little faith in me to be a good father?

Oh damn, I've just passed a pub. Shall I go back? No, it was a dive anyway. I'll walk on to the next one.

What did I care anyway? She's my ex-wife now. Ex. That's the operative bit. *Ex*-wife. I shouldn't be getting so het up about it all now, should I? Lily could do what she liked. She's a free agent. So am I. I could go settle down with somebody else if I wanted. Have a family. If there was someone for me to settle down with… If I ever found her… Shit. I hate self pity.

Where is the next pub anyway? Oh, just up here a bit. Good. I'll well and truly go and drown my sorrows.

As soon as I entered the dimly lit room I could smell the stale smoke. Luckily I didn't have to wait long to be served at the bar. I ordered three double gin and tonics and found myself a hidey-hole, away from the main seating area.

It was quiet for a Friday night. But I guess I was quite early. It would probably be heaving in about an hour or so.

126

Sitting there, I stared into each glass in turn, looking through the clearness of the liquids to the dark veneer of the round table. They didn't tell me anything. But they helped focus my mind on emptiness, instead of Lily's face. Her eyes. Her smile. Her warm nakedness next to mine. Her tinkling laugh. Her kiss goodbye before she left for work still on my lips. Her breath falling evenly as I watch her, fast asleep in the armchair, exhausted from work one evening. Lily stamping her foot in annoyance, thinking I'm not listening to her. Her perplexed frown. Her quiet voice in argument where I always felt in the wrong. My harsh retaliations. Lily's...

I thumped my fist on the table, making all three glasses shimmer in response. I downed one of them in two gulps, and nearly choked. Once my eyes had stopped stinging and my throat had stopped tickling, I gulped another one down. Glad of its bitterness biting my tongue.

Two down, one to go. I held the last one in my hand for a while, savouring it, letting the previous two slosh in my head, testing to see how much fogginess there was yet, how much Lily's image had diminished in my mind. Not all that much. I swilled it around, then stood, took the two empty glasses back to the bar and ordered another three. The barman looked surprised, but didn't say anything. I think my tortured, strangled, I'm-a-mess look kept him silent, and perhaps even made him a little sympathetic.

Thank God it wasn't work tomorrow. I was going to be in for a raging hangover.

I returned to my table to nurse my four small glasses. I made patterns with them, swapping them round, sliding them easily across the varnished surface.

First there was the square. Then a diamond. Then a triangle with a dot in the middle.

The first two drinks were starting to kick in now. I started to get bored with the limitations of the four glass arrangements. I gulped down my third, and became interested anew as to what possible shapes I could make by rolling this newly empty glass around. Or balancing it on top of, or under one of the other glasses.

Three more to go, three more to go. The stupid ditty

repeatedly ran round my head.

Lily never could stand spirits. When off duty she was a wine girl. Always a wine gal. Sometimes red, sometimes white. Red for evenings. Red with cheese. Red for twinkly evening guests and specially cooked meals. Red to make her heady and dangerous. Red to deepen the colour of her dark brown eyes. Red's bittersweet taste on her lips, last thing at night. Red's daring laugh and double entendre jokes with friends. But white was for day. Clear and sparkling. To be drunk with her light lunch, fat free. White with salads. White when she was alone. White to help her concentrate. White to make her playful, in the sober light. Always a wine gal. Always trying to educate me on the best wines.

In the wine shop, of a Friday evening. "You choose dear." "No, no, it's up to you." So I chose. And she winced. And would ask me to pick again. All too often I got a second wince, and sometimes a third. Occasionally I got lucky. But more often than not, in her exasperation she would end up choosing it herself. She chose to suit her mood, to enhance it. I liked them all. Wine was good. I didn't mind. But I was always much more of a beer man. Or a gin. Scotch. Even lemonade, for those times my stomach demanded I lay off the alcohol for a bit.

I enjoyed wine. Don't get me wrong. But I could take it or leave it. I could live without it. But whilst living with Lily, there'd never been less than ten bottles of wine in the house at a time. Five red, five white. Or six red and six white. Seven red, seven white. "All things need a balance, dear," she would say.

Time for another gin. I now had two empty glasses, and two full ones. My imagination whirred slowly through any new possibilities for making new patterns. I was getting quite good at this now.

Only two more to go, two more to go, der der, der derrrr! Don't think I'll be able to walk home tonight, never mind go on to a club! Have to, er, have to speak to barman. Gedim to, erm, get me a taxi or somert. That's it. A taxi. That'd be it. Good idea. Don't 'ave to do any walking then. Taxi. Yeah.

The glasses and table in front of me were getting very blurry. Bery blurry. One went smash. Oops! Wassit nempty one? Or a full un? Well, twer empty now. Last one then.

Poor sod. He'd passed out. Lucky for him, one of my staff knew his name, and where he lived. With a bit of help from Larry, we managed to haul him into a cab. Dead weight he was. Well out of it. Pam went with him, to help him out the car at the other end. It was her night off anyway, and she didn't have anything else to do. Glad I wouldn't have his head on my shoulders tomorrow.

Woke up. Bleary. Thirsty. Very loud banging. Very consistent. Wun't shurrup! Bloody neighbours. Tried to sit up. Big mistake. Ah, that hurt. Ah, my head. It was my head making that noise.

I laid still. Just concentrating on breathing. Hoping my head would quieten eventually.

What happened last night? I don't remember anything. Nothing. Zip. Oh, wait a minute. A pub. Lots of gin. Square shape, like on a dice. Diamond shape, like a kite. Yeah, I remember that. Then what? Things got real hazy after that.

Then I noticed a female form stood at the end of the bed, coming closer. Some light from the other room spilling on to her. Wearing my dressing gown? Apparition. Must be. Perhaps it was Lily? Come back to me. Ah, no. She's living in East Anglia. What would she be doing all the way back over here?

"How are you sweety?" Not an apparition then. And certainly not Lily. She never called me that. Who was she? She bent over me, but it was hard to look at anything for too long. Shapes and colours were still trying to make sense. "Do you feel all right?" Do I look bloody all right? What a stupid question to ask me at a time like this. I didn't say anything though. My lips were cracked and dry, stuck together. My throat was parched. One voice amongst the background of the cacophony inside my head, and blood pulsating in my veins, it was just as much as I could handle.

"Can I get you anything Ted? Would you like a drink of water? That's always good for the morning after." She loudly rustled away.

Recognition started to dawn on me. It was Pam. The girl who had served me a few times in the local pubs, as she flitted from one to another. I'd chatted to her a few times, when the evenings had been too lonely to stay home alone.

Had anything happened last night? I don't even remember how I got here. No, nothing could possibly have… I had been so out of it. I'd have been no more use than a sack of potatoes. Why was she wearing my gown? Perhaps she'd just stayed overnight on the sofa…?

She returned. Armed with a glass of water. "Here we go. Try to sit up now." She sat on the bed beside me. A well toned arm reached forth from the sleeve that was too big for her, holding the glass. I tried to shift my useless body into a sitting position. Not good. Nausea swept over me like a tidal wave. I just about managed to sort of sway myself over the side of the bed before it all came gushing out.

"Oh dear, never mind, most of it went in the bucket. Don't worry, I'll clean it up in a minute." Then after wiping my face with a tissue, as if I was a baby, she put the glass to my lips, and tried to hold my head in place.

My lips just about managed to open a slit, with some effort, and then the cold freshness dribbled into my mouth. I practised swallowing. I was starting to get the hang of this. My stomach was soaking up the non-alcoholic purity like a desert. Half of it spilt down my face and on to the pillow, despite Pam's best endeavours.

Glass empty, Pam took the bucket away, and went to get something to clean up the rest. The silence wrapped around my body like soggy cotton wool. But the regular poundings beating on my head like a drum punctuated the foggy silence with nauseating regularity.

I just wanted to die. I wanted to be more horizontal than the horizon. And just sink deeper and deeper into my mattress, until I became an innate part of the bed. I tried going back to sleep, but it was no good. I just kept wondering why Pam was here. I kept my eyes closed so they didn't hurt so much and tried to distance myself from my body, pretend it wasn't there.

I could hear Pam cleaning up. She was being awfully nice. I really hope I didn't give her any false impressions last night. No other impression than my being a drunken slob anyway.

She padded away, and returned with another glass of water. She tried to get me to drink again. I still couldn't speak, so I just groaned a feeble protest.

"Come on, Ted. Water's good for you." Death would be good for me right now. Go home Pam! Leave me in my misery. More water somehow managed to slip down my throat, and a lot of it made the pillow even wetter. Then with very kind cruelty, she took the wet pillow from beneath my head, sending fireworks shooting into my brain. She then plumped up a pillow she'd brought in with her, and forced it beneath my head. What was left of it anyway. It felt like an exploding rock by this time. She then padded away once again. I prayed fervently that my head would restore itself to some kind of order in the next few seconds.

I was determined to get back to sleep again, seek oblivion from the torture of this body I was attached to. But then I had a horrible feeling. A really horrible one. I needed a piss. The urge was getting worse with every passing second. I could *not* make it as far as the bathroom. I knew the world would do some serious nose dives, turn round, do a jig, then turn up-side-down again, if I tried to stand up. This was not good. I don't need the toilet. I don't. Shit. Perhaps I could ask Pam to bring a bottle or something. Oh god, how embarrassing! Wait a minute. I wasn't in my clothes. I was starkers. How did *that* happen? I can't think about this. Oh, it stopped me from thinking about wanting to urinate for a split second though.

I think I must've let out a strangled cry of some sort then, as Pam came dashing in and crouched by my side.

"What is it? What's wrong Ted?" I moaned again. "Do you need another drink? One moan for no, two for yes." I moaned once. "Something to eat?" I was going to be sick again, just at the thought of food. One moan. "The toilet, do you need the loo?" Two moans. "Hold on." What else did she think I was doing for god's sake? What was she going to do now? Make me walk to the loo? It was like asking a bee to fly to the moon and back. Oh no, she really was going to make me piss into a bottle. Not sure I can take this. Please, god, just let me die. Even wetting the bed would be better than this. Maybe. Well, perhaps not. Lying in my own cooling urine wasn't a pleasant thought.

Whilst holding the empty orangeade bottle in one hand, she flung my covers back. I shivered. I really wish she hadn't done that. Wish she wasn't about to do what she was going to do. She offered me the bottle for me to take it, but my arms felt limp, and my hands felt heavy. My head and stomach were in league against me attempting to sit up again. So she kept hold of the bottle and guided it to the tip of my penis. I felt the uncomfortable hard ridge against me as she held me in position for it all to flow out. The embarrassment of the situation was swallowed up by the immense relief I felt, not having to hold it in any longer. Then she threw my sheet and duvet back over me, and tucked me in just like my Mum used to do. I snuggled deep into their remembered warmth, and promptly fell asleep.

***

It must've been late evening when I awoke. It was dark out. I stretched and inhaled deeply. I lay still again. My head was quiet, it wasn't saying anything. My focus travelled down my body to my stomach. That wasn't saying anything either. Good signs. I gingerly pushed myself into a sitting position. Head was still in one piece. Arms weren't shaking. Stomach didn't heave. Signs were getting better all the time. Perhaps I could try standing up. What time was it anyway?

One look at my luminous alarm clock told me it was 9.35pm.

Was Pam still here? All seemed very quiet.

I stood up, switched on the main light, and I still felt fine. I called for Pam. My voice now worked! No answer. After gently walking round the living/dining room, the study and kitchen, it was abundantly clear she was no longer here.

Time for a shower. Followed by coffee and toast. Definitely.

Then after that I'll have to go and see Pam. Not the bit I'm looking forward to. But I'll have to find out sooner or later, what, if anything, happened last night.

***

All clean. All caffeined up now. Both head and tummy seem to be on good terms with me again. Now for the nasty bit. But then

132

the buzzer went. I went over to the intercom.

"Hello?"

"It's me. Pam." Oh god! I buzzed her into the building. She'd be up here in a few mins. What was I going to say? What did she expect? Christ! OK, don't panic Ted. Just stay calm. Act casual. Just be straight and to the point.

I opened the door to her. My old t-shirt and jeans met her black velvet evening dress, as she gave me a quick bear hug. Then she went past me and sat down on the sofa. Did she think we were now going to go out on a date? Did I arrange something that I should've remembered?

I shut the door and took my time turning round and walking the short distance over to where she was.

"Ted, you look worried. Whatever's wrong? Come and sit down and tell me all about it." I sat down in the armchair across from her.

"Well you certainly look healthier than when I last saw you. How do you feel?"

I cleared my throat. "Erm, good thanks. Yeah, much better than before."

"That's good. What's wrong then?" her very red lips said. Her face was now framed with her brown ringlets hanging loose.

"Well, er, nothing really. I mean, well, yes, something, but not really no, well, what happened last night?" There, I'd said it!

"What happened? Well you passed out in the pub. I brought you home in a taxi, as you were in no fit state to do anything! Then you slept like a log, once I'd finally got you into bed. And when you woke up, I gave you some water, and you had a piss. Remember that?"

I coloured somewhat. "Yes, er, I recall the last bit. But, er, you stayed over?"

"Yeah, I hope you don't mind, I just crashed on your sofa, as I'd an idea you wouldn't be fit to take care of yourself first thing, so I stuck around. Hope that was OK I went to work after you fell asleep again."

"Oh. Right." I felt relieved. That was it then. Nothing. All totally innocent. I felt a little disappointed too. "Right then."

Then she laughed. Merrily. "Oh, *you* thought..." More laughter. Well, it wasn't *that* funny! "Oh, I'm sorry. But honestly

Ted. If you could've seen yourself! You were in no shape whatsoever to get up to any hanky-panky last night." I managed to give a laugh. She was right of course.

"You're all dressed up, and I didn't know what to think…"

"I'm just about to go on a date with Charles. I'm taking him out to this new Italian restaurant. I thought I'd just pop by here first, make sure you were still in the land of the living."

"Oh right. Thanks. Yeah, I'm fine."

"Good. Sorry, I can't stay Ted. But you know, if you ever want to chat or anything, you know, about whatever was haunting your drinks last night, feel free to give me a buzz." And she handed me a piece of paper with her number on.

"Thanks Pam. That's great. Best let you go off to your date then. Don't want you to be late." I mustered a smile. She smiled back, gave me a peck on the cheek, said, "Bye Ted," and was gone.

I was left sat in my chair, holding the piece of paper she'd given me. Shame she had a chap already. Last night could've been the start of something. God, who am I kidding.

I looked at her number. If I ever wanted to talk about anything. Haunting. Yeah. My ex-wife. I suddenly realised I'd not thought of her at all in the last couple of waking hours.

I jumped up then, took up the letter she'd written, ripped it to shreds and threw every last scrap in the bin. There. Done. My heart still ached, and my gut still said there was a gap there, needing to be filled, but at least my head was now clearer.

Chapter Twenty-Eight

I look from sleeping Daphne to the cafe table. I can see resemblances of Ted. Patrick had asked about her father. He was a temporary love I said. He hadn't pursued the subject.

I didn't know what to think – thinking lots of crap, mobile goes off in middle of coffee with friend again on table opposite me, smell chlorine that my table's been wiped with, bright yellow light reflected off square tables, I look at my teacup, forgot teaspoon, remembered sugar, smell vinegar on someone's chips, reminds me how much I don't want food at the moment, tireless creatures.

I get up and rectify the spoon situation, bumped knees on chairs grounded too close to tables as always. Tinsel and glitter galore. Well at least they're not playing Xmas music at us, I can hear a kiddy louder amongst the rest of the hubble of few grown ups talking sense in a non-sensical way. The only one who sees and understands is the child.

Stomach churns through the wrangler again. Will this feeling never leave me?

Patrick. My mind goes blank again. Is my pot of tea ready yet, placed so carefully in front of me, I push it to one side and like the babble of the child a few tables down, hidden from view by the pillar. The adult nonsense continues. Xmas decorations aren't overdone, which is something. It can get awfully too much in your face this time of year.

Child counting aloud in unselfconscious way, all the way to ten and giggles. Someone's damn mobile again. I could strangle those things.

Clatter of knives cleared up behind me, and an occasional printing of till receipt. Is quite quiet actually, customer wise. Hum of air conditioning behind, ahead, up in the air.

Sicky feeling plaguing me. Why does it come and never

leave at such inopportune times?

I swallow it down and it still remains.

I decide to pour the tea but spill it all over the tiny yellow squares of the table, a child jumps past me and runs down other side of the cafe.

Some tissues on floor, they can mop up the brown pool. Feel cold even though it's warm. Little girl leaves. Feel sad. Little boy enters, he quiet. I suddenly think of Dominic and wonder. I don't think of him usually. I try not to. I don't like to. But sometimes...

There's a big red plastic roll attached to the wall behind me, labelled 'newspapers'. It's empty. It's an unusual thing to see. But somehow comforting.

Van Gogh painting on the opposite wall. The street one. Portrait shape copy. Better than the sunflowers I suppose. I could never understand how all that yellow was so attractive.

Feel desire stir below. I'm due for my period. Ted pops into my head again. My eyes follow the familiar puffiness of our daughter's face. She's nestled quiet in her carry cot beside me. So small and indomitable. So relaxed in sleep, beauty dreams, so adamant in her wants and needs when awake. Am hungry now. Am thirsty now. Going to wee now. Want hug now. Want to play now. Safe and comfortable world, everything new, everything to be tracked, see what it is, what does it do, how does it feel, yes I like that, no that one's boring. That makes a funny noise, like that one too.

I wonder at not remembering what it was like to be a baby, looking at Daphne makes me feel better. I like her otherness, yet her part of me-ness. Her dependency, yet individuality, when she laughs and gurgles, when she cries and screams. A whole new world. A whole new life.

Patrick thinks she's adorable. I know she's beautiful. And I know she likes her own way. Sicky feeling comes back. Patrick will never understand so what's the point in trying to explain?

Talk about the weather, the most common phrase ever said in England in the winter – isn't it cold! Like it surprises us, every day of a whole season every year. Yet strangers and acquaintances, even those in families remark to each other; isn't it cold! I do it too. You'd think we'd get bored of it. But I suppose people don't get bored of looking forward to the summer.

I unwrap my egg custard tart, but still my stomach insists it can't yet face it. I'll try again in a little while. At least I've managed to get some tea down me.

Rattle of spoon hits floor as she clears away, clunk and ching of plates on plates – hard wearing things. Lots of adult strange talk of nothing. Where have all the children gone? Oh, I can hear the little boy's loud comments on something, they make no sense but are true in their feeling.

Beeping microwave. Still feel icky.

I think about school for Daphne, a possible career, what she'll be like, when will I tell Ted and Isabel? It's a huge secret from them, yet it doesn't feel so weird. All of us single, all of us childless, that's our history together. Me as Mum doesn't quite fit the picture somehow.

Moving Santa model on the counter. Spooky thing. Holding a candle and a watch, in his stripy jim jams, rolling his head, bring his arm back. I remember learning about St. Nicholas in primary school. The original Santa, where it all started.

Custard's not so bad. Throat's swallowing, stomach accepting, tastes fine. Shame the seats aren't more comfy. Backs are hard metal shapes, not high enough. Pale yellow things, easy to look through and not notice.

Only half more cup of tea squeezed out of the pot. Might buy another one. Black tea. Strong and black, one sugar. Just how I like it. It surprises me, the people I meet, how few of them take sugar.

Children. Larger than life. So freer in body movement, louder in volume, louder in vocalisation, there's not so many rules to obey in what not to say. They can say anything. Almost. The censor develops too early. The deceiver comes in – not OK to do that, so I'll do it anyway, 'cause I like it and then not say owt bout it – they won't know – speak child speak – your crimes aren't punishable, they're a way of finding out, being curious, wanting more, ignorant of custom, of etiquette, of politeness, which are all strait jackets anyway.

Little boy walks past, studiously, diligently watching the tray with drinks on, treading carefully, 'I might drop it,' he says.

He doesn't. I knew he wouldn't. I trusted him not to. And when an adult trusts a child like that, then the child trusts themselves. And that's the best thing. And keep it, and nurture it, I send telepathic signals to his Mum, knowing she won't receive them, hoping anyway.

Even if he broke the trust, dropped the tray, spilt the drink, broke the cup, go on trusting him, and he'll feel OK. Knows it's OK that sometimes a trust is broken, but the honesty of the brokenness makes it easy to put right, clear up, mop it, pick it up, knows that sometimes mistakes are made whilst learning to trust in own abilities, learning to have faith in other's trust in you. It doesn't always happen, not every time, in every way.

Burning smell. Something's overcooked in the kitchen.

If the trust is held, even though the tray broke, the trust gets stronger, and the next million trays to follow will be sure footed.

If the trust breaks and the mother scolds, and the child cries, blamed, blameful, upset, done 'wrong', made mess, unforgiven, then a million wobbly trays will follow with more disasters to come, because the child won't trust her or himself again so easily, and neither will the parent. Or worse still, there'll be no more trays again ever. That would be the worst. The finality, the never to be trusted again, having fouled up once. The child will suffer the fantasy of millions of imagined broken trays and cups and spilt drinks. And that's much worse. The fear that's created. Better to give the child a second physical tray that they can learn how to master for themselves. Because with imaginary trays, the child can never move past that one real broken one, the accident, stuck in that trivial pained memory. So unnecessary. But if the mother's scared or too much in the depths of politeness, then she can be forgiven for scolding. Someone scolded her too one time. A million times. Perhaps it was a tray she broke.

Need some cushions on these dratted seats. Sicky feeling passed for a while, but is back now, now I can smell food and stomach recoils. I reject the image of Patrick's charming smile, his intimate eyes...

Lots of busy little children, passing up and down, between the counter and their trusting parents. Up to the strange end of food and cakes and lady behind the till, then back down again to safe, familiar circle of mother's love, so now can go back to excitement of stranger with the cakes. Still safe. Because Mum acted as such.

I look at Daphne. Glad she's peaceful at this time. I can sit and look at Daphne for hours and not get bored, not get sick of it. She's such an amazing miracle.

No doubt she'll have her hyperactive couple of hours when I get her home. Time to test mommy's patience and imagination. Both are getting lots of exercise.

A girl comes past, 12? 14? She's too thin. I look at her legs in narrow trousers. I suspect anorexia. Unnaturally thin. It pains me to look at her.

I suddenly think of a disabled chap I bumped into a few times in the local library. He'd been in an accident I think. Not sure now. He went about in a wheelchair. Or was it something more permanent? He was very nice to me, helped me pick a book. That I didn't want. Yet I remember being scared of him. Not wanting to talk to him or be with him.

It wasn't his disability. I didn't mind that. I was quite happy talking to a person in a wheelchair. It was his sentences I couldn't stand.

As he talked, I picked up on his own shock and horror of adapting to his situation, his mental pain of being robbed of his legs. His emotion of self pity, that no-one would find him attractive in the 'condition' he was in. I remember thinking what a load of rubbish. You're an intelligent person with love to give. People find that very attractive. You're not the wheelchair. You're still you. But his heaviness of loss swallowed everything he said. I couldn't bear it. Didn't know how to deal with it. It came off him in waves, great tidal waves, like high tide in the dusk. It was overpowering, his feeling of hopelessness.

I didn't need to spend that much time avoiding him though, fortunately, as he didn't seem to go down there that often, and I don't remember seeing him there again.

Feeling colder still now. That unnatural cold that persists, and gets worse if you try to heat the room.

Patrick's out climbing today, with Deirdre, Paul and Sophie. They invited me too. Well, Patrick invited me. I declined. He needs to climb without me sometimes. Or rather, I need him to climb without me sometimes, and for me to climb without him sometimes too.

The three he's gone with are good sorts. Down to earth. Friendly. But to themselves. Or perhaps it's me that remains unto myself.

It gets so dark so early now. Feels like the night goes on too long. Not enough daylight. Not enough sunshine. S.A.D What is it again? Oh yes, Seasonal Adjustment something, is it? Can't remember now. Dysfunction?

Can't hear the children now. Older couple sat at the table across from me, quiet, eating. The girls behind the counter gossip about people in common.

I think again of the tedium of working in a cafe or a shop. How my brain bleeds for stimulation.

But I have a fascinating job now. Taking adults and children climbing, giving instruction, ensuring their safety, watch them struggle and work out and overcome a difficult move, feel warm at the pleasure they derive from it. It's absorbing witnessing their absorption and I know I'm like that too, when I'm up there. The rock is everything.

It requires focus, concentration, agility of mind and body and also accepting the danger of taking the risk, feeling the rock, letting it guide you in its shapes and holes, its grips and strengths. Quiet textured strength of timelessness. The challenge to the climber. The safety of the slithering ropes and clinking gear.

It's a state of mind. Sometimes the fear grips and it's impossible to take the next step up, no matter how easy it is. Other times, harder moves feel fluid, as your body attunes itself and recognises the rock and the places and spaces to choose and the positions needed to reach them and balance the self.

Our 26th birthdays are up and coming. Why does that make me feel so depressed? OUR. Mine, Isabel's and Ted's. Have to sort something out, childcare for Daphne. At least it will be a break away from everything. Holiday camping round Scotland. Ted's idea. Should be fun. Should be. I don't feel very enthusiastic about things at the moment for some reason. I'm sure it'll be great though. It's the first time in *years*, the three of us have spent any decent time together.

It'll be the first time I'll have seen Ted since... I hope he doesn't/hasn't said anything to Isabel.

    A break away from Patrick too.

    Tea's gone cold.

    What time is it? No clock around here. Watch reads 5pm. Shall I get another pot?

    Yes, why not? Don't have to rush back for anything.

Chapter Twenty-Nine A

At last I'd managed to get my film developed. I've sent off copies to both Isabel and Phillippa too. Thought they might like them.

It had been such a fun couple of weeks together. I wish we were still there. Weather had been glorious, and the views spectacular!

I cleared a space on my busy (and still tea stained!) coffee table, and took a pile of books off the sofa so I could sit down. Tidy just wasn't in it. I was the guy in that advert, where that lass comes round and tells him he's been burgled, but really he hasn't, that's just the everyday state of his place. Still, I always knew where things were. Well most of the time anyway.

The first photo was a good shot of the two of them falling about, trying to put our new tent up. In a race against nightfall. Bloody long way to drive, Loch Lomond. Good job we all drive though, was fun sharing and singing stupid songs all the way!

Was definitely the best way to celebrate our 26th birthdays, even though they are nowhere near each other, date wise. Can't remember whose idea it was now, to go on a camping trip, just the three of us. Our little trio hasn't been all together in the one place for years and years. Not since childhood, no not since my wedding! Ah well... That seems like a lifetime ago now.

Yeah. Nice change to rough it a bit, have a laugh, get back to nature and all that malarkey. And just chill out! And complain that you have to get dressed in the middle of the night in order to go to the loo! And argue over whose turn it was to do the washing up.

Were a good tent though, that we bought. Three bedrooms and a dining area. Luxury really when you come to think of it.

Oh, sunrise over the Loch! It looked better in real life than in the picture, but isn't that always the way? Haven't stayed up all night, talking and waiting for the sun to rise since I was at Uni.

It really was just like old times, the three of us reunited, except better, because we could do what we wanted, whenever we wanted and not be expected home by such and such a time. It was also the first time me and Phillippa had been in each other's company since we spent the night together. I hoped that wasn't going to spoil anything. I'd been a bit nervous about that. Wasn't sure how I was going to react, if Phillippa was going to react to it in any way. I knew where we stood though, Phillippa had made it very clear. I was fine with it, but it still felt a bit strange. But it had all been fine, three friends together again. God, I sound like Enid Blyton!

Hah, we're all playing twister in this one. A fellow camper had snapped this one. Whose idea was it to bring that camping!? It was just like we were kids again. Big kids!

There had been the odd moment, just once or twice, where there had been something in Phillippa's eyes, and something in mine that acknowledged what had passed between us. I'd been somewhat afraid of uncomfortable silences, if me and Phillippa were left alone together at any time, but our usual banter and camaraderie was in full swing, and I needn't have worried. Phillippa was pretty laid back and happy within herself. In fact the happiest I've seen her for a long time. It might have something to do with the fact that she's now 'retired'. Neither me nor Isabel said anything about it, but secretly we're both as pleased as punch, to use a cliché. Phillippa knew we were pleased though, we didn't have to say anything.

Yes, Phillippa was bouncing along in her new life quite happily! Literally! She showed me and Isabel some photos that made our hair stand on end! Talk about vertigo city!

She tried to infect us with her obsession for rock climbing, but neither of us were tempted. She teased and cajoled, pouted, provoked, but we were not to be persuaded. Not one bit. It didn't strike us as a whole lot of fun to be left dangling at the end of a couple of ropes half way up a mountain side. No thanks! We both liked our feet stumbling along merrily on terra firma. Enough things to injure ourselves, just doing that!

She never gave up on us though. But we didn't give up

saying no either.

Though I think perhaps Isabel was beginning to cave in, and perhaps I might have too. Phillippa's damned persuasive when she wants to be, but we were strong in numbers, two to one. So, luckily, neither of us had to face the embarrassment of pooing our pants at great heights!

And I hadn't had a single thought of Lily, Steve or the baby the whole time!

Good shot of Phillippa here, basking in the sunlight. She could've been a model. Mmmm, no, maybe not, it would have offended her feminist sensibilities! I also didn't think of Phillippa in any romantic terms either, which quite surprised me. We respected each other, and what we'd shared, and it didn't impinge in the slightest.

What did surprise me was that Isabel was still single. Nice photo of her here in the pub we had dinner in. Our night off from our strange hotch potch of camping meals! She's such an attractive lady, yet she's still single after all this time. I thought I'd had bad luck with women, but Isabel doesn't seem to have any sort of luck with men at all. Though she chooses to be that way. I must admit she's happier and more comfortable with herself being single than I am. Still, after not seeing her for quite some time, I felt a revitalised tenderness towards her. The sisters I never had!

Another shot of Isabel, stood at the top of Ben Lomond, taken on the sly when she wasn't looking. Why does she protest so much at having her pickie taken? She's a beautiful woman. I still can't understand why some gorgeous hunk hasn't swept her off her feet yet. I asked Phillippa about this, and she just shrugged and said no-one measured up to Isabel's high expectations. 'That's Isabel all over,' she said, 'she knows what she wants, and she will never settle for second best.' 'And what does she want exactly?' I'd asked her.

'That's for Isabel to know, and men to find out!' was her mysteriously elusive answer. Isabel came back then from the washing up. So I never found out anymore. But I feel sure there's a special guy out there somewhere for her.

I wish we could have stayed there a whole month! Maybe longer! It was so great to get away from the everyday stuff and the pressures of reality for a while.

I suggested we did the same thing next year, in honour of our 27th birthdays, especially seeing as we don't actually get to see each other very much at all otherwise. The girls agreed enthusiastically enough, but when I tried to tie them down to any sort of dates Isabel was very evasive about it for some reason. I don't know why. Perhaps it's nothing, and she just doesn't like to forward book herself quite that much. Odd though, all the same.

Chapter Twenty-Nine B

Same again next year for our 27th birthdays – I think not! Though I couldn't say that to Ted. He'd want to know why. And what could I say? I'm in love with you Ted and it's bloody hard work pretending otherwise? That would go down well.

It had been a fantastic fortnight though. I'd just received the photos from Ted this morning.

Just us, the tent, the lake/loch, the mountains, basic food and camping stove, and the weather, which held out really well for us thankfully.

A totally different world from the hum drum and huzz buzz of journalism. So refreshing. Shame to come back, though I do enjoy work.

But to do it all again next year... It was hardest when just me and Ted were alone. It didn't really matter *too* much when Phillippa was there with us. I could then make believe that Ted and I were really a couple and Phillippa had come along with us. But we do still have that chemistry between us all as good friends, which I suppose so many people lose as they grow up. But continuously having to cover up my real feelings was a bit draining sometimes.

Phillippa did make it all easier though. We do make a good three point triangle, with ideas and feelings bouncing off each other. And Phillippa's always a good distraction.

I haven't seen her looking so healthy in years. She was positively blooming. I'm so glad she's changed 'career' path. Though I didn't mention it. Knew she wouldn't like it if we had.

It was scary thinking of her scaling those heights even with a rope, and she claims to be enjoying it even more without one! I don't like to think about it, so she told me not to. There's just no stopping her though. Not that I would want to really, but... Well, she loves it. And she's been spending a lot of her climbing time with a certain Patrick. I wonder if anything might happen there? She kept sneaking off to have private telephone conversations with somebody during that fortnight! She was very reticent about talking about it though. And she immediately poo-pooed any notions of romance with him. But still, you never know... She made at least one call a day to someone important, and Patrick and climbing were her main topics of conversation...

I think I withstood the effort of having to be 'just friends' with Ted in such close quarters pretty well. I caught Phillippa's eye when Ted was talking about it. And we both thought the same thing. She was very good at covering up any potential 'awkward' moments, especially when we got on to the subject of 'Why Hasn't Isabel Found Someone Yet?' yawn, yawn. Thank goodness I can rely on Phillippa. She's such a gem. I haven't felt so close to her like this for ages.

And Ted... it was so difficult at times, restraining myself from crossing that line, and instead of sisterly teasing, just wanting to put my arms round him and... But that's just it, isn't it! The futility of it all. The frustration! That he doesn't see me as anything other than a sister, a best friend from childhood. How on earth can I ever make him see me as anything else?

Still, we had a lot of laughs. I wouldn't have not gone. I wouldn't have missed it for anything in fact. I might get this picture framed, the one of the three of us, picnicking on the grass. We look so happy together.

Definitely the best holiday I've ever had. There's no-one like Ted and Phillippa to make me laugh till I cry!

I wonder what they're both doing now?

Chapter Twenty-Nine C

I wonder what Isabel's doing now? You'd like your Aunty Isabel. I'll let you meet one day.

These photos came out really well. Do you want to look at them too Daphne? No, dead to the world, for a change. Sleeping Beauty!

God, I'm so glad Ben agreed to take care of you whilst I was off gallivanting. I'd have been well and truly stuck if he hadn't! What a fucking fab time though! Sun, sea (well water anyway), no sex whatsoever (even better) and my two bestest ever friends in the entire universe, who I love more than anyone, except you of course, little one.

Great to have a holiday away from being a Mum though, even though I did miss you like crazy! Sneaking away to a phone box every night, to ask Ben how you were doing. If you missed me, were you sleeping OK, sometimes just to hear you gurgling! I knew you'd be OK really though, Ben loves kids, and you're very good with him, my sweet. Unusual, you don't take to everyone. Still wanted to check on you though. Who on earth would have thought – me – The Doting Mum!? It was the only time so far that we've been away from each other for such a significant amount of time.

But what a successfully happy happy time. What an absolute hoot! Just like ole times again.

And Ted was fine with us not mentioning or even alluding to the night of your conception. I think I would've died if he had. Izzy would never forgive me. But I needn't have worried, everything was as it should be!

Except, of course, for the fact that dear Isabel's totally gone on him, and he can't see it for shit! Was Ted born blind or what! When *is* he going to see that the two of them were made fer each other? WHEN? So maddening.

Still, I did see a flicker of interest there. I think he cares for her more than he realises. But Isabel's so fucking pessimistic about it all, she never thinks it's going to happen.

But it will. In time. I'm sure of it.

Was wonderful to be with the two of them again, and share everything together again. We should do it more often. Though I think Isabel would just burst if she had to go through that too many times. It must be hard being so near yet so far from the one you want to be with.

Still, no catastrophes, no, not a single cloud over the whole hols. Both literally and metaphorically speaking!

I am determined to get the two of them up a rope though one day, I don't care what they say. And preferably leaving them dangling there together, till they bloody well declare undying love to each other, and be done with it!

Uh-oh, feeding time is it, little one?

Chapter Thirty

Patrick sat down with my coke and his pint. I felt really whacked out. Climbing indoors was more intensive in a way, not as enjoyable as outdoors, but good practice. He'd brought some crisps from the leisure centre bar too, and I grimaced. I felt it was an insult to my body to eat such loathsome things. Stomach demanded fruit, veg., salads, organic pizzas, curries and tons of cheese, and bags of tomatoes. But not crisps. Occasionally chocolate, but that's it. I could never resist chocolate fudge cake if there was any on offer!

"How about coming up to Wales for a long weekend, and doing a couple of E1s or even E2s with me?"

"I don't know Patrick. What about Daphne? I can't exactly take her up on my back can I?"

"But there's some lovely climbs in Tremadog and there's a perfect camping spot right opposite the routes. Can't you get someone to babysit for a couple of days?"

"No, not really."

"Why are you being so dismissive about it? I thought you loved climbing. Aren't you at least willing to find out if you can make any provisions for her? What about your brother? He looked after her when you went up to Scotland with your mates didn't he? Or what about Celia, who's looking after her now? She'd do it. You could ask her at least."

"I could ask. Yes. But I'm not going to. Look, I'm sorry, I shouldn't be using my daughter as a scapegoat. The thing is Patrick, I don't think I want to go with you on a camping/climbing trip to Wales."

"Why not?"

"Because then it would stop being about the climbing and start being about you and me."

"I don't follow."

"Oh, let's stop skirting the subject. Sex. Relationship. Whatever. I get the feeling you're interested. And I'm not. So let's just keep it strictly climbing, eh? I'm happier that way."

"I thought we were friends."

"Don't play games with me. Just accept it."

"You're very self absorbed sometimes Phil. Anyone ever tell you that?"

"Insults will get you nowhere. I don't call it being self absorbed, I call it survival. There's a word for you."

"I don't know what you mean."

"I know. Otherwise we wouldn't be having this conversation."

Why did he have to be so antagonistic when talking about personal matters? As a climbing partner he was great; reliable, watchful, knew his stuff, a great teacher, enthusiastic, helpful. Even when talking about news or films, he was witty and clever. But with anything deeper he was a royal pain in the arse.

"What do you want Phil?"

"I want you to be straight with me. Is it just the climbing you're into, or is it me as well?"

"You're stunningly beautiful Phil." He looked at me, hoping to catch my interest, catch me unawares. I'd heard the line a million times.

"That doesn't answer the question."

He gave me a look as if to say 'Do I really have to say this?' "Yes I find you attractive. What man wouldn't for god's sake?"

"That still doesn't answer the question. Stop beating about the bush. I know I'm attractive. I know you find me attractive. But do you want a climbing partner who happens to be attractive, or an attractive partner who happens to be a climber?"

"Both sound good to me."

"Stop being so flippant!" I saw him glance at the couple at the nearby table. I didn't care about being overheard.

"OK, I'm sorry. I was just humouring you. Look I am not interested in seducing you into bed. You're fun to be with, and a hell of a good climber. I just thought a trip away would be fun. No hidden agendas. No strings attached. You make it sound like a crime."

"That's not a crime. But sex is just a no-go area. I do enjoy climbing with you, and that's as far as I want it to go. I don't want anything else."

"You've made that abundantly clear. I don't have any problems with that."

"Good."

"So will you come to Wales with me then?"

"No."

"How about if a couple of friends come too?"

"Maybe. I'd have to vet them first."

"You're a hard woman to please."

"So I've heard."

"Well, how about going for a drink tonight? It wouldn't be just the two of us, before you go jumping down my throat again. Ursula's coming. And she's a fellow climber who might like to come on a certain camping trip to Wales, it'd be the perfect opportunity for you to drill and interrogate her and find out if she's worthy or not. What do you say?"

"OK then. Where are you meeting?"

"Tonight, 8pm, Barnado's."

"I'll be there."

Chapter Thirty-One

"Oh Patrick, I can't, I'm babysitting tonight for my sister. I wish you'd called me earlier."

"Please Ursula, she'll *kill* me, skin me alive, serve me up for dinner and *eat* me if you don't turn up, and there's only the two of us there. This is the only way I can persuade her that I'm not trying to get into her knickers. She'll never believe me otherwise."

"And just whose knickers *are* you trying to get into, Patrick?" she laughed.

Yours actually, darling. "No-one's. Just please, do this for me? Please? Pretty please."

"Is it that important to you?"

"She's had a hell of a rough time lately. I don't want to ruin the friendship, but she's so paranoid about it all. She just doesn't trust me."

"I wonder why!" she laughed again.

"I don't know what you're talking about Miss Ursula Grey, I'm sure!" I said, pretending to be offended. "I'm totally trustworthy!"

"I know you are. I'm just winding you up. Isn't there anyone else you could ask?"

Yes, but you'd be the best possible person. "No, you're my last hope."

"OK, I'll see what I can do."

"Great. Thanks a million Ursula.

"I haven't said yes yet. I'll have to give Becky a ring and see what she says. See if I can re-negotiate! If she says no, then I'll have to say no too, I'm afraid. I'll give you a ring back when I've talked to her about it."

"Cheers Ursula. I really appreciate it."

"I can but try. Speak to ya soon."

"Bye."

***

"What time did she say she'd be here?"

"She said she'd definitely be here by eight, but knowing Ursula, that probably means half eight."

Phillippa was still looking at me dubiously, as if this was all a ploy of mine. Where was Ursula? If she didn't turn up soon, I'd have to fake a phone call to her, and pretend she's been held up.

Phillippa tapped her fingers on her white wine glass impatiently. She was on edge and I felt nervous. Conversation wasn't exactly flowing.

I looked around at the other people, smoking, drinking, their faces falling into the shades of the red wine colour of the walls and floor and small red lights dotted around the walls. Please hurry up Ursula, please.

"I'm just going to nip to the gents," I said as an excuse to break away from the nerve wrenching silence.

Just then the very welcoming sight of a familiar blond appeared. Her hair hung in a silk curtain down her back. She was so slim and petite, but a fantastic climber. She bubbled over to us, profuse in her apologies and grins all round. I wanted to hug and kiss her there and then.

I made the introductions, Phil mollified slightly now that she was in the presence of another female.

"What would you like to drink?" I asked Ursula.

"Pimms and lemonade if they've got any, if not, I'll have an Archers and lemonade."

"OK, back in a sec."

"Thanks Patrick."

"He's a real sweety, isn't he?"

"How do you know Patrick?"

"He and my brother bumped into each other on a mountain biking rally. Literally. Both ended up with some severe bruising, but nothing more than that. And they've been fast friends ever since." She looked tense. What could I do to ease the situation? "Has Patrick asked you about the camping trip?" She nodded. "A group of us usually go every year. It's great fun. And there's a good range of climbs round there. Not too good if it rains though, as I'm sure you can imagine, but there's always the pub isn't there?" I laughed. Phil started to visibly relax. So this is the woman that Patrick saved from the brink of self-induced death. I wonder what her story is. Her looks are as dark as I'm blond. *Why* doesn't Patrick want more than a friendship with her? I would if I was him.

"There you go." Patrick wobbly placed the Pimms on a place mat in front of her.

"Thanks Patrick."

I looked from one to the other of them. And suddenly my cocoon of blindness was pierced with a pin of clear insight. Patrick wasn't interested in me. Never had been. One look at the two of them together, it was so obvious. If there was any more chemistry between them, lightning might come down and set the whole restaurant on fire. I felt a flood of relief that Patrick wasn't interested in me that way. It removed all complications. It meant we could just get on with having a good friendship. I cringed internally as I remembered our earlier conversation today. Sorry Patrick.

As the evening wore on, I got very tired of being the fifth lost limb. They were both inclusive of me and friendly and curious of me. But I couldn't stand being in the way of their magnetic pull any longer. I decided to call it a night.

"You don't have to go Phil. It's still really early. I was thinking we could get a video out and a take-away or something and crash out at mine."

"I know I don't have to go Patrick, and I've had a perfectly lovely evening. And I'm sorry for earlier, when… Anyway, it's time I got back to Daphne anyway."

"I don't want you to feel like we're pushing you out," Ursula said in all genuineness. I couldn't help but smile.

"I know you don't, but the signals you two are sending each other tonight, just about anybody would feel completely surplus to requirements. I'd feel much happier letting the two of you get on with it, you've obviously got a lot *to* get on with." I didn't care that I'd just totally embarrassed them both with the unspoken. Honestly, some people would pussyfoot around for months, but their obviousness, even in their silences was far more embarrassing! "So you two fully enjoy the film and food and I'll catch up with you soon. By the way Patrick, if the offer's still there I'd love to come with you all to Wales."

He smiled warmly and I had his full attention for the first time all evening.

"We'd be delighted to have you along."

"So long as I can bring a guest…"

Patrick looked askance, then realised and nodded. "No problem. We'll do a turn each of babysitting."

"Thanks Patrick. For everything." I felt special and warm in a special and warm moment. I could see right through the whole thing and knew that Patrick had set this whole thing up to show me exactly what I never would have believed had he told me a thousand times.

"See you soon Phil. And make sure it is soon." Ursula got to her feet and gave me a hug goodbye, which totally took me by surprise. She whispered in my ear, "Thank you Phil, for everything," so as Patrick wouldn't hear. I understood the two of them were going to have a very very good time tonight, that had been too long struggling to come to fruition. Glad to be of assistance. Glad to stop worrying. Glad to be friends.

"You can count on it. Patrick knows where to find us. Take care of each other. See ya later." Patrick hugged me goodbye and I disappeared from their world before I'd even left the pub.

Chapter Thirty-One

"All ready then?"

"Ready as I'll ever be, yeah."

"C'mon then, let's go." I loaded mine and Daphne's things into the car, and sat in the back, and strapped her into the child seat next to me. We were going in Patrick's car with Ursula, and Deirdre, Paul and Sophie were following in their car.

Ursula's slight frame climbed into the seat in front of me, and Patrick started up the car. We were off!

I laid back, noting that Daphne was soon lulled to sleep by the drone of the journey's noise. I was happy not to contribute to the happy-climbing discussion going on up front. I watched the road go by for a while, the fields, the hills, other cars, too many unknown streets, and too many boxed in persons, impersonalised by their metal cases and flashing lights. We'd set off early, and the clouds were either chasing us, or we were chasing them. Not a good sign, let's hope there's not going to be too many of them when we finally get there, or else there won't be much climbing going on!

I dozed off myself for a bit, and when I awoke the flat fields of England were long gone, and so were the busy streets, and I watched the mountains pass us by as we swept up and then down the winding roads. The day was still overcast though, and the wind screen wipers were swishing in the annoying drizzle. A comfortable, intimate sort of silence ensued between Ursula and Patrick. It didn't take much longer to get there.

The rain held off long enough for us to park the car and set up the tents, in this field opposite the very rocks we planned to scale. There was a cafe and toilets only a minute's walk away. Together we set up the two-person tents and the slightly bigger three-person one. Sophie and Deirdre took one of the smaller tents. Paul got the other one, which we dumped all our spare stuff in. We decided to go have a coffee in the nearby cafe and discuss which climbs we'd do.

I let the four of them commiserate about the weather and the unlikelihood of getting any climbing in this afternoon, as I sorted out Daphne and what she would and wouldn't like to eat/drink, and try and sit her comfortably on my lap.

A consensus was reached that we wouldn't do any climbing that day, the rock face would be way too wet and dangerous. So we returned to the tents, we all went into the big one, and huddled up close to keep warm. We shared blankets as we sat on our sleeping bags. The rain lightly pattered on the walls of the tent, but it was all quite 'cosy inside. Daphne was very curious about everything and totally at ease with everyone. She was having great fun crawling under everyone's blankets and across everyone's laps, over knees and under legs. After a while she eventually settled down in between myself and Patrick with a scribbling book with dot to dot pictures in it. She had all her favourite colours with her, black and purple. She coloured/scribbled everything in them. Occasionally there would be a blue ball or a yellow flash on the page, but mostly it was black and purple. She seemed to be fascinated with those two contrasting colours. Black grass and purple trees would amuse her for a good while.

We chatted for a while, and we tried to play Pictionary, but people kept having elbows shoved in their ribs or faces, and losing their pencils and complaining they didn't have anything flat and hard to rest on in order to draw. I watched them from a happy distance. I felt comfortable and at ease, but a little apart. It was decided in the end we'd play scrabble in teams of two. Daphne and me chummed up with Paul, and Ursula partnered Patrick. Soph and Deirdre were warned to let the rest of us have a fighting chance, as they were both reputed to be good at it. I watched Paul hold the bag open so Daphne could put her tiny fist in and pull out a couple of letters and then a couple of letters more.

Daphne kept playing her own version of scrabble by herself with all the unpicked letters, so we made her Queen of Letters and she decided which letters we could have when we needed replacements. She handed out some very difficult combinations sometimes, without knowing it. Poor Patrick got given Q X Z all in one go. And she liked to give all the vowels to Soph and Deirdre. She held them up one by one, and asked us what letter they were, and if it was a vowel or not. Everyone laughed, amused with her antics. It made for a jolly hard game of scrabble though. Daphne was accused of favouritism, and she asked what that was.

"It means Mummy's your favourite person, so you want her to win, so you keep giving all the easy letters to her and Paul." Patrick explained to her. I watched him and wondered what he thought of the woman he'd saved from death, and the little girl she'd given birth to.

I noticed the physical closeness of Patrick and Ursula as their heads bent together to study their letters. I noted the accidental brushing of hands. I noticed the glances that passed between them. And the smiles in their eyes when they thought no-one else was looking. What had passed between them in the couple of weeks since I'd last seen Ursula? And in the car, whilst I'd been sleeping? There was an open acknowledgement between them now, of their attraction to each other. I was glad. They seemed to go really well together. The game continued, or rather it disintegrated, with Daphne swapping all our letters round, as if we were playing musical words/chairs. It was pointless keeping score!

After a while, Paul said he'd go set up the camping stove, and start sorting out some food for us all. Patrick and Ursula said they were going to go for a short walk in the rain before eating. Daphne orchestrated a new game of scrabble with some new and strange rules thrown in every now and again to keep me and the girls on our toes. And Daphne was keeping score too, so I ended up with three million points and Sophie got one million and one, and Deirdre was awarded only ten, because for some reason Daphne kept taking them away from her, instead of giving them out.

I watched the grins, smiles and laughs of the red headed Deirdre and the brown haired Sophie. They all adored Daphne. I guess I was lucky that I could come out with a group of friends who all included her so well, and didn't get annoyed with her curiosities and meddlings.

As the game came to a close, well all the letters had been dished out and ended up in strange piles on the board, Daphne decided she wanted the little girl's room. The other two went across to Paul's tent to help with the food. Me and Daphne under the shelter of Sophie's huge umbrella went on the short walk to the toilets.

As we walked along, I noticed two figures coming towards us, in the distance. Two wet figures walking along the roadside. Holding hands. They stopped and kissed, oblivious to the rain. They smiled at each other and kissed again, then continued their journey closer. Two figures who I knew were Patrick and Ursula.

"What are you looking at Mummy?" Daphne asked.

"Just watching the rain a while darling."

"Mummy, I need to go." She tugged on my hand. We went into the shelter of the ladies' toilets. I helped Daphne take down her bottoms, and sit on the loo to wee. All the time, my mind replayed the image of Patrick and Ursula, until they turned into naked silhouettes. I displaced Ursula in my mind, so that I was the one Patrick reached for, so our bodies could feel the outer skin of each other's souls. And to my complete surprise, I suddenly felt a hot stab of jealousy surge through me. And I laughed.

"What's funny?" Daphne demanded as I pulled some toilet roll off, and handed it to her.

"Oh, I was just thinking of a joke, that's all."

"What joke?" Oh, shit, now I had to think of a joke to tell her. It was funny though. All that suspicion and keeping Patrick at arm's length, and the relief I felt when I met Ursula, and all along, I realise I wanted to be the one in Patrick's arms. Yes, the joke was on me.

"Knock, knock." I knew she liked the knock knock jokes. And sure enough Daphne played the action of knocking on a door, and the sound effect to go with it.

"Who's there?" she duly asked.

"Boo."

"Boo who?"

"Now, now, there's no need to cry." Daphne still found that one funny, even though I'd told her it at least half a dozen times. But I suddenly felt like there was a need to cry. And I suddenly had an inkling of understanding of how Isabel must have felt at Ted's wedding. And I understood why she hadn't said anything. Well, I'd have to live with it, because obviously Patrick was already well and truly newly loved by someone else, and he was very happy in her love. And I had to share a tent with them for the remainder of the time here. Oh no, I wasn't.

I helped Daphne back into her things, and ensured she washed her hands. As we exited the toilets, there stood Ursula waiting to come in and use them.

We smiled at each other.

"Listen, would you prefer it if me and Daphne moved into Paul's tent?" I asked. Ursula looked half askance, half embarrassed. "I'm glad the two of you have discovered your mutual feelings." I smiled, and she smiled back sheepishly.

"We wouldn't think of turning you out like that, that's not fair."

"Don't be silly. I insist. We don't mind, and I'm sure Paul won't either."

"Well, listen, if you feel that strongly about it, how about me and Patrick swap with Paul, and that way you've got more space and don't have to bother moving all your things?" I watched the rain droplets run down her blond streaks and dribble down her face. She didn't seem to heed them at all. I felt gutted that she'd accepted my proposal so readily. Even though it was what I wanted, jealousy turned its knife in me as it was obvious how keen they were on each other, not to want to wait till we got back home in order to 'play' together.

"Yes, that sounds like a good idea," I agreed, "as long as Paul doesn't mind shifting his stuff over."

"I'm sure he'll be fine with it." She said good naturedly. No matter what my personal longings were, I couldn't take exception to Ursula. She was just so friendly.

"Yes, I'm sure he will." Unfortunately. What was wrong with me! Stop it Phillippa. "You're getting wet." I said lamely. She laughed, in a don't care sort of fashion, an I'm-in-love-and-everything's-OK sort of laugh.

"I'll talk to Paul after we've eaten, and we can sort it all out then."

Chapter Thirty-Two

"Hi! Ursula?"

"Up here, darling. My study." I looked up from my book, smiling in anticipation. Patrick popped his head round the door, but his eyes didn't twinkle my smile back. He looked worried. Almost fraught.

"What's the matter?"

"Oh, Ursula." He dumped his jacket on a nearby chair and sunk into the sofa bed next to me.

"What's up? Has something terrible happened?"

"It's Phillippa."

"Is she OK? She hasn't done anything silly again has she?" Patrick shook his head vigorously to dispel my alarm.

"Oh no, it's nothing like that." He took his hands in mine. They were cold.

"Tell me."

"We were just having a game of pool and a drink. And we went to sit down in our usual corner, like we do. And I told her about us planning to marry and wanting to travel, and she absolutely went off the deep end."

"How do you mean?"

"I've never seen her so angry. She caused quite a scene. I told her we could discuss it later, in a more private place, and she threw both our drinks over me." I noticed for the first time Patrick's damp shirt.

"Not raining then?"

"Only beer and wine," he smiled ruefully.

"But what did she say? Why was she so upset?"

"I'm not sure exactly. Things like she'd seen the way I treated you and it was never going to last between us. And other really strange stuff. She said you'd see through me in the end just like she'd done, and that you'd leave me with a broken heart and serve me right."

"You don't believe her, do you?"

"No, of course not."

I was reassured. "Just checking."

"But what does she mean though? Treating you like what? We've never even had an argument in private, never mind in front of Phillippa. She knows how we treat each other. That I totally love and respect you. She almost convinced me that I'd an evil twin or something, or that I really had been mean to you in some way and not seen it. I haven't, have I?"

"No, darling. Not at all."

"I just didn't understand. But every single thing I said seemed to make the situation worse. She was seething, Ursula, she really was. I thought she was going to hit me at one point. Well, she did actually. Well, a slap anyway, and called me a bastard."

"What did you say?"

"I just tried to reason with her. Calm her down. Ask her what all this was really about. But it was just a riddle to me."

"Was she OK with you before you told her about our future plans?"

"Yeah. Fine. A bit on edge, I guess. But otherwise just the usual friendly Phillippa. Why? You don't think that's got anything to do with it, do you?" He could see from my expression that that was exactly what I thought. "But no. How could it be? She's been fine with us as a couple. Why shouldn't she be? It was her who was worried about me wanting her, remember, not so long ago? Why should she suddenly be so upset about it all now?"

"I think that Phillippa's a little bit in love with you."

"Absolute nonsense!"

"Is it? Think about it darling."

"But how can you tell?"

"It takes one to know one, they say."

"But she can't be."

"Why not? I am."

"But she always said that…"

"She *did* see you as a good friend. And all her barriers were up to protect her from this sort of thing. I'm sure she'd no intention of falling for you. But somewhere along the line she has. You know, the more I think about it, the more it makes sense."

"I'm glad it does to you. 'cause it makes less and less sense to me. Does this mean she's jealous then?"

"Probably darling. And very upset."

"I should talk to her, explain…"

"You should leave her be. She needs time."

"God, I feel bad."

"Yes, so do I. Poor Phillippa."

"I never realised, I didn't even guess… I would've been kinder in breaking the news to her if I'd known."

"I know you would. But it probably wouldn't have made any difference. She'd still have been upset."

"True."

I saw the worry and concern in his eyes. I smoothed his hair back from his face. "She'll come to terms with it. She just needs time." I kissed him.

"I hope so. I hope she'll be alright with it. I really do."

Rage. I hadn't known the meaning of the word till now. I took off after Patrick's 'news'. Picked up Daphne. Held her for a long time. Took her to Ben's.

Could he take care of her for a few days? I need to clear my head. Gym's good for that. Good punch bag.

Punch, fist, hit, draw back, smack, again, again, again… Dancing round this huge black plastic padding, sweating round it, wishing it was his face. His goddamn handsome face I was hitting. And scratch out Ursula's mesmeric eyes, her concern and her kindness ripped to shreds. Punch, kick, dance. Heart beating faster, faster. Blood pumping harder, harder, trying to keep up. Getting hot. Want to take off these stupid leggings, this stupid fucking top. I wanna rip it all up. Till there's nothing, nothing there anymore. Kick. Punch. Kick again. Right in Patrick's face. Bring back, punch again.

It was his fault. I didn't deserve to be treated like this. How dare he? How did he fucking dare? How dare he treat me like this? He loved me as a friend he said. A friend. Some fucking comfort that is. When my mind and body screams out for something more. To be in his arms last thing at night. And first thing in the morning. Every night. Every morning.

He's a deserter. A coward. But we love each other, Phillippa, he says. As if I don't fucking know that! As if I don't already fucking know how blissfully happy they are and will be together.

And it's all his fucking fault. How could he do this to me? Punch, smash Brian's fucking nose, right through his face. Brian. Where had that come from?

I stand and stare at the swinging punch bag. I'm all punched out, and the room's gone blurry. My body's the punch bag now. Sobs punching out my ribs.

But I'm pumped now. I'm not going to take this lying down anymore. That punch bag is going to get beaten like never before.

For the first time... I feel free to blame Brian. Not myself. For what he did. What *he* did to *me*.

I went several more rounds with the bag, till I could see Brian bloody and bruised for his crimes against me.

Spent.

I sat to catch my breath.

Exercise bike next I think. Get a rhythm going. God, I'm an idiot. Poor Patrick. I really went for him in a big way. What must he think of me? I must apologise. I'll go see him tomorrow. Hope he'll still speak to me. Hope Ursula will too. I don't want to lose their friendship. I don't. And shit... God, I ache for him, to be *with* him. So this is how it feels. I always wondered. And now I know. Fucking typical. I get to the time I feel I can trust and open up to... and he belongs to someone else. And it doesn't help that it's a nice someone else.

I push hard on the up-hill climb I've set on the bike.

What right did I have to speak to Patrick like that? Every fucking right! I was voicing my irrational feelings. I've a right to do that. I've a right to love Patrick and be hurt that he doesn't love me back. I don't have the right to be raped. That's not my right. That's an abuse of my rights, Brian. Do you hear me? Can you feel my anger from wherever you are right now? Why did I hate myself so long? It's Brian I should be hating. And I do. And I still hate. Hate me. But not all of me. I don't want to blame me anymore. I want to like me. It wasn't my fault. *He* did it. He was the doer. I was the done to. Thank God for anger! Where the hell has it been all this time? Directed to the wrong place, that's where. Well not anymore. I don't want me beating myself up for this anymore. It's time to put the blame where it belongs.

OK, I think I'll ring first, before I see him again. Test the waters a little. Find out what damage I've done.

I dialled Patrick's number. A number I know so well.

C'mon, c'mon! Pick up!

"Hello?" At last! Time to face his voice again.

"Patrick?"

"Phillippa?"

"Yes, it's me. Hi." Now what do I say? I thought into the silence, wishing I could see his face. Silences on phones were always unnerving, there was too much going on in them that you couldn't see.

"Phillippa, how are you feeling?" His question surprised me.

"How am I?"

"Yes."

"Smarting from embarrassment, but a lot calmer."

"Do you, erm, do you want to meet up?"

"I thought that was my line to stammer and stutter."

"I did it for you."

"Thanks Patrick. Yes, I'd love to."

"Your place? Half an hour?"

"Er, yeah, OK then."

"See you then." I put the handset back with a shaking hand. God no! Now I'd have to wait for an agonising half an hour for him to come to me. I should've said I'd go over to his. But then it'd feel harder apologising on his turf rather than mine. Wouldn't it? Aren't I more in control here, in my place? Mine and Daphne's place? I don't feel in control anywhere. I'll ring him back.

"Hello?"

"Patrick? It's me again. Look actually I'll come to you. Would that be alright?"

"No problem. If that's what you want. I just thought it'd be easier if I came to you that's all. You know, Daphne and everything…"

"It's OK, she's at Ben's." Why are you so thoughtful and considerate and in love with somebody else all at the same time?

"Oh, that's fine then. I'll see you shortly."

"Will do. Bye."

My hand wasn't shaking quite so much now. Much better. I can do the doing bit now, instead of the waiting bit. I'm much better at that.

I knocked.

He opened the door.

"Hi."

"Hi." Don't you just hate those awkward moments?

"Come through, Phillippa. I won't bite, promise." He was so good at that. Easing difficult situations. How did he know how to do that? "Drink?"

"No, no, I'm fine thank you."

"Sure?"

"I can't drink and talk at the same time, and I've got some talking to do."

"Let's go through to the living room." I followed him through the pastel shades of his and Ursula's happiness. Even the rooms spoke of their love together. But I somehow felt it was easier, and I was less vulnerable apologising here than at my place.

We sat down like strangers, with an unusual bond between us.

"Where's Ursula tonight?"

"She's staying over at her sister's at the moment."

"Oh good." No, it wasn't supposed to sound like that! "I mean…"

"It's OK, I know what you mean."

"Patrick, about the other night. I'm so sorry. And I totally understand if you're pissed at me…"

"I'm not."

"Oh."

"I'm sorry I upset you so."

"But you didn't.. Well, you did, but you didn't mean to. You

167

didn't know it was going to…"

"It's OK."

"It's not though. God, I feel a fool."

"Listen Phillippa, I know you feel bad about it. And you've said sorry and I accept that. It's fine. I forgive you."

"Still friends?"

"Of course." No hesitation on his part. And a smile to go with it. A smile. His smile. His whole face smiled. Everything was OK with him.

"Then why do I still feel like shit?"

"Maybe you should stop giving yourself a hard time, and you forgive yourself."

"Maybe…" I look at him. His calm. Ease. Relaxed posture. More than just a whole room separating us. And I didn't know how to bring the closeness back again. There was too much something in the way.

"No maybe about it. Have a holiday from giving yourself a hard time. I mean it, Phillippa."

My turn to smile. Wryly. "Yes, I suppose you're right."

All this distance. We're friends, and he says it's all fine, but I can feel the miles rippling out between us.

"I should go."

"You don't have to."

"No, I know I don't have to. But I should. I need to go now." Our gazes met and said all the unspoken things that we dare not voice. I knew that he now knew my true feelings. And I knew he forgave me. And he knew I was having difficulty forgiving myself. For all sorts of things. And yet, we'd always have that bonding, me and my saviour. And we both knew the necessity of us being physically apart, yet he'd never push me away. I have to decide this and act on it. I have to find a way of living with this.

"I'm glad you came."

"Me too."

"Phillippa…"

"Yes?" I see thoughts I can't read flicker across his face.

"Nothing. I'll, erm, I'll see you out."

Standing at his door, it feels final somehow. He's left me. Left me for good. Yet everything's fine. Part of me understands that. And part of him will always be with me. And I can cope with the part of me that wants to reach for him, touch him... so long as I don't think about it too much. Yes we're still friends. But not like we were before.

"I'll see you later." His voice sounds normal, as if we really will be seeing each other later, at some other normal time, to have more normal conversations.

I swallow, and hope my voice won't give away my feelings of brokenness. "Yeah, sure, I'll see..." and then he's hugging me. Telling me to take care. I'm suffocating in emotion. I can't stop the sob that rises, the gasp. I can't stop smelling him, his sweater. I can't stop feeling his warmth. Emanating warmth. Enveloping warmth. As he rejects me. Tells me goodbye. Letting me taste the love I'm not allowed to feed off. The love he can't – won't give to me. The love I need and don't know how to ask for. The love he has, the love he's given to Ursula. I pulled away at last, after daring to taste as much of the forbidden fruit as I was able to stand.

"I'll be in touch." I nodded and turned. What a cold thing to say. A sentence to make your tongue blue. Yet how else would you end such a meeting? How else?

I only saw Patrick and Ursula once more after that. Just before they took off to France. To give themselves to each other. For life. Just before they went globe trotting together. Climbing, of course. Sharing. Experiencing together. They'll send me postcards and send me good thoughts. And if I ever want to talk, I can call them. Of course. Miss them? Miss her? Miss him?

Me left here. With daughter. Miss them? Miss him? Left here with what? A life. Climbing. Motherhood. But no partner. He left me with memories. She left me with a good friendship. He had given me some feeling of self worth. Yet denied me his love.

He left me with something else too. Something new that I'd not had before. Something I could learn to give myself.

Forgiveness.

Chapter Thirty-Three

I mentally shook myself. I was doing it again. I tried concentrating on the computer screen in front of me. But my thoughts kept returning to Isabel. To what Phillippa did and didn't say about her on our camping trip.

Here I was trying to work, trying to put all this code in place, and my mind continually drifts off to where Isabel is, what she might be doing now....

Why was I starting to think this way? And what way was that exactly Ted? What are we saying here?

The trip seems to have done us all so much good though. We're all in touch with each other more often. It seems we've mended some bridges, that I hadn't even quite realised were broken in the first place.

Am so glad me and Phillippa have kept our friendship. The way it is. That one night was, as it was. With no more to follow after. How strange. A stand-alone event. But such a turning point for me...

And Isabel... She seems so elusive at the moment, even though we're more in touch now than we have been for a good while. I wonder what she's doing now. I wonder what she's doing this weekend. If she's free. Probably not. But she might be. I'll give her a ring anyway. She can only say no. What am I thinking of? Of course Isabel can say no if she wants. Why should I feel so wary of it? So nervous of it?

And Isabel seems to be acting quite strange in herself. Sometimes so welcoming and friendly when we talk on the phone. Other times, when she's feeling down for reasons she won't tell me, I feel a wall between us. But the surprising thing is, I get upset about this wall. Maybe it's not so surprising. After all we've been friends for many years now. I don't like to think that she's blocking me out. But I don't contact Phillippa as much as I do Isabel. Phillippa's very much into her own life right now, and I'm very happy for her. Pleased she seems to have found some peace within herself after so much... But Isabel, she does slide into my thoughts at the most odd times. Like now.

I've really got to get this done. The client's not going to be too happy if it's not ready and fully functional by the end of today.

Yes, I'll call her at the weekend. What harm can it do? She might say yes. She might be free. And why do I feel nervous about that too? I've never felt nervous around Isabel. We've always felt so comfortable together. But it's not a bad nervousness, it's a sort of a.... Right, anyway, let's get this done. I need to go for lunch soon. And I haven't got as long as I'd like this afternoon to finish this. That damn meeting with Jerry at four. I really hope he's not going to ask me to commit myself to any work over the weekend.

Chapter Thirty-Four

A Busy Street In Leeds

"She just stepped out into road to avoid a cyclist on pavement. There was this great big truck reversing, that went back into alley way, and this other lorry just came from outa nowhere, speeding down main road, and smack!

"Shocking noise there were. He screeched to a halt, but it were too late.

"Someone called ambulance. But she were already dead. Poor lass. God bless her."

"I weren't goin that fast. I weren't honest! And she just stepped out right in fronta me. I couldn't do owt!

"I weren't speedin' or owt. I saw that lorry backin' into a side street, I'd slowed down fer that, I was well clear of it.

"One moment it were clear, no-one there. The next there was this woman stood there, too near fer me to do owt. I braked as hard as I could. I just went straight into her. There weren't nowt I could do. I did everything I could. It was useless. There weren't no time. No time!"

there she is... very familiar – yet totally alien... my case – my shell of 29 years – twisted and turned... bloodied and torn... yet her face is peaceful... framed by long dark hair... her dark eyes forever gone dark... nobody to scream her name...

there is a great raucous... parked ambulances... busying police... concerned doctors... stuck traffic... dawdling pedestrians... and at the centre of it all is a shell – the spirit absent – a vortex of peace – where the chaos swirls round and about her – unable to touch her – or disturb her... unable to

bring her back...
i am without body... but still within consciousness... still
aware... of free floating... like the wind...

daphne... she's attending the bleeding nose of what used to be
her Mummy... she doesn't understand... but how could she...
she's only three years three months two weeks six days fourteen
hours six minutes and forty-two seconds old...

daphne... i don't want to leave you... i'm being torn away from
you in a swirl of air that i can't touch or feel...

time and space suddenly unfold and makes sense to me now...
they're expansive and interconnected... not tied down and
restricted like they are when tied into a physical embodiment... a
'physical embodiment'... and i suddenly know right now – i can
understand dutch – french – german – swahili and every other
language in the world in complete fluency...

there is no spoken or written word anymore... only expansive
awareness... all communication is open and transparent –
'cause no-one has any cover... not covered by a body...

daphne... i love you... i always will... i don't want to leave you...
i'll always be with you wherever you go and whatever you're
doing... i'm always with you... you can feel me there in your
heart your blood your memories...

who are they over there... well – that group of girls and women
– sat floating in thin air – holding hands in a ring... my
goodness... they're all me... me as a baby... me at three years
old... me at six and at seven... me at... poor girl... i feel a
sudden overwhelming amount of comfort and protection fleeing
my mind – surrounding her image in a white fuzziness... she
knows... she's looking at me... they all are... me at 18... me at
22... me at 25 and at 26... healthier mes... their energies have
different moving textured colours...

they're approaching... or am i moving nearer – it's hard to tell...

what am i supposed to do...

slowly – one by one – each me unlinks themselves from the circle and dissolves into me... *the* me *without body... well none of them have bodies either... they are all different energies – delineated by a watery image of myself – like a reflection... they come forth and are absorbed into* me *as consciousness in flight – formless as the wind...* me *becoming all my ages...each age feels different as it unites with* me *and combines with my other ages also within* me... *the emotions – how intense... and some i can't even name... but it feels like a jigsaw – all the pieces coming together... i am understanding* me...

when 15 year old me joins me *after absorbing the younger mes – i feel such a deep sense of violation... my mind explodes with it... the violence is sheering... deep purples envelope me – the cuts the bruises – the injuries of scarlet purples glass cutting through skin – knives burying and twisting in open wounds – doing violence to an unmarked body – like tentacles part of me hunts for love amongst the blue purples... discs of metallic red within rebel – the thick strong snake of fear abuse wraps round and fights the equally strong thick snake of silk blue compassion – the feathers of wisdom shake a deeper blue... they meld together – moving – fighting and dancing through the whole range of purples from the deepest red of the spectrum – right through to the stronger blue purples... and the blues eventually take over swarm overcome searing fire flames – making them run wine colour – to disappear in misty rosiness...*

all my internalised feelings externalising themselves intangibly... all being expressed in space – through the medium of space... no time attached – except for this moment... *my spirit is safe in the knowledge that i can accept what was previously unacceptable... all these feelings that got buried and ignored – covered up – so my 15 year old could continue living day to day... i understand... and all my younger and older selves understand too...*

we can all see the emotion – a formless colour – travelling the

174

streams of the universe – swimming back and forth... almost a cloud... but engulfing my awareness – nothing but the feeling of purple... pure pain... i accept it inside me and give it love...

my 16 and 17 year olds are much less dramatic upon acceptance – more numb white in comparison – but they also draw painful emotions of jumpy – spiked – hard oranges and trickling rivulets of deceptive yellows – that fizzle with shame – self-hate – self-blame – more shame... as i accept other mes – i also accept the years of abusing myself – thinking that was what i deserved – the guilt – the shame – the covering up – the pretence at normality – all the crap... the bluntness of dirty yellow pillows of suffocation and the scars of muddied grey iron bars imprinting criss-cross prisons through me...

the intricate swirls of curiously rolling sea green hills – and comforting softness of sky blue angora wool wisping of isabel – her friendship – love and loyalty... a spattering of the darker edge of gem jealousy mixed in... i keenly feel the tenderness of ted – the precious kindling orange – unfolding – unwrapping in a delicate spiral of sand – in the whirlwind of autumn leaves...

the magnification of my joy and fear as daphne is born – and being a mother to her – is spun out in the kaleidoscope of intensity of the blinding twists of golden streams and the honest doubleness of velvet blackness... the rejection of dominic – i feel like the sharp side of a rust red sword swipe through me... i accept it... i understand it...

suicidal 26 year old me greets me with a total white-out white... there's numbness and pain wrestling and tormenting each other – swallowing everything – suffocating me – crowding everything else out... it is almost worse than 15 year old me... i didn't think it was ever going to end... like being enmeshed in soggy cotton wool – unable to see – breathe – hear – touch – move or smell anything... it takes me longer to accept this one... it is the most disorientating of all of them – the most divisive... there is nothing to focus on – nothing to distinguish one white space from the next white space – it is all one – too huge to comprehend... it is like being lost in complete darkness on a cliff – and the sky – ground and sea are all the same colour – and you can't see if your next step is going to lead you over the edge or on to more ground... except it is white – which is somehow more terrifying... it feels like i should *be able to see something – but the harder i try – the worse it is...*

a black spindling of hope yearns through the white – i face my darkness – gravestones sit hard and stone like then churn and disintegrate into rainbow slithers of flowing liquids that arch out the true colours of my life... if i still had breath to breathe – it would have been taken away... each me continues to pour forth and unite – until there is only one other me left...

we float opposite each other – closer to one another... she stares at my invisibility as i view her image... we are aware of each other's energy patterns – the intricate interlinking and interlaced colours of me *conjoined with my younger selves – and her simpler shades of an earthling life... she smiles – and glides into my nothingness – my presence – the space that is* me*...*

i feel complete...

i choose to go to my own funeral... a lot of people do... some don't... it's a personal choice... but your loved ones have come to say goodbye to you – or think they have... i doubt anyone's emotionally capable of doing it so soon after the death... anyway – the least i can do is turn up for them... even though they won't be able to see or hear me... perhaps they might feel me...

i didn't want to see the church bit though... never did believe in doing the end bit in a christian way – not when i'd never lived my life as a christian and thought the whole thing was... now you see if i'd been alive – i would've said bull shit... but i'm not... and from a dead perspective it's impossible for me to label it as such... i'll just say the religion has been tormented and twisted by human nature... and was forgotten to be updated...

i join my loved ones at the graveside for the lowering of the coffin – the encasement of my 29 year old shell... my loved ones... daphne – isabel – ted – ben... i ponder each of them and their feelings briefly... their emotions are mentally tangible – as if i'm moving through doorways and each room is a different person... curiosity takes me to mum and dad first... i stay with them but fleetingly... my long-suffering mother with no self-esteem... no drive... the loving door mat – forever hopelessly hoping... and father... a screw-up... ok – that's too narrowly defined – but his soul is not a comfortable one to address or dwell on... blind... ignorant... self-hating... he is his own living hell... isabel – loss – emptiness – feeling lost and adrift... sorrow and regret... wanting to lean on ted and be leaned on by him – but scared to let it happen... ted – loss – unhappiness... aching... needing comfort... loving... isabel... and trying not to – convinced she sees him only as a friend... ben – grief – love for an elder sister he didn't understand... i can feel gail's support for him... i'm glad he married her... she is true to him... they stand at each other's side as equals...daphne – confused – sad... but she can feel me... momentarily... on the edge of her senses... she knows i'm with her... she'll lose this ability over the years... i take a piece of daphne with me and leave a part of me behind with her...

Chapter Thirty-Five

Carpenters played soothingly in the background – their greatest hits. I love this album, just as it was well loved by the generation before me. Like Abba, they're cross-generational. I looked, as I often do in odd moments, at the cosy living room and the safe world I'd built for myself. I wasn't in touch with Felicity at all these days, not even birthday and Christmas. She'd occasionally call and tell me of her latest crisis but those calls got rarer and rarer. Mum had passed away about seven years ago now. Heart attack. I turned my thoughts away from that dark stone.

The grey drizzle of Phillippa's funeral replayed itself in my mind. And seeing Ted's face through its curtain. What did he think of the last time we were together? Did he think of it at all? The ripping ache of the loss of Phillippa had dissolved in my tears in the church. And now all I felt was a dull numbness of nothing.

Just then Bonny got up and barked. I glanced at the clock. 10pm.

"What's up girl? What is it?" The bouncy Labrador wagged her tail and barked at the window that had faint blue velvet curtains hanging across it. I went over and looked out. In the motion sensitive light that automatically comes on, it showed a familiar not so familiar figure. I gasped in surprise.

"It's OK Bonny, good girl." I patted her head as I went through to the hall and removed the chain from the front door and opened it.

Bonny sniffed the stranger suspiciously at first, then decided he had a friendly smell and licked his hand. Our eyes connected, and sought to check the reaction of the other, both feeling unsure of our ground. Words seemed suddenly inadequate. A moment longer, then he broke the connection, and bent to pat Bonny.

"Come in," I said, suddenly realising the cold of the night was stealing in and making me shiver.

"Thanks." He wiped his feet and Bonny followed him in. His voice was drier and crisper than I remembered it.

I shut the door. "Make yourself at home." He removed his coat and I hung it up. All followed in a perfectly natural order. I didn't feel perfectly natural though. I felt shy, surprised, curious. Where had all the words gone?

He took a seat on the new sofa I had just treated myself to.

"Ted"/"Isabel." We spoke simultaneously and smiled.

I: You first.

T: No you. *I felt uncomfortable in the ensuing silence.*

I: Er, would you like a drink of some sort?

T: Maybe in a minute. *God, this was hard.*

I: Did you say you were staying at the Lion Hotel?

T: Yes. I felt restless. *That explained everything then!*

I: It's a while since we last saw each other properly... *I can't think of anything else to say.*

T: Yes, it's been a while.

I: Yes it has. *OK, that's that established. Isn't there anything else you're going to say about it?*

T: You've got a lovely house here.

I: Thank you. *Oh god, let's not be quite so polite with each other, I can't stand it.*

I: Yes, it's great, I love it.

T: I can tell. *Oooh, first personal observation. What next? I've done the drink bit. Maybe some music or something to lessen the silences...*

T: I just had to get out of there. I don't know Isabel, I just miss her you know.

I: Me too. *I'm going to cry. I can't cry. Not now. But he did. He completely broke down. I went over to him, feeling awkward. I sat next to him, and put my arm round him. He turned into me, sobbed his heart out in patches on to my jumper. I hugged my arms around him. His sudden emotion was having repercussions in the well of my stomach. I held him till his emotions subsided, I passed him a tissue.*

T: Isabel...

I: Don't apologise. It's fine.

T: I won't then. But thanks.

I: You're welcome.

And the iceberg's broken and completely melted.

T: Can I ask a favour Izzy?

No-one else calls me that anymore. Stop pulling at my heart strings Ted.

I: Ask anything.

T: Could I crash here for a few nights? The loneliness of the hotel is driving me nuts. I feel I need to be with someone who also knew and loved Phillippa at the moment.

No, you can't stay. Why can't you go home – what are you not telling me Ted? I instinctively understood his wanting to share grief. But if that was his only *reason for wanting to be here... I'd really rather you didn't stay. Oh stop it Isabel. Stop being selfish. He doesn't love you, but he's just as upset as you are right now.*

I: Of course you can stay. I'll make up the spare room.

T: Don't feel like you have to Izzy, I know it's a bit of an imposition, and I'm assuming a lot here, and....

I: It's fine Ted. We're best friends remember?

T: Yes, we are.

I: *He looks at me. Brave smile. A few days. I can do it for a few days. I can pretend for just a little while, that I don't love him like crazy. He gives me a grateful hug.*

I: Come on, I'll get you some sheets.

T: Thank you Isabel, I really appreciate it.

I: Don't mention it.

***

It was the fifth day of Ted's stay. I was wearing a little thin with masking my feelings all the time. And Ted had noticed.

"Do you have a problem with me staying here?" Ted had tried to be helpful all day. It was driving me insane! I just wanted some space. To see as little of him as possible. But instead he insisted on helping with the washing up, help clear up the house, go to the shops with me, come out for a walk with me and Bonny, I absolutely drew the line on that one. Bonny's walks were strictly *my* time!

180

"No, not at all. What makes you think that?"

"You're acting kind of strange, sort of jumpy, like you're not sure what you're cross about." *Or like you can't bear to be around me. Why is that Isabel? I find I'm falling for you deeper, and you're pushing me away further. Why do I always fall for women who reject me? I must be a masochist of some sort.*

"I'm just tired and upset and lonely and missing Phillippa." And tired of loving you and having to hide it! Why can't you just leave me alone!

"You're lonely here?"

Did I say that? It must have slipped out. "No. Well, sometimes, maybe."

"You really don't like me being here do you? I've done nothing but get under your feet the entire day. Sorry. Look, I'll leave tomorrow if you like. It's no problem. You should've said if I was putting on you too much."

"No, no. It's not that. You're not really. It's been really nice having you here." Who am I kidding? It's been a torturous pleasure. I don't want you to go, yet I can't stand you being here.

"Well, something's wrong. I know you're grieving for Phillippa, as I am. But I dunno, you seem really edgy all the time." *God, I feel like a dog chasing its own tail here. Give me a break Isabel, please. Talk to me.*

"I'm just not sleeping too well. That's all." *Yeah, you're not the only one!*

"Well, you do look tired. There's nothing else on your mind?"

"No, nothing."

"You're a terrible liar, Isabel. Come on, you can talk to me. It's me remember?"

"I can't talk to you if it's about you." What am I saying? I want to tell him. Get it over and done with. But I can't.

"So the problem is with me. I thought it was. Isabel, have done I something wrong?"

"Yes."

"What?"

"I can't say this."

I could shake her. But I just gently put my hands on her elbows. I felt a frission. "Whatever it is, I'll make it up to you."

181

"You can't make up for this," I said adamantly. Why was he standing so close? Go away Ted!

"Try me."

"You made me fall in love with you." I heard him gasp, surprise and realisation in his eyes. I wish I could fly to another country and never see him again.

"Isabel," he laughed. The hurt deepened, and anger rippled. How could he laugh in my face when I've just told him what I had never never meant to?

"You can jolly well leave now," I said coldly, turning away from him.

"Isabel." His voice was soft in its caress of my name. But I remained silent. I thought he was going to go upstairs and pack his bags, then I felt his lips on my neck, and tantalisingly move up behind my ears.

"Ted, what are you doing?" I faced him.

"Loving you back you crazy woman. Both of us feeling the same way, and neither of us saying anything. You've gotta admit it's funny." He grinned inanely at me.

"Yes, very amusing," I wasn't convinced. And then our lips met, and conversation was no longer needed. His gentleness was seductive. I felt myself being drawn in. I could hardly believe it. I was going to wake up in a minute.

"I can definitely make up for that," he assured me, smiling.

"For what?" I'd forgotten.

"I can make up to you for falling in love with me." His eyes shone into mine. *I can love you right back. Why didn't we say anything to each other earlier?*

"Well, I think you better had," I said in all seriousness.

"How shall I begin?"

"Bow down to my every whim, breakfast in bed everyday for starters, and a body massage every night..."

"How about one now?" A flicker of doubt crossed my mind.

"Are you serious about me Ted?"

"Yes, of course I am. What's wrong Isabel?"

"How can I be sure of you?"

"Isabel, I've been in torture ever since I crossed your threshold a week ago. I didn't think you'd ever see me as anything other than a brother, we've known each other so long. But on our camping trip together, I started to see you differently. Things altered. I wanted to be with you, but couldn't broach the subject with you. I didn't know what to do. And all this time, when I thought I was just letting myself in for another disappointment, when to my joy, you turn round and say you want me too." *I wondered what else I needed to say to convince her.* "There hasn't been anyone since Lily. It took me a long time to get over her. I didn't know if there would ever be anyone after that. I hoped there would be, and that I wasn't just another reject on the shelf. But then I go and fall for someone I've known since childhood. Someone I thought would never see me the same way. But you have and you do. Unless you want to take it all back?" His hurt expression at these words told me all I needed to know.

"I don't take anything back. I do want you Ted. I've wanted you for so long." I reached for him. I needed him with me. I needed to feel he was real. Again the gentleness and tenderness of his touch made me open to him, want him more.

"You're so special. I can't believe I hadn't noticed before."

"I can't either." I couldn't help but smile, and he couldn't either. "Mind I've never had a body massage before. From any man." He caught my meaning.

"Then you will be treated with extra special care and attention," I read the emotion in his eyes and knew I could trust him. And I loved trusting him. I knew he understood what this meant. And I was glad I could trust myself to this.

"I look forward to it," I said. Our eyes reflected the smiling eyes of the other. He stroked my cheek. I felt very light headed all of a sudden. I let myself relax as I revelled in the warm touch of his skin next to mine.

Chapter Thirty-Six

You died too soon, she died too soon, I died too soon. The voices took up chorus in my head as I gazed down at Phillippa's grave. Twenty-nine days, twenty-nine hours, twenty-nine years. Words run round and round, up and down, wriggling round the pathways in my mind till they made no sense. Dead at twenty-nine, twenty-nine at dead, dead twenty-nine... I couldn't cry anymore. I've done some, some done, indeed more to come, but I'm frozen in this minute, wishing her alive, here, to see and laugh at her own grave to say it was all a hoax, for me to glare and grin and laugh and cry and shout at her and threaten her never to do anything like that again. An ache in my stomach splits the cliffs of the world as they yawn wider. Twentydeadnine, toosoondied, round and round, squigglydob. She had been the strongest person I'd ever known. She risked, dared, got burnt and hurt and risked again. She believed life was for living.

Leaves blew in a gust round her grave, and I huddled deeper into my thick coat, woolly and lined and 'best-buy' bargain.

She'd get so hurt, part of her would die, then she'd resurrect herself, and live again in a new way, heal and live through and come back for more helpings of heavy life. Phillippa celebrated herself, and it gave her strength, a deep inner strength, and I don't know how, but she would dig deep inside herself and pull through, and she would be self-protected. I hardly ever knew of Phillippa being down on herself.

"Isabel." I looked up. Ted was nearby. I hadn't seen him approach. I was glad to see him. I looked at his face, and I felt strange, like a sense of dread, something was up.

"I don't want to interrupt, but you've got a visitor. Walk with me a little." Puzzled, I walked with him round the edges of the small grave yard.

"What visitor?"

"Your sister."

"Felicity's here? Why?"

"I thought I'd better brief you first. She's a wee bit hysterical, shall we say. She wouldn't tell me why, but she demanded to see you immediately."

"It's always life or death with her, black and white, even when it's something trivial..."

"I don't think this is."

"You don't know what she's been like these past few years, Ted, she's always..."

Ted pulled up short and turned to me. "I appreciate she gives you a hard time Isabel, and she's not the most sensitive of people I know, but I really do think that you should hear her out this time." Here was Ted giving me advice on how to treat my own sister, as if he knew her better than I did.

I was annoyed, but there was such seriousness in Ted's tone that I didn't bite back, besides, the last thing I wanted to do was to have an argument with him.

"OK then, I'll at least hear her out." I concede.

"I'll take the car and pop into the village, if you like, pick up a few things."

"You mean steer clear of the battle zone?"

He smiles. "Something like that."

"You'll be OK? You won't get lost in all these country lanes?"

"I'll take a map."

***

She stood cluttering up the doorway. After a too-long pause I made my way over to my favourite chair by the fire. I didn't invite Sissi to sit down verbally, but I left her the physical space to do so if she wished.

There was a long uncomfortable silence. I stared out of the window in the far wall. Autumn gales blew the trees bent.

I thought about making us both some tea, and couldn't quite bring myself to commit to this polite civility. I wanted this over and done with. Plenty of time for tea later. I always felt self conscious playing hostess to Sissi anyway, like a part of her was always mocking me, sneering at me – for her thinking that I thought that I was above her.

Awkwardly, Felicity decided to sit on the sofa in front of the fire. She clutched a fist of wet tissues. She'd been crying heavily, and the previous sobs were still catching in her throat. Too many years of bad blood between us prevented me from giving her the comfort I would have done if she'd been anyone else.

"What is it this time Sissi?" I said warily.

"Don't call me that. You know people don't call me that anymore." Even when she was upset, her voice could still be scathing. Maybe she got it from Mum.

"Sorry Felicity," it came out sounding like I was protesting against using her full name. I hadn't meant it to, and I winced inside, and she cringed on the outside. I mentally kicked myself.

Silence maintained. We both stared into the roaring fire. It was pleasant to feel the heat on my face, especially after the unmerciful cutting wind. As the silence extended though, I began to feel uncomfortably too warm.

Just when I thought the two of us would sit like this forever, or until Ted got back anyway, and us not having exchanged more than five words to each other, she decided to speak.

"Izzy, I… well… I'm…" I flinch inside again, at the mention of *my* childhood name. She likes to enforce her position as Older Sister. It sounds like a gentle caress that helps heal old wounds when Ted says it. When Sissi says it, it's like the scab of an old wound ripped off.

"Spit it out Felicity." I say, not to be cruel, but to try and end this agony of waiting.

"I'm pregnant."

I'm shocked – pleased to meet you. I didn't say that of course. I knew, without any further elaboration that this was something she had not planned, and probably didn't welcome either.

"What are you going to do?"

"I don't know," she says blankly. I know she hasn't thought about this, and probably won't bother to either, she'll just go along with whatever happens in the end, just as she has in the past. I also know that an unexpected pregnancy would not bring Felicity 200 miles crying to my door.

I finally go and sit next to her on the sofa.

"Come on, Felicity. What else is going on here?" Silence. "If you wanted to have an abortion, I know you'd go ahead and have one. You haven't come all this way to ask my advice on an unwanted baby. What's really going on?"

"You always were blunt Izzy." The dig hits home, but I ignore it. Even though I know it's not true. My bluntness is new, and Felicity is only complaining about it, 'cause that's her way of making me feel bad. And it works. "The father's HIV positive."

The father. My mind hung on those first two words wondering what she was talking about. The holy father? Oh. The baby's father. HIV. Yes. HIV. What!?!

"What?!" HIV. HIV. The letters knocked on the door of my brain, and tried to gain access to comprehension.

"He's dying Izzy. He's dying," as if she was explaining it to a child. And she might as well have been.

"Dying," I say calmly. Not understanding what the hell she was going on about – my instincts already one step ahead of me, making connections that were too frightening to contemplate.

"Is that all you can say?" And there's a look of genuine hurt and horror in my sister's eyes, that pierces my heart.

"I'm sorry Sissi, what did you say?" I call her mainly from fondness rather than any bitter vengefulness. She doesn't pick me up on it this time.

"Shit Izzy. Christ. He's fucking dying! All right? Get the fucking picture. I dunno if I'm infected yet or what. I'm waiting for the test results." Her anger cascades over me and around me, and a sense of guilt flushes through me at my previous thoughts of wishing Felicity dead instead of Phillippa.

"Test results," I say like some stupid parrot.

"I can see coming here was a fucking waste of time – I dunno why I bother. I thought I could count on my own fucking sister for some support, wiv somert like this – even though, I know we don't always get on and see eye to eye and stuff…" She started sobbing again and she went into the hall to pick up her coat, making ready to go.

"Hold on. Felicity!" I dash through to her. I put my hand on her arm. It's our first physical contact of any tenderness for years and it slightly shocks us both. "I'm sorry, Felicity. Of course you can count on me for support. Look, I'm sorry, don't go yet. I was just, ya know, so shocked. Stay, please." She looks at me, trying to detect whether I'm being sincere or not. Fortunately, she hangs her coat back up, and I slowly follow her back into the living room. "Felicity," I say softly, standing behind her. She turns, and suddenly cries into my shoulder. I hug her tight to me, my body a soft buffer for the tumultuous emotions ravaging her body. I feel nothing and say nothing, as I continue to hold her. I was always calm in a crisis. It would hit me later.

***

I decided to look in on Felicity, see if she'd found the room to her satisfaction. I'd been thinking over all that she'd said. We hadn't had the greatest sister-sister relationship, but I didn't want to lose her.

I opened the door a crack, and gazed on Felicity's gently breathing heap of body under the bedcovers. I stood in the doorway, not wanting to disturb her, but not wanting to go either.

There had been one night, I recall, where there was tenderness and love between us, instead of the usual sibling hatred. I hadn't been feeling too well and Mum had been her usual indifferent self. She'd been slumped in front of the telly, and I couldn't focus on the book I was reading, as my tummy was in agony. I kept complaining to Mum about it, and in the end she'd got up and walked out of the house saying she never could get a moment's peace with us two around. That made me feel twice as miserable as I tried not to writhe in my seat from the pain.

Sissi had walked in just as Mum had left. "Well, that's that stupid Jake kicked into touch," she'd said as she entered. Jake being one in a long line of ex-boyfriends. "What's up wi' you, Grumpuss?" She called me that sometimes, as a bit of a spoof of Bagpuss. It was one of her milder insults for me.

"Don't feel well." I'd grumbled, holding my tummy.

"'Ere, have one a these," she'd tossed me a packet of pills from the mantelpiece.

"I don't think I should Sis, those are Mum's painkillers. She'll notice if one's missin'."

"No, she won't." I still wouldn't take one. "Please yer bleedin' self then." She'd switched the channel over, and plopped down in the nearest armchair.

"Just off to loo. Back in a tick." I paused. "Then maybe I'll take a pill." Sissi shrugged, as if she didn't care either way.

I went up to the bathroom. But me tummy was getting worse. I huddled into myself, my arms pushed into my gut as if they could force the pain out.

I reached the toilet, and sat on it. When I looked down, there was red in the bowl, red in my knickers. "Sissi," I yelled. "Sissi!"

"What?" she called back up.

"Sissi..." My voice trailed off. I didn't have the strength to shout any explanations down to her. I imagined her downstairs, trying to ignore my demands, being annoyed at my interrupting whatever crap she was watching on the telly. But thankfully, she made her way upstairs to me. She could hear me groaning.

"What?" she'd asked, impatiently.

"I don't feel well," I was starting to feel dizzy, as the world moved further and further away from me. It had been hard holding on to reality, keeping it real. My hands shook. My head swayed outside of itself. I stood up slowly, my hand still pressed to the wall.

"Sissi, I'm bleeding." I said faintly, as I weakly slithered to the floor. I felt Sissi's cool hands on me, guiding me, making sure I didn't injure myself. She laid me out flat on my back, and lifted my feet up into the air, as she'd seen on *Casualty*. I wondered what room I was in. My body was glad it didn't need to strain itself into an upright position anymore. Sissi got a damp cloth, and placed it on my head. Then she got a stool, to prop my feet up with, so they'd stay elevated. Then she just sat next to me, and held my hand.

I remembered that.

Dunno how long we stayed like that for...

...till I felt better. Felt like an age though.

"Fucking periods – they're a fucking nightmare!" This was possibly the nicest thing Sissi'd ever said to me. The single time that we'd concurred and empathised with each other.

I felt a rush of love for my sister, for being there, holding my hand, and for voicing my own opinion of periods thus far.

She'd put me to bed, once I'd recovered enough to stand and walk. I hadn't been able to stop shivering, so she filled a hot water bottle for me, to put in bed with me. She put both sanitary towels and tampons by me bedside and said I was free to use whatever I felt best with. Her generosity didn't feel out of place, as it might have done under other circumstances.

I really wish there'd been more times like that. I really do. I wiped the trickling tears from my cheeks, and allowed myself a small smile, as I shut the door behind me.

***

"Sissi, what's wrong? Has something happened? Tell me."

"Nothing. Nothing's wrong," she sobbed, "everything's great in fact. Well, nearly everything…"

"Then why are you crying?" I'd just brought Bonny back from her walk to find Felicity in floods of tears, still holding the phone. After unleashing Bonny, and having given her her post-walk treat, I took the receiver from my sister's hand, and placed it back on its rest. Her sobs were still coming thick and fast, but she was smiling through her tears.

"Who was on the phone?" But it was no use, I couldn't get anything of any use out of her till she'd calmed down. "I'll go make a pot of tea, then you can tell me all about it. She nodded, as she reached for the tissues to blow her nose loudly.

I toddled into the kitchen, wonderingly. Well, at least it seemed to be good news, whatever it was. I'd just put the kettle on to boil, when Sissi came up from behind me, and wrapped her arms around me in a massive hug. Surprised, I turned round in her arms and hugged her back.

"I'm clear! I'm negative! The test results are clear!"

"That's fantastic!" I hugged her even harder. It was the best.

"And David is going to be fine too."

"Who's David?"

"The baby."

I looked in to my sister's face. "You're going to keep him?"

"Yes, I sure as hell am."

"When did you decide this?"

"About five minutes ago. Life's too precious to throw away, Isabel. I'm fine, and I'm going to be a mum!" I was starting to cry now. We hugged and jumped up and down at the same time. We looked like we were doing some kind of mad jig round the kitchen.

"That's wonderful! I'm so happy for you Felicity. I really am."

"Thanks Isabel. Thanks for being there for me."

"Of course, what are sisters for?" And the years were forgotten, the years of fights, arguments and misunderstandings. It was all in a previous life. It was the first time I'd felt really close to Felicity.

"What was the 'nearly everything'?" I suddenly asked, just remembering.

She stood back and said, "Andrew's left me." Andrew, the father. The HIV positive. The guy I'd never met, who had almost passed on his fatality to my sister.

"He's left you? But why?" Felicity shrugged.

"Good riddance. Let's not talk about that now. Let's celebrate."

"Yes, let's."

"What are we celebrating?" Ted had just walked in the door.

"She's in the clear. She's fine!"

"And so is David."

"You know it's going to be a boy?" She nodded, her eyes shining. I felt a twinge of envy, but it was Felicity's moment, and I wouldn't ruin that for anything.

"Let's go out for a meal. What do you think? Let's really go to town on it. Go somewhere special?" Felicity grinned her agreement as Ted caught her in a big hug of relief and congratulations.

"Gets my vote," he said.

So we all went to the new Indian in town in raving high spirits. Then we went to the pub afterwards, and ordered lashings of chocolate cake, knickerbockerglories, and meringue.

Chapter Thirty-Seven

The phone started ringing. I put down the paper remembering Isabel had gone to the shops. A familiar voice was at the other end.

"Hello?"

"Is Isabel there?"

"No, she's not I'm afraid. Can I take a message?"

"It's Ben here."

"Oh, hello Ben. Ted here. How are you keeping?" His drawn and pale face at Phillippa's funeral came to mind.

"Not too bad. Listen. Maybe you could help. The three of you were very close weren't you?" he spoke haltingly. Ben was a much shier person than Phillippa had ever been.

"Yes, we were all very close," and I could feel a lump in my throat as I said it.

"Well, I don't know what to do, you see I was wondering if you could help, if I could ask your advice about something, it's very delicate, very important, you see neither me or Gail know what to do, perhaps I shouldn't be asking, but we weren't sure where to turn and we thought that maybe as you were her best friends, that you might have an idea what she would've wanted, but you see I just don't know."

Slow down a bit Ben. What's got you and your wife in such a tizz I wonder.

"Go ahead Ben, ask me anything. Anything that me or Isabel can do to help, just name it. We'd only be too pleased to help out."

"Well, thanks." There was a pause. It was so long I wondered if he'd changed his mind and had hung up.

"Ben, are you still there? I don't mind whatever it is. Ask anything, I'll try to do whatever I can," I reassured him.

"Well, it's about Daphne you see. And Gail's expecting, and

money's pouring out, and we're just in over our heads, and we don't know, we know Phillippa didn't want Mum and Dad to know, so we can't ask them, and we're just stuck, oh God, it's so awful, but we're like… sorry Ted."

"No need to apologise Ben. It's fine. But sorry, can we just back up a minute here? You said this was about Daphne. Forgive me for being really ignorant here, but who is Daphne?"

"You mean you don't know?"

"No. Should I?"

"Well, yes, I thought, I mean that, well, you know, *surely*, Daphne?"

"No Ben, I'm totally at a loss here."

"Her daughter."

"Whose daughter?"

"Phillippa's of course."

"Phillippa's got a daughter?" Could there be some mistake here? Was Ben being delusional?

"Yes. Didn't she ever tell you? I thought you and Isabel would have been the main people to know. Daphne's her little girl, she's not long turned three. I can't believe Phillippa never told you about her." Ben sounded as shocked as I felt. I did some quick smart mental arithmetic, and suddenly felt as if I'd been badly winded. But I could be wrong. I could be wrong. But if I am right, what does that mean? "Ted? Are you there? Ted?"

"Er, yeah, I'm still here."

"I don't know why she never told you. I just assumed… I'm sorry."

"No, it's not your fault Ben. She was the little girl with you at the funeral? I thought she was yours."

"Yes that's Daphne. No she's not ours. But I had to give Mum and Dad some sort of story about her. I promised Phillippa that they would never know about her. I thought you or Isabel might blow it, but you didn't even know… Sorry, I should never have called. Don't worry Ted."

"No, no Ben. If this concerns Daphne in any way, it's important. And you're obviously very worried about something. Tell me what it's all about." I hope I didn't sound as desperate as I suddenly felt.

"Well, it's all really awkward really. You remember my

wife Gail?"

"I met her briefly at the funeral."

"Well, she's expecting. And we're very happy about this, only…"

"You're wondering how this will affect Daphne?"

"Well, not just that, but, well, things are really tight at the moment. I know this sounds awful, but we really can't afford to support two children." He stopped. I was obviously supposed to respond with something, but my mind had turned into soggy cotton wool, and wasn't working properly. "We want this child, Ted, but coping with two is going to be so hard. Emotionally and physically as well as financially. I'm very worried about Gail's condition." He waited again. But I really wasn't sure what I was expected to say. "But we don't want to abandon Daphne, Ted. We don't. We're very attached to our niece, but…" he trailed off.

And my brain suddenly clicked as to what he was getting at. "You mean you're thinking of putting her up for adoption or something?"

I must have sounded accusatory to him, I hadn't meant to be, as he responded, "Well, it crossed our minds, but we really don't want to abandon her or anything, or give her away, we really don't, but we just can't cope with two, it's just too much…" His voice cracked. I didn't want to get into all the ins and outs of his domestic arrangements, I just wanted to know one thing.

"Ben, do you know who the father is?" There was another irritating pause. "Who is Daphne's father?"

"I don't know. I don't know if Phillippa did either, to be honest." See, I could be totally wrong, but my gut was doing funny things, and what I said next was purely instinctive.

"I'll take her Ben."

"You mean take Daphne?"

"Yes. I'll look after her. You don't want to give her to strangers, but can't cope with keeping her. Phillippa would have been happy knowing her best friends were taking care of her only child."

"Yes, she would. I'm sure she would be very assured." He pondered a moment. "Are you sure about this Ted? I was just going to ask advice about…"

"I'm dead certain."

"It's hard work looking after..."

"Ben," I interrupted, "I don't want Daphne to go to strangers either," (although I will be a stranger to her!), "I want her to be happy too. I could adopt her."

"It's a huge step Ted, I wasn't expecting you to..."

"Listen, Ben, I've always wanted a family. Let me look after Daphne. I'll bring her over to see you and Gail as often as you wish, of..."

"Oh, I wasn't worried about being cut off from her, I mean, not seeing her, not not seeing her, I mean..."

"It's OK Ben, I know what you mean. Look you can have a think about it if you like. But I won't change my mind," will I? Am I crazy? "But I would dearly love to take care of Daphne as if she was my own, and make sure her well-being is fully taken care of. As you say, I'm sure Phillippa wouldn't have any gripes about it."

"But she didn't tell you about her."

"No." And what could I say to that? I was as much in the dark as he was about her reasons for that. And what if Daphne wasn't my daughter? She could be someone else's. It's very possible. But it's still a little girl that's got nowhere else to go, and no-one else to turn to. And it's Phillippa's little girl. Even if she didn't tell me about her, I know she would want me to do everything I possibly could for her. And I would have a daughter, even if she wasn't mine. I would be a father to her. "Ben, if you have any reservations about me, let me know. I'll do what I can to set your mind at ease that your niece will be kept safe and healthy."

"Gail is due any time now. I want everything to be OK." He sounded worried.

"Everything will be OK Ben. What do you think, do you need more time?" Please Ben. Please give me a chance.

"When would you be able to pick her up?" I almost laughed with relief. And wondered at the tension I'd been feeling, not wanting to lose this little girl that I'd only ever seen once, when five minutes ago if someone had told me I was going to act as a parent, I'd have laughed in their face at the ridiculousness of it.

"How about tomorrow? Oh no, it's Sunday tomorrow, the

trains will be practically non-existent. How about Monday?"

"I'll have her ready."

"Are you happy with this Ben?" I suddenly felt completely exhilarated.

"It would solve all our problems, and Daphne would be safe with you?"

"Absolutely. But you can come down and check me out whenever you like in order to set your mind at rest. And whisk Daphne away again, if you're not happy with me, and make other arrangements." I laughed nervously.

"Phillippa always spoke well of both you and Isabel. Always. I think it might be the best possible solution. Are you still sure you're happy to do this?" he asked fearfully.

"Certainly. I would be deeply unhappy if you'd decided to do anything else."

"I'm very grateful Ted. I hope you don't think bad of us."

"Not at all. Let me take down your address details. I'll call you back when I've got the train times and let you know when I'm due to arrive."

"OK. Have you got pen and paper?"

Chapter Thirty-Eight

"Isabel?"

"Yes?" I nuzzled into him, smelling his scent deep into my lungs, whilst keeping the duvet tucked under my chin. I was sleepy after our love making. I'd just been drifting off, my head on his chest, listening to his heart beating away steadily.

"Isabel, there's something I need to tell you." This sounded ominous. He took his arms away from where they'd been holding me to him, as he sat up in bed. He looked serious. What terrible things was he going to tell me? I shivered slightly, even though I was warm. I sat up too, and pulled the moons and stars duvet up with me, hoping the warmth would ward off the fear. Was he going to say he thought we were a mistake, and shouldn't be together? Was he going to tell me that, oops, he'd forgotten, he really did have a girlfriend back home, and it'd, er, sort of slipped his mind?

"What is it Ted?" The suspense was killing me.

"Do you remember Ben and Gail at the funeral?"

Strange question. What had Phillippa's brother and his wife got to do with anything?

"Yes."

"Well, you remember..." he didn't finish.

"What?" I prompted, wondering why he was speaking of Phillippa's funeral as if it had been years ago, when in fact it'd only been a couple of months. "Ted, tell me, what is it?"

"You remember the toddler they had with them?"

"What about her?" I distinctly remembered them carrying a blond little girl with them. Ben had been very vague and dismissive towards me, so I hadn't spoken to either of them very much. But I didn't think it was anything to get upset about.

"She's Phillippa's daughter. Not Ben's."

"What?" Ted just looked at me. "But that can't possibly be

197

true. How could she have had a child and we not know about it?"

"It is true, Isabel."

"But… but…" How could that possibly be? "How do you know?"

"Ben told me."

"*He* told you? But when? How? Why?"

"He phoned yesterday. You were out getting the food shopping…"

"Why didn't you tell me?"

"I don't know. I guess I was shocked. I didn't quite know how to tell you."

"How do you know he's telling the truth? How come he never told us before? Why didn't Phillippa tell us?"

"Hold on. One thing at a time. I know this is a shock Isabel. Look, I'll go get you something hot to drink…"

"No, stay right here, Ted. I want to know everything. Tell me." Ted saw me shivering. He turned to me, cupping my face with his left hand. Warm hand.

"I'll be right back with some hot chocolate then I'll tell you everything," he said in steady tones. He gently kissed my forehead and slid out of the bed. He snatched up his towelling dressing gown from a nearby chair and barefooted downstairs.

The stillness of the momentary interlude helped me absorb the shock a bit more. But my head was spinning as questions chased after each other.

Ted came back with two steaming cups of hot chocolate. He didn't get back into bed next to me. I wish he had. I felt a distance between us, though I didn't understand why. I felt somehow alone.

Ted sat on top of the covers, and tucked his legs up under him. His profile was to me. I sipped the hot liquid, trying not to burn my tongue. Ted just held his.

"Well?" I said, impatient for more answers. "How come we never knew before?"

"I'm not sure why Phillippa never told us," he said carefully. "Ben and Gail were going to look after Daphne and…"

"Is that her name? Daphne?" What a lovely name. What a strange sound to hear coming from first Ted's lips, and then my own. Daphne.

"Yes. Well, they were going to look after her, but now Gail's expecting, and they don't think they can handle two children at the moment. It would be such a drain for them, and I don't think they've got enough money to support all four of them, so..."

"No! They're not just gonna get rid of her are they? Just put her up for adoption or something? Their own niece! How can they do that?"

"Well, give them a break, Isabel. He's only twenty, and she's only eighteen."

"True, but to let some stranger bring her up..."

"Well, not a stranger, no." Ted didn't look at me, and he didn't say anything for a few moments.

"What? Ted, what!"

"I said we'd look after her."

I felt like a bucket of ice cubes had just been thrown over me.

"You – did – what?" My words came out very quietly.

"Or that, at least, well, what I actually said was I'd take care of her. You don't have to be involved if you don't want to." He might as well have slapped my face and just walked out the door.

"What are you saying Ted? You're going to look after Daphne and run out on me?"

"No, Isabel. That's not what I'm saying." He now looked deep into my eyes. Seeking me out. He shuffled forward slightly and rested his hand on my covered legs. I felt his touch burn through the material on to my skin.

"I'm saying I really want to take care of Daphne. But I also want to stay with you Isabel. I love you, you must know that. I was hoping we could take care of her together."

I looked fish-like at him, my mouth open but no words coming out.

"Isabel?" His voice softly caressed me, implored me.

"You could've asked me first. We could've talked about this, before you went off and made unilateral decisions concerning my life."

"Yes. I know. I should've. I'm sorry." He paused. He looked sheepish, but I couldn't very well just take him back in my arms and go, oh, well, that's OK then, no problem. It was a problem.

"Look, I'll leave you some time to think about this," he said, rising from the bed. "I'm going to go and pick Daphne up tomorrow. I won't come straight back here. I'll go and stay in my flat in Bristol with her. You can give me a ring when you've decided on what you think is best for you to do." He looked sad. Regretful.

"Ted, you sound so cold. So distant." I felt suddenly very alone and vulnerable.

"I don't mean to be, Isabel dear." He came round to my side of the bed and crouched before me. He leaned into me, and our lips brushed. Brushed again. Deeper. My hunger for his warmth and love leapt inside me. But then he pulled away slightly.

My eyes sought him now, in his twin pool depths. "It means this much to you?" I whispered.

"Yes." His voice was hoarse. His eyes were moist. I was about to say something else, but he stood and walked away. "You've got my number." He turned to face me again. "I'll pack tonight and get the train down first thing."

"Ted…"

"Take your time with the decision Isabel. I don't want you to rush into anything that isn't right for you," he said in all sincerity. Then he walked from my room.

Chapter Thirty-Nine

A daughter.

A daugh-ter. Phillippa's daughter. The words echoed in rhythm to the train's wheels humming over the tracks, the vibrations trundling beneath my feet, making the carriage sway.

I stared through the fleeing trees and fields passing inside the silhouette of my reflection in the window.

And it was possible she was my daughter too. But I hadn't mentioned it to Isabel, just in case. I'd rather get that checked out and be certain first. Ben didn't know who the father was, but according to Daphne's age, it worked out at about... It was just a possibility. I might be wrong. But what if she was my daughter? My daugh-ter, the train reflected my thoughts back to me as it trundled on its way. I needed a drink.

I took my coat off, and bunched it up into a heap on the seat next to me, then made my way to the buffet carriage. Something strong. But not too much. I wanted to be sober when I went to pick her up. It wouldn't smell good, if Ben and Gail thought they were handing over their little niece to a man with alcoholic breath in the middle of the day.

I waited in line, idly looking over the Virgin magazine, wondering if there would be anything inside that would hold my interest for more than a few seconds. Probably not.

The man served me a G & T with a smile, and I decided to ask for a packet of ready salted too. Not good to drink on an empty stomach and all that.

I made my way back to my table, balancing myself between the seats as the train continued to sway. I was glad the train was fairly empty. I couldn't stand packed trains, too many people in too little space. And you could tell that the person sat next to you wanted your seat just to put their coat and bag on, and stretch their feet out to the opposite seat, and have their elbows sticking out all over the place, whilst they talked on their new Nokia mobile, irritating the hell out of everyone around them! Well, irritating all those who didn't have mobiles, like myself, or those who believed you shouldn't have private conversations in public like that, as it's so damn rude. Or maybe I was just getting stuffy in my old age? I could understand wanting to have a mobile in case of emergencies, and tell your loved ones that the train you were on was going to be a further two hours late. But otherwise, I was always overcome with the impulse to take mobile phones out of passengers' hands, and throw them off the train. I restrained myself, obviously, but it was tempting. I just had to make do with the fantasy. Perhaps I was just anti-personable. Perhaps I missed all the weird and wonderful conversations I usually ended up having with people sat around me, because now they were having business meetings on the train, or gossiping with their friends. Jesus, wasn't there already enough time to do those sorts of things?

A daugh-ter, my daugh-ter, the whisperings continued, as I settled myself in my seat again. But if it was my daughter, surely Phillippa would've told me about it. Or maybe that's why she *didn't* mention having a daughter, because she did suspect it was mine? That made sense in a backward sort of way.

So I might be a father. What I had yearned to be for the last couple of years. A father. The word hung in my mind, as if it was the only picture in a sparse gallery, it had always been there, but only now was it beginning to take on any real significance to me. Only now did I notice, that the artist's name might be Ted Hawkins, instead of some famous person, or anonymous signature that was impossible to make out.

I missed Phillippa. I wish she was here to talk to, to ask about... I wonder when she might have deigned to tell me and Isabel about her child, had she lived? She couldn't have kept it a secret forever. It was three long months since her funeral.

And how would Isabel take it if she does turn out to be my daughter? I hope she does take both me and Daphne into her life. I really do. I don't know what I'm going to do if she doesn't. It's so strange to think of us now. All this time we've known each other. All this time as just good friends. And now I can't think of living without her, of not having her by my side in life. I didn't think I could feel this way. It's much deeper than what I felt with Lily. It's very strange how life turns out. I never would have guessed in a million years.

And why am I so certain I want to take care of Daphne, even if she isn't mine? I don't know. I just am. Like a calling. Like an intuition, like I was meant to be there. Which is so bizarre, to say I never even knew of her existence until yesterday. Perhaps it's my paternal feelings coming out? Or maybe on some unconscious level, I already know she *is* my daugh-ter. But that's silly. Phillippa could have had anyone in her life, round about that time. It could all just be a funny coincidence. I so wish she had told us about Daphne. It would've been lovely to have got together, and take the little one out with us all.

I watched the countryside's blues and greens slow down as the train pulled into a station. I could see the half moon peeping through, not yet in its daylight bed. Why did that happen, when you saw the moon and the sun in the morning sky, sharing the same light?

Chapter Forty

i see isabel approach my grave... but she doesn't see me –
though it's me she's come to see...

Here I am, staring at the inscription on your grave, as
raindrops drip between the crevices of the lettering. My hand's
holding the umbrella and my feet are numb, I've been stood here
for so long.

It's been two weeks now. Two weeks since Ted went to
pick up your daughter. And I've done a lot of thinking. I've done
nothing but. He's called to reassure me he still cares about me,
and to reinforce that there's no time pressure. He's taken a
month's hols from work, to help her readjust, and to help him.
And also to sort out the legalities of it all, which Ben is going to
help him with.

I had no idea that Ted had such strong paternal feelings. I
could understand that he didn't want your child to be brought up
by God knows who, left stranded for possibly months, maybe
years, before someone would give her the loving home she
deserves. But it all just feels so drastic. So out of the blue.

I still feel stunned that you have a daughter. And that you
didn't tell me, well, either of us. But *why* hadn't Ben said
anything at your funeral?

A vague memory of the little girl filters through. I
remember looking down on her plump face, small silky blond
curls framing it. She had looked adorable. And so well behaved.
Though, of course, she hadn't really known what was going on.

Daphne.

How could I possibly stand in as Mum for you? Be a
substitute mom? It seemed like such a heavy responsibility. I'd
probably teach her all the things that you wouldn't, or miss out
the things that you would teach her. But I can't just guess at how
you would've brought her up, I would have to do it my own way.

But, I think, that you would've been happy knowing your daughter was being brought up by your two very best friends.

"Wouldn't you Phillippa?" I wait for your answer, but only the pattering rain says anything. *i'm here isabel... i'm listening... of course i'd be happy for you and ted to care for daphne... who else...*

The weather presenter had promised sunshine and showers. Well they got the showers bit right. They were never-ending today. And the sun? Well that was getting more like a distant stranger at the moment, just like you. I reach forward and touch the wet indents of the letters that form your name.

"What would you have me do, Phillippa? Why aren't you here when I need you? Why aren't you here for your daughter?" *you can't hear me... but i can guide you if you let me...*

I suddenly hear a distant roll of thunder. I look up from under my frail shelter at the deep grey above.

"And damn it all Fippy, why didn't you tell me about her?" I watch the drops starting to fall heavier on the grass and bounce off your gravestone. *open yourself up isabel... let yourself feel...*

Daphne.

Would she be the last link between us?

Can I be a replacement Mum for her? Replacing you? If I'd died, and left my only daughter alone in the world, and you wanted to bring her up, how would I feel? I think it would feel right somehow.

But do I want to?

What about me and Ted? Could it work between us? Would we make good parents together? Our love affair was still so new. True, I'd always wanted to be with Ted. And Ted seemed to want to go the long haul with me, but we'd made no commitments to each other. Not said *anything* about marriage or engagement or any sort of long term togetherness.

What if we broke up a year down the line? What would that mean for us? And for Daphne? I shivered in the cold, my body starting to feel stiff.

"Stop being so pessimistic Izzy," that's what you'd say to me. "Give it a chance. Things aren't written in stone you know, you just have to take a risk sometimes. Who knows what could happen?" *that's right... no living being knows...* But you were always so much braver than me in pushing the boundaries, making decisions, seeing what would happen if you just did this... I was much more the homey one, wanting security, familiarity.

Oh, Phillippa, help me see through this fog in my head. All these complications, all these different feelings. The right decision. What is that?

"There is no right or wrong Izzy. Just what you feel inside." I can hear your voice as if you'd only said it to me yesterday. "It's only as complicated as you want it to be." That was one of the other enigmatic pieces of advice you've given me in the past. Can it really be that straight forward? *yes it is – it's that straight forward isabel...*

Daphne's face swam into focus in my mind again.

And the doctor said I was infertile. "We can use an egg from your partner," she'd said. I hadn't said anything. I never told you about that Phillippa. I think I felt too ashamed.

But is Ted the right man? And we have never discussed having any children together. We'd not decided on anything like that. Well, you don't do you, if you've only been together for such a brief time. Funny, how we only got together after your death, Phillippa. I wish you could've been here to see it. After all that time I'd spent telling you about him, wanting him. And you said I should tell him. But I couldn't. I didn't. But I have now.

And now there's a child almost *thrust* upon me. Your child. The two things I always wanted. The 'stone age tradition' you always used to scorn. Here for the taking. My taking. So why can't I just reach out and pull it to me? Why am I so hesitant?

Your child. I feel like I'm being offered your shoes to stand in, and they fit funny. And I feel so guilty. Ted's determined to be the father, even though Daphne is as much a stranger to him as she is to me.

The father. Who is the father, Phillippa? I hadn't thought to ask till now. Do you even know who it is?

God, that sounds awful. To not know who the father of your child is. There I go again, judging you, even in death. Sorry Phillippa. I know you always played safe. Did something go wrong one time? Or was it a one night stand with someone you fancied? I'm sure you would have told me if there had been a long term guy in your life. Mind you, you never told me you had a daughter, so perhaps you wouldn't.

I do feel a sort of yearning for Daphne. I did when I first saw her. Before I knew she was yours. Yours. If Ted and I do take care of her, at least we can bring her up with the knowledge of you. We can tell her all about who you were, when she's old enough to understand. Because, after all, who knew you like we did?

I can picture me and Ted playing happy parents to Daphne, in the living room, in front of the fire, on long winter nights playing a game of some sort. I can see us on a picnic in the spring, smelling the freshness of first flowers.

But could I be a mother to her? And how do I do that? I don't know how to be a Mum.

Did Ted ask himself if he could be a Dad? Or was it a snap decision for him, that he felt he must do this out of a sense of loyalty to you? Did Ted *just decide* he was going to do the best for Daphne, seeing as Ben and Gail don't want her; *just decide* he was prepared to give it a chance with me, with the three of us? And here I am, still making up my mind.

"It's a big decision, Isabel," he'd said. A big responsibility. A big commitment. Something totally life-changing.

So, can I do it? Stand in as Mum for Daphne, whilst being a partner to Ted? I've just realised. I've stopped asking if I *want* to do it. I'm now asking if I *can* do it. So that must mean... that I do want to, but am scared I won't be *able to.* "Go for it," you would say. And you're right Fippy. You're absolutely right.

no – you're the one that is right – dear isabel...

Chapter Forty-One

I got back to the house, eager to call Ted and tell him of the decision Phillippa helped me make.

Bonny greeted me at the door, tail wagging. She'd been sulky that I'd gone out without her, but I didn't think she'd be able to contain all her bouncy energy, with such sustained patience, as I stood at Phillippa's grave.

I gave her some of her favourite dog biscuits as a treat to make up for it. Having hung my coat up, and stoked up the fire, I sat back in my comfy chair, to watch her munch happily on the rug. I smiled, and patted her head lovingly.

"What do you think Bonny? Having a little mite in the house?" I suddenly realised that I had assumed Ted and Daphne would live here with me, in Yorkshire. But we hadn't discussed it. What if he wanted me to move down to Bristol, to be with him? But his poky little flat wouldn't hold the three of us comfortably, like my home could so easily. I'd persuade him, if he didn't see the sense of it. I'm sure it will be fine.

I made my way over to the phone and dialled the number I knew by heart. It rang only twice, before Ted grabbed the phone.

"She's just gone off to sleep. I didn't want the phone disturbing her," he said conversationally, before I'd even said hello, before he even knew it was me.

"How's she doing?" I asked. Ted's didn't seem to be surprised to hear my voice.

"She's doing fine, I think. Better than I am actually, to say she's in a new place with a complete stranger and I'm the adult in my own home running round like a crazed loony." I smiled that Ted could still keep a sense of humour amid the stress and turmoil of the situation. "But I'm working on it."

"Listen Ted, I've come to a decision…"

"Hold on." I held, my heart clamouring. "It's OK. I thought

I heard her cry. I'm starting to hear things now. Sorry, Isabel, you were saying...?"

"Yes."

"Yes, what?"

"I'm saying yes, Ted. Yes to everything. Yes to you. Yes to Daphne. But we've got a lot of things to work out, like your having to move up here and..." I tailed off, my excitement met a dead silence at the other end. "Ted?" Please tell me you're happy, over the moon, that this is still what you want.

"That's great, Isabel," he finally said, with some difficulty.

"It doesn't sound like it." Here I was, just making the biggest commitment in my entire life, and he says, 'That's great, Isabel', in that sort of tone. What was he playing at? I didn't make decisions like this every day of my life, for just any old person!

"Listen, Isabel. I'm sorry. I didn't mean to sound so deflated. It *is* great. Really. I just think you should take some more time over this than you have. Cause it could be very messy to walk away from, once you're in it, and I'm not saying you would want to, it's just that... Shit. This is all coming out wrong. Look, you're right, there's a lot to sort out, Isabel. And there's a lot to discuss. More than I thought there was. So, I think it would be a good idea if you came down here for a few days, if you can get away from work. I can't do this over the phone. And I don't want to drag Daphne kicking and screaming to yet another new place. Isabel? Are you still there?"

"Yes, I'm here." No, I'm a million miles away. I feel exactly as I did when you didn't return to my side in bed after telling me Phillippa had a daughter.

"Will you come down? I really need to see you, darling." And that was my only indication so far, that he still had feelings for me. "Will work let you off a couple of days? Isabel?" He sounded unsure. So he did still want me.

"Yes. Yes, I can arrange it, but not as quickly as that."

"That's OK. That's fine. No rush. Is the week after next OK? Will that do? There's still so much I need to organise down here, and I'll know more about where I'm at then." I don't think I will though. I don't seem to know if I'm coming or going at all. And this topsy-turvy world seems to be the only way things are at the moment.

"I'll talk to my boss and see what she says. I'm due some time, so it shouldn't be too much of a problem. Have to see what's coming up." Momentary silent pause. "I'll let you know when I've got a date set then," I said lamely.

"That would be great." He sounded genuinely enthusiastic this time. Then another awkward pause. There didn't seem to be anything else to say, but I didn't want to let him go. Then he said the words I needed to hear. "I love you, Isabel."

"I love you too," my voice was husky with emotion.

"I'll speak to you soon, darling. Take care."

"You too. Bye Ted." And he was gone, with a final click. I sat there cradling the phone a moment. Bonny came up, and licked my hand. I put the phone back, and stroked her head. "What did he mean more things to discuss than he thought there was? Eh, Bonny? What do you think, girl? You want a walk don't you? C'mon then." I laughed as she sprung up, barked and panted after me, as I retrieved her lead from the book shelf.

**

It was a very romantic restaurant Ted had picked. I'd only just had time to drop my things off at his flat and change, before dashing out again. It had felt so good to be in his arms again, and feel his lips on mine. I hadn't realised quite how much I'd missed him. I didn't get to see Daphne though. Deborah was just reading her a bedtime story, so I didn't want to disturb them. Deborah was more attractive than I would've liked, but it was obvious they were nothing more than friends. I let my jealousy go. I knew it was silly. Everything felt much better now I actually had Ted with me in the flesh.

We went straight off to the restaurant, Ted'd made a booking and didn't want to be late. I wore my new black dress. Ted was in smart evening dress too.

It was good to get back into the warmth again. I tell him it's much nippier down here, than up north. He laughs. Our coats and scarves are taken at the door, and we're shown to our table.

The lighting is quite dim. The air has a rich aroma, something else beyond the whiffs of succulent food. We sit at a

210

corner table, big enough for four, but set for two. I take the wall side, Ted sits opposite. Behind him hangs a deep red, velvet curtain, separating us from the table behind him. Very unusual. Very cosy.

"What would you like to drink?"

"House wine?" I shrug, looking at Ted.

"Yes, that'll be fine. A bottle of red please." The waiter bows slightly, then leaves us to peruse the menus.

"This is all very extravagant." He smiles.

"Why not?" I smile back. "Who's looking after Bonny?"

"Andrea. My boss. She's a big dog fan. A big Bonny fan."

"That's good of her." I nod.

"Deborah lives in the flat above you, right?"

"Yes. She's a big child fan. A big Daphne fan. She's been really supportive." Though I'm smiling at him batting my words back to me, I feel a prick of jealousy again, but dismiss it.

The waiter brings the wine, pours for us, and leaves us once he's ascertained we haven't decided what to have yet.

Strange. Ted seems really nervous tonight. Jumpy even. Like as if this was our first date or something. I hadn't really noticed it when he'd picked me up, or when we were at the flat.

"I'm dying to see her properly."

"What Deborah?"

"No, silly. Daphne." He gives a weak laugh.

"What do you fancy?"

"You."

"That'll keep for later." Our eyes sparkle at each other, but I can still detect a certain uneasiness about him.

"What food do you fancy?"

He opts for the steak. I go for the vegetarian lasagne. The waiter returns and we order.

"Where were you thinking of us living?" I ask. My tummy rumbles and I wonder how long the food will be.

"With you actually. If that's OK. Your place is bigger and much nicer. Besides, you probably won't want to leave the magazine. And I can contract out almost anywhere." That was one big thing sorted then. That's good. Why do I suddenly feel like I'm navigating a minefield then?

"I think that would be best too." Dare I ask? About the 'm'

211

word? No, I daren't. "What do you see happening to us, in the future?" Well, that was a round about way of asking. Sort of.

"I see us… well, I hope to see us together?" He was asking me!

"Do you want us to be?" I ask, needing something a little more definite.

"Yes, of course I do."

"We've never even discussed children." Or marriage.

"I've always wanted children," he says wistfully, into his wine. "Lily didn't."

We'd not talked too much about his ex-wife. I knew things had gone horribly wrong in the end. Irretrievably. But Ted seemed to have come to terms with the fact that he and Lily were history. He had said it was fortunate that it had ended when it did. They had so obviously been on different tracks in life. I hadn't pushed it any further than that. He didn't like to rake over the past. I was content that he wasn't on the rebound, and that he was no longer carrying a torch for her.

"What about you?" he asks gently. I'd got lost in my own reverie, and forgotten what the original question was. "Have you thought much about having children?" he prompts me.

"Yes. I've always wanted them. And a career too. I want it all," I laugh. He doesn't join in. I ponder about whether to tell him about my previous efforts of trying for a child, but decide against it. Maybe another time. Ted was looking at me seriously. I soberly say, "Yes, I'd love children." I pause. He's still looking at me. "I'm infertile, Ted."

"Oh, I didn't know."

"Watch the wine!"

"Sorry," he hastily puts his wine down, so as not to spill anymore. He wipes his hand on the serviette. "I'm so sorry Isabel." His sympathy brings tears to my eyes.

"Yes, well, just one of those things," I dismiss it with a wave of my hand.

Just then the meal arrives. I tuck in hungrily, glad to have something neutral to focus on. It smells wonderful, and tastes just as good as the smells had promised.

We devour our food in appreciative silence.

The wine was good too, but I noticed Ted hardly touched

his. He asked for some water, and some was duly brought.

When we'd filled our fill, and our plates were almost empty, I was polishing off my third glass of wine.

"How's the legal side of things?" I ask. "What do you have to sort out? Will you adopt her?" I sip my wine, feeling its warmth mingle with the good food in my stomach.

"Er, no. I don't need to do that. I'm going to make an application to the court for a parental responsibility order." He stops, as if he's waiting for some sort of response from me. I wait for him to continue. "Ben said he would vouch for me."

"That's good. Will that be quite straight forward then?" Ted frowns. Was something wrong?

"Yes, it should be. I'll apply after Daphne has been with me a couple of months, so I can show the courts that I'm taking care of her satisfactorily." Well, that was good wasn't it? Why was he still frowning? Am I missing something here?

"So what's wrong then?"

"Isabel." I wonder what's coming next. "Isabel, I know who Daphne's father is." I gasp. Was he going to make trouble for Ted? Protest against him having Daphne or something? Is that what he meant?

"Who?"

"I am." *Now* I knew that the wine was having funny effects on me. I'd better not have anymore. I thought I just heard Ted say he was the father.

I laugh. "Sorry Ted, I think I misheard there. This wine's gone to my head. I thought you said you were Daphne's father there for a minute," I say, laughing. He waits till my hysteria has abated.

"I am Daphne's father, Isabel." He's having me on. He must be. But he looks dead serious. Well, he obviously hasn't drunk enough. Of course he wasn't Daphne's father. Cause that would mean that he and....

"But that would mean that you and Phillippa..." I can't complete the sentence. Ted just nods solemnly.

"But you can't have. You haven't. How could you? I would've known about it."

"Isabel, it was just one night, about four years ago..."

"But you *can't* have," I say with vehemence, as if by saying it, it would make him understand. Make him tell the proper truth. Make him admit that he and Phillippa had never been together, not even once about four years ago. "You can't have," I repeat stupidly.

"Neither of us said anything, because… I don't know why I didn't say anything before. I didn't think it would matter to you really, but now…"

Matter to me. Of course it damn well matters to me.

"I don't know why Phillippa never told you." No, but I do. I knew only too well why she hadn't told me. I suddenly felt very sober. Ted searches my eyes for some sort of understanding, but I'm just dumbstruck.

"Isabel? I wasn't sure how you would take this, but I…"

"Well, you want to know how I'm taking this Ted? I'm taking this very badly, that's how I'm taking this." My anger's bubbling under the surface, but it's having a fight with my tears. And I'll be damned if I'm going to cry about this in front of Ted.

"Ben asked me to give you this."

"Something else I should know about Ted?" He rummages in his jacket pocket for something. "Here it is." He places it tentatively on the table for me to take. It's a scruffy white envelope, with my name and address on it. I stare at it, not wanting to touch it. Not wanting to be here. Not wanting to be in a 50 mile radius of Ted. Or Daphne. I swallow down a wave of nausea, and try and focus on angry thoughts.

"It's from Phillippa. Ben and Gail only found it recently in some old clothes of hers. I said I'd give it to you."

"Oh, you did, did you? And have you read it too?" I just about manage to refrain from shouting. My accusation makes him flinch.

"No, but I… Well, Gail happened to read some of it, by accident. She didn't know what it was, but thought it was important you should have it. I haven't read it, but I've an idea what's in it."

"Any more nasty surprises?"

"No, I don't think so. It just explains… You should read it Isabel." An unknown force makes me reach forth and pick up the envelope with shaking fingers. I hold it stiffly, above the surface of the table.

214

"How was your meal, sir?"

"Delightful, thank you."

"Madam?" I realise I'm supposed to say something nice and polite, as the waiter clears away our debris.

Through gritted teeth, I say, "Yes, thank you. The food was delicious. Shame about the company." The waiter hurries away.

"Isabel. It was before 'us'. I wasn't sure how you would feel about it, but there's no reason why this should get in the way of our happiness. I mean we could…"

"No-reason-why!" I nearly choke on the words. "I suppose you're going to tell me it didn't mean anything." Ted has to strain to catch my words, but I was not going to repeat myself.

"No, I'm not going to say that. But it was then. This is now. You are now. You're the one that's important to me, Isabel. You're the one I love." His words were passionate and tender, but they don't reach me. I can't feel them. They belong to another person, another place.

"Yes, definitely *not* something to tell me over the phone, is it Ted?" I get up, making my way over to the doors.

He comes after me, grabs my arm. "Isabel, where are you going?"

"Don't touch me." I can feel my eyes spitting fire at him. "Don't come anywhere near me." I shake him off, and already I'm taking my coat and scarf from the hooks.

"But Isabel, I…."

"Leave me alone Ted!"

"You forgot this." He holds Phillippa's envelope in front of me. I'd dropped it in my haste. I thought of telling him to keep it, but I snatch it from him.

"Just leave me alone, Ted." I walk out. He calls after me. I ignore him. The waiter's already at his elbow, to ensure his 'delighted' customers don't run off without payment.

I rushed off down the road, not a clue in my head as to where I was going, or what I was doing. I had no idea where I was going to stay the night. Obviously, I couldn't go back to Ted's, and it was too late to catch a train home. I'd have to book into a hotel or something, somewhere.

Thankfully I had my purse with me. I stopped a stranger and asked them where the nearest B&B was. They gave me directions to somewhere not too far off. I focused my mind on just getting me there, remembering where to turn left, when to turn right.

I finally found it. A neat looking façade, hanging flowers over the door, and at the window sills. The sign read 'vacancies'. That's all I needed to know. I rung the bell.

A man in his sixties, slightly unbuttoned yellow shirt, old chequered trousers, smile on his face, welcomed me in.

"Bitter cold, isn't it?" I agreed. "Is it a single you'll be wanting?" I nodded. "En suite?"

"If there is one."

"I'll give you room number three then. Breakfast is at half seven till eight, if you want some."

"Yes, that would be great. I don't suppose you've any spare towels, have you? Only I hadn't planned on, erm…"

"Not a problem. No problem at all. I'll bring some up for you."

"Sorry to be a nuisance, but, could I also, no, never mind."

"Yes, I have actually. I keep a few spare. Just in case. I'll bring you up toothbrush and paste too." He'd read my mind.

"Thank you, that's very kind." I wondered if this happened often. If he'd seen all this before. Lovers had a fight. One of them needs a room for the night. They've not brought anything with them, as they rushed out in the heat of the argument. I can't be the only one it's ever happened to.

"Not at all. Is there anything else you need?"

"Not that I can think of." Yeah, a less complicated life!

"The key's in the door. There's a TV, and there's tea making facilities up there too. You go on up, if you like. I'll be up in a minute with the towels and that."

"Thank you very much."

"Could I just ask you to sign in here, and your address? That would be lovely."

"Of course." I scribbled down the information required.

"It's the first door on your left, just up the stairs."

"Thanks again." I stumbled up the stairs in my eagerness for some private space to collapse into.

I immediately slumped on to the bed and just laid there, staring up at the white ceiling. I could see where they'd painted over previous cracks.

There was a slight knock on the door. I went to open it. He handed me the soft, peach coloured towels, a brush and a mini tube of Colgate.

"Thanks."

"No worries. Do ya need a wake up call in the morning?"

"Er, yes. Would seven be OK?"

"Absolutely. Sleep well then."

"G'night." And the door clicked closed behind him. I stood still in the new silence of the room. The wallpaper stared its pale red stripes back at me. I turned round, the room swivelled. A flowery duvet looked at me blankly. I sat down into the softness of the mattress. I reached for the remote control from the bedside cabinet. The TV blared into life, making me jump. I turned the volume down quickly, hoping I hadn't disturbed anyone. I flicked through the channels. Newsnight. A murder/detective film. An old black and white. A stand-up comedy show. Adverts. I switched it off again.

I wished I'd brought a book with me. Not usually something you bring on a date with your lover though. Not really something you'd be expecting to use, is it? I wished the silence would stay, but the longer I sat there, the harder it was to keep unbidden thoughts from entering my mind.

Daphne: Ted and Phillippa's daughter.

No, no, no. Silence. Nothingness. Blankness. Ted and Phillippa in bed together, naked, making love, kissing, groaning, blank, blank, blank, blank! Their bodies writhing together under the sheets.

But she knew. She'd always known how I'd felt about Ted. Why?

No, it couldn't have not meant something. Hang on, was that right? Double negative is a positive… Well, anyway, it *had* meant something. And I might *never* have known if weren't for Daphne. Kind of an obvious thing really. Hard to miss.

The envelope. I remembered it for the first time since I'd left the restaurant. I took it out of my pocket, then shrugged my coat off on to the floor. I sat there, holding the thin pieces of paper between my forefinger and thumb. I wonder when she wrote it. Why she hadn't sent it. It had my full postal address on, but no stamp. A letter not got round to posting. A letter beyond the grave. A letter from my best friend, who I'd loved... Still loved. But was furious as hell with at the moment. A letter from the traitor herself. I placed it on top of the cabinet as if it was a delicate butterfly whose wings I might damage.

I peeled my clothes off, as if I was an orange, leaving the rind on the floor in a pile. Naked, I climbed into bed, bringing the covers up to my chin.

So what had she to say for herself? Did I care? Did I really want to know?

I picked up the envelope again, holding it in front of my face.

Yes I cared. Yes, I wanted to know. But at the same time I didn't want to know. It might be worse knowing. It would be so easy to tear it up, and throw it away, and remain blissfully ignorant.

A few hours ago, I would've ripped it open, dying to know what my beloved Phillippa had once written to me. But now... I wanted to hurt her, like I was hurting now. And this was the only way of doing it, by ignoring her, turning my back on her written words, not accepting them into my mind. How could she have done this to me?

I wished I could read it without reading it. To read it and forget it as if it had never happened. That way I would know if she said anything I needed to know, and simultaneously banish from memory anything I wished not to have read.

It was useless procrastinating. I wanted to read it. Scared of what her words might say, I slowly opened it. I turned over on to my front, so I could lay it out on my pillow to read it. My eyes slid from one word to the next. Her words of months ago, possibly years.

My dearest Isabel
Hope this finds you well. This is a very hard letter to write. So I'm just going to say it.
You know how near and dear to me, in my heart you are always. I know you love Ted. And you two are so right for each other. I hope you will come together some day.
I have something to confess. I hope you will forgive me. You

218

know I would never want you to be unhappy, so I feel I must explain this to you, & I'm writing it down, because I don't know how else to break this to you.

There's no easy way to put this.

I never wanted to hurt you. I don't want this to stand in the way of anything you and Ted will one day have together. I'm rambling now.

Isabel, this is what I'm trying to tell you. Ted and me loved each other for one night only. And Daphne was born of it. I never told either of you, for all our sakes. It just would've messed everything up.

I don't regret anything.

It wasn't a one night stand. It wasn't a love affair. It wasn't a relationship, and it wasn't casual. If I could make you understand… it was something that was right for both of us on that one occasion.

Ted was still mourning Lily. And I took something from it that I'd never had before with anyone, or ever again.

It was important that it happened. It wasn't planned. And it was important NOT to tell you, just as its important you should now know…

I know you'll be angry hurt upset. But there was never going to be anything long term between us. Me and Ted are not compatible that way. I didn't want or need a relationship with anyone, especially not Ted.

We shared some sort of love that night, Isabel. Not as lovers, but as friends in need of something, Friends in need of each other in a different way.

It probably all sounds like excuses, and it's not meant to be that.

It was the first time for me, that night Isabel. You know what I mean. you know my life… so it was with Ted, and you're probably thinking why couldn't it have been anyone but him, and your probably cursing me for it. I've always known Ted, It was the one time I chose. I know this is something you wanted for me, but it could only have happened with Ted… otherwise it would never have happened at all. I know I'm not explaining this very well, but Ted is not mine, nor ever will be, and that's how it's supposed to be. we weren't tied to each other that night, or after.

219

We were free. But I grieved for my loss, Isabel. not the loss of Ted. But the loss of love. I don't want you to be trapped by that night, Isabel. By the hurt and pain you must feel. Don't let it suck you in and drain you.

But I found a new love too. Daphne. Her beauty shines from within. You would love her too I'm sure. I think she's going to have my dare-devilness with a dash of Ted's sensibility to keep her in check, so she dun't go off the rails like I did – ha, ha!

I'll probably not even send this, you may never read it. I'll tell you when the time is right, like when the two of you are married or something, then it won't matter as much... I believe in you two, you're what's helped keep me sane, even though we don't talk so much these days. and now I have Daphne too.

Stay well and be happy. thinking of you.

All my love, Phillippa. xxxx

And I cried. I cried for Phillippa, for what she'd lost and for what she'd found. I cried for myself, having lost Phillippa and Ted to each other. I cried for Daphne, having lost her Mum. I cried till I couldn't see the words anymore. Couldn't even make out the shape of my pillow. I cried myself to sleep, the letter still in my hand.

Chapter Forty-Two

I'd spent the last couple of days in a tumultuous sea of thoughts and feelings, and ignoring all of Ted's calls.

It was Friday evening and I'd finally found enough courage to give my sister a ring, after starting to dial her number then hanging up about ten times.

"Felicity?"

"That's me."

"It's me, Isabel."

"Hi Sis. What can I do you for?"

I looked at Bonny laid out in front of the fire and wished I could be as carefree as her.

"I just wondered how you were doing?" I lied. That wasn't the only reason. Not the main one.

"I'm doing just great."

"How's the preparation coming along for little David?"

"Getting there slowly, but surely. Ya can easily spend a small fortune on a newborn. I'd no idea how much stuff! But this receptionist job I've got pays quite decently, well more than many others, so bit by bit I'm makin' progress."

"Heard from Andrew?"

"No. The shit. Don't care anymore." But I knew that she did. That was just her way of dealing with it. So Andrew was not a topic to be discussed anymore. "How's you? Still miss Phillippa?" Her sensitivity surprised me. I didn't think she'd even remembered my telling her that, amidst all her own troubles.

"Yes, I still miss her." I sighed.

"Time heals ya know."

"Does it?" I doubted it very much, but wasn't going to start an argument about Felicity's little 'gems of advice'.

"Sure it does. How's Ted? Keepin' that twinkle in yer eye, I hope." I was glad she couldn't see me blush.

"Er, not so bad." A bloody mess actually. "Listen, why don't cha come up and stay a couple a days? I could do with the company."

"Uh-oh."

"What?"

"Has he left you?"

"No. Not really. It's complicated. Could you get time off, say a long weekend or something?" It was strange, but even though Felicity had only stayed a few days last month, I missed her. I really did. I surprised myself.

"I'll've to check. But I think I cud get this Friday and following Monday off. Will that do ya?"

"That would be great."

"Except…"

"What?"

"I can't really afford the train fare, and yer know I can't travel on coach without puking my guts up every two miles…"

"I'll transfer ya some funds over if you like, Felicity. It really isn't a problem. Would that be OK with you?"

"That be terrific. Are you sure you can spare it?" Isn't it funny? I never would've guessed, even a month ago that I could be having this conversation with my sister. The politeness, the friendliness! Unheard of!

"It's fine. I can cover it. If you gimme your account number, and I'll do it now."

"OK, and I'll call you back when I've got the train times, and let you know what time I'll be arriving. Are you sure you want to see me twice in the same year?"

I laughed. "Yes I'm sure. If you're sure?"

"Hey, I'm easy. OK, got pen and pad?"

"Shoot."

***

I'd taken to leaving the answering machine on all the time now, even if I was in. Ted kept ringing. I didn't know what to say to him anymore. Phillippa's letter had explained, sort of. And I sort of understood, but I was still hurt. But what really got to me the most was that Ted couldn't get to grips with why I was so upset

222

about it all. And I wasn't sure if I could explain it to him, or even if I wanted to.

I looked at my watch. Time to go pick Felicity up. I took Bonny with me in the car.

***

I cooked spaghetti bolognese for us both, but I couldn't eat mine. I wasn't eating a whole lot these days. Felicity had scoffed everything on her plate, and almost licked it clean! She teased me into trying to eat more, but my stomach churned at the very thought.

Felicity put her knife and fork neatly on the plate, side by side and pushed it away from her a little. "I get some great bargains from charity shops and jumble sales. There's loads a stuff goin'. So it's not been too bad. One shopkeeper was a bit pissy though, 'cause I bought somert in pink, though I'd told her it was for a boy! But it were in such good condition, and cheap at the price. Besides, David ain't gonna know if he's in pink, red, black or shit colour till he's quite a bit older. I don't see as it makes any difference either way."

"Shall we go through to the lounge?" We took up positions on the couch in front of the now roaring fire.

I couldn't quite believe the transformation I'd seen in Felicity. She was a new person to me.

"I totally agree. I think girls-pink, boys-blue is such a lot of crap. Do you remember when we were kids and Mum making us wear pink dresses? I hated pink."

"Me too." And there was a silent moment, where we just listened to the fire crackling, as we sat and thought of Mum.

We hadn't talked about her death at all. Or our childhood. Or Dad. Or anything. I was scared of broaching any of these subjects, should it upset our new fragile friendship. We skittered around the edges whenever we touched on any of the taboos. I suppose we were bound to face our ghosts at some point, but neither of us were quite ready yet.

"So, anyway, you don't want to listen to me rabbit on 'bout baby stuff for 72 hours…" She gave a self-deprecating laugh. And again, I was surprised at her sensitivity. Was this new? Or had it always been there, but I'd never noticed?

"I don't mind. Really. I think it's great I'm going to be an aunt." And I did. I loved the idea. I was very much looking forward to baby-sitting and holding young David in my arms. I had once upon a time looked forward to being a Mum too. But that wasn't to be... Well, there was Daphne, but... Dangerous ground again.

"Come on Isabel. Time to spill the beans." I looked at her, but no words came. "I've been here all of three hours now and not mentioned Ted once. You've no idea how much effort that's taken for someone as nosy as me. So c'mon. Where is he?"

"He's in Bristol."

"Back in his own flat?" I nodded. "How come?"

"He's with Daphne."

"Oh shit. Another woman." I laughed dryly. Felicity frowned her puzzlement.

"Not exactly. She's not more than four years old."

"Double shit. Child by another woman."

"You got it in one," I said ruefully.

"But, hang on, if the kid's a couple a years old, well, you guys have only been hanging together a few months, so what difference does that make?"

"The other woman is Phillippa," I managed to tell her in a level tone.

"Oh. But Ted and Phillippa? I don't get it." So I filled her in on the little I knew, and surmised what Phillippa had said in her letter to me. Even though she'd never sent it.

"So are you pissed at Phillippa then? Or Ted?"

"Both."

"Well, I can understand why ya'd be a bit put out by Phillippa. After all, she did know how you felt about him. But, Jesus, Isabel, she is dead. Ted isn't, and can't carry on owt with her anymore. And it was ages before you two got together. Other than the fact that they din't tell you about it – what is it about it that's got you so worked up?"

Although Felicity was blunt, at least she hadn't said I was stupid and had no reason for getting so upset. Still, I felt insecure about continuing to confide in her. Even though we'd not got on, and not been in touch with each other for ages, I knew that she knew things about me, about the two of us, our growing up together that no-one else did, and that gave us a common ground to work from. I hoped. Instead of divided ground, as it once used to be.

"I don't know if I can explain this properly,." I said unsure, wondering if it had all been a big mistake after all, inviting Felicity up. I really would be completely crushed if she thought me stupid and without reason as Ted so obviously did.

"Try me, Isabel."

"Do you remember when I was younger, and you were dating, and Phillippa was going out with guys, well at least till she was 15 anyway, and Ted went out with other lasses? But I never went out with anyone?"

"Yeah. I remember. I asked you if you were gay." I nodded. "You mean, you are gay?"

"No Felicity. I am not gay." I refrained from sighing. Life would've perhaps made more sense if I had been gay. "I just never felt *comfortable* round any guys. Except the ones I couldn't have!"

"Like Ted?"

"Well, I didn't fancy him then. It wasn't until much later that I realised I harboured any feelings other than friendship for Ted." I paused. "This sounds so stupid."

"C'mon Iz. I'm not gonna laugh."

"But it is stupid. And you won't understand." The crackling fire filled the silence. I didn't know how to continue. Felicity didn't seem to know what to say either. I searched for the words, but they didn't come. The image of Phillippa in bed with Brian, her silent pleading eyes, and I'd thought she'd just had a mysterious boyfriend that she'd kept a secret. I hadn't known. Not understood.

Felicity interrupted my thoughts. "Well, it's obviously something big. Big serious. C'mon Sis, you can trust me. I can handle big stuff now. I'm a big girl now, ya know." I smiled, and she smiled back and our new intimacy drawn from the experience of nearly losing my only sister to AIDS, glimmered in our eyes, and I felt a new confidence to continue my explanation.

"Phillippa was raped when she was 15. Several times." I felt

225

sick just saying it. Felicity remained silent, watching me, her face listening. "It terrified me, Felicity. I somehow got it into my head that all men were like that. I dunno why or how. Stupid I know, but... Well, I just thought that it could happen to me too. Anytime. Anywhere. By anyone with a penis. And I didn't think I could live through it, if it did happen. I'd have killed myself. I'd rather be murdered than raped. I really didn't know how Phillippa survived. But she did. She survived so much. But I couldn't cope with it, if it had happened to me. I'd have... given up."

"I'd no idea..." Felicity began, but didn't finish. Tears crept down my cheeks. My sister moved closer to me on the sofa. She pulled me back into her arms, and I felt her warmth, her reassurance. I felt a security I'd never felt in childhood. Why hadn't Dad stayed around? Had it been all my fault? Why hadn't Mum loved me like she had Felicity? I cried, and she held me, stroked my hair down my face. I felt loved and cared for. I wish the child of me had known/felt this.

We stayed like that for some time. Fire crackle and wind howl were the only other sounds outside of my heart beat, Felicity's heart beat, and her fingers combing through my hair.

"What does this have to do with Ted though? I'm not sure I understand," she said kindly.

"Sex was such a taboo for me. Phillippa's pain impacted on my perception of men, and the threat they posed. Like, any man could get it if he wanted it. It was very difficult for me to match up sex with love, even though I could never have one without the other. Anyway, you know I had this idea of Mr Perfect, right? Who would love me, and no-one else forever? Well, I could never imagine myself sleeping with anyone but him. I could never see me sharing my body with more than one man, ever. And Ted's my Mr Perfect right? Well I could just about handle the fact that Ted had slept with Lily. After all, he had thought she was his one and only, but then to discover that he and Phillippa... for that one night... what they'd shared... I feel so jealous of Phillippa, that she knew him in that way, that he knew *her* in that way... I just wanted that intimacy to be all mine, not belong to anyone else, for me not to feel..." I started crying again. "Am I making any sense here?"

"Yes, I think so."

"I just feel so betrayed. Even though I know I wasn't. Ted had no commitments to me then. And Phillippa... I just can't get my feelings to act logically."

"Who can?" I gave a small laugh through my tears.

"Do you think I'm mad?"

"Absolutely fucking starkers! But I won't hold that against you, Izzy dear, 'cause you always were mad anyway." I laughed again. I looked up into my sister's loving face.

"What am I going to do now?"

"Well, you've got a choice Isabel." Hadn't I heard those words somewhere before? "You can either forgive Phillippa and Ted their one night of comfort they found together, and go and tell Ted ya damn well love 'im, and want 'im back, little girl an' all. Or you bear your grudge for all eternity, and be a very pure but sorry saint, living a fucking lonely life."

"You don't make it sound like much of a choice at all, Felicity. It sounds more like anyone would be mad to choose the latter!" I protested.

"Good. That was how it were meant to sound!" She grinned back.

"I think you and Phillippa would've got on really well together in a different time and place."

"Maybe. I doubt it."

"Put like that, it does begin to make more sense to me."

"You're beginning to see sense girl."

"And you're starting to sound like an older sister," I teased back, affectionately.

But Felicity didn't smile when she said, "Well I think it's about bloody time I did too. Don't you?" It was reproof of herself, not me. I was quite taken aback.

"What's up Felicity? What are you thinking?"

"Just stuff. Us as kids. Mum. Dad leaving..."

"*Was* it my fault Dad left?"

"No. Don't be silly. Whatever gave you that idea?"

"You did."

"Oh."

"Felicity?" She moved away from me slightly, and stared into the dancing reds, yellows and blues in the grate.

"I'm sorry. That wasn't true."

"What is true then?"

"I don't really know for sure what went wrong between Mum and Dad. Lots of things. Money, well, lack of. Going from one job to another, not being able to find owt steady. Another woman. Dad had an affair. Two in fact, that I know of, anyway. He said he wanted to be with someone who was happy, not bloody miserable all time. But I think Mum was depressed. She thought being pregnant with you would make things good again. It did for a little while, but it didn't last. After a time, things just got worse. That weren't your fault. It was just that they couldn't really afford another child, and Mum and Dad, well, they were so hung up on criticising each other, and arguing all time, instead of lovin' each other and us, well… Mum kicked him out when she found out about the second affair. And that was that."

"Did Mum blame me?"

"No, not at all. I think she just got very bitter after that. She just seemed to shrink into hersen' and not really wanna talk to anyone." I thought back over my memories of Mum. She'd never talked about Dad. Never. Only to say a piece of dog turd was worth more than him. I don't remember her being happy. Usually, she'd been quite distant.

"Did *you* blame me?"

"I guess I did sometimes. But I shun't a done really. You weren't to know. weren't your fault Mum and Dad couldn't get it together. You were such an innocent. You still are." She ruffled my hair as if I was still a kid.

"I always thought Mum loved you more than me."

"What tosh! She admired you, Izzy. You did what neither me nor her did; got to college, got a career. She was dead proud."

"Why didn't she ever show it then?"

"I think she were scared of you."

"Scared? Of me?"

"She din't know how to relate to ya. Probably felt a bit dim in comparison to your brains. I know I did sometimes." This was all news to me! "She thought you'd got it all from Dad – crafty bugger she used to call him. I think seein' him in you put her off. Put her on her guard somehow. Not your fault, just Mum being

228

weird."

"I wish I'd known."

"Don't beat yourself up about it, Iz. It's not worth it. There's nothin' ya coulda done anyway."

"I feel really guilty now. That I wasn't nicer to her, that I didn't spend more time with her before she died."

"Jesus, Isabel! Ya'd feel guilty for killing the neighbour's cat, even if it were them that had run over it, and you'd been living in Italy at the time. Give it up. It's not good for ya!"

"Yes doctor." We both laughed. I put my arm round her, and she took hold of my other hand in my lap. "Thanks Felicity. You're just what I needed."

"Glad to be of assistance," she squeezed my hand, "sister dear."

"Do ya fancy a game of scrabble or something?"

"Yeah, OK. No doubt you'll whip my arse though. I'm not so good at word games."

"You'll enjoy it. I'll go easy on you, promise," I laughed.

"OK, so long as you promise to do something first."

"What's that then?"

"Phone Ted." I looked at her. "C'mon Isabel, put the poor guy out of 'is misery. He's so obviously head over heels for ya. Ya need to put yoursen' out of your misery too." I hesitated. "Do it now and get it over with."

"What am I going to say?"

"Tell 'im how you feel, you twit. Get together. Talk it all over. Go on. And then I'll dig the scrabble out for ya. Otherwise I'm just gonna sit 'ere and stare at ya till ya do it."

"OK, OK, you win." I laughed, nervous as I was.

"No, *you* win. And Ted wins. Get on with it."

"I'm a getting, I'm a getting." She watched me go over to the phone and dial his number. She waited with me while it rung. She heard me respond to Ted's salutation. Then she came over, squeezed my shoulder, gave me a wink and a smile, then disappeared upstairs.

My throat went dry and I felt slightly sick.

"Isabel, are you there?"

"Yes, I'm here."

"I didn't know if you were ever going to talk to me again."

"Neither did I."

"I'm sorry Isabel."

"What are you sorry for?"

"I'm sorry that what happened between me and Phillippa hurt you. I didn't know, never realised…"

"I know, but it did."

"Can I ask forgiveness?"

"Yes."

"And will you forgive me?"

"I'd like to."

"I feel like I betrayed your trust somehow Isabel, but I'm not sure I understand how. Is it because we never told you about it?"

"Partly. But also because…"

"Because what?" he prompted gently.

"Because I've loved you for so long. And because Phillippa knew that."

"Are you angry with her too?"

"Yes. I have to say that I am."

"I don't think she meant to hurt you either. It's hard to explain Isabel, but that night… we both needed someone."

"And so you just happened to be together at the time when you both needed it?" I couldn't help but sound a little scathing.

"Did Phillippa's letter help explain things for you?"

"I can understand Phillippa's feeling the need to be loved, and that it was important she'd found that she could trust you as a man, as a lover…" I stopped, breathed, continued. "But why did *you*… And do you still feel… something for Phillippa in that way?"

"Not in that way, no. Not for a long time now. It's strange, but we were both our own persons. I accepted that night as it stood – alone. I never really wanted to be tied into a relationship with Phillippa. It was complete in and of itself. I didn't need or want anything more from Phillippa. I did want to be intimate with a loving partner, but it wasn't going to be Phillippa."

"But why did you…?" I couldn't say the words to describe what they'd done, they stuck in my chest.

"I never really told you much about the effect Lily had on me – our divorce I mean, and her consequent remarriage and

230

child with Steve. It tore me up and broke me down in more ways than I thought possible, more than I could initially comprehend. And my confidence was totally shot. You might think it silly, but I worried if I'd be single all my life, as everything I had to offer Lily wasn't enough. Wasn't enough to keep the relationship, the marriage going. Phillippa made me realise that I was not forever to be categorised as a 'failed marriage man'. Just because I couldn't make Lily happy, didn't mean that I could never find happiness with any other woman ever. Phillippa ended the generalisation of my pain, made it specific. She gave me hope again. I saw things in a different light – a wider perspective. One failed marriage started to mean something different than Ted is a failed person. And that was a revelation to me."

"Couldn't I have given you that?"

"That's a tough question, Isabel."

"You mean no." I challenged him. My hands shook as I said it.

"What I mean is… because it was Phillippa, and because it was one night, no relationship ensued, then I was free to take from it, to discover something new about myself without falling into old patterns of behaviour. I'm probably not explaining this very well, but I came away from that night with Phillippa with new knowledge of myself that helped enable me to enter a relationship later down the line as a healthier person… Is this making any sense?"

Tears coursed silently down my face. "Yes, it's making sense."

I couldn't have given Ted what Phillippa did. Not because of any possibility of Ted's having any deeper feelings for Phillippa than for me. Not because Phillippa may have been a better lover, been so special to Ted. But because I could never have needed Ted in the same way as she did which helped him find his self esteem again. And I could never have only slept with Ted for one night and then been able to let him go, which was the trigger that enabled him to be free.

"Isabel?"

"Yes, I'm here."

"Are you OK?"

"I've felt better. But I've also felt worse." My jealousy had abated considerably. But I felt a shock wave of loss wash through me. Not *my* loss. But the loss I sensed Ted had felt in losing Lily. And the devastating loss that Phillippa had experienced was suddenly coming home to me. I'd never consciously acknowledged it before. Phillippa had always scorned needing a man in her life, and perhaps that's not so surprising. But how much of that was due to her own need for independence, and how much due to what Brian had done? I pulled a tissue from my jeans pocket and wiped my face dry and blew my nose.

"So what happens now?" I asked, unsure how to proceed with the conversation.

"That rather depends on you."

"What do *you* want to happen?" I needed to hear it.

"Isabel, you know what I want to happen." And I did, it was all there in the quiet intensity of his voice. "But is it what *you* want?"

"Yes it is, Ted," I said without hesitation. "I do want to be with you. And Daphne."

"*Are* you OK with Daphne?"

"Well, I think it'll take time to adjust, but I would like to give it a try. She deserves a loving home."

"I love you Isabel. I love you so very much."

"I love you too Ted." I blew my nose again. "When would be a good time for you to come up?"

"There's still a lot to organise and finish up. So it'll be a couple of months before we can move in, assuming you still want to do that?"

"Yes, of course." More than anything I wanted Ted to wake up to every morning. I wasn't so sure about Daphne. But I guess doubts are natural.

"But I can come up to see you this weekend if you like?"

"I'd like very much." The heat of love and relief beat through my body, and my stomach rumbled happily as if to say, 'Now all that's sorted out, I feel like food again now'. "What time shall I expect you?"

Chapter Forty-Three

I'd counted down the hours to the following weekend, and now he was here. I picked him up from the train station in Vivien, my trusty Volvo. We went into the nearest town for dinner, I'd been too full of nervous energy to cook anything. He'd left Daphne with Ben and Gail for the weekend, so we could have some time alone just to concentrate on the two of us, which I was really thankful for.

Dinner was full of nervous energy too.

We got back to my place about ten. We sat in the lounge, and after I'd set the wood on the fire and made us coffees, I curled up in my chair, and Ted sat in the middle of the sofa. There was still an emotional space between us, and we were both trying hard to please the other. God, it was like a first date!

"Do you still have doubts, Isabel?"

"There's some stuff going on in my head."

"Tell me," he invited me in that gentle way of his.

I could feel my pulse quicken as I haltingly told him all I was thinking, well not *everything*. "I feel like... she stole you from me." Your body. "Your affections." The intimate knowledge of you. "She knew you before I did. And was able to give birth to a child that I never can. I feel cheated somehow." And you *knew* her. "How can I compete with that?" How can you love me now that you've known Phillippa? "I don't want to be compared with Phillippa." Do you compare our bodies? – the way we act in bed? – the way we kiss? I can't bear the thought of that. I'm possessive Ted. "I want you all for my own." My very own with no-one else's heat on your lips, no other woman's taste in your heart. I can't stand the thought of it. She's broken in and torn my ownership apart, my claim to your soul. It's now sullied. Second best. Second hand. "I guess what I'm trying to say is I don't want to be second best in any way." No longer first, top

233

priority. No longer the only, but one of many – devalued. And how can I compare with Phillippa and her expertise, after so many many men? I can't. You'll think me silly, unknowing, naive, not want to know. But I know. I know my own body, I can teach you. If you'll let me.

"I love you for you. Why can't you understand? I don't compare the two of you. You're both very different. Of course you are. With different wants and needs. Different feelings. Different sorts of love. Different time frames, different sorts of commitment. I was a different person then. I was a different person with her. I can't say what happened with Phillippa meant nothing. It meant I was no longer criticised, no longer forced to adhere to this higher standard I could never reach. I was no longer required to be all fire all the time, but that tenderness and softness and even weakness was acceptable to Phillippa, that I could love in my own way, a different way than I'd loved Lily. I gave to Phillippa the love that she craved that night. And it was enough. I learned to trust in giving again.

"And from that I now have the courage to love *you* in the only way I can. In Ted's way. In my own way. And to find a woman who needs the sort of love that I can give, to find that our two definitions match, are compatible, fit into each other, like pieces of a jigsaw. And I feel we both belong to the same jigsaw.

"With Lily, I hadn't even come from the same jigsaw shop, never mind the same box. We didn't speak each other's language. We tried to learn each other's, and we learned a few words here and there, but fluency didn't come naturally, and the harder we tried, the worse it got.

"But you're you Isabel, and you're all I want."

My stomach flip-flopped at his words, but I had to ask, "Would it have made any difference to what happened if you had known my feelings for you?"

"Yes, it would have made a difference." He said firmly. I wanted to believe him. "Phillippa hasn't stolen me from you Isabel." Ted was earnest in his need to convince me. "I was never hers. She never took me. She just gave me back to myself. I can't do this if *you're* going to be comparing yourself to Phillippa all the time in your own head. I'm not. There's no such thing. No competition, nothing *to* compete. You're both very different parts of my life, and just because I spent that one night with Phillippa does *not* mean that I could never truly love you. Because I already do, and you already are. You may have both touched the same body, but you do *not* hold the same knowledge." He'd read my mind. "I love you Isabel. You're a part of me, of who I am, I can't imagine existing without you in my life. Phillippa never knew that side of me, and never could. I'm giving you parts of myself that I never gave to Lily. That I've never given to Phillippa. Only to you Isabel, because you love all of me, the way I am. I don't need to play any games, or play any roles with you. And I'm offering you my everything for you to take to make you happy. When you shun me, it hurts."

"I'm sorry Ted. I…"

"Only *you* can convince *you* Isabel. I can't think of any other way that I can."

I pause before saying, "And Daphne?"

"We'll bring her up together, as her parents, her guardians, whatever she'll accept us as. She's still getting used to the new word 'Daddy'. And of course, she knows Phillippa as 'Mummy'. And she's scared and confused and upset, because her one big person world has collapsed, disappeared, and we're both strangers to her. But she needs us Isabel. She needs love to get her through this. She needs someone to rely on and depend on and help her through the loss of her Mum. The rock of her life. I want to do that Isabel. More than anything. I've always wanted a family and I find I have one already, and I damn well want to make the most of it. I'll go it alone if I have to, but I'd rather have my wife with me."

My stomach turned a series of somersaults. "Your wife?"

"I mean, I meant you… I'd rather have you with me." He said befuddled.

"As your wife?"

"Yes, I would like to have you with me as my wife." His eyes connected with mine, trying to glean my response.

"I would too."

Chapter Forty-Four

It was a nervously exciting, anticipatory couple of months, the wait for Ted and Daphne to join me in my place – our place. I felt like I was getting to know Ted all over again from scratch. And there was a lot to find out.

He sold his flat in Bristol, and tied up his business affairs down there. And I started thinking about how safe/dangerous was my home for a three year old to wonder about in. There was a lot to organise and prepare.

Felicity was over the moon when I told her about us getting married. We stayed in pretty regular contact these days. And she was preparing too. For her little one. I was going to be a 'mother' and 'aunty'. And live with the man that I loved. I felt happier than I had in a very long time.

Getting to know Daphne was sometimes a joy, sometimes very nerve racking. She's a very boisterous and adventurous child, very friendly and open though.

But it was hard knowing what to say sometimes. Like the early nights, soon after the two of them had moved in, when she'd wake in the middle of the night asking for her Mum. Where had Phillippa gone? Why wasn't she coming back? Did Mummy still love her? Could people die of nose bleeds? When would she see her again? How would she die? When would me and Ted die? What was heaven? How come she still felt Mummy with her sometimes?

She was as open in her grief as she was with everything else, which I found quite hard to deal with at first. Daphne provoked outbursts of grief from both Ted and myself, when otherwise I would've grieved alone, in private. I guess it helped really, felt better for it afterwards, but it was scary at first.

But Daphne would put her small hand in mine and Ted's when she saw either of us cry and say, 'It's OK to be sad about it.

It is very sad." She made us laugh through our tears, our little adult-child.

It was a big time of change and adjustment for all three of us.

And there was also the wedding to plan. It was going to be a small affair, just immediate family and friends. And Daphne was going to be bridesmaid, which she was thrilled about. She wanted us to wed on her 4th birthday, but we didn't want to steal her limelight So we agreed a date in the spring – May 6th.

And thankfully Daphne was settling in just fine in the local infants school. She was highly intelligent and so into everything. She just soaked up new information like a sponge and wanted to bounce on to the next thing.

Chapter Forty-Five

"Right, now this afternoon I want you all to pick one thing you'll be doing this weekend or one place you'll be going to, and draw me a picture of it. Now hands up if you know what you'll be doing tomorrow or Sunday."

"Miss I'll be going to the park with Mum and Dad and play on the swings and slides with Divvy my best friend and Samuel my cousin and my aunty'll be there too and Samuel's sister Diane who always cries when you call her dirty die."

"And how will you draw that then Claire?"

"I'll draw the park Miss and us all playing and going high on swing and jumping off and wizzying round and round about until we puke."

"That's very good Claire. What about you Daphne? What will you be doing this weekend? Or will you be going anywhere special that you could draw us a nice picture of?"

"I'm going to a wedding, Miss."

"That's exciting. Who's getting married?"

"My Dad and Bella."

"OK then."

"And I'm going to be bridesmaid."

"And what are you going to wear?"

"A pretty blue dress with lace round the ends."

"Well, you'll be able to draw us a very colourful picture of that, won't you? I look forward to seeing it."

"Why do you call your Mum Bella?" Sandra who sat next to me asked me.

"She's not my Mum Mum, but sort of a second Mum. She's called Isabel, but that's too long, so I call her Bel or Bella 'cause Daddy says that's Italian for bootyfull. Sometimes he calls her trés Bella to me, 'cause that's French for very and he doesn't know what that word is in Italian. He's silly sometimes."

"It's silly not calling her Mum." I didn't like her saying that. I didn't talk to her for the rest of the afternoon. I shared my colouring cranes with Neil instead who sat next to me too. Sandra called me stuck up, and I called her trés uglifia.

**

I've not been to a marrying before. I was happy in my blue dress with lace at the ends of it. Daddy was smiling and laughing and Bel was very Bella. Aunt Felly came. And so did Daddy's Mummy. Bel hasn't got a Mummy or Daddy. I felt sad for her. Uncle Ben and Aunty Gail came too. He gave me a big hug. His jacket felt smooth on my cheek and he wore after-shaving lotion which I could taste when I kissed him. Aunty Gail was carrying cousin David in her arms. She said I was that small once. I said that's not true, I'm always the same bigness. I would've remembered having no hair on my head and not having anything to brush in the morning and last thing at night. I've never had no hair I told her.

"He hasn't got no hair, Daphne, it's just very fine. He'd a lot less hair when he was first born." I pulled a face then and she laughed. Or she tinkled. Aunty Gail was very tinkly. She kissed me on both cheeks and said I would have lots more hair when I got bigger. I said I'm not getting bigger, I'm the same.

Bel was wearing blue too. She said it was Sky Blue, which is light blue. I said I must be wearing Skier Blue then, as my blue dress was lighter than hers.

There were lots of cake and chatter and everyone smiled at me and there was lots of flowers and Daddy was in blue too. Bel said it was Navee Blue.

"Daddy, did you marry Mummy?" I asked him.

"No sweetheart."

"Why do people marry?"

"Because they love each other."

"Didn't you and Mummy love each other Daddy?"

"It was a different sort of love."

"What sort of love?"

"There are all sorts of love, Daphne, and we don't know what they are till we feel them."

"Do you and Bel love each other in a marrying way then?"

"Yes, we do."

"I wish Mummy was here now."

"I do too sweetheart. She would have been very happy to see me and Isabel together at last."

"I think she is here Daddy. I think she's watching."

"Well if she is, I know she's smiling."

"Do you think she's wearing blue too?"

"I think she would be wearing deep red."

"Why?"

"Because she liked to be bold in her feelings."

"What does bold mean?"

"It means your Mum was bold enough, daring enough and brave enough to do something as wild as rock climbing, whereas Isabel is more cautious, and would prefer to watch your Mum climbing than do it herself."

"So blue is corshus then?"

"Sort of."

"I'd go climb rocks. Why aren't I wearing red then?"

"Cause that wouldn't match Isabel's dress." Then the camera man clicked up to us.

"How about a special photo of groom and daughter? Just there. That's great. Smile now. That's great." We smiled into the clicks. I could see my Mummy stood behind him. But she wasn't wearing red like Daddy said she would be. She was in a blue jacket and blue trousers and black top. Darker blue than mine and Bel's, but not as dark as Daddy's. I smiled at Mummy and she smiled back. I knew she was here. Then Bel came over to us then, and clicky man clicked us three together. I looked again for Mummy but couldn't see her. Clicky man then clicked me and Bel together just us two. Daddy went to get more cake. And Bel called him a greedy guts.

"Daddy said Mummy be wearing red today."

Bel looked at me and said, "Yes, I suppose she would be."

"But she's not. She's wearing blue too." And I told her the sort of blue she was wearing. Bel said it was called royal. Royal Mummy. Then Bel raced me over to the cake, she said we had to stop Daddy eating it all.

***

"How are you feeling?" Isabel asked as she lay with her face on my chest. I could feel her warm nakedness breathing next to mine. I could smell the subtle scent of her lightly fragranced perfume delicately lacing the air I inhaled...

I sighed contentedly. We'd finally managed to get Daphne to settle down for the night in her own bed. She'd been quite hyperactive after the wedding, quite the 'restless wanderer' as my mother would've said. She'd also say she knew where her granddaughter got it from!

"I feel very cosy, lying here with my new wife." She gave me a slight squeeze with her body, which made me think of all the delicious things I'd like to do to her.

"And how is Mrs Hawkins?"

"She's very happy thank you."

"That's what I like to hear..." I snuggled down deeper into the bed, and bent to taste her kiss again, to feel her kiss all over...

***

We laid joined together for a while after, feeling each other's heavy pulsating warmth.

"Would you like something to drink?" I asked, suddenly feeling very thirsty.

"So long as it's not more champagne!" I laughed.

"Hot chocolate?"

"Sounds good." I donned a dressing gown and went to make some. I peeped in on Daphne on the way; sleeping soundly.

"Here we go then," I put Isabel's on the bedside cabinet, and went to sit in bed beside my wife.

Married a second time. Yet the word wife meant something quite different to me now. With Lily, I remember the wedding and the immediate nights after being very frantic and anxiety ridden and exciting. With Isabel it's dreamlike, comfortable, intimate. No racing round madly, no competitiveness, no danger.

Just us. As we are.

241

"Have you thought about adopting Daphne?" I asked.

"Yes and no. I've thought of it, yes, but is it too soon?"

"How do you mean?"

"For Daphne, I mean."

"Oh right. I don't know."

"I think we should give her more time to get used to us, and to me. And then ask her how she feels about it."

"OK, we'll do that. I'm sure Daphne would be happy with it though. You two get on very well."

"Yes, but it's still too soon I feel, after Phillippa's death."

"I'm sure Daphne would let us know if she didn't like you!"

Isabel laughed. I watched the corners of her mouth rise, her white teeth show through. I watched her laugh lines crease at the sides of her green eyes. I gently picked out a silk pink petal from her hair, that had clung on long after she'd put the bouquet down.

"Yes, I'm sure she would."

"There you go you see. And no complaints in that department." I reached for Isabel, pulling the small of her back towards me, so I could feel her skin all along mine and hold her to me. "And no complaints in any other department either."

"I should jolly well hope not!" Isabel relaxed into my embrace and I smiled at the thought of being like this in many future nights to come.

Chapter Forty-Six

The months passed and we easily settled into a routine. Sunday again. Housework day. Again. Oh, well, I guess it had to be done at some point. Ted was cleaning and hoovering downstairs with the help/hindrance of Daphne, and I'd taken the upstairs with the help/hindrance of Bonny.

Our bedroom first, put all the clean clothes away and sort out the dirty ones. Fab job!

Felicity had been astonished that Ted and I didn't have a romantic honeymoon away together the week after the wedding. We had a family holiday instead, we couldn't leave Daphne. She'd offered to have Daphne with her, and even suggested we could have left her with Ben and Gail for the week. But Felicity's into the late stages of pregnancy, and David's a handful on his own. Besides, a week's a long time for Daphne to be separated from us, and I didn't like to upset her new found building blocks of familiarity and security.

So it was off in the car, with the tent, down to the south coast for a very sunny week of fun and frolicking. It had been great. Lots of sandcastles, burying Daddy in the sand, sand in the hair, sand in our sandwiches and in our socks (are these socks mine or Ted's?) and underwear, lots of swimming/paddling, kite flying and ball playing with Bonny. Daphne has fallen in love with Bonny big time.

I think that's helped this transition period for her a lot, having a big bouncy, furry, friendly animal to cuddle, talk to, play ball with and order about. She loves ordering Bonny about. Ordered to sit, to beg, to roll over and play dead. Though Bonny isn't very good at the latter, she just looks at Daphne intelligently with her head cocked on one side, panting, as if to say, 'I think you're great Daphne, but you want me to do what?'

(How does all this washing manage to pile up so much in a

week?) Daphne was very protective of Bonny when she cut her paw on something and limped for the rest of the day. Personally I think she did it for effect, just to get the sympathy vote, but Daphne made a fuss of her anyway.

Bonny's protective of her too and actually barks if a stranger comes up to her. I felt slightly jealous about that! Bonny never barks whenever strangers approach me! Obviously I'm not young and bouncy enough to warrant protection! Charming! Ted said he'd bark when strangers approach me if that would make me feel better! I said he could sleep in the kennel if he was going to start picking up strange bad habits!

Yes, Bonny just laps up all the attention from Daphne. She's like a dog with two tails!

(Right, now for Daphne's room. What a tip! "Bonny – stop getting under my feet!") And Daphne didn't have any nightmares at all on the camping trip.

But she's started having them again, now we're back home. Not as regularly as before though. Only once or twice a week now, instead of every night where she'll come and seek solace between our sheets, and one of us will get up and make her some 'special drinking chocolate' and sit with her, read to her or talk with her till she falls asleep.

I think we've shown Daphne all the photos that we have of Phillippa now. Photos from childhood, and also from the camping trip in Scotland. She enjoyed looking through them. I don't think she believed us at first though, that her Mum had ever been a child, or that any of us had. She says you're either born an adult or born a child. And she was born a child, and we were born as adults, so there you go! She loved hearing our tales of all the things we got up to, the three of us. (This bed needs remaking!) I noticed the other day a photo missing from one of the albums. The one of Phillippa making a funny face at the camera, on the last night of our trip, and she's pretending to have a wrestling match with a great pink teddy bear that she'd won at the fair that afternoon. Phillippa was declaring that Pink Ted had been trying to steal her sleeping bag. I'm laughing in the background, though I'm a little out of focus.

And here it is. The very one, just fallen out of her pillow case…⟩

I stare at the photo and want to laugh and cry. Kiss it, and rip it to shreds. I want to burn it and give it a special frame and hang it on the wall. I want to crumple it up and stamp up and down on it then throw it in the dust bin. I want to erase that beautiful smiling face, and replace it with mine.

I want to reach out and feel Phillippa's arm through mine, and hear our shared laughter at a shared joke. I want to grab the laughing woman in the photo and shake her and scream why.

Insecurity suddenly clouds in and shrouds me in its clingy cloak of ink. Fingers of doubt scrape their way down my inner-emptiness. Phillippa was Daphne's Mum and always would be. I didn't want to replace Phillippa in Daphne's heart, but I wanted... Daphne's love. And damn it! – I missed Phillippa too, why did she have to die?

I shake the pillow case viciously, and another two photos fall out, face down. They have writing on the back. One says 'Daddy'. I turn it over and I see Ted's laughing face as he tells Ben some humorous story at the wedding reception.

I turn to the other photo. It says 'my 2 Mummys'. I catch my breath, and I feel my eyes well up. I turn it over. It's me, in my wedding dress, long silk, sky blue. And stood at my side, at my left elbow is... but that's not possible!

I see a half transparent figure, royal blue trouser suit, black silk blouse, long black hair, galaxy chocolate eyes... It's just not possible! What was it that Daphne had said...? That Phillippa wasn't wearing red like we presumed she would have. Darker than Ted but lighter than me. What sort of blue is that? How did she know? How did this happen? This photo didn't used to look like this I swear. I blinked, and looked away at Daphne's normal room, and back at the photo, but the same mischievous grin was gazing up at me. I sat down heavily on Daphne's bed, feeling kind of strange.

"Isabel? Isabel? Oh there you are. I've been calling you, didn't you hear? Are you OK? You look pale."

"No sorry, I didn't hear you." I said not looking up.

"What's that you've got there?" Ted took the photo from my limp fingers before I could say anything.

"And you said you didn't think she cared. Yet here she keeps a photo of you close by her, and look at the back... that's

245

so lovely!"

What was he talking about! Couldn't he see the mysterious figure next to his bride in the photo?

He hands me back the photo. I looked at it. There was only me there. No ghostly figure. No Phillippa. Just me and the solid clear background of a long table with a white tablecloth with food on it.

"But..." I turned it over to reread Daphne's childish handwriting. 'my 2nd Mummy' it now read. I could've sworn it hadn't said that a few seconds ago.

"Isabel? Darling?" He sat on the bed beside me, his arm falling into place round my shoulder. He felt real. "Is something wrong?"

I looked into the depths of his blue eyes, reading his concern there and his love for me. I recalled the words he'd just said to me, that Daphne cared about me, and how lovely that was. My shock allowed me to absorb the feelings of these words slowly. A warm feeling began to spread through me.

"Yes, it is lovely, isn't it. I guess she does care." Ted kissed my lips gently.

"How could she possibly not?"

I ask Daphne later. Just out of curiosity. "What colour was your Mummy wearing at the wedding?"

"Royal Mummy. Royal Blue."

"What colour was her top, Daphne?"

"Her top? Er, she wore a black top. All shiny." I can't have imagined it, as Daphne didn't mention the blouse at all, and certainly not the colour of it, before now. Are we both seeing ghosts?

Chapter Forty-Seven

It wasn't until my daughter turned eight that the adoption finally came through. But more importantly Isabel felt happier in her role as mother, not because of the adoption though, but because Daphne had decided to call Isabel by the name of 'mum' on an everyday basis.

I remember the startled joy on Isabel's face when she first said it.

Daphne was just playing with her Lego on the rug in front of the fire, I was listening to the radio, Classic FM, and Isabel was writing an article for the magazine, when Daphne, without looking up, suddenly said to the world and all and sundry, "Bella, I'm going to call you Mum 'cause now I know you better it seems too formal to call you Bel anymore." I almost laughed out loud.

'Formal' was Daphne's 'grown-up word' of the week.

I held myself in check, as Daphne had said it with such a studious face. Isabel's mouth was agape in surprise and her eyes lit up with emotion. Daphne then suddenly got up and ran over to Isabel and put her head in her lap and said, "is that OK mum?" Isabel found voice enough to answer definitively in the affirmative. In retrospect, I wonder if she was asking Isabel that question, or Phillippa. But I'm sure Phillippa wouldn't have minded.

Daphne seems very happy though, and comfortable in her new use of the word, and Isabel feels like a more complete 'mum' now and not Bella anymore – though she's still as beautiful as ever.

Chapter Forty-Eight

I hadn't had the nightmare for a long long time. But I had it again last night, which was Mummy's sixth death anniversary, the very last day of July.

Mummy was there in the museum with Dad, and I was lost, wondering round trying to find them. And I did, but they hadn't even noticed I was not with them anymore, and every door was made of glass, but I tried to open it so I could get to Mum and Dad, it wouldn't open, and they couldn't hear me yell at them, or hear me bang on the door. Then Mummy turned into Isabel, and I went up to her, but she gave me a look and then she was holding hands with Dad and a little boy, my age. Dad put him on his shoulders and swung him up to the lowest bough of a tree, the relics in the museum now standing in a green field. I kept asking Isabel who he was, as Dad was still ignoring me, but she kept shaking her head and laughing. So I went up to the little boy, I chased him up this really tall tree, right to the very top, it went on and on and on up and up. He smiled at me cheekily, and I walked up to him, easily balancing myself on a thin bough, not thinking at all of the long distance to the ground should I fall. And I pushed him. He fell. Silently. In a draft of wind. And I heard Mummy scream. I don't know how I know that it was her scream and not Isabel's, but I just knew, even though I couldn't see anyone else down below, just his body falling, falling. His face crying, but he remained soundless in the wind. And then the long note of Mummy's wailing scream.

And then I'd wake up.

Chapter Forty-Nine

Yes, it was a scream. No, more of a yell. Coming from Dominic's room. And another one.

My right hand automatically found the switch on my bedside light. I jumped out of bed, and raced down the hall to Dom's room. I went straight through the open door. Samantha was already there, at his side, trying to wake him up.

I grabbed a glass of water from his bedside table and threw it over his face.

He woke up, coughing and spluttering.

"It's OK Dominic. It's all right. Just Sheila trying to drown you," but she grinned at me as she hugged Dominic to her. I passed her the box of tissues from his dressing table, and she took a few and wiped his face.

I sat on the other side of his bed, creasing up Spiderman's face in the duvet.

"Was it the same dream again, Dom?" I ask. He nods.

"Do you want some hot cocoa or something, Dominic? I'll get Sheila to bring some up."

"What am I? Your slave or something?" I demanded.

"OK, you sit with Dominic. I'll get him a drink." Mum and Dad had gone out for the evening, so Samantha was 'in charge'. She hadn't kicked up a fuss like she usually did. Normally she wanted to be out on a date with 'hunky' Timothy, who did A-levels at the same college as her. Maybe her diary had been empty tonight.

I go sit round the other side of Dom, where Samantha had sat.

"Was it the same girl again?" I ask.

"Yeah. Exactly the same. I don't know why I keep dreaming it."

"Maybe she's your true love, who you're going to marry."

"Don't be silly. I'm only eleven."

"You can be any age to dream about that sort of thing. I sometimes dream about the guy I want to marry."

"But that's girls' stuff."

"Is not!"

"Is too!"

"Stop it you two. Here you go Dominic." She handed him his drink.

"Can I have one?"

"You can make your own Sheila."

"That's not fair!"

"Get over it." I turn my back on Samantha, keen to ask Dom more questions about his dream.

"What was she doing?"

"The same as what she's always doing."

"Tell me again." He sighs.

"Well, she's about my age, as you know. And she's playing tennis in her back garden, on a sunny day. And then she's kidnapped by this man in grey. And she screams. But then she's at this graveside, and it's raining and dark. She's really sad and she's crying. Then she disappears into the ground, down into the grave. She's being hugged by this smiling woman. And I'm there, watching them. But they ignore me. I want a hug from the smiling woman too, but she doesn't notice me. I shout at the little girl, and she makes a sign to me to come closer. So I do. Then she disappears. But the smiling woman's still there. And I yell, but she doesn't even look at me, she just walks right past me, as though I'm not there. And then I'm above ground again, and it's sunny. It's spring, all the flowers and trees are out. And she's there, dancing round, singing. It's warm and the birds are singing. I call out to her, but she's so far away, even though she's not really, and she can't hear me. No matter how much I shout out to her, she never hears me anymore."

"What does she look like? Is she pretty?"

"I suppose so."

"Oh, boys are no good at describing things! Do you know her name?"

"I don't know."

"You said you call out to her in your dream."

"Yes, but I don't know what I said."

"How can you *not* know, it's your...."

"You ask too many questions this late at night, young lady. Time you were back in bed."

"Oh, stop trying to be so goody, Samantha. It doesn't suit you."

"And I'll not take any of your cheek. Go on. I'll tuck Dominic in, you get back into bed."

"Sharn't!"

"Sheila!"

"I wanna stay up and talk to Dom."

"Well, you can't. Look, it's midnight already. Go to bed, Sheila."

"Only if you make me some cocoa." My sister stared at me. I stared back.

"OK, OK," she gave in.

"I'll talk to Dom whilst you make it and then I'll go to bed." She started to protest. "Promise I will. Promise."

She sighed. "All right then." I watched her slip out of the room in her black silky night-dress. I tried not to giggle, she probably thought it was sexy.

"I don't get it. It's always the same girl. Exactly the same things happen, every time."

"And you always dream it in the last week of July, every year. Have you noticed that? Maybe you'll get married in July."

"But who's the woman?"

"I don't know," I said, looking at my cute brother. We were both blond. But Samantha and Mum and Dad were darker. Both me and Dom'd been adopted though. We knew Mum and Dad loved us though. And me and Dom saw them as our proper Mum and Dad. They'd had us since we were very little. They wanted us, 'cause they couldn't have any more kids after Samantha was born.

"Maybe she's your biological Mum," I said. I purposely didn't say 'real mum', 'cause we already had that.

"Maybe. I don't know." He stared past me at his blank TV screen in the corner of his Spiderman room.

"Do you think you'll ever want to find out who your biological Mum was?"

251

"No. Do you?" He answered quickly. I shook my head.

"It's sad isn't it?" I put my arm round him, as he nodded. Neither of us needed to say anything else. I crawled into bed beside him and snuggled down under the duvet.

"Here it is," Samantha was back. But Dom was already falling asleep, and I was yawning.

"Can I sleep here tonight? Please Samantha. You know Dom doesn't have bad dreams when I sleep in here." Her image was fading out of focus, as my eyes kept closing. She stood there, cup in hand, hair down to her waist. She was trying not to smile, I think. "Please Samantha. Mum and Dad won't mind."

"OK, Sheila. Just for tonight." She gave us both a peck on the cheek, then switched off the main light at the wall, and closed the door to after her.

"Night, night Dom." But he was already snoring.

Chapter Fifty

"Gosh don't the years fly by?" I said to Ted as we sat down at the dining table, after having done the washing up and drying together.

"They sure do."

"I can't believe Daphne's coming up for her GCSEs next year. Time's just flown. I don't feel it was all that long ago since you and Daphne first moved in here. Although the place itself has changed somewhat!"

"Well it's nice to expand, that extra room and the conservatory at the back have given the place extra character..."

"And more rooms to have privacy, or more rooms to avoid each other when your teenage daughter is having one of her 'everything you say is hateful and you don't understand how I feel' moods."

"Indeed. And just think, the place would be a lot different if we'd let Daphne have her way with the decor of the house!"

"Yeah, not sure black with purple striped zig-zags would've sat easy on the eyes last thing at night."

"Or first thing in the morning."

"But she had a good old sulk about that one!"

"She sure did. I wonder if Daphne ever feels like she missed out, not having a brother or sister?" The sun streamed in through the window, and the green of the fields blazed.

"And have *two* teenagers in the house knocking things over, squabbling with each other and tearing our heads off – no thanks!"

"I have to admit, that doesn't sound very appealing – but I mean from Daphne's point of view, do you think she feels, I dunno, lonely sometimes?"

"She has lots of friends and does plenty of things with them. And at the end of the day Daphne has always liked her own private space to retreat into. I don't get the impression she's lonely. Why do you think she is?"

"No, not particularly."

"Isabel, stop giving yourself a hard time about this."

"About what?"

"I know you. You're trying to blame yourself for a situation that doesn't even exist. Daphne's fine. She goes out, studies, gets all our devotion (and money) and is at her rebellious stage of development which is very healthy. It's not because she secretly wants brothers or sisters to get up to mischief with, and it's *not* your fault that she doesn't have any. Stop punishing yourself darling."

"I can't help it sometimes." We held hands across the table, as he rubbed his thumb across the back of my right hand. I gazed out of the window to the blue contrast on green. "I do wish sometimes still, that we could've had more children."

"We just about coped with one."

"Yes, I know but…"

"It's not too late, you know."

"Too late for what?"

"To adopt another child, if we wanted to."

"Yes it is. Forty year olds? Come on!"

"It *could* happen…"

"It's too late emotionally as well, anyway. I know I'd just resent having our freedom tacked back down again, and having to have the patience, time and energy to bring another youngster into the family. And we wouldn't know what their background was before they came to us, what their parents had been like, or anything. I couldn't do it all again, not now. Besides we've had this discussion before."

"I just want you to be happy and if you're yearning for more children, we could still look at options for doing that."

"No, I'm not yearning. Not anymore. I don't think we were meant to have any others. But just occasionally…"

"You feel the odd twinge?"

"Yeah, I guess."

"You know, we should be out in the sunshine on a day like this. What are we doing stuck in here? Let's grab a rug and lay out on the grass."

"Good idea." We proceeded to do just that. "Let's do it naked." Daphne was away for the weekend, staying over at Teresa's house. It *would* be nice to take full advantage of her absence – and face the yawning fields in our birthday suits!

We stripped off, leaving our clothes in a pile on the kitchen floor. We laid out bare on the rug, our bodies turned to the sun, feeling her warmth drape over us kindly.

"So you don't think she wants a brother or sister then?"

"Oh Isabel!"

"Well we don't know do we? If it's something she'd really like to have or not."

"If you like, I'll ask her."

"Would you?"

"If it'll set your mind at rest."

"Well it would do, if she says no."

"OK, I'll tell you what. I may or may not ask her. If I do, and she says she didn't care a jot, I'll tell you, and if I ask and she says she might've liked one possibly, I won't say anything, and you can act as if I haven't asked her, because you won't know, will you?"

I laughed. "Of course I'll know. If you don't say anything I'll know you've asked and that she does mind, or I'll just remain paranoid about the whole thing!"

"OK, I'll tell you one way or the other."

"Honestly?"

"Yes, honestly."

"OK then."

"But seriously Isabel, do you want to explore further avenues…?"

"No, I don't think I do actually. As you know, I did want to try in the early years of our marriage, but it either didn't work, or we were too busy to really commit ourselves to another child. I'm really happy with what I do have. I'll just feel even happier if Daphne doesn't feel hard done by it."

"OK then Mrs Hawkins, I still have one question for you."

"Oh yes, and what's that?"

"Well, now that you have me naked…"

"Yes…?"

"Would you like to rub some sun tan lotion on me?"

I laughed and said, "If I had a cushion to hand right now I'd throw one at you."

"Oh no! Not a cushion! Not again!"

"Oh you're so hard done by."

"I am, I am. You're always beating me up with cushions."

"Well give me a long, luxurious and sensuous massage all over my back, and I might retract my threat!"

"How could I refuse an offer like that!"

"Or you'll be sleeping in the kennel tonight, and I'll let Bonny slobber over your side of the bed instead..."

"OK, OK you win! Massage it is!" He laughed as he got up to get the massage oil from the house. "And I *don't* slobber!" he called back.

I smiled as I rolled over on to my front, stretching out in delicious expectancy of his warm hands smoothing themselves over my body.

Chapter Fifty-One

"Dad, do you miss your Dad?" Daphne asked.

"I never really knew him. I was too small to remember him." We were having a heart to heart about my past, as we sat on her bed. I could see the clouds skip across the sky like streaks of teased out cotton wool. I breathed in what little breeze there was coming through the open window. Another hot day.

My gaze fell inside her room once again and I was struck by the fact that Daphne was no longer such a little girl. Her bedroom attested to that. Half of the walls were painted red, with stencilled green dragons on, that six year old Daphne had jumped up and down and insisted upon. The other half was a pastel blue, that the 14 year old Daphne had decided was much more 'her'. Not quite having got round to finishing it off yet. Boy band posters, and female singers tried to cover up as much of the dragons as possible.

"I missed having a father in my life though. A fatherly presence or influence, if you like."

"Did your Mum tell you much about him?" I looked over Daphne's curiously intent face.

"Yes. Some things. She loved him very much."

"Did you miss not having brothers and sisters?" Daphne looked so like her mother sometimes, like today, it was almost like being haunted.

"I don't think I thought about it much to be honest. I always had your Mum and..." Your Mum and your mum! "...her best friend to hang round with, and the guys to play footy with. So I don't think I ever felt lonely as such. I quite liked having my Mum all to myself perhaps. Except that she could be *majorly* overprotective sometimes. We didn't half have some arguments when I hit about your age and beyond. But things got better when I moved away to college. Do you miss not having brothers and sisters, Daphne?"

She gazed across the room, and met the eyes of her reflection in the mirror of her dressing table, and pondered.. "I sometimes wonder what it would be like. I don't know. I haven't really thought much about it either. I think I'm quite happy as things are." I smiled at her as she turned back to look at me. Daphne returned it with a cheeky grin, so like Phillippa's.

"Did your Mum ever embarrass you?"

Ted laughed. "All the time!" I felt relieved that I could put Isabel's mind at rest. "Look why don't you change into your sports gear, and we can run over to the tennis courts and have a match?"

"But Dad, it's way too hot for anything like that!"

"Let's head for the lido then, Miss Lazy Bones."

"I'm *not* lazy!" I laughed at her defiance.

"C'mon then. Prove it. I'll go get my stuff together, and last one ready has to do three laps round the tennis courts as a warm up exercise."

"Three laps! That's way way too much."

"Betta get moving then hadn't you!" I laughed as I made a hasty escape with Daphne throwing one of her teddies after me.

Chapter Fifty-Two

"Mum, I think I'm gay."

"Oh." I paused. "Oka-ay." I wasn't sure what she expected my reaction to be as I tried not to drop the plate I was drying up. Daphne didn't look at me, as she continued washing the cutlery, wiping it with the cloth, dipping it in the water. She didn't seem to notice that she washed and rinsed the same set of knives for the third time now.

"Is it anyone I know?" I asked, thinking what I might ask, if she'd just said she was heterosexual, but somehow that didn't seem to fit!

"A girl at school." she mumbled, as she dipped the knives yet again.

"How long have you felt like this?" God, now I've made it sound like a disease! I cringe to myself, and hope Daphne doesn't take umbrage. But she just shrugs. "Why don't you invite her round for tea?" That's definitely something I would say if she said there was a boy she was interested in.

"Could I? Would you mind?" She looks at me now, her voice lifted in surprise.

"Of course not. Why should I mind? So long as you are happy with who you are, I don't mind at all." I felt a funny twinge inside. But I guess that was because I've never fancied another female, so I don't understand what it would be like. But if that was how Daphne felt, I would not judge her on that.

"What about Dad?"

"What about him?"

"Will he mind?"

"No, no, of course not. I'll tell him if you like. I'm sure it won't bother him either."

"Thanks Mum, you're the greatest!" And with that she dripped the wet cloth round my waist as she hugged me enthusiastically. It was nice to be hugged, didn't get many of them these days, from the unruly teenager that she'd turned into. I hugged her back gladly. When she pulled back slightly she looked really worried though.

"What's the matter?" I asked.

"Do you think…. Well… Do you think that *Mum* would mind?" And I suddenly understood her dilemma of feelings. But Phillippa was always an open topic between us. It was an easy question to deal with.

"No, I'm sure she wouldn't mind at all. She would always have been on your side, and stuck up for your right to choose things for yourself, and follow where your feelings lead you."

"Are you sure?"

"Positive!" I laughed. And that more than anything seemed to reassure her.

A happier daughter and a surprised mother continued the washing and drying.

"I think those knives are clean now, darling." Daphne at last put them in the drainer, and started to wash the remaining cups and plates.

"So who is she?" I finally said, racking my brains for appropriate questions that wouldn't offend, but that would give me some more clues as to what was going on.

"She's called Teresa."

"What's she like?"

"You know. Teresa! Blond, my height, very pretty."

"And is she in any of your classes?"

"Mum, you have met her, don't you remember?"

"Oh yes. Oh *that* Teresa. Put my foot in that one didn't I? Why the long face then?"

"I don't know if she likes me."

"Have you talked to her about it?"

"God, no!"

"OK. Well, do you know if she's… single?" Yes, that's the right word to use.

"I don't even know if she likes guys or girls."

"You like her a lot?"

Daphne hesitated. "Yes. A lot."

"Well, there's only one way to find out."

260

"But I could make such a fool of myself."

"Or you could die living in suspense. Take a leap, Daphne and find out. If it's a no, well at least you'll know where you stand, rather than spending all your time wondering about something that will never happen, and in the meantime missing out on opportunities to be happy with… someone else."

"But if she rejects me…"

"You'll live with it. I promise. Yes, it will hurt. But don't run from that. Otherwise you'll never get anywhere."

She looks up at me, still surprised I think that I'm accepting her sexuality as easy as this. "How come you got to be so wise?"

"Oh, I've lived through my mistakes. Believe me, it pays to take a chance." I smiled at her, thinking of how the three of us wouldn't be where we are now if I hadn't have taken a chance. And I would have been the greatest fool to have rejected and missed out on all the years of Ted's love. And Daphne's. She smiled back. A happy mother/daughter moment. I just wanted to hug her to me tightly. But I felt Daphne's 'independence cloak' back in force again, and refrained.

"OK. I will take that chance. I think I can." I half wish I'd had the courage and presence of mind to go after what I wanted so early in life.

***

I told Ted that evening, after Daphne had retired to her room to read/play music/dance round her room/watch dvds or whatever.

"Oh. OK," he said, dumbfounded, as he sat heavily on our bed.

"Yes, that was my reaction too," I said.

"How long has she felt like that?"

"Yes, I asked her that question too."

"Oh. OK, well what did she say?"

"Nothing very much. I told her she could ask her to tea."

"Fine."

"Strange isn't it?"

"Yes." He paused. "What else did you say to her?"

"Just that I was happy if she was happy." I replied as I brushed my hair in the mirror.

"I just naturally assumed Daphne *would* like guys."

"Yes, so did I. I guess parents do assume that about their kids though."

"Gosh it makes me feel weird." I went to sit beside him.

"What sort of weird? Redundant?"

Ted laughed. "I dunno. Cut out. Cut off somehow. I don't know. How does it make you feel?"

"Well, I was really surprised to say the least, as you can imagine. But now, I sort of feel a little disappointed that perhaps I won't have any grandchildren." I laughed. "But no, really, other than that, I feel pretty OK with it all actually. I'm just very curious as to how it's all going to work out."

"I just can't imagine me fancying another guy."

"No, I know what you mean. I can't think of myself in the arms of a woman."

"Not unless I was watching anyway!"

"You cheeky bugger!!!" I pushed him playfully.

"No, I'd just find it so bizarre if I'd have liked another man. I wouldn't have liked it at all," he shuddered.

"I wouldn't have liked it either," I reiterated forcefully.

"Do you think it's permanent?"

"What do you mean?"

"Could it be a phase she's going through?"

"Well, it could always be that, hormones jump all over the place at her age. I remember having had lesbian fantasies in the past."

"You did? You *never* told me about them!"

"Well, I think it's natural to sort of wonder about what it might be like. But never fear, darling, I'm not going to turn gay on you, I find you far too attractive for that!"

"Well thank you!" He gave me a playful kiss. "Glad to hear it!"

"Or maybe she feels that that is for her, and guys don't do anything for her. We'll find out in due course I'm sure."

"Yes, I'm sure!" he said ruefully. "Well, now how about doing some heterosexual things with your beloved husband, or is that all too by the way now?"

"Oh, yes, definitely by the way, I'll have to go out and find myself a girlfriend this minute…"

"Well, we'll see about that!" Ted dived under the bedcovers. I soon forgot about any 'girlfriend' provocation I could retort in turn.

Chapter Fifty-Three

"Teresa?"

"Speaking."

"Hi, can we meet up?"

"That you, Daphne?"

"Who else?"

"Didn't recognise your voice for a minute – are you OK?"

"Well, I'm not sure, yeah, well no, well I think so."

"What's biting you, Daph?"

"Can we meet? Go for a chat?"

"Course, I can be at your place in…"

"No, not here. I want to be totally out of Mum and Dad's hearing."

"Oh, OK."

"Can I come to yours, do you mind?"

"Course not. I'll even get out the toasted bagels with cream cheese."

I smiled. "What about the salmon?"

"You'll have to come and see."

"OK, I'll be there in about half an hour."

"See you then then."

***

I looked round Teresa's blue carpeted, blue walled, blue curtained bedroom. It was very restful, and you hardly noticed it was all in blue unless you consciously focused on it. It was all different shades that lived comfortably together in a quiet background.

I leaned back on Teresa's bed. She was sat on her favourite bean bag in the middle of the room.

"Chuck me a bagel will you?"

"Come and get it yourself lazy."

Teresa rolled her eyes heavenward in a good humoured way. I laughed as she climbed on to the bed next to me.

She reached her hand into the bag of toasted bagel chips, (garlic flavour).

"There's only one left you pig! You ate all them!?"

"Hey, it wasn't me. Must've been a ghost or something."

"Ha bloody ha!" She munched on the last one, giving me a mock dirty look. She looked so attractive. So pretty. On impulse I said, "how would you feel if I gave you something?"

"Depends what it is."

"A present. A surprise."

"You know me, I love surprises!"

"You have to sit up and close your eyes."

"Is this some sort of mean joke or something?"

"No, no, honestly. It's something nice. Now, no peeking."

"OK, OK. Just hurry up will you? I can't bear the suspense."

I looked at her, with her eyes shut. Well here goes taking a chance! I closed mine, and placed my lips to hers. She started. I stopped. She looked at me, and a deep flush of shame reddened my cheeks. "Sorry," I mumbled, turning away from her.

"No wait. Close your eyes again," she said. I did as she asked, my heart beating ferociously in my ears. And then I felt her gentle lips against mine. It felt nice, and fluttery.

"I've wanted to do that for ages," I admitted.

"Have you?" I nodded. "Well you should've done it ages ago then."

"I was afraid."

"But you liked?" I nodded again. We explored each other's lips some more, holding each other close. I felt my body flood with relief and excitement. I wanted to burst out laughing and not stop. I wanted to run a thousand miles, I felt so full of energy. I felt her gentle warmth next to me, our barriers coming down. I felt flushed with pleasure. I couldn't stop smiling, and the best thing was seeing Teresa smiling right back at me.

We laid back on the pillows of her bed, in each other's arms. She stroked my cheek. I noticed that the only light in the room was from her lamp. The unseen stars shone outside her window, but because of the light, the window only reflected back to us ourselves and the room.

"Do you want to stay the night?"

"Yes." I answered, wishing I could just stay and stay and stay.

"Will you need to ring home, and tell them?"

"Yes."

Then Teresa left my side and I watched with curiosity as Teresa started to undress in front of me. It was interesting seeing another female form naked before me, in such an open way. Her body invited mine. She laid back down on the bed, next to me, not touching. I looked down her body, over her forming curves, not dissimilar to mine.

She turned her face to look at me. She smiled. "Feel free to join me, if you want to." I felt a bit scared, but wanted to please her. I hesitated. "Please join me," she asked. And she looked vulnerable. That gave me the courage I needed.

I started to enjoy the feeling of her eyes on me as I slowly peeled away my layers. I liked looking at her, and she liked looking at me. Our gazes locked and I felt really light headed as my heart rate increased.

Once I was stood naked to her, I watched her eyes travel the full length of my body. My skin tingled. "Daphne," she whispered. I smiled warmly at her, as her eyes returned to mine. As I moved towards the bed, to lay next to her, I began to feel more nervous. Our bodies lay out full length, on our backs, looking up at the ceiling.

"Do you want to do anything?" she asked me.

"Like what?" My mind raced and blanked out at the same time.

"Do you mind if I touch you?" When I didn't say anything, she continued. "Please just say no, if you'd rather I didn't. I don't mind." I turned my face to look at her. Her eyes stared into mine, then fell away to appraise my body, then stared back into me again. I felt tingly, and could feel myself becoming wet.

"I'd like you to touch me," I said honestly.

"Tell me if you want me to stop." I nodded, entwined in her spell. She sat up slightly, and drooled her fingers down me, as if they were combing water. I felt them tickle along my skin, starting from my neck, working their way down the centre of my body, between my breasts, and stop just above my pubic area, then repeated the trail a few times over. My body was tantalised, I wanted her touch all over. But she continued that same path way, her fingers starting to massage me more, stroke me, but they didn't waver from their short narrow path.

I didn't feel brave enough to take her hand and place it where I really wanted it. So I whispered, "Touch me further." She nodded her understanding. Her hand gently cupped my right breast, and I shivered. I saw her tongue wet her open mouth, unconsciously. I nodded to her, she bent to me, and sucked my nipple into her mouth. It was delicious torture. I arched up towards her, holding her head down on me. She licked and nibbled, and I groaned. My wetness increased. She lay her body on top of mine, and I felt the full weight of her settle on to me. I welcomed her weight, her intimacy touching my intimacy. We kissed deeper this time, and it felt natural to hold her in my arms as we did so. My hands travelled down the length of her back, caressed her buttocks. Daringly, I slipped a finger between her legs, amidst her hairs, and was delighted to feel her slipperiness as wet as mine was. My curiosity and desire drove me onwards, as I teased her intimately, spreading her wetness, feeling her get more excited. I slipped my finger into her and she gasped.

"Is that OK?" I asked, suddenly nervous again. Her eyes shone, as I looked up into them.

"Oh yes. Don't stop," she said so softly, I almost didn't hear her. I slipped another finger in, and felt her tighten around them. My body answered hers with its own shudders. I wanted to kiss and suckle her, as she had done me. I wanted her touch down below, to feed my hunger. We could feel each other's growing need. She slid off me, and rolled me on top of her. Hungrily my mouth sought her breasts, and was pleased to hear her gasps. I revelled in the warmth of her body beneath mine, her legs open to me, wrapped around me, holding me into her. I could feel the sheets beneath me getting damp from my desire. I moved up her, so our heads were level once again, and reached down with my hand, to fuel her need even more. She rubbed her wetness into my hand, relishing my touch. "Do you want to kiss me down there?" she asked. I thought for a second. I shook my head.

"That's OK," she reassured me. "Do you mind if I kiss you there?" Her hand teased my clitoris, and I spasmed against her in pleasure. I wasn't sure what to say. "I'll try it and see if you like it." I didn't stop her, as she fluttered her kisses all the way down my body, over my stomach, between my legs.

She ran her tongue along my thighs, my aching increased. She was holding out on me, sharpening my anticipation. Then she carefully licked me, my shudders becoming stronger. She dipped her tongue into me, I felt trembles cascade through my whole being. Then she sucked all of me into her mouth, and I orgasmed almost immediately. After I'd peaked, she kissed me gently down there once more, then made her way up. She wiped her face on the pillow, and looked into my eyes. I felt very embarrassed, and I could feel the heat rise up into my cheeks.

"That was great. You're great Daphne," she said as if she could read the insecurity and doubts in my mind.

She kissed me once on my mouth, then went over to her wardrobe. I wondered what she was doing. When she came back to lie with me, she had a dildo in her hand. How on earth had she managed to get hold of one of them? She put it in my hand. It felt rubbery, and smooth, a perfectly formed black penis. My mind suddenly went blank, and I wondered what I was supposed to do with it.

"Tease me with it, Daphne. Make me arch for you to put it inside me," she instructed me. I obeyed gladly. My curiosity piqued once more. I ran it between her inner lips, her juices making it wet, and easy to slither round her, making her gasp and moan. I rubbed it against her clitoris, and down the whole length of her wet cunt. What a naughty word, I thought, but somehow much sexier than vagina. She dripped on to it, making it glisten slightly when it caught the light. She rubbed herself against it, wanting it more and more. I was starting to feel excited all over again, just watching her.

"Now, Daphne, now." But I withheld, taunting her with it. "Please," she begged. And I was suddenly afraid I would hurt her with it, if I slipped it in. "Daphne," her voice was more commanding now. I nuzzled it against her opening, and pushed it between her lips, it slid in easily. I pushed it further, watching her face anxiously, hoping it wasn't hurting her. "Push it in more," she said, and I did, as I watched her body writhe on to it, swallowing it up. I moved it deeper into her, and eased it in and out. She called out. I was afraid her parents or her sister downstairs might hear. I kept going until she'd spent herself on it violently. As her body shuddered into calmness, her desire completely sated, I made to withdraw the dildo. "No, leave it in for a while." So I did, then laid down next to her, her breathing still heavy. She opened her arms to me, and I lay in them, contented. She kissed my forehead. "Am I beautiful to you Daphne?" Her voice sounded uncertain.

"Very beautiful," I said admiringly. She pulled the sheets up around us, to warm our cooling bodies, and we dozed on and off in each other's arms.

Chapter Fifty-Four

"What do you think will happen to the relationship Daphne's built up with Teresa?"

"How do you mean?"

I looked at Ted, spoon in one hand, just about to hit open the top of his boiled egg, and newspaper in the other, absorbed in the print of others' words. We'd both taken the week off work, just to relax, and Daphne was out at college.

"I mean now that Daphne's applying for Uni. but Teresa's staying here?"

Ted folded his paper and put it on the table. Sunlight streamed on to him through the blinds. It was going to be a gorgeous day.

"Why are you worrying?"

"Well, I was just remembering what you said about Uni. when you were there, how so many couples broke up. How the distance made such a difference, and meeting all those new people."

"Yes, but that doesn't mean to say the same will happen to Daphne and Teresa. Besides, if it's meant to be, it will be, if it's not, it's not."

"How can you be so laid back about it? I can just see myself trying to comfort a broken-hearted Daphne, in tears over the phone at two in the morning."

"I can be so laid back darling, because it might not ever happen, and if it does, we'll have to cross that bridge when we come to it. Worrying about it won't prevent it from happening."

"I hate it when you're right."

"Well, I have to make the most of it, it doesn't happen that often!" I threw a place mat at his pouting face, and he caught it. "I don't know, I get told off when I'm right, and told off when I'm wrong. A bloke can't win."

"That's right," I said, as I went over to him. I stood behind his chair and put my arms round him, and he leaned back into me, his arms going up my back, round my waist.

"Honestly, darling, there's nothing we can do about it, if they do happen to break up, then all we can do is mop up the tears, and come out with awful clichés that won't be of any use whatsoever, you know all the cringeworthy things like 'there's plenty more fish in the sea' and then Daphne will scowl at us and stomp off saying she has hateful parents who don't understand her."

"Thank you darling, I feel oh so much more reassured now, knowing that we're powerless to do anything of use for our little girl, should it end in tears."

"You're welcome. That's what I'm here for, to be absolutely reassuring on things like this!"

"Watch it you!" I tickled him.

"Oy, that's not fair, you're taking advantage."

"Damn right I am." Ted struggled out of his chair, and chased after me round the kitchen table, trying to tickle me back. We ended up penning each other in, in the corner next to the bin. "If I get any of that dirt on me, you can jolly well lick it off!"

"No, but I'll jump into the shower with you, and wash you down."

"Oh, you will, will you?"

"It's a promise."

"How long before Daphne comes back?"

"Long enough," he smiled impishly at me.

Chapter Fifty-Five

I put the phone down and looked again at the essay covers I was holding in my hand. Mum and Dad had been thrilled that I got 64%, 65% and 69% in all three of the English modules I'd taken in semester one. But Teresa didn't seem to be so impressed. In fact, she didn't seem to want to talk about it at all. We don't seem to want to talk about the same things at all anymore. I felt a bit deflated.

Just then there was a knock on my door. That was the good thing and the annoying thing about halls of residence. You were surrounded by people pretty much all of the time. I threw the papers on my bed and shouted come in.

Peter burst in, grinning all over his handsome face.

"What did you get?"

"All 2:1s. What did you get?"

"Two 2:1s and a 2:2. A gang of us are going down to town to buy some booze and pizzas and stuff. And we're gonna stay up all night tonight and party. What do you reckon?"

"Yeah, great," I said plopping down on my navy blue duvet, thinking of the blues of Teresa's room. I stared out of the window at the sunshine glancing through the leaves of the weeping willows.

"You don't sound very enthusiastic," he said, sitting down beside me. He put his arm gently round my shoulder. I turned to face him, his face very close to mine. I looked into his dark dark eyes, and felt an unexpected *frission* race down my back.

"No I am, well I was, I mean, I dunno..." I trailed off, not really knowing what to say.

"The party'll cheer you up, why don't ya come down into town with us, we're all gonna pile into Jake's car."

"I don't really feel like it right now, but I'll join in the festivities when you all get back. Promise."

"Or I could just give our orders to Jake, and he can get what we want, and I can stay here with you, and really get you into the party mood."

I could tell from the way he said it, and the way he was sitting so close to me, exactly what he had in mind to 'get me in the party mood'. I felt another *frission* race after the first one. I'd never slept with a guy, there had only ever been Teresa. I wondered what it would feel like.

I felt a sudden stab of guilt for even thinking about it. I loved Teresa. She would be really hurt if I did this. I felt Peter's hand trickle down my spine and up and down again. "What do you say?" His smooth angular face glided closer, to nestle next to mine. I watched our faces turn into each other, and our lips meet.

His kiss tantalised me, and I felt desire awaken. No, no, I couldn't possibly do this. I wanted to celebrate my good marks with Teresa, and hold hands with her and... His fingers started to undo the silver buttons of my pink blouse. His kiss drew me in deeper. Well, Teresa would never know, this could just be a one off, just to experiment and see what... Oh, that feels nice. His warm hands had found their way into my bra, and the teasing was setting off all sorts of electrical impulses in my brain. I started to feel moist, and I wondered what his cock would look like.

What was I thinking? This was no good... Teresa, I'm sorry, I... I unzipped his trousers, eager to caress his firmness.

***

We lay together afterwards. It had been 'nice'. I was a little disappointed that the culmination of our desire hadn't been as spectacular as the foreplay had promised, but never mind. It was only the first time.

First time? Was I going to do this again? Did this mean I wasn't gay anymore? Did this mean things were really over for me and Teresa? I suddenly felt a strong pang to be lying in her arms, and not Peter's. I looked at him. A stranger. One of many at Uni. One of the many sexually active strangers on campus. And now I'd joined them, instead of remaining aloof, faithful to

Teresa. I hadn't been tempted to be with any other lass since coming here, and now this…

What did it all mean? I suddenly felt like I didn't want to be anywhere near Peter.

I got up, and started to put my clothes straight. Peter didn't notice my closing up against him.

"Are you coming into town then?"

"No, like I said, I'll join you all later, there's some other stuff I need to do this afternoon."

"Well, I certainly hoped I put you in the party mood, I sure as hell am."

"Yeah, you did actually Peter, thanks," I lied, I actually felt worse now than I did before.

Peter started to zip up, and tuck in. "Glad to be of service." I wondered how only half an hour ago I'd found him so desirable. I now felt cold to the core, and wondered at how I had felt so tempted. "Hey, what's up Daph? You're still not smiling."

"Nothing, I was just thinking, well… does this mean we're in some sort of relationship now? Cause I really don't want to be committed, ya know?"

"Hey, chill, Daph, that's fine with me. I'm not into the commitment thing either." And he seemed to be totally at ease with the whole casualness of the thing. I felt shocked and relieved at the same time. Relieved that he didn't expect anything else from me. But shocked that he… could discard the whole thing as if he'd just handed in a troublesome essay that he no longer had to spend time thinking about. I suddenly felt very used. I'd just let this guy in, on a physically intimate level, and we didn't even know each other, let alone have any 'finer feelings' for each other. What the hell had I expected? I hadn't wanted anything anyway. And there was Teresa… God! Why had I just done what I'd done?

Maybe it was just the fact that I suddenly found Peter incredibly unattractive after all, and I hadn't even been drunk at the time. How had my feelings managed to turn around so quickly?

Peter gave me a peck on the cheek, "See you tonight darling," and banged the door closed after him.

I went to the sink next to my wardrobe and retched. I

washed the yellow thickness of lunch down the plug hole. I really wish he hadn't called me darling. I'd never heard the word sullied in such a way before. Well, I guess I'm still gay after all. I wish I could have two simultaneous lives, and that the other Daphne had experimented with Peter to discover what a guy was like to be with, and this Daphne was still true to Teresa. Perhaps I should tell her. Maybe she'd forgive me, and then we could just carry on... as before? Before I went to Uni. and before we'd run out of things to say to each other?

Then a horrid thought shot through my head. My heart beat very fast. I started to sweat. We hadn't used any precautions, what if I was pregnant?

Yeah, I certainly had some other stuff to do this afternoon, I'd to get myself to a chemist and get the flipping morning-after pill. The very last thing I wanted right now was to mess up my degree and end up with a kid on the way!

***

I tried calling Teresa again, when I got back from town. She wasn't there. She was out on a job interview. What would I say to her anyway? I'm miserable 'cause I just slept with this guy and realised that all I really wanted to do was be back home with you. Talking about everything. Kissing. And talking. Understanding each other. What should I wear for the 'party' tonight then? I looked dismally at my wardrobe, and decided I'd go back to town, and buy myself something outrageous. Why not! I'd ask Sally if she wanted to come too. She was always one for shopping!

Chapter Fifty-Six

Dear Diary

3 weeks into 2nd semester now.

Teresa was really distant over the few days we spent together when I went back home. Almost as if she knew that I'd done the dirty behind her back, even though I never said anything. I hate it. But I don't seem to be able to... I dunno. She was quite reserved about touching too, which is really strange, 'cause we're normally quite huggy and at ease with each other. Maybe she's telepathic, or someone's told her about Peter.

I'm just being paranoid now. There's no possible way Teresa could know about Peter. Is there!?

And now I feel doubly guilty, 'cause since being back at Uni. after inter-semester break, I've now been seeing another guy called Shaun. And we've even slept together a few times.

He's very different from Peter. He's such a laugh to be around, and we have so much fun together. He's so good humoured and good natured. And he's more sensitive. We're not exactly having a relationship, we just sort of see each other on and off whenever we like, sort of casual friends/lovers. We're committed to having fun together, but nothing else. I feel comfortable with that, and with him. And there's never any big questions hanging over whatever it is we do.

I still love Teresa, and I'm not in love with Shaun. It just feels good to do whatever we feel like doing, and there's no obligations on either side. We both agreed that if we fall in love with other people, we'll stop being lovers – no, not lovers, we're not that, we're just sexual friends. Well, anyway, if either of us found someone we wanted to get serious with, we'd just be friends friends. And that suits me fine.

Teresa writes less and less. She writes just as regularly, but her letters are shorter and shorter. I asked if she was upset about anything when I saw her, but she just shrugged it all off. I don't understand.

And I don't know why I feel so comfortable with Shaun, and yet simultaneously want everything to be back on track again with Teresa.

I have to stop thinking about it, or it'll drive me insane. Maybe if I write my diary, it'll help sort my thoughts out.

Dear Diary
4th week into semester.
Got letter this morning.
Teresa's broken up with me...

I shoved my diary aside and reread Teresa's letter. I couldn't believe it!

I smudged the ink with my wet fingers. I tried to stem the tears, but they kept coming.

She'd met someone else. Anna. They had more in common. She didn't feel we 'connected' with each other anymore.

I missed her so much it hurt. I wish she was here to hold now.

Knock-knock. Who's that now? Go away!

"Daphne, are you in there?" Knock-knock.

It was Vanessa. She was nice, Vanessa. Perhaps she wouldn't mind if I cried on her shoulder.

I opened the door and let her into my disgruntled abode.

"Daphne! What's the matter?" She immediately enveloped me, upon seeing my tears. I gave her the letter. She kept an arm round me and made lots of sympathetic noises.

"Listen, it's Square Peg Society meeting tonight. Why don't you come along? Take your mind off things for a bit? Meet some new friends. I'm going with Charlie, but I know she'd be pleased to offer you some support too." Charlie was Vanessa's girlfriend. They'd done A-levels together, and then come to the same Uni. together. They couldn't bear to be separated.

Square Peg Society was for gay and bisexual students. I didn't fancy being pigeon-holed as such. I just liked who I liked, whenever I liked them. I didn't think of myself in terms of labels of sexuality. But going to the meeting would be better than moping in my room all night. And Vanessa and Charlie would be cheering and sympathetic company.

"OK then."

"Great. Look, why don't we get you cleaned up a bit? Then we'll call on Charlie and we'll all walk down together?"

"Sure."

"C'mon then." I bathed my face at the sink whilst Vanessa picked out my grey chiffon top and white jeans for me to put on.

***

The meeting went on in its own sweet way, I really didn't pay all that much attention. I let my eyes wander round the Students Union bar. The newly painted purple seating, and the peeling, cigarette stubbed floor. The square rails drawn down over the bar. The pool tables being unused for once. Backs of black plastic chairs. My bored eyes roamed over and over the same familiar shapes.

I just couldn't focus on what anyone said, my thoughts continuously returned to Teresa. Teresa and Anna. All that time. It hadn't been her picking up on my guilt over sleeping with Peter or Shaun. She'd been attracted to someone else. Falling for someone else. Somehow it felt like the bigger betrayal of the two things.

The meeting, I noticed, was breaking up, and everyone was chatting socially, making arrangements for tonight.

"What about it Daphne?"

"What?"

"Come out to Bar Icon with us tonight. We're heading out there in about half an hour. Come on, it'll make you feel better, take your mind off stuff." Vanessa put her arm through mine, and smiled at me.

"C'mon Daphne. I promise you'll enjoy it."

"If I keep saying no, how many more times are you going to ask me to come?" I knew how persuasive Vanessa could be. She just never gave in.

"Several million. I'm going to drag you kicking and screaming if I have to."

"But you'll try and match-make me, I know you."

"Moi? Sweet innocent moi? Would I do such a thing? You're nursing a broken heart at the moment, but I'm here to remind you that the world does continue, and that you can still have fun, with or without Teresa."

"Yes, but just because I'll be there, and single," I'm now single, how terrible! "And lots of other single lasses will be there, I'm serious Vanessa, no setting me up with any blind dates or anything!"

"Now, you're being paranoid sweety. I know you know what I'm like, but I'm not that insensitive. Just let a few of your good friends cushion your fall, and remind you that you're not the shitbag you feel you are at the moment, just because the love in your life has come to an end." I couldn't help but laugh. Vanessa could always be counted on to be forthright with you, that's one thing I could say about her.

"Who's going?" I asked.

"Me and Charlie of course, and Parminder and Patsy are coming too."

"Great, I'll be the oddball then."

"No you won't. We'll look after you." I smiled at her 'motherly act'. I knew what she said was true. Even though they were in couples, I never did feel left out with them, they were always very inclusive of me, and friendly. Besides Patsy and Parminder were fun to be around, especially when Patsy's humour was on top form.

"OK, you twisted my arm."

"Great. Are you going back to halls to get changed then?"

"Changed again? No, I can't be arsed."

"Fair enough. We're meeting at the front of the SU in a couple of hours, but I'll come knock on your door. We'll order a big taxi."

"OK, see you in a bit." My attention wondered to the two guys who had just entered the SU and were making their way over to the pool tables. One was Shaun. I suddenly felt like everything we'd done together, the laughing, enjoying, pleasuring, it rang hollow inside me. What had been fun, now felt empty and meaningless. Why did my feelings keep changing about so many things all the time? What did I really want? Did I really know? I want Teresa.

279

***

Bar Icon. Even though it was a Thursday, it was still absolutely packed. Event night – had a live band on. It was loud and heavy and smoky. Normally I would've enjoyed it, but tonight I just couldn't get into it. I'd bought a round for everyone and was tip-toeing and juggling my way through the heaving, jumping, sweaty bodies to our table. The girls were all up and dancing. I was happy to watch and drink my beer. Vanessa beckoned for me to come and dance. I shook my head. She plonked herself beside me, breathless.

"C'mon, on the dance floor with you!"

"After I've downed one of these."

"OK."

"I watched the dancers, jigging around in time to the beat. I felt like I was watching from a million miles away. I saw the men dancing with the men, and the girls dancing with the girls. Everyone was jovial and smiling. Laughing and joking. I felt tears spring to my eyes. What *was* it with me? I didn't care about Peter and the others. All I cared about was Teresa, even though I'd done the dirty on her. I missed her friendship, more than I thought I could. She was probably blissfully happy, all curled up somewhere cosy with Anna. I nearly choked on my jealousy, as I tried to swallow some beer.

I needed some air, but first a trip to the loos. I told Vanessa where I was off, then started the ballet dance across the club to the toilets. There was a huge queue for the ladies, as per usual. I thought fuck this for a laugh, and went in the gents instead. Why didn't we all just have mixed toilets anyway like they did in Holland? The memory of that weekend in Amsterdam with the girls came crashing back to me. God, that'd been fun!

I went into one of the smelly cubicles and locked the door. Just as I was finishing, I thought I heard a sob in the cubicle next to me. No, couldn't be. I went and washed my hands, and I heard it again.

"Are you all right in there?" I asked.

"Leave me alone," the vicious reply came back.

"OK, fair enough. Just asking." I was just about to go when

the gravely voice said, "you're a girl."

"Ten out of ten," I replied.

"This is the gents."

"Ten out of ten again. You're good at this." I wasn't usually so sarky with complete strangers, but he had just refused sympathy from a miserable person, what did he expect?

"Are you laughing at me?" And suddenly the door swung open, and a gangly young man, in a crazy patterned rainbow coloured sweater stood there, glaring at me. He had short spiky brown hair, and a large thin line of a mouth. Shit I was in it now.

"No, not at all. Sorry I disturbed you."

"Well, you damn well *should* be laughing at me. I would. What's your name, Lady of the gents?"

"Daphne," I said, startled.

"Well, Daphne, why aren't you laughing at me? I'd be cracking my sides open by now." He seemed to genuinely want an answer. I was a little taken aback by him, but still pretty irritated myself.

"What on earth are you talking about? *Why* should I be laughing?"

"Because it's bleeding well happened again, hasn't it! AGAIN!" He went over to the sinks and stared into his brown eyes in the mirror. I wanted to go, but felt awkward leaving the toilets as if I was in the middle of a conversation with this strange stranger.

Finally I said, "What's happened?"

"You mean you don't know? I thought everyone bleeding well knew. Every-bleeding-one! Including you, Miss Lady of the Gents." He poked a finger in my direction.

"Will you *stop* calling me that! And I don't bleeding well know what you're bleeding well going on about. I don't even know your name. So stop trying to hang whatever your shit is on me."

"Feisty Lady of the gents," he said as if it was the salutation at the start of a letter. "Have you ever died of a bleeding heart? Literally. Have you ever felt the wound of love so deep? Fair Lady of the gents, has your love ever been quashed underfoot, right in front of your face, by the very person you entrusted it with? Have you ever swooned and gaped and bled, bled, bled, dear Lady of the gents?"

If he hadn't been so pissed off with me, under other circumstances I think I would've laughed.

"Well let me tell you, Poet of the gents, you're not the only one in the whole history of humankind to have their heart broken. So fuck him, whoever it is. Find somebody better. And get over it!" Why was I sounding like such a heartless cow all of a sudden? Because I was angry with myself for feeling exactly the same way he was.

I thought he was going to go mad with me then. But hey, a good argument clears the air doesn't it? Even if it's with a loony stranger in the gents of a nightclub?

But then he burst out laughing. In fact he doubled up in laughter. Tears were starting in his eyes, and he'd to hold on to the sink to stay upright.

"What's the fucking joke?" I was annoyed. And I felt very self conscious that I was the one being laughed at now.

"Oh, sorry," when he got his voice back. "Did *you* fuck her, find someone better and get over it?"

"What?" Had Vanessa blabbed? Did he know all about her? Oh God, who *was* this awful person? "What are you talking about? Who told you?"

He sobered up then, as he gently said, "I don't know what you're talking about. No-one's told me anything. You're as strange to me as I am to you." I was taken aback anew by his unexpected reactions to me. "I'm guessing from what you've said that you've been shat on too, from a great height. You're a tonic, Daphne. Let's get out of here, and I'll buy you a drink." And he motioned for me to go ahead of him, out of the room.

"What if I don't want a drink?"

"Don't you want one? I sure as hell do." He waited again, for a reply from me.

Did I want one? Yes, I did actually, and despite his total off-the-wallness I thought it'd be a damn sight more interesting than getting slowly drunk and watching the girls dance the night away.

"Where did you have in mind?"

"Somewhere quieter. Sedater. More melancholy. Somewhere you can hear what the person shouting in your ear is saying to you." Sounded good to me. We grinned at each other, as if we both understood something.

"I know just the place."

"I thought you might." He raised his eyebrows at me.

I went and shouted in Vanessa's ear that I was off for a drink with someone.

"I knew you'd meet someone," and she gave me a hug. Not an attractive female to fall in love with, Vanessa dear, but a very strange weird guy who seems kind of interesting. I couldn't tell her that though. I'd burst her bubble tomorrow.

Me and The Loony went out into the biting fresh air of the night. After the momentary relief from the buzzing club, my teeth started chattering.

"Which way, Lady of the gents?"

"Hey Loony, would you stop calling me that?" I started to briskly walk in the direction of the Ryeworth.

"Loony eh? That's not very nice you know." He pretended offence, pouting. I suddenly felt like we'd been friends for ages.

"Neither is Lady of the gents."

"What's wrong with it?"

"C'mon Loony, hurry up. Need to keep the blood pumping, or I'll turn into an icewoman."

"Oh no, you could never be ice, with the hot blood in your veins," and he linked arms with me as we went round the corner, and trotted up the street to the welcoming sign.

He ordered us a couple of pints, and we went and took a corner table, just near the open fire. Hmmm. Lovely. Nice and quiet too. And light enough to see the opposite wall and the pictures hanging on it.

"So, Mr Loony, tell me about your broken heart," I invited.

"Poet of the gents was a better name. Please call me Michael." His emphasised politeness was amusing.

"OK Michael."

"I don't want to spend the whole evening lamenting over how could Victor do this to me, and I remember when Victor and I did this, and oh but when Victor did that, wasn't he a sweetheart, and what have I ever done to deserve what Victor's done to me. He was just a Darling, and then one night I discovered he was vicious Victor, vampiric Victor, vain Victor, viperous Victor. Viperous *is* a word. I just made it up. So that's me sorted. What about you Daphne Dear?"

The whole conversation had taken an unexpected twist again and I took a moment to think about how to respond.

"Oh, it was someone back home," I sighed, "she…"

"That's it! That's all I need to know. I can guess the rest."

"You're very rude Loony," I pointed out.

"Poet," he corrected.

"Michael," I recorrected.

"Yes," he admitted solemnly. There was a silence and I wondered why on earth I'd agreed to go for a drink with this enigmatic guy. Because of that, I guess. He was enigmatic. But what on earth were we going to talk about now? I needn't have worried. Michael was one of those sorts of people who can talk nonsense for hours, or sit in perfect enduring silence with an inane smile on his face.

"I have the idea. The perfectest, most bestest idea ever. Why don't we both turn straight and date each other?"

I laughed. I knew he was joking.

"I've already tried that, didn't work."

"You most certainly have not. I would've known if you'd been trying to date me." I laughed again.

"No, the other one."

"The *other* one? What are you speaking of now?"

"I've tried the straight bit."

"Always a mistake. One must learn to sway with the bends. Nothing's ever in a straight line."

"Do you ever talk seriously about anything?"

"Never. Why do *you?*" he asked incredulously. I couldn't help but laugh.

"You really are a loony, Loony."

"Thank you, gents Lady." And the rest of the evening continued in the same zany vein.

After the pub, we taxied back to campus and walked back to my halls.

"Do you want a coffee or tea or something?" I asked once we'd entered my very messy room, where you could just about make out the furniture from under piles of clothes, books and papers.

"Nope. Don't drink. I'm an alki-totaller. Bad fer yer elf, all that caffeine." He cleared a space on my bed, and plonked his arse on it.

"You're a drama student aren't you?"

"I take offence at you stereotyping me as such." I sighed and laughed. Getting a straight answer from Michael on anything was like trying to get your buttered toast to fall on the right side!

"Which halls are you in?"

"Greenwich."

"Oh no, the security chamber!"

"The very same."

We talked the hours away till 5 am. Hardly seemed any point in going to sleep. But he finally kissed me on both cheeks in an ostentatious French way and bade me goodnight.

When I got into bed, I was smiling. As I turned out the light, I was smiling.

And as I went to sleep, I was still smiling. I'd found myself the kind of insane friend I'd always wanted!?!

Chapter Fifty-Seven

Graduation day at last! It dawned bright and clear. Although I was all happy and smiling now, last night I'd had the nightmare again. I haven't had it for years and years. Dreamt of mother and her nose bleed, those last moments together... And a boy who I keep pushing away and hurting. I don't want to, I don't mean to, but I always do, and then mother is always really upset with me. And I'm still a child in the dreams, I haven't aged at all. And the little boy is my age. I don't know what he looks like, but it's always the same one.

Bella (strange, I just couldn't think of her as 'Mum' today) and Dad had driven me and Michael up in the car. We'd all arranged to meet with the rest of our friends outside the front of the hall. All six of us, with our families. Except Michael had disowned his family. No, not the other way around. He didn't like to talk about them too much.

We all hugged. Vanessa, Charlie, Parminder, Patsy, Cecelia, Jennifer, Michael, and of course Keith. Yes, Michael had finally fallen in love again. Funny, but both me and Michael had spent the last two years or so completely celibate. I'd given up on relationships completely, except for the occasional get together with Shaun and Sam and Sarah (rebounding from Teresa) and Terry and David... OK, so I hadn't been all *that* celibate... But Michael had, that is until he met Keith during the third year. Then I didn't see him for a solid two months even though we were living in the same student house together. He was always at Keith's. Good job the girls were around in the house to have fun with, or I'd have been quite lonely during that time.

And now we were all graduating, robes and mortar-boards and all!!!! And didn't we look smart! And funny! Then we had to go out into the real world – oh no!

I wish Mum could've been here to see me. I found a poem the other day, that described just how I felt:

Presence of Absence

The seats sit there,
one awaits you for its private satisfaction,

Your arrival is an initial impossibility,
it looks an uncomfortable grey in a clear glittering day.

I stand and stare at
the chair as its space claims my heart

I don't want to
think of tears on such a pleasant day

But, oh, how I wish
you here, to see, to watch, to know

Fantasy, my well sought
oblivion from life's disappointments...

I imagine you there,
feeling proud, full of hugs and congratulations.

The vision clears to show an empty
chair, so I'll ache and imagine you there.

So, in my head, I set up an empty chair to rest next to Bella's and Dad's chairs. In honour of my mother.

Chapter Fifty-Eight

"Daphne?"

"Yes, Mum?"

"Me and your father are just going to go for a run out in the country. Want to come?"

"No thanks Mum."

"It's lovely weather for it," Mum smiled at me, wondering if I could be coaxed.

I shook my head. "Then you and Dad have a good time then," I smiled.

"OK. We might be going out for dinner tonight, so will you be all right fixing yourself something?"

"Yep, don't worry about me. I know where the oven and fridge and freezer is," I said good humouredly.

"Fine. I'll see you when I see you then." We smiled at each other and she left. I sat on my bed, looking into the mirror across my room, the large one over my dressing table. It felt so strange to be back at home again after Uni. Very strange. Almost like it wasn't home anymore. What *was* I going to do this afternoon? I heard Mum and Dad's voices and the front door slamming shut. I'd looked in this mirror a million million times, and seen myself at all different ages in it. And slept in this bed as a little girl and as a teenager. And now as a young woman. I heard the car rev up and drive away. I suddenly felt really restless. *What* was I going to do with the rest of my life, more to the point. I felt like I had no goal in life, now that I'd got my degree. I still wasn't sure what I was going to do. I decided to ring Michael. He could always cheer me up. That's if he was in. And wasn't gallivanting off somewhere with Keith. Or gallivanting in with Keith!

I went to the phone downstairs in the living room. I looked out at the surrounding hills, the green ones, the greyish ones, the yellow ones, as I waited for Michael to pick up at the other end.

It rang and rang and rang. I was just about to give up when I heard Michael's gruff voice on the other end. I must've just woken him up. He always sounded gruff first thing. I looked at my watch. 1.30pm. Michael's usual waking up time.

"What do you want?" Yes, he'd definitely just woken up!

"I wanted to talk to my best friend if that isn't too much trouble."

"Who might that be then?"

"Michael Twigger is his name, ever heard of him?"

"No, never heard of him."

"Otherwise known as Fruit Loop?"

"Oh *him*. Yes, I've heard of him. Why didn't ya call him by his proper name before?"

"Sorry. I know sometimes he likes to masquerade as Michael Twigger. I wasn't sure if you knew his real name or not."

"Of course I know his proper name. Me n him is on very good terms thank you *very* much."

"Well, would it be possible to talk to him?"

"I dunno about that. I'm not sure I can locate him for you."

"Try having a look in your bed, maybe he's still there, sleeping."

"Good idea. Hold on a minute."

Silence. "Michael?" Now *what* was he doing? Unbelievable. He really had gone back to his bed probably to see if he could find himself!

"Hello there Miss?"

"Yes?"

"I looked, and you were right about one thing, there is a body in there, but when I asked him his name, he said it was Keith. That sounds nothing like Fruit Loop to me, does it you?"

"Nothing like" I agreed.

"Maybe I heard wrong, I'll go ask him again."

"No wait. Forget it. How about I just talk to you instead, and you can relay it all to Fruit Loop later?"

"Fair enough. Who are you then?"

"You know who I am."

"I'm not a mind reader."

"OK, Daphne," I said playing along.

"Don't know anyone of *that* name."

"Do I *really* have to say it?" I asked.

"Yes."

"OK, it's Lady of the gents."

"Ah-ha, now I know who you are! Well what can I do for you then?"

"I wanted some career advice."

"Ah, hold on a minute. I think Michael's entered the room. He'll be better at talking to you about this than I."

"You reckon?"

"Hi Daphne. Sorry about that. Can't stop my shadow from talking to people."

"Good job I know you, or I'd have to have you committed!"

"Committed to what?"

"Never mind," I sighed, suddenly feeling tired of the game.

"What's wrong Daphne?" That was the good thing about Michael, he knew when it was time to make me laugh, and when it was a time I felt like crying.

"I've found you a lap dancer for the club you and Keith are going to open up," I joked, my humour returning to me.

"Really? That's great. Who?"

"Moi."

"Sorry, Daphne, you don't qualify."

"Why not?"

"You're female."

"That's sex discrimination."

"No, it's a gay club, remember?"

"Worth a try anyway," I laughed.

"Don't know what to do with yourself?"

"Got it in one!"

"Well, you got an English Lit-er-a-ture degree. You could be a manager?"

"Nah."

"Don't fancy that? Well how about an accountant?"

"Mich-ael!"

"OK, you could retrain as a lawyer!"

"Very helpful, I'm sure, but I'm minus a few grand, not plus a few grand. The bank wouldn't like it."

"Sponsorship?"

"Uh, no! I don't want to be a lawyer anyway. I couldn't handle losing a case. You know what I'm like, too much of a perfectionist!"

"Yeah, you'd end up shouting and swearing at your own client *and* the judge, knowing you!"

"I have a little more tact and decorum than that," I pretended to be offended.

"Yes, of course you have, how silly of me. You'd only scratch their eyes out and then pee on their legal papers."

I was about to deny this, but thought what the hell. "No, you're wrong there, Michael. I'd go into court totally naked, painted all over in black body paint and interrogate every single judge as to their prejudices racially speaking and gender speaking and then defecate in their laps for all being closed minded white middle class men!"

"Daphne!" Michael exclaimed in mock horror. "I think I'll take out an injunction against you becoming a lawyer then!"

"Good idea," I laughed.

"OK, so you need a rebellious job then."

"No, not a rebellious one, just one in which I can be fair and just to people."

"Ah, well for that you need something very special..."

"What's that then?"

"A space shuttle in order to take you to the next galaxy, where they have such jobs!"

"Mmmmm, except I could be waiting a very long time for one of them."

"Well, how long did you have in mind to wait?"

"Not *that* long!"

"Oh, well, you could always work for charity!"

"And what would I do for money?"

"Really, Daphne! You're so materialistic! What does money matter?!"

"Well, you know, it's kinda helpful if I want to eat and have somewhere to live and shit like that, but other than that, it's absolutely no use at all!"

"Oh, you want shit like that do ya? Well, you can still work for a charity and get paid you know!"

"OK, I changed my mind, I want a job where I can be really

shitty to people, after all I'm no good at admin stuff, or organising people."

"What utter bollocks you talk sometimes Daphne!"

"This isn't getting me anywhere!"

"You know what you've got don't you?"

"No, what?"

"No nothing-itus!"

`"What *does* that mean?"

"It means no matter what I suggest, you're going to find something wrong with it, so I'm wasting my time giving you ideas."

"No, that's not true."

"Yes it is." A silence ensued. If we'd have been in the same room together, we would be having a staring-out war and whoever spoke first would lose the battle. I held the phone to my ear, searching the fields for grains of knowledge, truth, some sort of direction to take. I began to wonder if Michael was still at the other end and hadn't walked away, but I knew if I said his name, then I'd lost. I thought about what he'd said.

"OK, you're right," I finally said, longing to break the silence.

I waited for Michael to gloat, but instead he just said, "I've a friend you might be interested in meeting."

"Who's that then?"

"I'll fix you up a blind careers date, what do you say?"

"What's one of them then?"

"You'll have to come and find out won't you?"

"OK Michael. You nutty nutty arse! Who, when and where?"

"I'm not going to tell you who. But I'll sort out the when and where and let you know."

"Michael, what does this person...?" He hung up. "Michael? Michael?" The NERVE of the man! I slammed the phone down, then immediately rang his number again.

It rung several thousands times, before a sleepy Keith answered the phone.

"Hello?"

"Keith, is Michael there? Can you put him on please? It's Daphne."

"Sorry, Daphne, he isn't here."

"Ha-ha, very funny Keith. I was just talking to him. Put him on."

"No, honestly Daphne. I know he *was* here, but he's just raced from the house like a Fruit Loop possessed! I can't bring him to the phone if he's not here."

"You'd better not be lying to me Keith?"

"Would I?" He asked astounded.

I reflected a moment. No, he probably wouldn't, he knew I'd beat him up if he did! He would honestly have said that Michael was there, but wasn't coming to the phone if that was the case. I scared Keith a little bit. He was as steady as Michael was off the wall.

"No, you wouldn't. I know you wouldn't."

"Thank you. How are you anyway?" After the initial hostilities between us had abated, when Michael had just met Keith, we'd finally found some common ground, and actually got on with each other fairly well these days. Most of the time anyway. We were still slightly unsure of each other on occasion.

"Fine, just worrying about my life."

"Take a holiday, and think about it after."

"Easy coming from someone who *knows* what they're doing."

"True." Still we weren't best buddies or anything, and conversation could still be awkward sometimes. Especially over the phone.

"Anyway I'd best get off, sorry to disturb your beauty sleep."

"No problem. See you again soon, Daphne."

"Sure will. Bye Keith." And I was left to wonder at my blind careers date that Michael had in store for me. And whether he was actually serious, or whether I'd end up being a clown at a kids' party, which I think would suit Michael's sense of humour right down to the ground!

Chapter Fifty-Nine

Lunch hour. Five minutes to breathe and stuff my sandwiches down my throat.

The office was strangely quiet. No phones ringing. No-one bustling round doing 101 things. Where was everyone? On various assignments no doubt. Well, Francine had certainly been right. And so had Michael. My blind career date had certainly paid off. Went off to the London College of Printing, did my MA in Publishing/Publishing Production. And through the college's contacts managed to land a job here. And have loved every minute of being an editorial assistant for Unicorn Publishing House.

Oh, one other person still here. My eyes followed the movements of Adrian Shelton. New boy. Only been here a couple of weeks. And boy had he ever caught my eye. My eyes rested on his face, as he typed away at his desk. I had a naughty but nice idea.

"Adrian, could you come up to the top floor with me a moment. There's some stuff I need to dig out, and it'll be quicker if there's two of us."

"Sure," he said obligingly.

He followed me up the stairs. And thoughts of his nakedness followed in my head.

I waited till he was absorbed in looking through an old filing cabinet, then made my way round the back of him.

I stood right behind him, not touching, my lips at his ear.

"Let me fuck you."

Adrian stopped what he was doing and froze.

I moved my hands up his inner thighs, gently stroking. "Do you want me?" I whispered in his ear. My hands wandered to and stroked his groin to see if I was having the desired effect. I was. "Like I want you?" I stopped. "I'm wet for you," I said gently. I slowly moved round to face him. Our eye contact was intense and unblinking. Our breathing was very loud in the stillness of the room.

I stood very close to him not touching. Just feeling his warmth emanating, letting him feel mine. I wondered how long he'd hold out. A whole four seconds I think was all it took, before his mouth was on mine, passionately exploring. I lifted his hands to my breasts, and they easily found their way to my buttons. He took one and then the other into his mouth. He felt good, I knew he would. There'd been that electric attraction building between us ever since he joined the firm, only a fortnight ago. I'd just been waiting for my chance. Just the right time when the balance was dead right between surprise and desire. When I knew he'd respond happily to my demands, when I was ready to have his body in my hands.

I stepped away from him, and let my skirt slither to the floor. "I'm not wearing any knickers," I told him, watching his expression. Yes he was still with me, yes he wanted me, good. I touched myself with a sly finger, then lifted it and sucked it slowly. "I'm absolutely sodden." He started to move towards me, his hunger growing.

"No, wait." He stopped, looking at me, waiting, wondering. "Let me watch you undress first." He proceeded to hastily undo himself, in order to throw them on the floor. "Slowly," I remonstrated, "I want to savour you." Yes he liked a woman in command, but only to a point, and I knew exactly when to press the button. I watched him take off his shirt, enjoying the sight of his naked muscled torso. He worked out, obviously. His dark good looks were the first thing that had caught my attention. He had enough model good looks, thrown in with a bit of rough, just the way I liked them.

He was just unzipping his trousers, and he said, "How's your cunt?" So he could play ball too, good.

"Dripping." I saw him smile. "How's your cock?"

"Hard."

"How hard?"

"You'll see in a moment." He looked at me, to check my response, and he saw my smile.

When he was fully unmasked from his clothes, I ordered

him to touch himself. He obeyed. "Does it feel good?"

"It would feel better if you did it."

"In good time."

He continued to rub himself, as I walked round to the back of him, and kissed my way gently across his toned shoulder blades, and back. Still behind him, not touching, I whispered in his ear, "I want you to fuck me hard, against that wall over there. Do you think you can do that?" He turned to face me. I wondered how he would rise to the challenge. He put his hand on my wet sex, and my body immediately responded.

"Yes, I think I can handle that."

"Good. I like to play rough. Do you want to play?" I stopped his hand, and slid it upwards, to cup my breast inside my loose hanging shirt.

"Yes," he said with naked lustful eyes. He walked forwards and I walked backwards. We paced ourselves in a slow dance till we came to 'that wall'.

"What about pregnancy?"

"I've got a cap."

"You were that sure of me?" He raised his eyebrows.

He might not be offended by the presumption, but to be on the safe side I just said, "I was prepared."

"What about STDs?" I asked.

"I'm clean."

"You'd say that anyway," I pointed out.

"What about you?"

"I'm clean."

"You'd say that anyway."

"Touché." He cocked his head on one side, as if to say there you go then. "I would never play around with something like that," I told him in all seriousness. "Neither would I." And it was foolish of us both really, but we trusted each other. Perhaps it was the way it was said. Perhaps because we both knew we hadn't gone too far, and it would be so easy to stop. And we would've done, if either had felt any threat in that way.

So that was the health and safety necessities out of the way, now it was time for the seduction to take over.

"Fuck me deep, Adrian." But first he had to feel and taste my mouth and chest more, it was his turn to tease me, and I let him. I massaged his buttocks, drawing his hard length along my softness, our juices mixing. "Show me how much you want me," I demanded, my body aching as his urgency built.

"Beg for it," he said, as his cock titillated my clitoris. And I was pleased at the switch over point of power. I knew the shy, gentleman-like Adrian was really a primitive animal, just like myself. Well, I didn't always know, sometimes the guy I picked would follow all my orders like a sheep, but it was always more interesting if they played ball, much more exciting. He repeated his order, and we pretended that he wouldn't enter me till I did. I doubted he could hold out very long now.

"I beg you to fuck me, I want to feel you deep inside me now," I growled. Still he held out, and teased. I was impressed. "Let me draw you deep into me, down into my hot wetness." He groaned in anticipation. I was amused, he was still pretending he was in control. "Fuck me now," I commanded, my desire now hitting frenzied heights. And I expected a hard thrust, but instead, there was a gentle nuzzle, as he inched his way, then dipped in and out slowly, making my desire spiral upwards ever more. He then burrowed himself within me, feeding his hunger, and then stopped, and let me feed mine. It was wonderful torturous pleasure. But I didn't tell him how good he was. I wasn't there to massage his ego.

After we shook to climax, I held him to me, breathing in his musk and his sweat. He gently kissed my shoulders and neck. Fantastic. Just what the libido had ordered.

"How about dinner tonight?" I asked him. "Take it or leave it, I don't mind." I did mind terribly if he did say no. But bravado was everything.

"You're on."

"Indian do you? There's a great restaurant just down the road from me." I watched his body ripple back into his everyday mask. What a shame. If I had my way, I'd have him wander round the office all day naked.

"And then back to your place after?" he asked, half playful, half serious.

"Now that would be personal," I teased, "I don't mix food and sex."

"Only work and sex?"

"That's more fun."

"Food and sex is fun too."

"Maybe when I know you better." He was amused too. Adrian had turned out better than I had expected. Still, he had to pass the meal test. If anything else was going to happen, or else he'd just end up on the reject pile, like all the others. But if Adrian proved to be as much fun in other areas, then who knows where the affair might lead...? And hopefully he wouldn't bore me like all the others did. I often got bored of men. They just so often had nothing else on offer, nothing that made the appeal last beyond a few weeks. And the sex got boring too.

"So is it a date?" I asked nonchalantly.

"It's a date, Daphne," he smiled warmly.

Now I was fully clothed, yet what *was* that tingling down my spine, just when he'd said my name?

Chapter Sixty

We'd been seeing each other for a few months now. And I thought we'd been getting along famously. Lots of fun. Lots of laughs. Adrian was very good natured and easy-going. And fucking great in bed.

And this was supposed to be a romantic evening in, but things weren't turning out quite as planned. Why the hell was Adrian so fucking argumentative all the time?

He'd cooked a gloriously wonderful meal, by candlelight too. Nice touch. He'd found his way round my kitchen easily. Too easily.

Now he had to go and ruin it all. Just because I suggested we give the theatre a miss. OK, so the tickets were already reserved and paid for. But what did that matter? I thought bed would've been more exciting. But Adrian wasn't just not in the mood, he was... "Is that all you think about. Sex?"

"Isn't that my line?" I teased, hoping to win him back on my side. Bad move.

"Don't be so bloody facetious Daphne."

OK, humour didn't work. Time to fight fire with fire. "Don't you dare speak to me as if I was a raging adolescent who didn't know what I wanted."

"But that's just it Daphne. *Do* you know what you want? 'cause I sure as hell don't. If it's just sex, if that's what all this is to you, nothing more than a frolic in the hay, then forget it! We can call the whole thing quits here and now."

"Don't you fucking take the moral high ground with me Adrian Shelton. You don't fucking own me."

"No, you're right. I don't. And I don't want to. That's not what this is about. Why do you keep avoiding the issue all the time?" He sounded tired and agitated. I can fight anger with anger, but what do I do with this?

"And what is the issue exactly?"

"I can see I'm going to have to spell this out for you in loud letters." He shook his head sadly. He turned away from me.

I couldn't stand this. "Adrian?" No response. "Christ! Talk to me, will you?"

He turned to face me and said quietly, "Do you love me?"

"Oh, Jesus Adrian…"

"That's all the answer I needed. Goodbye Daphne." He went to pick up his coat from the hall. My heart gave a terrified jolt.

"No, wait. Adrian please."

"What?"

"Don't go. I need you." My voice cracked. That was a big give for me. Couldn't he see the sacrifice I was making?

"I don't think you know what you need at the moment," he said without anger. He made as if to go anyway, but stopped. I went to him, but I couldn't touch him. Couldn't bring myself to do that. His eyes stared into mine, and he said with tenderness, "Admit it Daphne. You're running scared."

"Of what?" I said defiantly, trying to hold back the tears that were threatening.

"Being close. Of intimacy."

"We've been intimate lots of…"

"God damn it! You know what I'm talking about. Stop going round the fucking houses with me." His anger was back in full force. I stood my ground. He was so pig ignorant and self satisfied sometimes. I wasn't about to be bullied into any statements of undying true love. I couldn't vouch for my sincerity on that. And I wasn't even sure if I believed in it. Not for me anyway.

"You're such a bloody steam roller sometimes, Adrian. Just going your own sweet way and expecting others to fall in with you. My feelings don't always fit in neatly with yours when and wherever you feel like it. I'm not going to stand here and have your terms for my feelings dictated to me."

"That's the first meaningful thing you've said to me in ages."

"Meaningful my arse! Stop being so fucking patronising. I hate it when you're like this, thinking you're better than everyone else, and nobody else has any reason whatsoever to behave any other way than how you think they should. I'm not a dog Adrian. I don't do tricks, and I sure as hell won't jump through hoops for you. So get used to it!"

"I'm not asking much Daphne, I just want to know where…"

"Yes, you ARE asking a lot Adrian. And that's the problem. You don't realise just how much you are asking. You talk about love as if it's a gift you can buy in a shop, that you keep under your bed, and just hold on to, till the 'right'," I made a sixty-six ninety-nine sign with my fingers, "person comes along, and just decide to give it to them. You can't simplify like that. Just because you have no troubles wearing your heart on your sleeve, don't expect it to be so easy for everybody else."

"I'm sorry Daphne." I thought he was apologising to me at first, but then realised he was just sorry about the whole situation. "But that's not it at all. You think this is easy for me? I would've thought you were the one who had it easy. You've always it had easy Daphne. You've no idea how lucky you've been in your life. You're one spoilt lady, but you can't even see it. You ought to try looking at things from someone else's point of view for a change, instead of giving out critical tirades like the journalist you are. I'm not a fucking case study, I'm a person, and damn it, I have feelings too you know. But if I have to point that out to you, then that speaks volumes doesn't it?"

"You're jumping to conclusions again. You're always doing that. You don't know my whole life history Adrian. You don't know if I've had it easy or not. And you're the one that feels it necessary to point out you have feelings. So you can't stand there and make presumptions about what sort of state our relationship is in from that. Why don't you come down off your high horse for once, and treat me like a fucking equal?"

"I always treat you as an equal, you're just too blind to see it."

"You're not treating me like one at the moment."

"That's because you're not behaving like one."

"You're right Adrian. You should just go." I wasn't going to be insulted like that.

We stood a moment in silence. Eye to eye. My blue to his green. We were at an impasse. The electricity between us was tangible. I still wanted to whisk him off to bed, and show him how I really felt about him. But that wasn't an option at the moment. I wasn't going to open myself up to a second rejection tonight.

Unexpectedly, he gently said, "Will you call me?" The tears sprung up again, I blinked them away. He cupped my face with his rough hand. If we kissed, I wouldn't be able to stop myself, I'd be fire in his arms.

"You could call me," I say.

"These days of equality…"

I smiled. "And what would we say to each other?" I whispered.

"I don't know. I really don't know." I looked into his sincere green. He bent to kiss me. I stepped back. If I couldn't have all of him right there, I didn't want any of him. I looked into his hurting green, and felt a corresponding pain in the pit of my stomach. "We might say we loved each other," he finally said after some time. He looked like a wounded animal, but he was pushing me again. And I wasn't ready. He sought reassurance in my blueness. I wanted to reach out for him, but I resisted. Not yet. Not like this. Damn it! – I wasn't ready for this.

I couldn't rebuff him the way I wanted to. "We might," I conceded.

"Or we might not." He stood up straight, his voice clipped. He thought that was the answer I had really wanted to give. I bit my lip, no longer knowing what to say.

He went through to the hall way. I watched him put his coat on. His hand was on the door. I was going to let him walk out. Walk away. He wasn't going to stay.

"Adrian," his name was out of my mouth, before I could stop it. He faced me again, but his green was now impassive and cold. "I'll call you," I said lamely, feeling terribly vulnerable. I thought he was going to reject me, reject my offer, say goodbye for good. Damn it, I wanted him. I wanted him back. But not like this.

"Please do," was all he said. I was surprised and relieved, even though the politeness grated on my nerves. Our blue and green battled for communication. I couldn't read him. I don't know if he could read me.

I closed the door after him, and stood with my back to it, resting against it, wondering at what had just passed. Could it be mended? Could *we* be mended? I couldn't think about it anymore, it was all such a fog.

Chapter Sixty-One

I was flopped in one of Michael's comfy chairs that had seen better days. Keith was out. Somewhere. I sighed deeply and Michael looked at me with that sort of "I know what's wrong with you Daphne, but you gotta admit it to yourself" look. That infuriating look.

D: *Why* am I so miserable?

M: Because you love him.

D: Who? What?

M: You're so miserable Daphne, because you've fallen in love and you miss him like crazy, and want him back.

D: That's absurd. Of course I don't love him!

M: OK. So *you* tell *me* why you've been Miss Misery Dumps ever since Adrian walked out on you.

D: He didn't walk out on me. He said for me to call him.

M: And have you?

D: Not yet.

M: Why not?

D: Because I'm still angry with him, that's why.

M: Because he's got under your skin.

D: Yes. No! Well, maybe. I dunno. Michael, do you think I'm spoilt?

M: Is that what he said? No, I don't think you're spoilt. A little insensitive and harsh sometimes, but not spoilt.

D: Thanks Michael! I think I preferred myself as spoilt! At least it sounds like it's not my fault then!

M: Hey, you know you can always depend on my honesty, Daph.

D: What am I going to do? I wasn't supposed to fall in love. That wasn't meant to happen. It wasn't in the plan!

M: You don't plan for love, Daph Dear, it just happens to

you.

D: But I'm not ready for it yet. I can't do this.

M: Not ready for what? Not ready to open yourself up to the enormity of the potential hurt that you could face?

D: That's right.

M: Not ready to risk being in love, for the fear of losing it again?

D: Yes.

M: Not ready to commit to such a powerful relationship, because you've never been in so deep before?

D: Yes.

M: Not ready to be loved for all that you are by some gorgeous hunk who will make mind-blowing love to you anywhere you like?

D: No, yes, I mean, hey that was an unfair question!

M: Thought that would get you!

D: Michael! *What* am I going to do?

M: What do you want to do?

D: Take him to bed and shag his brains out.

M: Yes I know the feeling.

D: Hands off! He's mine!

M: Is he now?

D: I wish he was.

M: He could be, if you wanted him for more than just sex.

D: Why do you both think that sex is all I ever want?

M: I know it's not all you ever want Daphne Darling, but I can see how Adrian might interpret it that way. You use sex to express yourself, well everybody does, but… what I'm trying to say is you use sex to *relate* to people and think that explains everything, how you're feeling, who you are, what you think of the other person. But sometimes your romantic other, your partner, whoever, wants to feel you love them in other ways, not just in bed.

D: Or the shower.

M: Or the haystack.

D: Or in a lift.

M: Or the kitchen counter.

D: Or on the rug in front of the fire.

M: Exactly.

D: But I do love him whatever, not just in bed. So what am I *supposed* to say to him?

M: Yes, I know that Darling. But apparently he doesn't. You don't really have to *say* anything specifically. Just *being* with him in the garden or the cinema, holding hands, so you both know you care about each other whilst doing simple things.

D: God you're such a slushy romantic, Michael. I know Keith's a lucky chap having someone like you, but I do wonder how he stands it all!

M: Yes, well I was fortunate to end up with someone who could stand all my romantic ideals and dribbling.

D: I just get so awfully insecure sometimes, and...

M: I know you do.

D: ...and I feel I have to be sexual such a lot of the time, otherwise I won't be accepted. Like he won't love me if I'm not sexual.

M: Hey, Daph, you'll always be sexual Darling. You're a fiery temptress! But you don't have to be orgasming 24/7 in order to be loved.

D: Don't I?

M: No Sweetheart. And that is what Adrian's trying to tell you, you blind pup. He's telling you he loves you anyway, no matter what you're doing. He just wants to feel the same thing back from you, and that he doesn't have to perform orgasmically in bed for you everyday in order to be loved by you. He wants to feel that you don't just want him for sex.

D: I don't though.

M: No, I know, but that's the bit that scares you. All the other stuff that goes with the sex. So you push him away. 'cause sex is your only outlet to express your need and desire for him, and he's chucked it back at you, so you feel stuck, like a dictionary without any words.

D: That sums it up rather well. How do you do that? No, don't tell me, I don't want you rambling on, praising yourself on your insightful insights into my psyche. You still haven't answered my original question. What do I do now?

M: What do you want to do?

D: We're going round in circles here. Stop it!

M: But if I tell you to do something, you'll find one hundred

306

and one reasons or excuses against it. You know what you want to do Daph, you've just got to find the courage to do it.

D: I want to call him.

M: OK. So what's holding you back?

D: I just see this picture of us, eating and drinking at a restaurant somewhere, maybe. And feeling really awkward. Not having anything to say. Feeling inadequate and useless. Not being able to tell him the 'meaningful' things he wants to hear. And scared of being rejected.

M: Welcome to the human race Daph. It's not so bad feeling inadequate you know. You just haven't had enough practice at it. You need to stop being Miss Perfect Goddess for a minute or two each week, and realise what us lesser mortals go through grinding along on a daily basis.

D: You're being silly.

M: No, I'm being dead serious Daph. He'll still love you even if you feel inadequate and useless. The thing is for *you* to know that you're *neither* of those things, even if you feel it sometimes. And that someone can still love you, even when you're being a miserable pain-in-the-arse! Like now. And I still love you.

D: Yes, but not in *that* way.

M: No, not in that way. But you're changing the rules, just because you've slept with Adrian and you haven't slept with me. Sex always makes things look more complicated that they have to be.

D: Is that true?

M: Of course it is! I'm being your guru for today, so everything I say is gospel! *We both laugh.*

D: So it's really not so terrible?

M: What?

D: Feeling inadequate? Ya think I can handle that in front of Adrian?

M: I know you can Sweetheart. There's the phone over there.

D: Yes thanks Michael. I know that. *He looks at me. I sigh. I go over to the phone.* Are you going to listen?

M: Damn straight I am. I know what you're like.

D: Don't you trust me?

M: No.

D: Thanks for the vote of confidence.

M: You're welcome. *He stays sat there fixedly. I was going have to go through with it. Michael was such a bastard! I rung his number and waited. It rang and it rang, and then an answer machine clicked in. I hung up.* Daph-ne!

D: It's on the answering machine. I hate them horrible things.

M: Leave a message!

D: No.

M: Do it, or I'll ring him myself!

D: You wouldn't dare!

M: Watch me. *Michael makes a grab for the phone, and I hold it away from him, laughing.*

D: No, no. Get off, Michael. OK, OK, god, you're worse than Adrian.

M: No, I'm not. He's definitely worse than me. Definitely!

I rung a second time. I waited till after the beep. My mouth went suddenly very dry. "Adrian. Er. It's me. Daphne. Just calling to say… Oh shit, I dunno what I want to say. I hate these damn things. Listen, Adrian, I want to, well, if you could just call me back on…" I saw Michael's disapproving look. He wasn't going to let me cop out just because I was talking to his fucking answer phone! He was most definitely worse than Adrian! Why on earth did I let Michael push me into this? Some best friend! "OK, so you know my number Adrian. I guess I want to say I'm sorry. I'd really like to meet and talk. And if we make it a date for sometime next week, or even next year sometime, so then I'll have had time to think of maybe a few more sensible things to say. Depends on how long you want to wait, but…"

"Hi Daphne." Words dried up on me the instant I heard his voice. "Daphne?"

"Adrian?"

"I got all that. Look, I'm sorry too. Are you free tonight?" His apology threw me off completely. I suddenly felt very giddy.

"That's a bit soon isn't it?"

"For what?"

"For me to think of something meaningful to say. You

know it might take some time. Not sure I can do it under that sort of time pressure."

"You seem to be doing just fine." I could hear my heart pounding wildly. Why did he have this effect on me? Nobody else ever had. I tried to hold the phone steady.

"I am?"

"Just fine. Anyway tonight's a long way away from the last time we saw each other. I don't think I can wait any longer."

Fifty-six miserable hours ago. Not that I'd been counting or anything.

"OK," I agreed.

"Where do you want to meet?"

"I don't know, you choose."

"Are you feeling OK?"

"Yes fine, why?" I lied.

"'Cos normally you know exactly where and when you want to meet." Don't make this any harder Adrian, or I might have to accidentally on purpose drop the phone on you, even if Michael is watching.

"OK. Let's meet at Brady's Bar at seven," I decided.

"I'll see you then then."

"Yeah."

"Oh, and Daphne?"

"Yeah?"

"I'm glad you called. I look forward to seeing you tonight." And he clicked off.

"See? That wasn't so bad was it?" Michael grinned inanely at me.

"No, it was worse. You lied. Feeling inadequate is bloody awful."

"Yes, but it was worth it wasn't it?" he said, still with a stupid grin on his face.

"No you wretch! Now I have to go through it all again tonight!"

"Some people are never happy." That was it! I caught up the nearest cushion, and proceeded to beat him over the head with it, or anywhere I could reach. He grabbed another one and retaliated happily.

Chapter Sixty-Two

"Why are you acting so strange about it? So huffed up about it all?" I looked at Dominic. He didn't understand at all. I watched my brother holding his birth certificate and I just wondered if there was any point in dragging up all these skeletons and all this pain. Was it really worth it?

"*I'm* not going to look for *my* biological parents." He looked hurt at my curt tone. I hadn't meant to sound as harsh as that.

"Why not, Sheila? What's so wrong with it?" he asked me tentatively.

"I just don't see the point." I couldn't help myself from being so short with him.

"Don't you ever wonder why? Don't you sometimes feel that you want to know?" he asked reasonably.

"Mum and Dad gave us everything. They made us who we are. I would never want to turn my back on that." Why was I being so defensive? But why couldn't he see how this hurt the rest of the family?

"Well, it's your decision not to," he said carefully, "and this is mine. I don't love Mum and Dad any less. I just feel like an interrupted narrative – a story without a beginning, and I feel I need to find those missing pieces. I need to get them back. Fill in the blanks, so to speak."

"And what happens if you do find your 'real' parents?" My scorn erupted. My nerves were raw. "What happens then eh? In your duplicity, having two sets of parents, possibly two sets of siblings? People you've never even met – who might not even know you exist! Have you thought of that?"

Dominic considered my words a moment. "I've thought about it all endlessly. But I didn't create this duplicity, Sheila. My parents did. I've run through in my head a million different case scenarios of what could happen, what it might be like. To be honest, I just don't know. I don't know who I might find at the end of my search, or even if they'll want to know who I am. But I have to take that risk. There's this restlessness, this yearning almost, that's egging me on. It won't leave me alone. It's difficult to explain to you. But it's just something I *need* to do."

There speaks my brother, the lawyer. Of course he'd thought it all through. Every single logical argument to the bitter end, no doubt. And his instincts came up with the same answer every time – to find his parents. The ones that *did* bring him into the world. What was all the mystery with the origin of our genes anyway? I pretended I didn't understand. Part of me did. Part of me understood all too well that indefinable, inexplicable need to find my parents. But a bigger part of me wanted to maintain the status quo and not upset the boat. A bigger part of me wanted everything to stay as they are. A bigger part of me wanted to deny I'd ever been adopted in the first place and that Mum and Dad were Mum and Dad. Dominic's pain was too real sometimes, and I DIDN'T WANT TO KNOW.

I saw Dominic interpreting the steady silence that I greeted his words with.

"Please don't hate me for this, Sheila."

"I don't hate you…"

"I feel a 'but' here."

"But I can't help feeling a new distance between us because of it."

"I still love you Sheila. You'll always be my sister. Just like I'll always love Mum and Dad and Samantha. And everything we've shared and still share, I hold so dear to my heart, and always will. But…"

"Your niggly genes keep getting in the way."

"I don't want you to see this as a rejection. God knows I feel enough guilt about this. I don't want to lose you."

"You won't lose me, Dominic. But don't expect others to accept your decisions and the effects of them so readily. It's a tough one to swallow, OK? Just give me some time to adjust to this. And Mum and Dad and Sam will need time too. So promise you won't go jumping down their throats with all your well-thought out arguments and reasonable conclusions, because all our different feelings cloud it all up. And it's still hard to see what's right and what's really going on."

"OK, I promise."

"Listening to you sometimes, I can't help but feel a sort of reverse guilt, for *not* wanting to find my own parents, when they were the ones to reject me in the first place. How crazy is that?"

"Maybe it just isn't right for you to trace your origins, Sheila. Don't give yourself a hard time about it."

"You're being very generous about this."

"It's tearing me up, Sheila, and I don't want to tear others up with it."

But you are, my dear brother, you are anyway. And there's no avoiding it. "I love you, Dominic. I just want you to find peace within yourself." We hugged each other tight. We hugged through the distances between us. Through the different hurts we were both feeling. Yet it was the same hurt. We'd both been adopted. Both in the same boat. But we weren't rowing together, we were going in different directions. I didn't want to be on the opposite side of the river to him. I really didn't.

"Love you too." We looked into each other's eyes. A tear escaped and ran down my cheek. Dominic stopped it with his finger. There was no perceptible movement from either of us, almost as if time had stopped, but there was something a little too intimate in his eyes, in his look. What was going on here? I pulled away.

"Good luck with your search, Dominic. I don't hold it against you that you want to search. And I hope what you find doesn't bring you unhappiness." I half lied. I did wish him luck and happiness. But I also did hold a grudge against him for wanting to look. I didn't want to. I tried to fight the feeling, but it wouldn't go away.

"Thank you, Sheila. Your support means a lot to me."

I faced him again and smiled. "You are very welcome," I said. He smiled back. My heart ached for what he may or may not find out.

Chapter Sixty-Three

"Daphne, are you having an affair?" I avoided Adrian's eyes. My eyes fell on the pair of long slim white stone textured vases that Mum and Dad had got us as moving-in presents. Their pleasure at me and Adrian 'settling down'. But we'd never really 'settled down' to anything. Sure, we were living together. But...

Everything *had* been going great. All the usual 'fantastic-in-loveness' that you get at the start of new relationships. And Adrian had lasted longer than I'd expected. But these past few weeks, something had been wrong. And we'd both been ignoring it.

He seemed to want something that I couldn't give. He just never gave me enough space. He said I was being remote. I said he was being possessive. He said I was cutting him out. We both wanted each other, but... not in a way that seemed to be compatible.

And then I'd bumped into Teresa. My old 'flame'.

She was raw from having split with her long-term relationship. She'd been with a lass, Beatrice, for nearly four years. But it hadn't worked out in the end. And I found Teresa consoling. I found she didn't ask for that secret centre of myself that Adrian seemed to be so in demand of all of the time. And our passion in the bedroom department rekindled all too easily. And I found some sort of reassurance, perhaps *revenge?* – in Teresa wanting me again, after the hurt she'd caused me, back in those oh-so-innocent days of university. I relished every moment with her, I can't deny it. And yes, I've seen her a few times now.

But I'm a slightly different person now to the one I was back then. I learned a few things along the way. And to my dismay, I found that Teresa didn't fill the void in my life anymore.

But Teresa couldn't let go.

There had been one too many hung up phone calls. Teresa had pestered me to see her again. She wouldn't take no for an answer. But I just didn't want to see her anymore.

She reawakened my longing for Adrian. But it still wasn't working between us. I felt so frustrated and confused. And now he'd twigged. He knew. I guess it wasn't that hard to put two and two together.

"Daphne, I asked you a question. *Are* you having an affair?"

"No, not anymore." I admitted. Guilt was written all over me.

"So you were having an affair!"

"I saw someone a couple of times."

"Did you sleep with him?" Of course he assumes the gender.

"Yes."

"Do you love him?"

"No."

"Do you want to be with him?"

"No."

"Is it someone I know?"

"No, you don't know her."

"Her?"

"Teresa." I had told him previously of my earlier experimentation in my teens.

"Are you gay?"

"No."

"Are you bisexual?"

"I'm not a fucking label. I'm just the way I am."

He didn't say anything for a while, as he sat on the bed, his head in his hands. I felt like a berated school kid, having been caught by the teacher for doing wrong. The silence was awful, clotting, almost solid. I couldn't think of anything to say, but he didn't say anything either. I had to break the silence, I had to stop it.

"Adrian?" He didn't answer. I stood there, wondering what to do. Feeling terrible, wanting to be sick, legs wobbling. I felt like a tower block with no foundations, ready to topple at any second. I wanted to go to him, touch him. Tell him I want to be with him, no-one else. Wish it all away, all my stupidity, my temptations, my fear. But my feet wouldn't move, they were lead weight, dead stone, frozen.

After some time he said without looking at me, "Why, why, why, why, why, why?"

"I was stupid, I was scared."

"Of what?"

"You."

"But I love you Daphne."

"Yes, I know."

"Do you?"

"No. Yes. Sometimes I can't *feel* it. I can't feel you."

"You have been pushing me away a lot lately."

"Yes, I'm sorry."

"What do you want Daphne?"

"I want to be with you."

"Yet you insist on hurting me."

"I can't help it."

"Damn it! Don't say that." I jumped.

"Sorry."

"And stop apologising." I bit my tongue. What else did I have to say except sorry?

He looks at me expectant. I can't say or do anything. My loss of words and action is an alien thing to me. Usually I am so sure of what I want, what I'm doing, and get on with it. Now everything is so uncertain. Except for the fact that I love Adrian, and now I risked losing him. He came over to me, putting his hands on my hips, kissed me gently. I fell into him, my tears cascading. He held me gently. I could feel his stomach rising and falling rhythmically, his warm chest and arms cushioning me, my face hidden against his jumper, feeling its woolliness absorb my tears. I can smell his musk, that he uses in the shower.

He finally says, "I think we should spend some time apart. I'm not saying this is the end of us, Daphne. I'm not saying I'm reconciled to the situation, but I think we both need some space to clear our heads a bit. And then we can meet up and discuss our futures and see how we feel then."

"I don't want to do that."

"I know. But I think you need to Daphne. And I do too."

"When will we meet?"

"I don't want to put a definite time limit on it. That would be unreasonable. I think we can just phone each other when we're ready."

"What about… living arrangements?"

"You can stay here if you like. I'll rent a room or something for a while."

"No. Don't do that. You stay here, and I'll go stay with Mum and Dad for a bit." I didn't want him moving out, he might never move back in again. And I certainly didn't want to stay here without him, it was *our* place, not mine.

"Are you sure? I don't want to push you out."

"I'd feel better if you stayed. It'd be good to see my parents, haven't seen them for a while. And you never know, they might talk some sense into me." I laughed self-consciously, but Adrian didn't smile.

"I want you to do what you think, not what Isabel and Ted think."

I felt a surge of anger. "And since when did I ever do anything they wanted me to, that I didn't want to do myself?" He smiled then.

"Never."

"Right." And that somehow gave me the strength to pull out of his embrace. "I'd best pack a few things then." I couldn't look at him.

"Daphne?" Our eyes met. "Call me whenever you want to. I don't want us *not* talking to each other. I just need some room to breathe and think."

Room without me in. Yeah, sure! But I couldn't protest, I was the guilty party here, he was the one who'd been wronged, so I couldn't really deny him this. Not if I wanted us back together again.

"Will *you* call *me*?" I asked him directly.

"Yes, of course I will." My gaze turned to the cluttered dressing table; make up remover, lipsticks, nail varnishes, hair brushes, cotton buds.

"OK, good. Well, I can't pack with you standing here watching, so I suggest…."

"You don't have to do it now, Daph…"

"Yes I do," I said firmly, pleased that my voice didn't break.

Adrian didn't argue, knowing this was hard for both of us. "So I suggest you take a walk or something and I'll be gone by the time you get back. I'll call you when I get to Mum and Dad's to let you know I'm safe."

He didn't say anything for a moment. "OK, yes, that's probably best." Well go already! Go! Before I change my mind and beg you to let me stay. "I'll speak to you tonight."

"Yes, I'll speak to you tonight Adrian." I thought about saying 'I love you' but somehow it didn't feel appropriate. I concentrated on standing still, until I heard the bedroom door click behind, until I heard his receding footsteps down the stairs, until I heard the front door latch and bang shut after him.

Then I was free to pack and cry.

***

I got to Mum and Dad's and unloaded the car.

The torrent of questions was withheld. They knew not to pry, that I'd open up in my own time. It was said without words that Adrian and I had split somehow.

I loved the familiarity of coming home. If I stayed too long I would begin to feel restless and want to move back into my own space, but right now, it was good to be enveloped once again in the family space.

It wasn't until my third evening there that Mum broached the subject with me. We sat on my childhood bed. Dad had taken Lee-Lee out for a walk – Bonny's descendant.

"Do you want to talk about it?"

"Why isn't it working mum? Why does it keep going wrong between us?"

"Perhaps you're not meant to be together. Or perhaps you're just not on the same wavelength. Perhaps you need to talk things over more? I don't know darling. You tell me."

"I want him back."

"Do you? Why?" Mum's philosophy was that people held the answers to their own questions. This was sometimes helpful, sometimes incredibly infuriating.

"Because I love him."

"And you love Teresa?"

317

"A part of me does." I said honestly.

"Which part? Your childhood part?"

"I guess. I don't know."

"Did you think of Adrian at all when you were with her?"

"A little."

"What did you think of?" I looked out of my bedroom window to the familiar shape of distant hills that my eyes had run over and played with a million times. "Do you feel guilty about the answer to that question?" Mum knew me too well. Knew my silences very well. I nodded. "You may or may not want Teresa back. But however much you may or may not want Adrian, part of you rejects him. Would a reconciliation with him really make you happy? Or would you still be ignoring something unresolved within yourself?" I looked at Mum wondering at what she might be getting at. As if she could read my mind she suddenly said, "I don't mean whether you're straight or gay or whatever. I mean you giving yourself time alone to discover how *you* can make *you* happy, regardless of whether you're with Adrian or not, or with Teresa or whoever. What do you need, Daphne? What's missing that's making you so unhappy?"

It felt peaceful talking to Mum, but at the same time I felt agitated. I didn't know the answers to these questions. God knows I wish I did. I don't know what I want. I don't know what it is that I feel I'm missing. I don't know what I need, why I'm not finding it with Adrian. I don't know why I had the affair with Teresa. Why I still feel something for her. Why I want Adrian back. I don't know, I don't know, I don't know.

Mum stopped my fingers fidgeting restlessly, by putting her own hand over mine. I stopped biting my lip and looked at her.

"I'm not asking you to give me any of these answers now. I'm just prodding you to have a think about them. But don't think too hard, going round and round in circles will just stress you out. You've got as much freedom as you want here Daphne, to just do what pleases you for a while. Follow that, and see where it takes you. But you won't find 100% fool proof answers, so don't kid yourself!" We smiled to each other, sharing the continuous in-joke of my semi-obsession with perfection. "Just take some time to see what your feelings are. Where they will lead you. So what do you want to do now?"

"I don't know!" I half screamed, half laughed. She laughed too.

"Decisions, decisions!"

"They're too hard!"

"Well, I can hear your father coming back, so you can shout the toss with him as to whether he should convert to your vegetarianism, and help him make tea. It's his turn tonight."

"Cheers Mum."

"You're welcome."

I went downstairs to meet a very lively waggy dog and an exhausted father. Looks like *she* took *him* for a walk again. I armed myself with all my anti-meat arguments, ready to take full advantage of his momentary respite.

Chapter Sixty-Four

"Clive, I'm going out for lunch." Clive looked up from the reception desk to see who was going out for lunch.

"Back in five minutes then, Dominic?" he joked.

I smiled. "No, I'm jolly well going to take my full lunch hour today. The full hour."

"Good for you. Watch it, I'll be timing you! A *full* hour!"

"I'll try not to be early."

"Yes, try not to."

I exited the building into the sunshine, and breathed in the non-office, non-stale air.

I needed time out. Time away from my desk. From the phones, from the dictation tapes. From the computer. From time. From criminals. From witnesses. From statutes, precedence, case law. From Sheila.

I walked through town, crossed the bridge and went down to the river.

I sat on the sloping grassy bank, just before it fell away to the water. I was surprised it was so quiet. There were a few ducks to ignore me, and a wind that rustled nearby trees that didn't touch me. The sun shone but didn't warm me.

I put my head in my hands. I wondered what the hell was I doing?

"Lovely day isn't it?" I heard a stranger greet me.

I looked up at an attractive woman. Blonde. Self-assured. And obviously a tourist. No-one from round here said hello to complete strangers.

"Is it?" And I was shocked at myself for breaking the golden rule of pretending to be happy and full of joy with the world, when talking to acquaintances, strangers, and even friends.

"You sound like you've got the only cloud in the sky

hanging over you." She smiled.

I could've remained silent but smiled back and nodded. She would've continued walking and I would've continued being miserable. But I felt the need to reach out to her and respond.

"You got it in one."

"Is it that bad?" And she sat down beside me as if I was an old friend. I was most surprised, but didn't feel uncomfortable with it.

"'Fraid so."

"Girl trouble?"

"You could say that. Amongst other things." I looked at her, but she was watching the ducks. "Yes, I've suffered from that too," she empathised. It took me a moment to comprehend. And then she registered my surprise, and laughed. I wondered at my easy assumption that this beautiful woman was heterosexual.

"Not with your own sister though."

"No, I have to admit I haven't suffered that. But then I don't have a sister."

"Neither do I."

"You're not making any sense."

"She's my adopted sister." I felt the hot shame burn through me. I felt awfully exposed, and so stupid.

"Oh I see. What happened?" Her sympathy was the last thing I'd expected.

"There wasn't even a kiss between us. Just a feeling. A moment. Where something lingered in the air that shouldn't. Not between brothers and sisters. She was upset, I was upset, and we were just hugging…."

"So now you're raging against yourself for your 'despicable behaviour'?" She made a sign of sixty-six ninety-nine with her fingers as she spoke.

"Yeah, you could say that."

"Have you spoken since?"

"Only over the phone."

"*Do* you feel that way about her?"

"No, I think the moment just overtook us, but I just feel so…"

"Guilty?"

"Yeah."

"Guilt's a real shitter isn't it? But I don't think it's so unusual to feel a moment of strangeness and wonder for an adopted sister or brother."

"Do you really think so?"

"Absolutely. Families are very funny things."

"There speaks the wise oracle." I half laughed.

"No, I'm just a woman enjoying the sunshine and the greenness and the earthiness. And I came across a man who couldn't enjoy any of these things and asked him why."

"And *how* are *you* enjoying these things?" I asked. "I noticed the sun didn't seem to touch you either."

"Well apart from my boyfriend breaking up with me due to a stupidly mindless affair I rekindled with an old girlfriend of mine, everything's just fine and dandy. So, we're living together, sharing this great house, and he's totally in love with me, and although I can't live without him, I can't live with him either. I guess Teresa was a way of trying to make up for my insecurity. But there's nothing between us anymore. I want him back. But how? How can I feel comfortable with myself staying with him? How do I stay connected to me and to him at the same time?" Then she laughed. At herself. "Listen to me. What do I sound like? A woman who has it and doesn't know what to do with it! How bloody untragic is that!"

"It has its own tragedy."

"Don't say that just to be nice."

"I don't pretend to understand. But your feelings are valid, whatever they may be. Just have a proper listen to them and see what they say."

"Easy for you to say."

"Yes, it's easy for me to say." We sat in a comfortable silence, listening to the rustling leaves and the occasional happy quack from the ducks.

"Is there anyone else in your life? Romantically speaking?" she asked.

"No, why do you ask?"

"Why isn't there?"

"There just hasn't been anyone that I've met."

"Maybe your expectations are too high."

"Maybe I just haven't found the right person."

"Or maybe we're both running and hiding from things. From the things we want. You're protecting yourself by wishing for the unobtainable, and I'm throwing away what I already have."

"What are you talking about?"

"Putting obstacles in your own path to happiness."

"But there isn't anyone else to be with."

"Exactly." I tried to figure out the enigma behind what she was saying, but couldn't grasp it. She hardly knew me anyway, so how could she possibly make any such pronouncements on my life and assume she knew what she was talking about?

"Exactly nothing. You know nothing about me."

"No, you're right. I don't." I expected her to stand and go then, but she didn't. I watched her become mesmerised by the flow of the river, and its shimmering reflections of trees and blue sky.

I returned to my own thoughts, wondering how long this woman was going to sit by me, and yet I didn't want to get up and leave either.

After a while she said, "You need to find a female darkness to match your own darkness. Then you'll be happy." My darkness? I was as fair as she was.

"Darkness?"

"Of spirit." What strange words to utter. And even stranger to say them to someone you don't know.

"Female darkness?"

"You'll know her when you meet her. You'll illuminate each other's way, and understand each other's depth of darkness, and respect your different darknesses."

"Are you a tortured artist, a fortune telling gypsy or an escapee from the local asylum?" I couldn't help but ask.

"Neither. I'm a publisher."

"That's much worse then." Thankfully she shared the humour and smiled.

"Have you ever felt your world up-turn slightly because someone close to you gets deeply hurt, yet you're divorced from it by a long distance of time, and from not really having known that person very well?"

"Or felt that you were talking to someone who was madder

than a publisher can be?"

"Only when the wind is blowing north north-west."

"You know a hawk from a hand-saw." My favourite Shakespeare play.

"Spot on."

"And who is this person that you're so close to, yet hardly know at all?"

"My mother."

"I see," I said, not really seeing at all. "No, actually I don't see. What do you mean?"

"I've just found out that someone hurt my mother very badly, before I was even born. And, I don't know why, but I find it very upsetting, as if her pain was passed down to me through her genes."

"Perhaps you can see how her pain affected her life."

"That's just it though, I don't know how it affected her. She died before I'd even turned four."

"That must have been devastating."

"Yes, it was." Birdsong, breeze and ripples once more filled our ears, traffic humming in the distance, as the ducks bobbed for food and paddled around. "She was devastated too. Some men are just total bastards."

"I agree with that one. I'm dealing with one right now."

"You are?"

"Someone I'm prosecuting."

"I should've realised you're a lawyer."

"How? Have I got that 'sharp nothingness look' about me?"

"Yes, but I haven't known 'a lot of everybody'." Her parents liked the old eighties films too.

"Point taken." I ventured a question. "Do you know who it was who hurt your mother?"

"No. I've never met him, nor am I likely to. He could be dead by now for all I know."

"What did he do?"

"I don't want to talk about it," she said very firmly.

"Fair enough." There was another long pause. "Perhaps you're recognising her pain, even though you weren't there. Perhaps you need to recognise her healing too."

"Perhaps that's what it is." The splashing of the ducks

bobbing and skittering across the river as they quacked to each other coloured in our silence.

"Is your pain, and your mother's pain what's driving you away from the man you love?"

"Well, that's an idea I hadn't entertained. But the thing is I turned him away before knowing what happened to my mother."

"Or maybe it's the loss of your mother that's preventing you from settling into love."

"How do you mean?"

"Losing a parent/parents, well I mean, that's your first love isn't it? The primary love, so to speak. If you lose it, then maybe you're scared of losing this love. His love."

"Don't go giving me any of that Freudian crap now."

"No, I'm not. He didn't even occur to me. I was thinking of myself actually. I'm adopted. So both my parents are dead, except they're not. They *chose* to reject me. And I think that..."

"That it doesn't help you find and trust the love of your life?"

"Right."

"But I have a loving father and a wonderful step-mum."

"Well, I have wonderful parents too, adopted ones that is. But that doesn't mean we forget the earlier tragedies in our lives. All we forget is the way that they imprint themselves on us, and the way they affect us for the rest of our lives. Like an interrupted narrative. A story without a beginning... Feelings without stories to give them a context, a reason."

"You mean like you're feeling all these strange things, but you don't know why?"

"Yes. Feelings without stories. That's what is so confusing."

"Did you know that I'd read somewhere that the opposite of love is not hate."

"What is it then?" I asked.

"Fear."

"Well, people often do hate the ones they love..."

"But you don't love the people you fear..."

"Don't you?" I wondered.

"You can feel love and hate at the same time, but not love and fear." I digested this new piece of information in silence. I turned it over in my mind like a precious gem, seeing how it looked in the light. And what if I turned it this way, did it still look the same? Still ring true?

"So who's this bastard you're dealing with then?"

"Attempted rape. Assault. He denies it of course. And she's just…"

"Just what?"

"Shocked I think. Shell shocked." She nodded as if she understood. "Is the river helping to resolve your relationship difficulties then?"

"It's soothing. But not helpful." She paused. "But I found some words from a dark man sat in the sun helped." Her smile twinkled in her blue eyes.

"Funny, but I found some wise words from a woman down by the river who has helped me."

"Good luck, Dark Man, finding your dark love." We both rose, our bodies posed in the opposite directions our feet were going to travel, taking us away from each other.

"And good luck, River Woman, accepting your lover into your life."

"Thank you." I watched as she walked away. Wondering who she was. Wondering why she felt like some sort of kindred spirit. Wondering how we'd managed to understand some emotional truths about each other when we didn't know each other at all. She looked back and waved. I waved back. Glanced at my watch, time enough to grab some snack food before returning to the office.

Chapter Sixty-Five

"Why are we always doing this to each other?" I asked, despairingly.

"Because we love each other?" His voice was heavy with irony.

Me and Adrian were at our usual battle stations. Things had been really good between us again for a while. After I'd mulled over thoughts sparked off from my strange conversation with Dark Man, things shifted into a slightly different focus for me. But even that wasn't enough to keep me and Adrian from ripping each other apart.

"Adrian – this is going to be the end of us. I've got to stop being in the wrong all the time. It's just not working."

"You're right – it's not." I'm right for the first time, would you credit it!

"Tell me Adrian, just how many women have you slept with?"

"Perhaps a dozen or so, why?"

"And how many have you had relationships with?"

"Five."

"And how many have you truly loved?"

"One."

"Don't give me any bullshit."

"OK. Two."

"I don't believe you."

"There's you. And someone I was with before – Helen."

"You've told me about Helen. I still don't believe you."

"Which part?"

"I don't believe you've ever really loved anyone at all."

"That's not true."

"Isn't it? I think it is. You're a good actor Adrian, and you're very good at making someone feel like they're the only one in the world that matters, but I see through it now. I see you clearly Adrian and I don't think I'm the one for you."

"You think I've only acted as a lover to you? How dare you assert that? Who the hell do you think you are Daphne? You're not the only important person in the world, you know. Other people have feelings too. Are you deliberately trying to hurt me?"

"This is hurting me too. But I'm not just your lover Adrian. I'm me as well. And you don't like that. But I do have a life outside of you, and you can't handle that. You're too possessive. And it constrains me."

"Constrains you? That I give you my love and my attention? Well, if I'd have known that's how you felt, I wouldn't have bothered in the first place. I'm just sorry I've wasted such a lot of time and effort on you."

"Adrian, you're very generous in love, it's one of the things I love about you. None of it's wasted. It's just *too much* for me. I've never spent so much time apologising as I have in our relationship. I've never felt so insecure, and I'm not an insecure person. I need my own time and space, and you want to be my Siamese twin."

"I can give you more space. More time. Or is this all an act of yours Daphne, when what you're really trying to say is you don't love me? That you never really have?"

"I didn't pretend anything Adrian. You've got to believe that."

"On top of your other lies. Yes, am I meant to believe them too?"

"What lies?"

"Teresa, and God knows if there's been other affairs too that I haven't yet found out about!"

"There isn't anyone else *to* find out about!"

We stared at each other. Hot. Breathless. Anger. Not enough air in the room. I tried to rationalise it for him. "Your love is wonderful, but your arrogance and possessiveness is suffocating. It just leaves me feeling empty and lonely. The more you obsess, the more it pushes me away. I don't need it and I don't want it." I expected a round rejoinder, but he said nothing. He strode towards me, covering the short distance between us. The room grew smaller, as his figure became larger. I looked up into his face inches from mine. He was sweating. I felt devoured by his intense gaze. I felt angry, and frightened and excited. My pulse beat hard and fast as I returned his stare, looking into his glassy grey blue eyes. I could hear his breathing. My anger fluctuated as I read his gaze, could see his anger welling, his hurt, his questions. His defences were down, but he still wore his suit of... self-righteousness is too strong a word, but his conviction of him being the only wounded party here. I couldn't understand how sometimes he was so sensitive and so intuitive and other times he was totally blind to my feelings, my motivations. Like he could only really see my true colours for a limited amount of time, and then he'd lose his spectacles and he'd make up all these fictions about me that weren't true, and expect me to wear them. Well it was time Adrian stopped playing victim, when he most certainly wasn't. I was tired of being confused by his differing attentions, his need for me to fall in with him, even when he pretended to give me space, I could feel the expectation, tangibly in the air for me to come back and say 'I'm sorry, you were right, I was wrong'.

"What *do* you want Daphne?" he said softly, dangerously.

"More than what you can give. Less than you do give." I responded just as softly. Time spun out in the narrow gap between us. I only had to lift my hand slightly and I would be touching him. Feeling him, revelling in the intensity he wraps around me like a blanket, a blanket with fasteners, fastened tight, claiming me, owning me.

"Tell me you don't want me Daphne. Say it." I did want him. And he knew it. But I didn't want 'us' like this. Not in this way. Not the way we had been. I would miss him, I knew I would. But it was time for the games to stop. I remembered the emptiness I felt he'd created within me. I wanted him more when I was with him, than I did when I was alone. Which is the wrong way round. I never felt fulfilled with him. Well I am not here to *be* Adrian's lover and nothing else. I'm me and a lover. Not one or the other. I could feel confusion creeping up on me again as I remembered his kindnesses to me, his generosity of spirit, all the things he did give me. Maybe he was right. Stop it, stop it, Daphne. I need to get out of here. But what if Adrian is the right one for me and I'm throwing it all away? For nothing. Am I making the right decision here? *There is no right or wrong. Just what you feel inside.* That's what Isabel said that Mum had told her. I don't know why that came into my mind just then.

"Adrian…"

"Say it Daphne." He was asking for honesty. He was asking for a final choice to be made. Was this to be a definite division for the future, alone in our separate worlds? Or was this to be the beginning of something new and fresh between us with a different understanding? I read his need in his eyes, his longing for me. I wanted to answer that call, I wanted to be there with him, but something held me back. Deep inside, I knew I would feel trapped again with him, knew I wanted something different, needed something else. But I didn't know what it was yet. So should I just stick with what I did know? But that would be unfair, dishonest and cowardly. I had no right to 'have my cake and eat it' and it would just make us both miserable in the end.

I couldn't lie to Adrian and say I didn't want him, but I couldn't give my assent either, knowing the weight with which Adrian attached to my answer. "It's over Adrian. There's no more 'us'." I expected him to fight me on this, refute it, throw it back at me, argue me ragged. But instead he stepped away, and I was upset to find that there were tears in his eyes.

Impulsively I kissed him. He held himself stiff at first, but his arms came round me and held me tight. We kissed, like we had done before, like we wouldn't ever again. We tasted each other, and felt the sweetness and the bitterness.

He slowly held me away from him. And shit, I felt like apologising all over again, but I held my tongue, I was bored of that line.

"How can we want each other like this, yet not be good for each other?" An overwhelming sense of relief washed through me that he openly admitted the misfit of us as a pair, but simultaneously I felt a lead weight of sadness settle in my gut. There was no going back now.

"I don't know," I breathed. I was fighting my body's desire to be held within the passionate prison of his wild and tender desire for me. But I remembered the wanting never ending when I was locked in his arms. And all the wanting made me not want him at all in the end. Like a need that never gets satisfied, it wears out in the end and gives up.

"I *do* love you Daphne," he quietly insisted.

"I know," I whispered, my vision getting blurry. Don't say it Daphne, don't say it, don't say you love him too, or you'll never break free.

To my surprise, he placed his lips gently on mine, as the sands of time ran away from us. It was our goodbye kiss. We both knew it. I wanted it to last and last. It lasted too long and too short. When it did stop lasting, the pain that ripped through me seared hotly. I treasured the pain of our parting, taking the love that we had, with it. Because it was impossible to not have one without the other.

Chapter Sixty-Six

and so she leaves him – to travel... to travel...

finding out more about the world... the heats and colds of other places... the different birds and how air smells different in other countries... how feet touch the ground no matter where you are... and you are always you with the same history and memories and passions and regrets no matter where your bed is placed... so she finds and searches and loses herself again... meets others who she can be confused by... click with... find kindred spirits with... goes on and on from one town to another spending foreign currencies in new museums... new to her... old to history... she talks with the mona lisa but doesn't find anything new... takes in broadway and wonders at the stage...

watches the changes of her perception in the rippling lakes of mountainous regions... tastes the sands of pyramids in her clothes and hair... feels the nausea of the ferry trips on rough seas...

she's wondering... watching all the time...

but at night... when she shuts down her visual input sensors her mind overcompensates with regular beautiful and horrific dreams... of other lives she'd like to lead... how a different skin might feel... a part of her yearning for the twin she doesn't know she has... but she's not lonely... she feels my presence in a myriad of ways... she talks to me sometimes... asks herself to remember what little there was of the intensity of new born and new mother... she recalls a laugh... looks at old photos of me... one she carries with her... to look at now and again... i'm a reminder of her insecurity... her power and strength in survival... and i'm testing the limitations of her memory... isabel and ted keep me alive for her...

and she wonders and misses... and yet loves too... she missed ted before she met him and wonders at my choices... what I chose and why... she loves isabel... and wonders of what might have been had i been with ted... as her birth parents... i can't tell her the resentment and the struggling silences that would have been the background of her life had it been so... the staying together just for the child... although i know isabel suffered and wanted her Dad around... and i don't agree with what he did... deserting them emotionally long before he walked out... i don't ever believe in staying together for the children... unhappy parents equals unhappy children... so the children won't like parents separating either... but pick one... pick one... bad situation... make the best of it... there's no perfect answer... give the child as many tools as you can to live with the separation and grow from it...

and ted and isabel have always been there for daphne and always will be... no matter who she is... or what she decides... they love her unconditionally... i miss not being there to give you that love too my dear daphne... i didn't want to leave you... i didn't want to go... i didn't want to go... she wallows in an emptiness of rejection sometimes that has no physical embodiment outside of her head... i am here daphne... in your heart... your blood... your veins... in your parents' heads... you're contacting me now and now and now... let it all flow... even the pain... accept that... it's very important to who you are... who you are then... and now... and in this next moment as you're carried on a train past the landscape you wish to inhabit... let it in... let it work... it needs you to feel it... to acknowledge it... so you can learn to be more yourself... denial is the worst... don't let that take hold... it will deceive you of your life... cheat life from you... let it all flow through you... as michael said... go with it... go with it...

searching for meaning in a open space... there is no solid writing to tell you why... you have to take that leap of faith and

trust in yourself... in your own life... in what there is around
you... trust yourself... within your body... in its existence...
believe in its power and beauty... and pain... so that you can
carry through to wisdom about yourself... i love you daphne...
take care... take care... take care... take care...

I decided to spend the last few days of my holiday in
Tunisia. Why there? I don't know. Because it's somewhere that
wouldn't normally be on my mental map of places to go?
Because Paris, Egypt and New York didn't quite fulfil? Because
I heard from a friend that Tunisia had been bliss when she'd
gone there? I don't know. Or was it a fate of some kind?

The heat is dry here. And you don't feel as though it's
eighty/ninety degrees. Haggling in the market. Trip into the
desert and being outcrowded by stars. Bumpy ride of camel.
Swimming at night. Walks along the beach at sunset. Hit upon
by dozens of men. After all, western women were easy. The
place of holiday romances. Is that why I'd come here?

There was one man. And we'd actually talked a little while
before he hit on me, unlike other men there. In broken English
and French we communicated. We went to my hotel room. He
massaged my whole body. And it was sensual. And a tease.
Though I could have been any body to him. And I was unusually
passive. I let him caress and rub my back with lotion. And work
his way downwards. He didn't touch anywhere that he
'shouldn't'. It was torture. My desire licked at me within. If I'd
been at home with any other man, I would have taken over and
initiated. But for some reason I just relaxed into the bed,
breathing in my pillow, feeling wetter, wondering when on earth
he was ever going to get round to… But he did.

And then he asked.

"Shall we make love?"

Once the condom had been coaxed on he was ready. And so
was I. I was still lying on my front. I hadn't moved. I let his silk
hands move over me once more, readying himself. And he
entered me, I felt the initial fizzle of pleasure and then… I wasn't
sure what happened. My mind somehow couldn't follow
through. It was somewhere else. My mind no longer desired
what my body did, and it started to feel uncomfortable. I told

him to stop.

"Are you all right?"

"No, it hurts." He stopped and withdrew. I faced him. His face was full of concern.

"Did I do something wrong? Are you angry?" This seemed to be the first assumption that men made here. You weren't allowed to be upset or down. If you didn't like something, he assumed I was angry. I found that ironic. Back home a woman's anger was always the last thing that was assumed.

"No, I'm not angry," I assured him, for all the good it did. "I'm really sorry. I'm not going to do this." And to my own amazement, I slipped on a sundress and walked out. He could release himself in my bed if he liked. I didn't really care. It wasn't really my bed anyway. It was a stranger's bed. It wasn't even that. It was a bed for strangers. It didn't belong to anyone. And neither did I.

The beach was too crowded. With children. With couples. With other men out for easy sex. It was too sunny. The place was too happy. I didn't feel happy inside. I didn't fit in here. I was tired of it all. Was there nowhere to get peace in this place?

In the end I reached the bar, which was deliciously cool and deliciously deserted. Everyone preferred to be out in the sun's kiss. I bought a beer and a coke with ice in. If I had two drinks in front of me, no-one bothered you. They assumed you were going to be joined by someone in a few minutes. I reached to drink the beer and then thought better of it. Instead I picked out an ice-cube from the coke, and sucked on it. It melted slowly in my mouth, making my tongue and inner-cheeks go cold.

As I sat there, I allowed myself to think thoughts that I'd been avoiding these past few weeks. "Was Adrian thinking of me right now?"

yes he is... he's learning to let you go... when you need him to... he misses you too daphne darling...

Chapter Sixty-Seven

I'd thought a lot about River Woman's words. The things we'd discussed. And what sort of meanings they could hold for my life. Was I afraid to love? Would I never heal from the hurt of abandonment and rejection by my birth parents?

I'm late again. Why can't this sodding taxi go any faster?

At last I could see the hotel/mansion from the end of the drive way that we entered. Frustratingly the speed limit dropped to 10mph now, as we snailed up the gravel.

And here I am. Where am I? Why am I doing this? But I've found love now. Haven't I? Or was this still running away? After all, I can only be Kelly's lover in secret. I mean, I doubt her husband is up for having an 'open relationship'.

I looked at my watch. I was only ten minutes late. But it was ten minutes less spent with her. Ten minutes deprived of her, of the too short a time we got together anyway. Her scent raced in my veins, and I didn't care anymore if this was running away or loving. I just knew I wanted to be with her.

"Mr & Mrs White," I panted as I reached the reception desk.

"Your wife's already up there," the bemused receptionist said, "Room 10, top of the stairs, second door on the left."

"Thank you." I sprinted off, feeling embarrassed for participating in such a cliché, but at least we hadn't signed in as Mr & Mrs Jones!

I opened the door, and saw her figure outlined beneath the duvet, curtains drawn, main light off, only a small bed lamp lit the room. In spite of everything, Kelly had made the room look somehow cosy instead of anonymous.

"Sorry I was late, it's just…"

"Shhhhh, Dominic," she said. She slipped out of the bed, and let me hold her nakedness against me. She kissed my lips, not allowing me to speak.

"Let's leave the real world outside the door. I don't care why you're late. I care that you're here. Now get into bed, and let me hold you naked too." I flushed red. She could make me feel like such a naïve adolescent sometimes.

She wouldn't let me undress at first, but led me to the bed, and made me feel what she felt like in all the right places, teasing me, before she started to relieve me of my shirt and trousers.

I was so hungry for her. Mad for her. Once I was naked, she let me make the running, and I teased and tormented her. I drew back from letting her pleasure being outrightly fulfilled, and let my focus wander to different parts of her, and of me. I relished her gasping and writhing with pleasure. She was totally unabashed in her arousal, so utterly confident in her power to arouse and to be aroused. Her rawness made me want to please her even more, and drive us both to the brink and back again. Unable to hold back any longer, I gave into the satisfaction we both craved.

After our initial passion was spent, we sat in bed and talked. Sometimes we'd have a drink, if we were in the sort of place that provided room service. Sometimes she'd read, and I'd watch her, trying to read too. She liked to pretend the room, wherever it was, was really our home, and wanted us to act and behave as if we were around each other in our own place all the time.

She once asked me about other women I'd slept with. Our post-coitus chats were very frank sometimes. She laughed when I told her there'd been no others. Then sobered a little when she realised I wasn't joking. And then we'd kissed, and kissed some more, till we were so caught up in each other again.

This time though, I wanted to talk about us. About Brooklyn. Or possible lack of.

"Darling, I don't want to talk about him. He's a separate world. He's not a part of this one." I felt mildly angry and frustrated in her avoidance of the subject.

"Kelly, I need you..." I began to explain.

"I know," she cut in, her hand reaching between my legs, stroking, teasing. In spite of my best efforts, I felt myself starting to respond, as always.

"I want us to be together."

"We are together darling."

"I mean properly. I mean always. I always want to be by your side Kelly. I love you."

"And I love being with you too Dominique," (she liked to pronounce my name that way), "but we can't be together always. It's just not meant to be. We'd be no good for each other darling."

"How can you say that? When you've, when we've just... you know, doesn't that mean anything to you?"

"Of course it does. I love your fire. I love getting lost in you Dominique. Why do you always want more? Don't spoil it."

"I'm not."

"Then come here then, and spoil me."

And only later did I realise that she'd used our passion as a way of avoiding answering my questions. Again. But I loved it when she took me over. When I took her over. I just wanted to bury myself in her, feel her burst around me explosively. But afterwards, I'd feel vulnerable and somehow incomplete. She'd stroke my chest, and my hair, and I'd doze in her arms on and off, nuzzling into her.

But her passion and love for me somehow never quite hit the mark, never quite set me at ease fully. There was always an irritating niggle, doubts playing in my head. That she wasn't all mine. And I didn't know how to make it so. How can I give her everything her husband does and more, so she can finally see that we're meant to be? Finally see the way clear for us to set up together, formally, externally, for other people to see. To make a life together.

What was I competing with? And how could I win?

Chapter Sixty-Eight

"I'm just going out, Brooklyn."

"What was that sweetheart?" I watched as he did up his tie in the gilt framed mirror. More business for him to rush off to. On a Sunday afternoon. Really, what could possibly be outstanding, or of such urgence that couldn't wait until tomorrow?

"Have you heard a single word I've said?"

"Of course I have, Kelly. I've been listening."

"Then where did I say I was going then?"

"For a walk in the park."

"Right."

"OK, sweetheart. I'll see you when I get back."

"When will that be?"

"I'm not sure, sweetheart, but don't wait up." He kissed me goodbye. A peck on the top of my head. As if I was his mother! And left.

I waited till the car had well and truly gone, then threw on my casual jacket and made my way to the swings in the park. On second thoughts I took gloves and a scarf too.

Yes, I'll go play on the swings. Always makes me feel like a little girl without a care in the world doing that. Watching the world go up and down, continuously seeing different views as you move back and forth.

It was cold enough to see the air as you exhaled, but it was a good half hour brisk walk to the park, and that set my blood moving, keeping me warm.

When I got there the park was deserted. But then it was mid afternoon, all the kids were in school still.

I made a bee-line for the swings. Going higher. Faster. The air whooshing. I saw the fields and the slides, and the houses on the fringe of the park drift upwards and downwards.

I couldn't help but think about Dominic today for some reason. He didn't usually play on my mind so.

He's such an impossible man. So feverish. So frantic, never stopping to see the sun. Just wants to soak it all up and *be* the sun. Instead of letting go. Letting it be the sun, admiring its light as you stand shaded by the tree. Not thirsting for it, craving it, grasping it every second of every day. Letting it be. Just letting it grow, to be true only in its temporary truthfulness. To live and breathe and die, and only come back as something new that you can't behave the same way with, because it won't understand you.

He doesn't understand. He wants permanent. Still. Labelled. Pinned down. The same. Forever. Like a dead butterfly, captured in its beauty. But then he complains, cries, doesn't understand his wrong doing when it deteriorates and crumples and turns to dust, nothing but dust, that he can't admire, and can't hold, and can't trap, and can't gaze on and can't want anymore. Where did his butterfly go? Why didn't it stay? He doesn't comprehend that his need to keep it stamped in the same place and time, stamped in his memory, his brain, in his sight, in his touch, always, that that is the very thing that destroys it. As naturally it's living and breathing and flying and flitting and here one second, gone the next. It's fluid and out of control. It's not needful of his desires, and wants and emptiness and desperation to hold. It eats where it can and flies where it goes and moves on.

And I'm his butterfly. He doesn't comprehend that the only reason he wants me is because he can't have me. Be together. We can never *be together* in the way that he wants us to be. I'm already *together* with someone. And that's why I want Dominic, because he's not that. He's everything but that. And that's what makes the relationship. That's what gives it its flavour. Its intensity. Its passion. Throw all that away? Not in a million.

Yet I soak him up. I love his energy, his want of me, his ceaseless wonder and fascination with me. It's bemusing and flattering. It's feet sweeping and blissful. His energy is storm like, dark and uncontrolled. It's strong and vast and he doesn't even realise his own potential. He thinks it all comes from me. That I make him feel this. But he's wrong. It comes from him, emanates from deep within him, resonating throughout his being, and it draws me in every time. It claims me every time. I can't say no. He has no idea of his power of me. He thinks I'm always in control, pressing all the buttons, holding all the cards, pulling all the strings, knowing what's going on, allowing myself to say and do at arbitrary times, as discerned consciously as to whether I feel like it or not. Feel like him. Feel like I fancy him for lunch or dessert. Like a snack. Or an addictive drug.

But I'm not as callous as he thinks me. I don't rule his world as much as he thinks I do.

He overrules mine. And I can't stop it. He says he can't either. But he's lying. I know he is. And that makes him dangerous. He says he drinks of me every time, could not, cannot deny me anything. But he lies. He loves his illusion of my power over him. It give him permission to be dark and dangerous and devil like and treat me how he likes.

But I could never ignore his need of me, like he plays with my want of him. And he does play me. He plays me all the time and my body sings and dances to his fluent fingers. And it slumps and moans to his withdrawn silences.

'What if I told your husband?' is his latest recurring threat. His blackmail. His endless selfishness. And he doesn't understand. I coax and tempt him. I want him in my bed, but he'll say no. He'll walk away. Turn his back. Say he doesn't want it like this anymore. 'How do you want it?' I ask. 'With me begging and crawling on the floor at your feet? Is that how you want it?' He might turn. Might look sad. Might shed a tear. He would say, 'Why do you do this to me?' As if I do it deliberately, as if *I could* turn it on and off at whim. As if all I ever thought about was how to punish Dominic, make him feel bad. I can't cope with his reprieves, his reproachfulness, his dalliances.

I love his anger and his storm and his fretting. His violence, his whirlwind, his demonness, the arguments and the fucking. I can handle all of that. I can love him then.

But not the lies and the blackmail. The pretending always, that he's the weaker party and I'm the cat playing with the mouse. Not true. He could walk away anytime, and I could do nothing.

Nothing at all. I can't walk away, but he doesn't believe me. He gets paranoid.

When he retreats and plays me, as if I'm the cruel controller, and he hides from me and won't let me touch him, I say; 'Perhaps we'd best not see each other anymore!' And it breaks my heart, but it always works. He comes to me then. Always. He'll reach for me. 'I couldn't bear it,' he says. He'll stroke my body, stoke my desire and need of him. 'I can't not see you,' he'll say, and we'll be drawn together, like we always are. 'I want to be by your side, always,' he'll say.

He wants to usurp my husband in order to become my third husband, without realising that if he did that, I would take another lover. It's a lover I want him to be. But somehow he doesn't see this as a compliment.

He thinks he can make me a happy wife! But he can't because Dominic is not a happy person. He's morose and moody. Which makes a perfect lover, but a lousy husband. And, laughingly he thinks *I* can make *him* happy. But I can only need him. Give him loving. I can't make him *happy*. Only he can do that.

He thinks I'm the answer to everything, to all his prayers, all his problems, all his everything. He's wrong. I am the sum of all his problems. I illuminate the questions not the answers.

I just want his body next to mine, sweating between the sheets, I want his breath in my ear saying he loves me truly and no other and never will, not like this again. I want his body in mine, plunging my depths, needing me more, more than is possible to ever satisfy, ever satiate, ever even get close to. We always run out of breath before we even get half way near. But I'm always satisfied. Satisfied with everything he gives me, even though it's poisoned. Poisoned with his need and want for me to give him even more, ever more. I love his poison, I relish it, even though it hurts me, can destroy me. I love to take it. I love to flirt with danger, drink the danger, taste its blood, run its course through my veins in his head.

He wants me. And I need that.

But if my husband ever found out, I'd deny everything. Cut all ties. Never see Dominic again, and beg forgiveness from my husband. Because freedom-giving husbands like Brooklyn are much harder to find than moody lovers who are good in bed.

With my husband I'm free. And he loves me with spaces.

Too many spaces sometimes. I do love the freedom and security I have with him, but he doesn't give me the attention I yearn.

But Dominic does. I love how Dominic feeds off my neediness, even though I hate the power it gives him over me. But he makes me ache and ache and then he pleases me to distraction till I burst everywhere, all over, all at the same time, and I can ride that cloud of bliss for hours. But he spoils it with his demands for more. Accuses me of holding back when he already has all there is to take.

He doesn't appreciate, stop, think, reflect, it's gotta be do-do-do, faster, harder, deeper than ever before, as if he's in some kind of competition. Like he's got to prove something, like he's letting the side down, like he's got his own private audience in his head watching all his moves over his shoulder, everything he does and says, whether they approve or disapprove, judging, weighing things up, criticising. He cuts me to shreds sometimes and hold me afterwards. But his pity and sympathy are worse than his bite. I won't shun him. I'll never do that. But I won't respond either when he's like that. When he thinks I'm a dog to pet and forget about, when he patronises me, it turns me cold. And I'll not talk, not kiss, not respond. If he accuses me of anything, I'll ensnare him outrageously, saying, 'My husband never treats me like this. And I won't take it from you either.' This drives him insane. He hates being compared. Especially to my husband. He wants to be first in my affections, in my heart, in my head, in my bed. He hates coming second.

He'll pinion me to the bed. 'And I bet your husband never treats you like this does he?' Sometimes he'll tie me up, arms outstretched – wrists tied to the headboard, ankles crossed together, and make me take my words back and beg him to come inside me, deep deep inside, deeper than my husband could ever go, or even know. He only does this, because he knows I love it. It turns me on more than I can say. So this time we're both pretending he's in control, though we both know *I* am. There's no deception. Just our bodies talking to each other, like they know how to. Like they want to, fluent in their vocabulary, easily left to their own devices.

And I swallow up his energy, his storm. And he brings me calm and peace when all is done and spent. But I cannot bring *him* calm. Or peace. I cannot give him these. And he desires this above all else.

I fuel his anger and his neediness for me wherein he fails to let me give him what he needs. He fails. Yet he sees it as my failure, and will make love to me again, just as strong, just as violent, just as needy. But I give myself. I cannot give myself and more. There is only one of me. My body responds to his needs, it always does. His anger and need excites me, turns me on, reaches into my heart and draws me out in all my clinginess.

But he leaves me exhausted. Wiped out. No smiles. He gives a lot, but takes more.

He stops eventually, knowing there's nowhere left to touch this afternoon/evening/morning. Nothing left to say. Or do. Try again on our next calendar meeting. He hates that. The diarising of lovemaking. So cold and calculated he'll call me. How can I be so distant? But it's just practical. And necessary. You can't be a romantic about everything, all the time.

It's quite nice to have secrets, and secret meeting places, and secret memories, and a secret world away from the prying eyes and thoughts of every single other person on the planet. I like him – my secret. My secret passion. And that's how it will stay. Or nothing at all.

I stop the swing, my cheeks flushed, my ears burning. My body frozen in swing pose. I can't feel my hands or feet. Time to walk home, get the blood moving again. Time to stop thinking about Dominique, he's taking up too much space in my head.

Chapter Sixty-Nine

I watched Dominic as he picked out a sandwich and custard tart from the self help counter. I sighed inwardly. Another chance to try and talk sense into my brother re his love life. The mess that it's in. But he doesn't think so!

"And what does our Big Sis say about of all this?"

"Samantha just goes, 'Oh Dominic' with that tone of voice she has when she's very disappointed in you, and arches her eyebrows to heaven in a resigned sort of 'what are we going to do with you then?'"

"Yes, I know the one you mean. Did she say anything else?"

"She said plenty of things. Things like; 'She doesn't appreciate you... She just uses you and throws you away like a paper cup...' and 'you shouldn't let yourself be abused like this.'" Dom looked like he'd been stung. But golly, Sammy was right.

"I'll get these."

"No, no. I insist." Dom paid for our sandwiches and pot of tea and we took a corner table in the window.

"Will you stop looking at your watch every two seconds? You've only just left the office, we've got a whole hour together. It's not going to disappear that quick."

"Sorry Sheila. Guess I'm just a little jumpy right now." I felt my own eyebrows raising to heaven in a 'no, really!' sarcastic sort of way, and stopped myself before he noticed.

"You *have* got a full hour for lunch I assume?"

"I have today anyway," and he smiles his winning smile. And again I wonder why Dom can't date an unattached woman who would also find his smile incredibly attractive. Why was he so stuck on Kelly?

"I made sure my colleagues understood I'd be gone a full hour in order to spend time with my favourite sister."

"Damn right!" I said, mockingly annoyed. Samantha didn't approve of Kelly either. But Samantha's very straight laced about affairs of the heart, especially when it comes to extra-marital ones!

"I just can't get her out of my mind Sheila. It's like she's taken over my very existence. I find I'm always imagining her there, whatever I'm doing, wherever I am, whatever I'm saying, and what she would think of it. What's wrong with me?" He took a bite of his egg mayo sandwich, chewing it distractedly.

"You're obsessed Dom. That's what it's called; an obsession."

"But I love her. I just want to be *with* her. It's driving me nuts, all this secrecy and remembering lies and sneaking around. But the thing that gets me most is not being able to see her and talk to her whenever I want to. It's all got to be so carefully arranged, so that *he* doesn't suspect. I want to take her out to the pictures on impulse one night, say, or call round with a present and take her out for the evening. But no, it's got to be a set date at a particular time, for a certain length of time, and not before and not after. And if I've to cancel for some reason, I can only get in touch with her via certain means and more importantly, it would mean I have to wait even *longer* before I get to see her again, and be with her. It's torment Sheila. It really is."

"Poor you. You're really suffering aren't you?" I sipped from my too-small cup as Dom tried to work out if I was being sincere or patronising. "I mean it Dom. I hate seeing you so… you're so fidgety, distracted, irritable. And deprived of the wholehearted love that you crave. You're here punishing yourself… Look at what she's doing to you! Your attention span's shot to pieces, you can't focus on anything except her. It's not healthy. You're denying yourself the opportunity to find someone else who would really love you." He sighs, like he's tired of explaining. He looks unhappy. Why is he doing this to himself? Does he *really* love her? "How does she feel about you? What has she said about the whole situation?"

He runs a distracted hand through his wavy blond hair. He stares out to the street and unattached strangers passing by, hurrying about in their lunch hours, grabbing food, doing a spot of shopping, racing round in order to be back to the office in time.

"She loves him."

"Her husband?" Dom nods glumly. "Yes, but what about *you*? How does she feel about you?"

"She says she needs me. That she loves being with me. That I make her feel alive."

"But she won't leave him?"

Dom stopped eating altogether, and looked like he might throw up his half eaten egg mayo. "Occasionally she says she might. But the problem is he's got her firmly where he wants her, and she feels she can never get away from that."

And *she's* got *you* firmly where she wants you, but I didn't say it. Dom was talking to me about it all at least. Perhaps Sammy would have had more luck talking some sense into him? Perhaps not, he would've just flounced off in a huff, and been as deaf to her warnings as he is to mine. But really, the situation is hopeless.

"It could go on like this indefinitely Dominic. Do you really want to keep living your life like this?"

"What choice have I got?" He looked at me despairingly. I hadn't the heart to say, 'all the choice in the world, it might hurt, but you should give her up as a lost cause.'

"She's hurting you like this."

"It's not her. It's the situation." Oh, the *situation!* Not Kelly's fault at all, that she's married and continues to string you along. Not her fault that she won't cut you loose and be faithful to her own husband till death do them part. Not *Kelly's* fault that she won't cut the husband off in order to make a go of it with you. No, not her fault at all! How did such an intelligent man as my brother end up being so blind when it came to matters of the heart?

"I've been over this a thousand times in my head Sheila. I know all this. But..." I waited. Why couldn't he see her as the dead end that she was? That the only way out was to turn round and leave Kelly behind? "If I wait around long enough, perhaps she will leave Brooklyn..."

"Wait around long enough? What's long enough? A month? A year? Your whole life is on hold for her." OK, stop there Sheila, you're being rather hard on him. But dammit, if I couldn't make him see sense, there was nobody else around to do so.

"Well, you know, sometimes, things change, she says she wishes he was different, wishes she could just take off with me somewhere and relish me to her heart's content."

Sounds like a wife looking for a somebody to relieve her boredom, and keeping her bait dangling. "Sounds like sandcastles in the air to me." Dom looked hurt. "I'm sorry Dom, it's just, well... you're stuck between a rock and a hard place, and I want to see you either move to the top of the rock and surpass it, or go find a softer, comfier spot to reside in."

"I know you do." He smiles but it doesn't reach his eyes. And my words have not reached his ears. He hears but doesn't listen. I can't forcibly drag him away from seeing Kelly ever again. He's just going to have to learn the hard way. Oh Dominic! I hope for your sake you'll see the end of this soon.

Chapter Seventy

"Will you stop it!" Kelly sounded really annoyed for some reason.

"What?" She moved her nakedness from mine, my hand dropped from stroking her back. My body felt the loss of her heat against me. "What's wrong? Why are you suddenly acting like I've been dipped in shit?"

I wondered if the River Woman would've picked up on my *Sex, Lies & Videotape* reference, if we still watched the same films. I needed someone as dark as me, she'd said. Was Kelly dark enough for me? I didn't think Kelly was dark of soul at all. Perhaps that was the problem.

"No. I just wish you'd go away. That's all." Here we go again. She has these bouts of guilt from time to time. Guilt over what she's doing behind her husband's back. It trips her up every so often, and I get the brunt end of it.

"You mean you don't like it when I do this?" I curled up to her from behind and let my hand stroke her thighs. "And when I do this?" I kissed her neck and her body started to arch into mine. I rubbed my hardness between her bum cheeks. She wriggled into me.

"No. I mean it. Stop it." And she rolled away from me again. I was very surprised. And hurt. She'd never rejected me before.

"Don't you want to?" I asked, feeling her wetness on my hand, knowing well indeed that she badly wanted to, but was fighting it. I didn't know why.

"Damn it Dominic! Can't you leave a girl alone when she says no?" The remark stung. I got out of bed and got dressed.

"You know very well I would never..." I started to say.

"Yes, yes, I know Dominic. I'm sorry. I didn't mean it." She looked vulnerable all of a sudden, hiding herself under the sheets. I sat in the chair in the corner of the room.

"What is it then?"

"It's Brooklyn. I think he's starting to suspect." I stayed silent. All the responses I wanted to give I knew would not be welcomed.

When she didn't continue, I said, "What makes you think that?"

"He's been quite off-hand lately and that's unusual."

"I thought he liked giving you space. And that you enjoyed having it?"

"Oh it's not that. It's different. He gives me this curious searching look sometimes, that I've never seen before. I don't like it."

"Have you asked him about it?"

"Sort of, but not directly. He responded ambiguously, but suspiciously."

I felt the torture wind round my mind as always: leave him, stay with me, but she was never persuaded. She just got colder and colder on me when I started talking that way.

"What are you going to do?" My nerves were on edge.

"I think we should stop seeing each other." This wasn't the first time she'd said this, but it felt different this time. I felt a surge of panic well within me, my fear mounting. I went to her. I lay beside her, barely touching.

"Kelly," I whispered. She rolled over to face me. We kissed gently, then deeper, but she kept her body aloft. She wouldn't mould to me as she always did. I put a hand on her side and she removed it. I could feel her need of me in her kiss, yet she wouldn't melt to me. She was keeping still, keeping her distance. My hunger for her turned to despair. I was really losing her this time. "Kelly, you're so cold."

"Your Ice Queen."

"Talk to me," I could feel myself almost begging.

"I can't talk to you anymore Dominic. You're threatening my life, and I like it the way it is."

"But what about us?"

"There isn't any us." I felt shocked with the finality that she said the words. She'd never spoken in this manner before.

"Nothing? It's all nothing to you now? How can you say

that?" She got out of bed, and I watched her naked form slide over and into her dressing gown.

"It's all over Dominic. It's time to say goodbye to each other. I always knew this time would come and here it is. Now."

"Is there someone else?" Jealousy bubbled within me. She laughed. It sounded horrible in my ears, echoey and flat.

"There's always been someone else. My husband."

"But no other than him?"

She laughed horribly again. "No, there's no other bit on the side, other than you, lover." And I hated her use of the term, as if the word was dirty and sullied.

"Why now?"

"As I said, I think he's starting to suspect. I don't like that, and I don't want to lose him."

"But you want to lose me?"

She sighed and sat on the bed. "You'll never understand Dominic." I noted I was no longer her 'Dominique'. I hated her tone of voice too, as if I was a child.

"Do you love me Kelly?"

"Not anymore." Her straight and simple refutation cut me open inside.

"Did you ever?" My voice broke as I said it.

"Of course darling. Of course." And her gentleness was there. That gentleness that I'd believed in, been teased with, tormented with, fallen for hook line and bloody sinker. I knew she was telling the truth, but I still resented it. Resented her.

"How can you give me up?"

"Because I don't need you anymore. This is to be our last time together lover," and again the term felt like an insult, "our goodbye lovemaking."

"This isn't lovemaking," I suddenly snarled. She came to me, and offered me her kiss, but for the first time I was repulsed by her. I still ached for her, but somehow the attraction was tainted, and the taste didn't sit well with my stomach.

I turned from her.

"My lover rejects me now?" She looked almost hurt, and I almost gave in. But there was something else in her face too.

You're protecting yourself by wishing for the unobtainable.

She doesn't appreciate you... thrown away like a paper

cup... abused like this...

The voices of the River Woman and my sister came through loud and clear in my head. And for the first time I could hear their words without blocking them out. I could feel the truth behind their words for the first time. I could listen to them and gain strength from them.

"Your lover is already rejected," I replied.

After a moment she said, "He doesn't control me. He never has. No matter what you think of him." She was talking about Brooklyn now. And I had the same clarity of thought about her words too, and saw them for what they were, and for what I was. I'd been kidding myself all along. Of course he didn't manipulate her. She manipulated him. How could I have been so stupid for so long?

"You love him."

"Yes."

"As you never could love me."

"Yes." her honesty hurt, but it was refreshing also.

"Why did we even start this thing up anyway?" God, now I sound like John Travolta in *Staying Alive* and he plays such a tosser in that film. I winced at myself, but apparently Kelly didn't catch the nuance. She didn't watch the same films or read the same Shakespeare as me and the River Woman.

"It was beautiful Dominique, don't spoil it."

"It's already spoilt!" and for the first time I felt truly angry with her. A distant objective anger, not a raging jealous anger.

"I love you when you're like this Dominique. Come to bed again. Let's make our last time together memorable." She always did love my raging passion for her. 'Love'.

"You don't love me at all, you've just said so. I'm *not* going to do a 'one last time for old times' sake', I'm not as cheap as all that. I didn't think you were either."

I'd shocked her this time. I'd never criticised her before. I'd always been the blind obedient following puppy dog. Not anymore.

"If that's how you want it Dominic." She slipped out of her gown. Her beauty hurt me. She slowly got dressed, testing me, and though I still wanted the feel of her skin on mine, because I knew it was a test of hers, my resolve remained strong. I wasn't in the mood to be played with anymore. If this was the end, so be it.

"I'll miss you Dominique," she said looking at my reflection in her mirror as she brushed her mousy bob.

"Will you? I won't miss you," I lied, but had the satisfaction of seeing her look hurt. So she did still have some feeling towards me. But she was still ending it. Well I wasn't going to play the pining, panting after her part anymore. I wasn't going to give her anything more.

"I hate saying it's been nice knowing you," she said. I couldn't look at her anymore for fear of caving in after all and begging her to see me again.

"Then don't say it," I said bluntly.

"I still want you," but the fire was no longer there when she said it.

I counted to three, slowly in my head. I had to lie again. "But I don't want you anymore." I glimpsed her frown of puzzlement.

"You're taking this very well Dominic."

"I'm not taking anything, and I'm not giving either." My chest felt big with hurt, but my gut felt clear and sure. Yes this was the time to end it all. Walk away from it, and somehow rebuild my life without Kelly in it. I can do this. I can.

This is as good a time as any for a good clean break. I didn't recognise this new clear voice that spoke out against Kelly. For months now, all my thoughts had been absorbed by her, wanting her, needing her, but now they rebelled, and I gleaned strength from their rebellion.

She stood about to go. About to say something before she left.

"Don't say anything Kelly. Just walk away." I couldn't bear to hear any more of her lies or truths. I didn't want to hear her voice again, unless it was to tell me that she loved me still.

She did as I asked and went out without another word.

I felt relieved. But then the pain kicked in, and stole my breath and punched me in the stomach. I laid on the bed. Mistake. I could still smell her. I howled into the pillow. The pillows limply absorbed my heartache.

Chapter Seventy-One

a couple more things left to do... i think of him – and in an instant i'm here...

and here he is – lying in his stuffy bed – tossing and turning – fitful – trying to find some peace – some escape from the terrible events that have unfolded... it's ok dominic... everything will be ok...

he looks so much like a younger version of ted... the blond locks – the chiselled cheeks – but my eyes – and my nose... and the similarities are there too between he and dear daphne... i'm going to stay by your bedside tonight – dominic – that i never did when i was alive... i'll guide your dreams – and offer you the love and comfort you need... though you can't understand – i am sorry... but i'm with you now... i have understood and accepted my 25 year old who gave you away... and now i understand my infinite self – as i help you reclaim yourself... your soul is dark – little one... dense darkness – yet the flecks of light in it are like diamonds... like a dark starry sky... i'm going to knit your diamonds together and see what they say to you... relax dominic... let your mother's protective soul release you of your burdens for tonight...

i stay till dawn... i stay past dawn... i watch him breathe... feel the images that run through his mind and body... i stay till he wakes... wakes to face this new saturday in a way that dear dominic has not faced a day before...

I lay in bed for a while. Savouring the warmth of my bed. Breathing easy, I suddenly decide I'm going to have today off. Just to myself. No working this weekend. My case load was easier at the moment. And I'd reserve this day just for me. I don't know what I'm going to do with it though. Phone Sheila? Immediately the River Woman slips into my head for some reason. And then I remember that my first thought of today was not about Kelly. For some reason I don't feel the usual discomfort and terrible longing that normally plagues me when I think of Kelly. This morning she doesn't touch me at all.

It occurs to me that I asked and asked of her and she never gave. Yes, we shared our bodies, but how much was she ever really there? In her head? I thought she was at the time. But if that was so, why had I felt lonelier after lovemaking than before?

Oh, golly, I dreamt last night. So many dreams. I felt so much peace. Vivid colours and feelings spun away from my dream memory.

I look over at my familiar wardrobe. The shape it has in the sunlight splitting the curtains apart. I didn't feel like wearing anything today. Just my bathrobe maybe. Unheard of for Dominic Maguire! I smiled to myself. Lounging around in a bathrobe for a whole day! What would Sheila have thought of that? She probably would have thought I was coming down with something – flu maybe? Even on weekends, I always wore a shirt and trousers. It wasn't that I didn't have any jeans or other casual clothes. It's just that my formal wear made it out of the wardrobe into my hands first.

Out of the wardrobe. That reminds me. Last night, I dreamt of a woman standing in my wardrobe. I opened the door. She smiled strangely at me. Almost as if she was a vampire. Her clothes parted at her overripe stomach. I watched in horror as her stomach expanded, bulged and split. And out climbed a skeleton of a baby. It flew through the air, straight at me. Straight through me. I think I screamed.

How horrible. I shivered involuntarily.

Straight through me.

I turned on to my right side. The hard lines and right angles of my desk and law books and papers sat firmly in place.

Straight through me.

That reminded me of another dream. A little girl had sprang from my body. As if she was a ghost moving out of my body.

We were both kids. I don't know how young we were. But her ghost walked out from my little boy body, her head from my head, her arms from mine. And we'd played together. She was the little girl from dreams ago, when I had really been a boy. The little girl that played with the smiling woman in the grave. It was the same one. But it was just the two of us now. We were running and chasing through a playground, and then raining woods, and through flowery gardens of a Lord and Lady's estate. And then we were both picked up and given piggy backs by parents. They were Mum and Dad to us both, yet she was a stranger to me. They weren't Mum and Dad who have really brought me up, and love Samantha, Sheila and myself. They were total strangers. I've never seen or met them before in real life or in dreams before. They raced down a tree lined lane. Me on her back. Her with auburn hair. And the girl on his back. Their blond looks together. We ran on forever, laughing. It was really comfortable and loving.

Comfortable and loving.

So, what *am* I going to do with myself today?

I think I'll call Edward, see if he's free for a game of tennis. But no hurry. Think I might just doze off again…

Chapter Seventy-Two

I looked at my watch. God. 9.30pm. I really will go home in a minute...

"Hey, Mr Workaholic, what's keeping you here so late?"

"Uh, hi Fiona. R. vs. Thurston. I think the bastard's going to get away with it."

"Away with what?"

"Attempted rape."

"Why are you being such a pessimist? What's the evidence like?"

"Not good. Her word against his. He's 74, would you credit it? He's visiting an old friend, and the old friend's daughter is this attractive 22 year old. She's alone in the house. He tries it on with her. She did sustain some bruising however. So we stand a good chance of getting him on assault. But attempted rape? The defence is painting her as black as can be. Though she does have a steady boyfriend, so he can't label her as a slut, but he can label her as 'up for it'."

"Who's the defence?"

"Our good old friend, Mr Van Hessen."

"Shit."

"Yeah. Wish he'd work for our side."

"Not a chance. They're the underdogs, remember? The state is the bully."

"Yeah, right." Fiona raised her eyebrows mockingly. Fiona was very attractive. What did she do outside of her court life, I wondered.

"Fancy getting out of here and grabbing a drink or something?" I asked on impulse.

"What! You're leaving work before 10pm? Are you feeling all right Dominic?"

"No, I don't think I am. I don't know why, but this case is

bringing me down."

"Uh-oh, not one of them!"

"One of what?" I asked.

"One of those 'did I choose the right career?' cases mixed in with some 'are we really doing more harm than good?' thrown in with a bit of 'we need to reform the penal system again, 'cause it's really all a load of shit'."

"How did you guess?"

"Oh, I've had a fair number of them myself. You get them from time to time."

"Yeah," I said glumly. I remembered Kirsten. Her face. Ashen. So young. Not just age wise, but mentally. She was the kind of girl who thinks everyone is a happy doggy, but now she's been bitten hard by a vicious rotweiler. She'd no idea such violence existed, let alone how to deal with it. Innocent she isn't anymore.

"Are you all right? You look pale."

"Too busy living the life of a vampire I guess," she looked askance at me. "You know, stuck indoors during daylight, and starved of blood."

"I see." She smiled. "Do you want to go for that drink then?"

I was about to say yes. Thinking what a good idea it would be to pour out to her all my misgivings and frustrations about this case. How I felt repulsed by Thurston, when I'd seen him in court the other day. How Kirsten's life ahead of her had been somehow sullied. And how I felt so helpless to help her.

"What do you do when you get one of them cases then, Fiona?"

"Oh, I get through it somehow and battle on to another case, my righteousness re-instilled. That inner-certainty reinforced that we do all we can do within the existing system to help make the world a better place. And feel glad as hell that I don't work for the other side."

"But what if a case really gets to you?"

"I don't get emotionally involved Dominic. I can't afford to. God, if I did, I'd be a nervous wreck by now. I do my best. And sometimes all my hard work pays off. And sometimes the system is stacked against us, and you have to let it go. This case isn't *really* getting to you is it?" She asked in surprise. When I didn't answer she said, "it's not as if he's a serial killer or anything."

Isn't he? True enough, Kirsten is still alive, and bodily walking around. But he'd definitely killed something within her. Perhaps something that *might not* ever live again. And why was I feeling so emotional about this case anyway? I wasn't sure. But I didn't like it.

"You're right. No, of course it's not really getting to me quite that bad. I'm just tired, and as you say, having one of those doubting-career cases." But I knew that wasn't it at all. Like a sixth sense I found something very disturbing about this case.

"Great. Drink then?"

"I'll pass actually. Think I'll just go home and crawl into bed."

"OK. Hope you're having a sleep in tomorrow. Looks like you could do with it."

Chapter Seventy-Three

it was now time to visit brian thurston...

brian looked pale against the white pillows... brian the free man... unconvicted of anything... free to destroy... free of recrimination... free of punishment... free of understanding... he'd suffered two heart attacks now... and he is going to suffer a third and possibly his final one... but that will be his choice...

poor dominic took it hard when the not guilty verdict came in... kirsten took it even harder...

this wasn't unlike the time i'd been in hospital... the white linen... the nondescript blinds – the white sheets and pillow cases – as if everything could be clean and white and purified and cured...

ᐟ

but really the white was an irritation – a nuisance – annoying – taunting... it had made me feel very uncomfortable in that maternity ward... it had all been a lie... white lies... everywhere...

the light green curtains that pull round each bed for privacy – they weren't allowed to be a dark colour – a rich colour – with any texture... that would be too truthful – too real... the whiteness of the sheets at the abortion clinic too... what a stupid idea – easily dirtied – always to be washed... all sheets should have been red – burgundy – coal black – not the numbing whiteness of bandages tied too tight...

i look at the face of the man who stole my body... made me intimate with violence – like a rose slit in half by a knife... the man who had fed me the death of love... made me feel like an empty can drained of beer... used up and thrown in the gutter... kicked down the street... stood on and squashed... to be swept up and kindly placed in the bin by a cruel road sweeper... so the world did not have to look upon me – the broken glass of society...

but i crawled out of the bin i learned survival – and gained knowledge... i can feel the purple bullet bomb sparks of my 15 year old... tinged with fiery red – fighting ocean blue... edged purple knives fresh from the fire – scorching and burning my body from the inside out – creased silken shreds blowing in no wind... blacker prongs of anger needling through... her rebellion... the unfairness... unjust... sick yellow desert sun of self blame revolving – erasing – purging...

i'm acting as your key brian... just as ted was my key that night – all those years ago... i enter your dreams and i open your floodgates to feelings – humane feelings...

his mind feels loathsome... his own self hate... his own powerlessness... a bucket lost down a forgotten well... toilet white... the sides of the well have been clawed... and in the shallow water lies the rusty pennies of his victims... pennies he thought he'd earned... pennies he thought would make him feel better... us pennies may have fed his rage and power like a bandit swallowing money and time... but we never produced the hand to lift him – up to take him to the moonlight... we made his whiteness blinding... and made him remember our pain in the red scrapes and scratchings on his plastic surface...

i drown you in my purple torture – as you feel all that you inflicted – all that you violated... you are now the violated instead of the violator... feel every nightmare i ever had... you now experience female fear – an identity turned inside-out – the denial of love – a life destroyed... you feel the painpainpainpain rip your very self apart – the pain of years you left behind in a 15 year old girl... feel the tombstones of tears drag you down from the neck every step you take... the endless despair of

crumbling walls of all you've ever known become soured –
scoured – sore from scabs inside your body... wretched in a man
trap of remembrance or lost in a fog of forget... to shower twice
– thrice a day and still not feel clean... to reject what you want
most... you feel all that i felt... falling through holes with
nothing to land on... you feel the threat of every male gaze –
every song about sex – every advert showing a sexy woman...
you feel the receiving end of violence forever tied to what should
have been love pleasure solace intimacy... you weaponed it –
now you feel the weapon on your feelings – your emotions and
body denied – trapped in the plastic bag of suffocation and fear
tied around your neck – breathing in hate – hating the feelings –
hating yourself for feeling it... you feel the worthlessness – the
victimhood – the powerlessness – the constant fight to live
another minute with the horror of what you know... you feel
your wrongness your rightfully accepted guilt your own anger at
yourself for being the criminal for criming and robbing and
stealing in the worst possible way... feel the struggle of claiming
your own life back... you admit you rape... you know you are a
rapist... you acknowledge your crime... feel your pain of
responsibility of guilt... as you went on to live your life and the
choices you made to violate others... feel the retching of the
female bodies trying to rid themselves of the dirt you forced into
them... retching morn and night to eject the misery... the self
deadness self imposed – you learn – because there's a point
when it's too much and feelings need to be stopped... we learn to
feel again – to find pleasure – to allow love affection tenderness
trust back into our lives... you stole a thousand things a
thousand times everyday of our lives but not forever... because
we take it back... we take ourselves back... and eject you the
perpetrator the liar the thief the criminal... from who we are...

brian – i will now show you the beauty you never had and could
never steal from us... the love i gave myself when ted and i came
together... the rippling peace of a blue lake... the gentle touch of
black velvet against the skin... you feel the equality respect
affection a moving deep within the soul that you never never
felt... a gentle pinksilk blossoming tenderness that you never
knew existed within the human heart... the possibilties of love...

362

the lapping sea of treasured openness... the cradling of a vulnerable being – the smell of a new born's hair nestling against your face... to be needed for who you are – a snooker ball accepted cosily into the corner pocket – your being held in its own individual place in the universe... the tangled silver threads spinning out to the stars encompassing your very own beauty – freshness flooding through – encapsulating you safely – letting your black-self-rose breathe and explore... growing hurting healing – ebbing and flowing in tides seeking the moon – as a child seeks its mother and father... the precious fragile glass petals of self entwined with another...

you never had that brian – you denied it – forgot it – so you abused your power over others... you understand your own lack – what you are missing – your own misdirected anger – your violence to women... you raped brian... and now you know – accept it – and use this crushing knowledge – use it well... of the swords of pain you wrought slashing through my life – our lives – remember the contrast of navy night falling on hard repeated lies of crystal white snow – needles green trees prickling signs of consciousness as your shadow makes footprints – the soft frills of carpet green ruffling in a spring breeze – hard compact brown earth under honest feet and the grey learning that travels in between... for now i depart and leave you to the sentencer and executioner within yourself... he'll awaken you to the nightmare that you gave to me and to others which I now give back to you...

Chapter Seventy-Four

"Dominic Maguire?"

"Speaking."

"I need you to do me a huge favour."

"Sorry, can I ask who's calling?"

"You're not going to like it. But I need you to give a letter to my daughter. I don't know where she is. We haven't been in touch for years, and I haven't time left to search for her. It's of utmost importance."

"I'm sorry, but I still don't know who you are."

"I haven't got much time left to live, I fear. But it's desperate that she gets this. But she's living in Australia the last I heard."

"Sir, I don't specialise in probate. I'm a criminal lawyer."

"Yes, I know that. I was in court too you know. I'm Brain Thurston."

I hung up. What the hell did that scum think he was doing? After all he's done! All the lies he told to the court. After everything he put my client through. Why on earth get in touch with me?

The phone rang again. I looked at it suspiciously. It was him again.

"Listen, don't hang up. I know you don't want to talk to me. But you were right. Kirsten's right. I'm as guilty as hell. And I'm sorry. I'm also guilty towards other women too, and I need to make it up to one in particular. My daughter."

I hung up again, feeling sick to my stomach. I picked up the nearest coffee cup and threw it against the door. It split and cracked, but didn't smash into nearly as many pieces as I'd like. I did it again, with another cup.

Then Fiona came in, and waved a white piece of paper at me, in mock flag style.

"Wasn't me your honour. I'm innocent." I couldn't raise a smile. "Something serious?"

"You could say that. I'm going for a walk. A long brisk one."

"Want company? Need to talk?"

"No." She looked offended at my brusqueness. "Thanks for the offer Fiona, but I just need some time out."

"No problem." I felt her eyes on me, as I left the office. I didn't want her concern, I wanted Brian Thurston locked up behind bars for all the despicable crimes he'd committed.

***

A couple of days later I received a letter in the post, with a further two letters enclosed with it. One was addressed to Roberta Thurston. The other was addressed to me. A matron at the general infirmary had sent them to me. She said in her covering letter that Brian had been most emphatic about my receiving these letters, and that he'd had another heart attack and passed away in the night.

I couldn't believe the audacity of him. I felt no grief in his passing, wished it had happened earlier, would have saved my client a lot of heartache.

Now I was left with this additional responsibility. I wasn't his damn lawyer. Why leave it to me?

I tore open the envelope addressed to me, wondering if I should just burn the whole thing.

I read through it quickly, resenting his post-humus invasion into my life.

With this letter is another one. For my daughter, as I said on the phone. Please can you track her, and make sure she receives this? It's a letter of apology. It doesn't ask for forgiveness, but lets her know that I'm the one in the wrong, and always was. I didn't realise before. The intention is not to hurt her, but hopefully to help her heal. I've realised a lot of things these last few days that would surprise you. They shocked me. And am finding it difficult to live with this new understanding I have.

You may not believe me and may hate me still. I don't blame you. I hate me too. But whatever you think of me, well because of what you think of me, I hope you will be honest enough to do this for me, and help me to help Roberta, in the only way I can. If you throw this away, you're denying Roberta, not me. The letter will upset her, no doubt, just because it's from me. But the words need to be received, need to be heard.

I could beg you on my knees, and you might still say no. Please don't.

I can't change the past and I can't take back what I have done, but I can try and ease Roberta's pain a little. Pain that I have caused.

And some more in the same vein. Even though I despised the paper he'd held in his dirty hands, and loathed the writer of the words I held before me I somehow felt responsible for this letter now whether I liked it or not. I just hoped I was doing the right thing.

***

"I didn't come to the funeral to say goodbye. I came to dance on his grave." Roberta, a very serious, defensive young woman, now sat across from me. Round about my age. We were sat in the restaurant part of the pub, just two minutes walk down the road from the graveyard. It was very quiet at this time, mid afternoon. Her grey green eyes regarded me across the table, studiously trying to fathom me out.

I shifted uncomfortably, questioning again, if it was wise to comply with Brian Thurston's last wishes.

I was stuck for words. 'I'm sorry for your loss' didn't seem appropriate. I stared down into my black coffee, too hot to drink.

"What is it you wanted to talk to me about Mr Maguire?" Her voice was waspish, but I probably deserved it. I felt her distrust of me, purely on the grounds that I was a man. She'd ensured that we'd remained in a public place, with people around the whole time. This whole thing left a nasty taste in my throat, and I wished I could gulp down some of the coffee to drive it away.

"I have a letter for you, but perhaps you won't want it. But I was asked to ensure that it was delivered into your hands."

She regarded me again. "Did you *know* Brian?" I noted she didn't refer to him as her father.

"No, I only ever saw him in court. I have personally never had any dealings with Brian Thurston. Until now. And it is not something I relish." She gave me a curt nod as if I'd passed some sort of test.

"Then why are you doing it?"

Good question.

"I did think about not doing as your fa... as Mr Thurston requested, I'm not his lawyer after all. I'm sorry, Ms Banks but I find I cannot answer your question sufficiently. I guess deep down his words to you might indeed be able to offer you some comfort, in the way that he promised it would, in his letter to me."

"Comfort," she scorned. And I deeply regretted being here and doing this. In the silence that ensued, I could hear my heart beating erratically, and I was just thinking it was perhaps a good idea for me to leave and take the letter with me, when she suddenly said, "Give it to me." Her words were precise and firm.

I brought out a long narrow white envelope from my inside pocket, her name scrawled on the front.

She took it from my hand, ensuring that none of our fingers touched. She smiled unpleasantly, as she looked at the writing. "He couldn't even get my name right." I thought at first she meant he hadn't spelt it right, but then realised she was talking about her changed surname. To my horror and deep consternation she started to open the letter.

"Don't feel like you have to read it now. Perhaps you'd like to open it in your own time, in your own privacy," I gushed.

"Perhaps I want you to know if Brian has indeed brought me any 'comfort'." I felt trapped by her words, as if she was saying, this is your deed and now you have to accept the consequences. I sickeningly felt as if I was a party to the crimes that Brian had committed against her, as if I somehow condoned it in some way. I felt sullied. But there was nothing I could do now. There was no escape.

She slithered the lined paper from its casing. I could see

Brian's scrawl had reached to seven sides of notepaper.

She proceeded to read it in front of me. She glanced up a couple of times. Perhaps to ensure I hadn't run away. Perhaps to check to see if I was feeling uncomfortable enough. I'd a sudden urge to dash to the gents, but I dared not leave my seat for fear she'd read it as desertion, cowardice, not being able to take my medicine like a good boy.

As she got further into the letter though, she forgot I was there completely. I was left stranded in that dreaded silence of worry and wait. I wondered how bad the damage was, that I had wrought. I wondered if this was how defendants felt when they were waiting for the jury to come back with a verdict.

I saw her face, a closed mask. I studied my swirling coffee with new interest, watching the light reflect from its dark depths. I wondered what Brian had written, what sort of effect it would have, how I could possibly plead innocent in the face of it all, when I was as guilty as hell. Guilty for delivering it. 'Don't shoot the messenger,' I felt like saying. But why not? I didn't have to be the messenger. I could've decided not to. Roberta wouldn't have been any the wiser. Instead I'd be feeling guilty for my silence, and wondering if there was something I could've done to alleviate this young woman's distress in some way.

I lost either way. Damn Brian Thurston for putting me in this position.

I suddenly felt a slight difference in the surrounding silence. The verdict was in. I felt a hush, though nothing was said. The letter slid from her fingers. I dared to let my gaze travel up from her fingers to meet what I thought would be condemning and accusatory eyes. But when I looked up, she was crying. Streams silently coursing her cheeks. This was much worse. I looked at her, but she seemed to see right through me, like I wasn't there.

"Ms Banks? Ms Banks?" My voice seemed to bring her back to her earth and her eyes focused on me properly.

"Bastard," she said in lowered tones. Then, "Bastard!" she screeched at me, and upturned the table on me, my hot coffee burnt through my trousers to my thighs, then she was raining punches on me, and trying to scratch at my face. I held my arms against₁ myself to deflect her. Then she suddenly stopped. I slowly lowered my arms. Roberta had sunk to her knees on the floor, uncontrollably sobbing.

And I noticed a waitress and a barman hovering at the edges of my vision, staring at us.

I knelt down in front of her.

"Is there some sort of problem?" The barman cautiously approached.

"No, it's fine. This young lady's just had a hell of a shock. Can you get some brandy or something?"

"Yes of course."

"Ms Banks?" I daren't touch her, though I wanted to put my arm round her, and offer her some support. "Do you wish to go to your hotel room? Would you like me to call your mother?" I asked gently. She shook her head.

"I... want to... to go back... to his... grave," she managed between sobs.

I was surprised at her request. "Are you sure that's..." She nodded furiously. "OK." The barman returned with a glass of brandy, but Roberta pushed it away.

"Have you... a match... or a lighter?" I wondered if she was starting to lose it. I nodded to the barman, and he went to get some.

"He's a bastard... and he... admits it." Her sobs had slowed, but they still came from the gut, making her shake.

"Yes he is a bastard," I readily agreed, and then wish I hadn't.

"You. Don't Know Him," she emphasised each word as if it stood by itself.

"No." There wasn't any 'right' thing to say here, I decided.

"You don't know... what he was like... all the things he did." Wisely I kept silent, respecting her private grief. "I wish I had your ignorance."

The barman returned, held a small box of matches to her. She just sat there and stared at them, as if she was wondering what they were, and what they were for. I reached for them, but her hands suddenly sprang to life and snatched at them before I could touch them.

"Come to..." she paused, "the grave with me." It was more of an order than an invitation.

369

"OK." Though I was surprised she wanted me with her. Surely I was the last person she wanted to see anything more of at the moment? She got to her feet and took her coat from the back of her chair. She stood there waiting for me. I rose too and slid my jacket on, feeling very strange.

I walked unsteadily to the exit. She followed, her body language refusing any assistance I would have offered.

The air was biting and crisp and I found myself shivering. But Roberta was now rigid. We strode in cold silence to the graveyard. Cars passed by. Passers by passed by.

At the open grave, we stared down on Brian Thurston's casket.

Roberta then held aloft Brian's letter as she stared to the mid distance. I was entranced and thought of nothing. The pages were still and dead in her hand. She then gave the sheaf of papers to me, and got out the matches. Very deliberately she lit one, and took the top page from my freezing hands. She held the hungry flame to the naked paper, and watched at it licked at it, and took hold. The flames ate it slowly, as if relishing its destruction. The ashes fell over his coffin. Once the whole page had been claimed by nothingness, she proceeded to enact the whole slow ritual again with the next page. She did it a piece at a time, till there was nothing left to burn.

Brian's last words were no more. Noisy silence continued to spread out from us. I thought the moment would go on forever. Years and years would pass and I'd still be here at Brian Thurston's grave, stood frozen solid next to his ashen faced daughter.

Suddenly she turned to face me and said, "Thank you Dominic Maguire," and then turned and walked away.

I didn't follow. I waited till she was out of sight, then I strolled back to the office, not really comprehending what had just taken place, and not understanding why she'd thanked me.

Chapter Seventy-Five

A warm waft of air greets me after the cold of the street, as I enter. BBC Radio 2 plays discretely in the background.

A smiling assistant attends me immediately. "What name is it please?"

"Roberta Maguire."

"If you'd just like to take a seat over there, and Shelley will be with you in a minute."

"Thank you."

I seated myself down. I'd decided to treat myself. Hair change time again, equalling face change, equalling personality change, equalling refreshed Roberta, equalling smile at world again. Such a simple thing, yet so dramatic upon feelings and appearance – hair. Do hairdressers know of the happiness they hold in their scissors, shampoo and water as they religiously transform each customer?

I look uninterestedly at the uninteresting magazines on the interesting table before me, as Shelley finishes with her current customer. I wander back in time to the other significant times I went for a hair change.

I am surprised and relieved to find that the most vivid memory which floats by is a happy one. The day after our explosive meeting.

Our very first meeting, I died. And after that I... I don't know.... I don't want to say relived, or re-birthed, as that's so cliché, and it implies a return to something, when I didn't return anywhere. I went on to somewhere new.

"Hello there. Roberta is it? Would you like to take a seat over here? Shall I take your coat? Right there we go then. What is it, a wet trim? And some styling? Oh you want it layered, OK, no problem. If you'd just like to put this round your neck, I'll tie it up for you, right then if you'd just like to put your head back, rest it gently on there, that's it. OK. Good." I let Shelley chatter on, nodding in the right places. She was a happy chatterer who didn't need much prompting.

I closed my eyes to the bright lights and dark wood furnishings of the room, as the warm water jettisoned on to my head, running through my brown hair, feeling the massage of fast pricks of warmth rush my scalp. I revelled in the vigour of Shelley's fingers shampooing in, rubbing foam into, massaging all my unique bumps and shapes that made up my head.

That first day. I can see his eyes again, blue blueness. I never thought our paths would cross again, after that time. The sombre lawyer. His shocked blueness. His familiar concern of strangers, yet he'd delivered the message of damage and help. His person having been plunged centre stage into my drama, my life, just where he didn't want to be, this unsure stranger with this aggrieved woman. Why had I thanked him, he later asked me. I enlarged his perspective. He differentiated mine. Our lenses crossed and coloured and lived happily if warily for a long time. Wariness, caution always follows a great calamity though. Only time brings freedom.

But perhaps it's unfair of me to remember him as such a dark sombre figure, when the occasion did call for a degree of sobriety and regard. God knows he wasn't in an easy position, and he put me in an even uneasier position.

He'd piqued my curiosity. I looked to the papers to find out more, the trial, the lawyer, the 'defendant'. How the trial had gone, how it had been obstacled, how it had not gone, how it fell apart. Jury unconvinced. Lack of proof. Absence of witnesses. Too much about the victim, not enough about the perpetrator. Brian's act, his role of innocence.

Wilson Phillips' calming tones lilt into *Hold On*. One of my favourite songs. I did a lot of that – holding on for one more day, waiting and hoping for that 'someday' and 'somebody' to make me 'turn around and say goodbye'. Goodbye. Madonna's right, there's nothing more powerful than the *Power of Goodbye*.

Brian's funeral was someday. Not the only someday. There was a lot of leading-up-to-somedays. Brian's was the last page of a book of 'somedays'. And Dominic was the 'somebody'. The second somebody. The first one was me. I was the somebody, all along. Dominic was my catalyst.

I did say goodbye to Brian after all, that day. Not goodbye to pain, hurt, self-blame, and self-shame he'd caused, they were diminishing and returning things, part of my past and sometimes present kaleidoscope I viewed and felt through to the outer world.

But I found a way past, a way to break the taboo. Break my silence. Break through the silent silences. The chains of tied gags. Everybody's silences. Their overwhelming silences, the awkwardness', the disappointments, the fears, the misunderstandings, the not-wanting-to-knowness, the shame and the blamefulness, it's my fault, it's their fault, sometimes his fault, their powerlessness in league with my own, their anger and my silent response. Why didn't I have anger? I did. But not at first. I found people who were not afraid of the silences. People who I could talk to and could talk about the unspeakable. That was my release.

I see a crocheted cloth laid out on the counter. Someone's made it. A member of staff. It's new and she's proud. It looks good, patterned and light. Something that paper will rest on gladly and people won't be able to write on it properly because of the unevenness it makes. My life, a patchwork of knitted memories, pain, trying to find the thread of stories to fix it all back together, where the narrative kept getting interrupted and I lost time and special moments, I lost where I was supposed to be, where I was at the time, lost a way of keeping track of things, lost a girl who was more than innocent and I lost her reactions and trustingness in things, in life, in people. I caught at threads, dangling pieces of string, clawing them back together, tying them up, making them fit together. But sometimes I couldn't find any threads at all. And the material wasn't just unravelled, it had disappeared. Seeing the fragments was just the first step, before I could even start to sew them together.

Brian's death was an added revelation, and yet it wasn't. His letter was a full stop at the end of his behaviour. So many things culminated in that moment of the letter. His admitting of his crimes that I battled all my life to see straight and fix the blame firmly where it belongs. Battling the way he made me a perpetrator in the crime against me. Divided me against myself and the rest of the world.

Shelley towels off the drops, and I don't look at my reflection as she snips and clips and combs and snips and combs clips, jigs my head, pinches the hair. I'm too much in my own thoughts, not wanting to let the outer world disturb my concentration and the sensations of her hands on my head, in my head, through my head that will breathe a different life into it, into me. An enhanced one.

I remember the hairdresser in Australia. A tight short bob. My first hair cut in a new country. The country without Dad. I suddenly realise what I've just called Brian. Realise I've deliberately not called him that for years. Realise there was a time long ago, when that had been his everyday name on my lips, just like Mum. Country without ritualised pain and terror. Country with courage, country with talking, counselling, healing, friends, shared experiences, not talking, outrage, hiding myself, disappearing myself, denying my body, denying feelings, denying the world. I hardly believed I existed at all. I was surprised when people looked at me, and answered a question I may have asked, as if they were addressing some*body*, a body, a person with a body. How could their eyes tell me they were looking at a person, acknowledging the existence of Rapee Roberta when I didn't exist to myself. I had no body. I wasn't there. There was no body for them to address, for them to look at, for them to answer. My voice was disembodied, had no body to come from or return to. I was voice, and eyes. I could see others. I could not see me, so how could they? How could they address a *no-body?* I didn't understand.

Dominic and I met, the second time, an accident, fate, a faith, in the park. Frosted grass, the earth's hair gone white. Bare trees, earth's spiked and knobbled fingers, skinned of skin. He was listless, ghost-like – apt, seen as he had raised and killed ghosts last time we'd met. To see me, he was taken aback, ill at ease, upset, avoidance wishing, lacking in words. What words are there for such situations? What can words possibly do? What need is there for words? Sometimes they just are not needed. Sight and feeling is all. Other times there is nothing but the words, and the words must be writ large, for everyone to see, for all to know, so that I can't ignore, and my mother can't ignore,

374

and my friends and my strangers can't ignore, because validation and recognition of the *importance* of feelings, of the experience, of my body, are *essential.*

The day was a Monday. The start of a week. The start of new relations.

New lives, for both of us. He's quit work. Ex-lawyer. His time-out. His 'what-am-I-going-to-do-with-my-life-now' time. How was I keeping, he asked. "Well." Words had deserted me too.

"How long are you here for?" I can't quite remember his tone of voice, but I remember feeling like a tourist for a second.

"For good." I'd answered, which surprised him, and absolutely amazed me! His awkwardness cried out for reassurance, and I felt it being drawn from me. I gave it freely, not wishing him to suffer the guilt that was Brian's. I remember being aware of that for the first time. I had learned painstakingly to differentiate some males, friends, from the men that rape, from the cloak of wrong-doing of my father's that had shrouded and ensnared every man in my sight for a passage of time.

Oddly I had then invited him to walk with me. He acquiesced. He was bound in devoted servitude to amend for the tears his actions had wrought. It was his own creation. I could feel his want to amend, his lack of knowledge as to how. Within myself I rejected all ideas of amendments, there were none to make. I could give him healing. He was wounded. And my body, my mind, discovered a new power within me, the power to give. To this man.

The power to receive was something I had been working on for a long time, to receive the love I didn't think I deserved, to receive help, to receive guidance, to receive my body, to receive my being still being and existing. Receiving is a hard thing to accomplish. Receive compliments. But I could be the rescuer too. I could rescue him. I felt the need to find out, to explore, to find the tools, to help him. I wanted to know him. To receive this stranger's company until he was no longer a stranger.

Snip-clip-comb-tug-tug. What was Shelley talking about now? Holidays. What a strange topic to talk about. How light and frivolous and perfectly wonderful. I couldn't recognise the now playing tunes of the happy DJs.

I advised him on the dangers of not being dedicated to teaching as he bounded the word in the air, trying it out as a career, not really knowing anything of it, except that it was not being a lawyer. He knew right away that that was what my chosen profession was.

His tinged red ears badly needed a hat to protect them from the numbing cold. He needed protection. What from? I needed to rescue. I zoomed in on this new power of mine, in my gut, testing it, mentally prodding it, tasting it, what it was like in its newness.

We shared our first laugh together. I forget what was said now, I wish I could remember it, something to do with teaching. Something. "Are you materialistic, Mr Maguire?" I'd asked him. How had that come up? Oh, yes, I told him TEFL teaching was more lucrative and less paper weighted than school teaching.

We'd passed the lifeless swings in the park, shimmering ever so, every now and then in a frosty breath of nobody, frozen memories of t-shirt and little dresses, kids, snotty faces, and cries of delight in the wooden seat, the metal chains. As we passed them, he informed me his drive in life was no longer passion but listlessness. I could see that. It was all about him. As soon as he said the word, it became him, who he was, how I saw him, how I looked at the world imagining seeing it through his eyes. He was walking Listless. Mr Listless. Without a list. No list, nothing prescribed. An empty space, a blank page, looking for his pen to write with, not knowing, not knowing how to know what he would then mark down on that vacuum of whiteness. I had encountered that. Lots of them. Vacuums.

He'd asked me to call him by his first name. Call him Dominic. He asked politely, with great respect. He asked in earnestness. But mostly he asked the question as if answering no was a possibility, an option, and it was an answer he would respect and comply with, with no judgement. He would've accepted no, had I said it. He knew it was my right to, but further than that, deeper than that. He would not have held me any grudge, any forbearance, any emotion of dislike had I said no. And I remember that moment clearly.

The air crisp around us, as if it was frozen and could not move, only we moved, and stirred the coolness around us. Only our steaming clouds of rising breath altered any shift in the air around us. Our steps crunching down in time, my body warm through the travelling blood of walk, but my feet stiff with continued combing of earth's hard cold hair.

It seemed a long pause of air and space before I answered his question, his polite and respectful request to call him Dominic instead of Mr Maguire. Many thoughts held and swam and hovered and whisked round my head. I hated that line, let's be friends, call me by my first name, let's be lovers, let me turn you on, let me use you, I know your name now and can use it, reel you in and abuse it, let's be intimate, let me impose upon you to make myself unstranger to you, let's get close, let me tear you apart, I'm asking a lot, but you won't mind, when you call me by my first name you're obligated to let me call you by yours, that's the way it works, even though I made you the offer you didn't realise I'd kindly deceived you into letting me do the same, a trap you fell into, whatever comes next is all your fault, you let me in, you made it so, even though the question was for you to use *my* name and not the other way round, nothing comes for free you know, quid pro quo you know, swap names, but I hold the power as I was the one that asked, I initiated, ball in my court, and your granted permission gives me permission also.

But there was no rape in his question. I often thought of people's sentences and actions as smaller actions of rape, an enforcement of another to your disadvantage, an unnoticed violence, an obtuse permission opened wide and abused and turned in upon the victim. Blame reassigned to the wrong person. Keep your own guilt. Keep your own responsibility for your own actions and words and behaviour. I don't want them. They're yours. Accept your own wrong doing. But his words were kind. He spoke deferentially. No was an option, and he valued that. He respected that. There was an authentic choice. And there was no obligation for me to then say, 'Please call me Roberta'. It just wasn't there. I tested the air for it, swept his face and step in one glance. He owned the responsibility he had for his own actions in coming to father's funeral, in seeing me, in delivering the letter. He blamed me not. And he was offering me the use of the word of his name for me to do with as I pleased, and still retaining the power of position of Ms Banks in his vocabulary, 'Roberta' still remaining off limits to him, without question, judgement or imposition.

So I called him Dominic. I felt a small tug of fear as I did so. I had his name, and he didn't have mine, yet it drew me to him. I didn't want it to. I fought it. But it was there. The fear was there because I liked saying his name for some unknown reason. But more importantly the fear was not because of any fear *of* him.

Blow drier time. It drowned out the radio and Shelley's continued chatter. She never stopped. I briefly wonder at what other light conversational words I've missed that tripped off her tongue so easily.

I used the power I had, to ask personal questions. I asked if his lack of wife/partner and children bothered him. But the balance needed to be redressed, he knew personal things of my life, that I had not volunteered to him, or given any consent for him to know about. Somebody else had told him, Brian, without me even being in the country. Perhaps I shouldn't have asked, shouldn't have been curious, perhaps I shouldn't apologise for asking.

He admitted to a stranger, a woman, a woman who had known abuse and had the power of creation within her body, admitted to me his guilt for thinking of kids as if they didn't apply to him, because he did not have the body needed to give birth.

And somehow we both disclosed to the other that we were in search of a soul mate and hadn't found one yet. How had the conversation got so personal?

"Soul mates are very hard to find," he'd said like it was some dark prophecy.

"Have you looked hard?" I'd asked.

"In all the wrong places it seems."

"Well, now you know where they are, you can start looking in the right ones."

He laughed bitterly, saying, "Yeah, like not in other men's marriage beds for one thing."

"Oh, that sort of wrong place." I couldn't hide my disapproval of such behaviour.

"Yes. That sort. Bad idea. Not one I ever wish to repeat."

Well he hadn't tried to excuse himself.

But as I got to know Dominic better over the following days, weeks and months, my disapproval of his past extra-marital affair lessened. I came to understand him, understand his initial bitterness. I understood his list-less-ness too. I found his pen for him, gave him the will to start to write his life, his next few moments, I helped warm the ink so it could begin to flow once again, so he could dare to formulate plans and thoughts for the future again. His future. Our future.

Fields opened out to either side of us as we'd continued walking, more dog owners showed themselves, more kids on dare devil bikes, more couples and couples of friends, sauntering, running, getting somewhere, breathing in the cold air into their lungs, exhaling warmth, wrapped in their t-shirts, boots and scarves.

I suddenly felt starved for knowledge of other post humus letters of my father. Had the girl from the trial received one too? Dominic Maguire informed me that she had. His secretary had informed him. The girl, Kirsten Dubois, had complained about the letter, not wanting it, rejecting it, blaming him – the lawyer, the third party, the safe fence between right and wrong, the fence had splintered and let through some of the badness to the good side. Not allowed. Then he started to make excuses, to ramble, over his bad feelings about it all, I told him to stop it. I ordered him to stop that. And put him absolutely straight there. Brian's fault. Brian's blame. Brian's actions. Not his. Not Dominic's. I separated out Brian's dirty fingered deeds and Dominic's innocent helpfulness as plainly as I could for both of us to see it, right before us.

Shelley got too close with the drier and my skin on the nape of my neck started to get hot. She didn't seem to notice as I shifted my head in discomfort, but thankfully, she decided that other areas of my hair were in need of a roasting, and continued to waft the hot air around me.

I remember feeling anger. Knowing my anger was valid. Why hadn't Dominic done more? Why hadn't he put the bastard behind bars? I listened to my angry voice hollering around inside my head. I didn't give vent to it. I listened to another voice in my head that intuitively knew that Dominic had been berating himself enough for it, and still was.

Our verbalised words between walking silences continued as naked trees and disguised grass continued to pass us by, and black silhouettes of passers by on the path beside, and in between trees ahead of us, behind us, and away to the distances at either side of us.

Shelley proceeded to briskly brush out my hair. She then noticed my scowl. Her brushing became gentler.

Somehow our words followed ideas on appreciation of various forms of literature, of different types of music, of the formulating and formless shapes and pictures of art, of going to the art gallery together next Friday as they were holding their annual book fair.

And our relationship began. It began without us almost. Without us noticing. We talked little, shared silences in libraries, book shops, more art galleries. We read each other's collection of books, and listened to each other's record collections. We read each other's characters in the doodles of borrowed books, in well thumbed pages with corners turned down, in the underlined words selected from a favourite passage, a passage of meaning. We discovered each other's natures in the tattered record sleeves, in the moving lyrics, in the moving notes. We grew to understand each other's internal picture galleries of families, likes, fears, loves in paintings and sculptures we loved and hated. The information was not in the agreement or disagreement of our likes, but in the ways we liked and disliked various formats and why.

He introduced me to cinema, and I introduced him to theatre. It wasn't that neither of us had never been to the respective above, but that we both shunned that one particular medium or other. I found things to criticise and engage with in the films, and he found things to admire and objectify in the theatre.

And one day, I broke our shared silent communications of written, visual, audio culture and directly said: You don't need to blame yourself for having given me the letter from Brian. You don't need to feel indebted to me that you were unable to swing the jury towards truth.

From time to time, I still felt the remnants of his guilt and bad feeling about it all hang in the air between us. He asked me why I'd suddenly said this to him.

"Because sometimes I can still feel an apology ready to spring from your lips. Because I want our friendship to be genuine and equal and not based on your feeling you have to atone for something all the time. I want our friendship free of my feeling any need to punish you for what Brian did and what the law courts didn't. Free of my feeling that I need to reassure you constantly, so that you can look up from your guilt trodden shoes, and look me squarely in the eyes. I need our friendship to *be* simply because we like and enjoy being together."

He took note of what I said. He held it to his heart, and retrained himself and eased the burden of what was not his responsibility. He worked at it.

He fell in love with me.

That sentence still makes me shiver internally with pleasure. Sometimes I hold the six words of that sentence physically in my hands in disbelief, and gently remind myself how to receive.

"I love you Roberta. Do you believe me?"

"I do." Registry office. Family and a couple of close friends only. And all the celebrated days that followed. Simple wedding. Touchingly enacted. His family opened their arms to me, like a flock of birds receiving their long lost missing relative.

And Dominic himself... My husband...

Silence of the taboos are no longer taboo with him... all my pain already speaks in his head and whenever a 'little earthquake' of mine steals moments of time and joy from my life, he is there listening, holding my hand, respecting, waiting, loving.... when I take him into my deepest horrors and he holds me whilst I'm there... his patience holds the roof of the tunnel up, so I can traverse towards the light at the end....

And I envelope him in a total acceptance of who he is.... He has access to all the love in my heart, all the love that he needs.

And we laugh so.... Like two parts of a broken bridge meeting in the middle to make a whole, we can see the bigger pictures of things... And fun, humour, irony begin to find ways to exist in our union that neither of us could access alone.

From our very second meeting, I knew he was the one. Love at second sight.

"There we go. All done. What do you think?" Shelley indicated for me to look in the mirror, for me to look in the mirror reflecting the other mirror.

Straight faced I turned to her and said, "I think you've done a bloody horrendous job Shelley and I'd like my money back." She fell silent. An achievement. I couldn't tease out the moment of her suffering any longer though. I smiled broadly. "Shelley, you've done a fantastic job. As usual. It looks great. I look great." Her beaming smile returned. And so did her 60 mph chatter. I didn't mind.

I made an appointment to see her again in two months time.

Chapter Seventy-Six

I wish Roberta was here today. I thought of ringing her at her mother's. She's only gone for a few days, yet without her I feel my understanding of myself stray, fading like words in the air. They're still there, but without my wife here to witness them, their shapes transmute into scary feelings or vanish all together. Leaving me without a joined up history again.

And today. Well, today I was going to the literature festival. To talk about my own book. A collaboration of my legal experience and Roberta's emotional wisdom. A book that makes so much sense to me. And only now do I understand why my last case, with Kirsten, R vs Thurston, why it had been so personal.

And my editor is going to be there. For moral support, she said. She knows I feel nervous about it all. Just as she's known other things about me. Intuitively. Funny, funny world. That my editor should turn out to be none other than the River Woman. Daphne Hawkins.

Who is also…

I can't swallow. And my stomach's doing funny things. Food. Absolutely not.

I could ring Roberta. She'd know just the right things to say to soothe me. But somehow this feels like my pre-history coming together, and I need to…

Daphne Hawkins. River Woman. Friend. Editor. And…

Sister.

I'll never be able to speak to my real Mum. Died when I was three. And I feel a strange sense of loss streaming next to my anger of unanswered questions. Sheila needn't have feared. Mum and Dad, although hurt, were very supportive of me trying to find my biological origins. My other parents.

Yes, they were hurt. They tried to understand, but somehow

couldn't. And they're afraid. For me. For Sheila. For themselves. Afraid of what I might find. Afraid Sheila might eventually want to do the same search one day. Afraid that they might lose me, their only son. I can only love them. And hope they forgive me. The relief of it not being a secret anymore does not assuage the guilt, but at least we can openly be there for each other.

But I found my sister. Even before I knew that's who she was. My twin.

I feel like one half of a ripped heart.

Does she know? Does Daphne know? I feel curious, scared, angry, affection, nervous and suspicious and... what? I don't know.

And I have to face her today. This of all days. Not as a friend. Or an editor. But as a blood relative. How am I going to feel? What will I say? What will she say?

I want to put this moment off forever, even though I've waited, wanted, searched for it for so long.

What if she knows? What if she doesn't want to know me? What if she can help me find my missing pieces? What if she can, what do I do with them? Does she know she has missing pieces too?

I hear the ticking of our grandfather clock stood in the corner of our living room. It's ticked all my life. And continues to tick as my life becomes something new. Something different. I don't know what's going to happen, but I'm going to take a deep breath and meet my sister.

Chapter Seventy-Seven

Raped by Law, Raped by Society by Dominic Maguire. The red and black cover of his book stared back at me from the empty table.

I switched my gaze to the face of my twin brother. *The Dark Man.* Dominic, my brother.

Author of many of the injustices I wanted to put right. The injustices as pertaining to victims of rape in a court of law. The treatment by the police. Sentences for rapists. Date rape. Repeat offenders. Serial offenders. Incestuous rapists. How both the offenders and the victims should be treated. The sort of support needed by victims prior to, during and after the case hearing. A much needed redefinition of terms. Rape is not sexual. Rape is violent. Rape is about anger and power, not sex. The focus of the crime is in the wrong place. The education needed from schools to the lay person in the street as to how the act affects the perpetrator, victim and every single individual in society. A society of rape. Of silence. Of taboos. How to break down the barriers, and create understanding. Realistic goals. Everyday implementations to re-enable both victims and perpetrators to integrate the pain in their lives. To even dare to say the opposing sides in the same sentence. It was a break-through book. Clear. Concise. And empathetic.

I felt a sudden empathy with the emptiness that now lingered in the scattered chairs. Yet they were solid. Familiar.

I glanced at the clock on the wall. It told me the next writer was due in here any minute now.

"I prosecuted the man that raped our mother." His words free-floated in the room. The cyclicity of it blew my mind. Two significant occurrences in one sentence. *Our mother.* No longer just *my* mother. I'd never shared her before. And that Dominic had actually stood opposed to the man who hurt *our* mother.

385

Without even knowing it.

"There's so much to take in…" I said after a moment.

"Yes," he replied, and met my eyes. "What was she like?"

"I don't have very many memories of her. A lot of them come from Isabel and Dad and how they knew her." I shared a father with him too. Such easy words, yet so hard to grasp.

"Do you think they know?" His voice was edged. Guarded. *Did* Isabel and Dad know about Dominic? His adoption? Well I couldn't say for definite. But I felt pretty sure they didn't. They'd been pretty straight with me on all matters concerning Mum.

"No, I don't think they do. I think they're in for as big a shock as the one I'm feeling now. I can hardly believe it!" He smiled warmly, and the tension ebbed from the room.

"Neither can I."

"So did I pass the test?" I asked tentatively.

"The test?" He raised his eyebrows.

"Do you still want to know me? Can we start to know each other as…" I was hesitant about using the words. The labels didn't fit yet.

"As brother and sister?" he completed the sentence for me.

"That's what I wanted to say, yes."

"I feel like I've been searching for one half of a pair of shoes all my life. I've been carrying this tatty old left shoe with me, looking for its partner so I can fill in the blanks of who I am. And here you are."

I felt tears prick my eyes, but I laughed and said, "Well, I've never been someone's shoe before!"

"How about I try you on for size?" he asked, smiling. We stood in unison. The spaces of time and distance disappeared between us. We met each other in a warm heartfelt, but strange embrace.

"How does it fit?" I asked, tears slowly traversing my cheeks.

"It's a little uncomfortable, but I'm sure it'll wear in. We'll get used to each other."

Just then there was a light knock on the door, and it swung open. It wasn't time already was it, for the next author's talk?

A familiar figure stood framed in the doorway. He took a step into the room. My stomach did a flip flop and performed some sort of fuzzy melting trick that made me feel heady, and my legs feel as if they weren't quite attached.

"Hi Daphne," he said in his quiet tones.

"Adrian..." We hadn't seen each other, spoken to each other for months.

"I'm sorry to disturb... erm, you're busy, I'll leave you to..."

"No, don't go." I stood outside of Dominic's embrace. He looked more gaunt than how I remembered him. His eyes looked haunted. He searched my face questioningly. But I couldn't think of anything to say. Thankfully Dominic came to the rescue.

"So, you're Adrian. I've heard so much about you. I'm Dominic," he took a step forward, extending his hand. Adrian looked at him strangely. "Daphne's brother," he explained.

Adrian looked in disbelief at the two of us. "I didn't know you had a brother."

"Neither did I until about an hour ago." Adrian, thankfully, did shake Dominic's hand.

A little dazed Adrian said, "Your Mum told me you'd be here. We bumped into each other, and er, had a chat."

"My mum?" My head was full of Phillippa still, and I wondered how... "Oh, Isabel. Yes, Mum."

"She told me how important this book was to you, and I just thought I'd come along and erm..."

"I'm glad you did." I reassured him.

"I'm sorry..." We both apologised at the same time.

"You first," I said.

"Sorry for not being in touch, I er... Sorry I pressurised you so much."

"And I'm sorry for giving you such a run around."

Our blue green communications twinkled at each other. My body responded to his words before my mind did. It knew when something fitted. More than I did.

Dominic, sensitive to what was happening, said, "Why don't you two go to lunch. Seems like you have a lot of catching up to do." I turned to him.

"So do we."

"We can wait. I know where you are now. We've got lots of time. I think the needs of the River Woman are a little more important at the present." We smiled at each other. I gave him a

387

big hug and kissed him on the cheek. "Go on then. I think your lover is waiting," he whispered to me.

I walked the short distance between my brother and my 'lover'. Then I turned back to Dominic before leaving the room.

"Are you my younger or elder brother?"

"Younger. By seven minutes."

"That doesn't make any sense. You're like the older wiser one, and I act more like the younger, flightier one, who needs looking after."

"I wouldn't say that. You look to be doing just fine to me." His gaze slipped from my face, and I followed his eyes down, as they came to rest on my hand. My hand that had somehow found a way of interlocking with Adrian's hand. My eyes flicked upwards and met Adrian's. There was a smile in them.

I indicated the door, "Shall we go?"